FROZEN WITH FEAR

"They've spotted us. The Russians must have known all along that we were hiding under the ice pack. Now we're right where they want us."

"We must get moving, admiral. There's still time to shake them off," Captain Laycook conceded.

The admiral listened carefully, but his orders were clear: "No engines are to be turned on. The Soviets are listening to every sound we make. We will not be detected!"

"But, sir, we can't make it above the peaks at this depth. We have to correct our course!" Laycook cried.

But Admiral Awesome was as immovable as the frozen waters in *Amundsen*'s course.

The first berg hit sharply; the others that followed were even more violent. How long could *Amundsen* endure such punishment without puncturing? No submarine was designed to withstand it; she couldn't tolerate it much longer.

The admiral clenched his teeth, Laycook was numb with fear. As the submarine drifted into surface waters, both men remembered *Titanic*. But there was one big difference—*Amundsen* had no lifeboats . . .

GHOST
SUB

ROGER HERST

ZEBRA BOOKS

KENSINGTON PUBLISHING CORP.

ZEBRA BOOKS

are published by

KENSINGTON PUBLISHING CORP.
475 Park Avenue South
New York, N.Y. 10016

Copyright © 1979 by Roger Herst
Library of Congress Catalog Card Number 77-27707
Published in cooperation with Doubleday & Company, Inc.

Third Printing

Printed in the United States of America

GHOST SUB

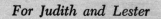

For Judith and Lester

CONTENTS

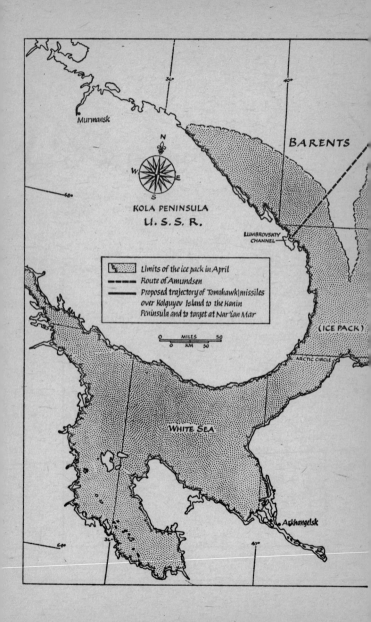

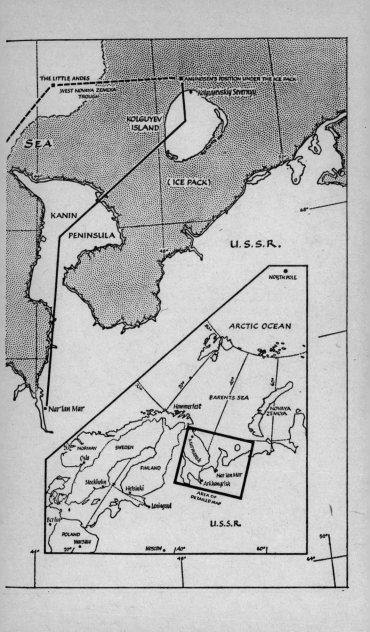

1

LUMBROVSKIY CHANNEL

(Patrol Polynya: 60th day plus 21)

You could always tell when a nuclear submarine was nearing the end of its routine sixty-day patrol: fresh food was nonexistent; movies were reruns; conversations were stale and repetitive. Irritability was even a better barometer. If there were going to be fights, that's the time they would erupt. After two months on a crowded sub you became obsessed by the thought of feeling sunshine on your cheeks (at Squadron base in Holy Loch, Scotland, the fog substituted), to stretch your legs, to talk with a female, and, of course, to have a good screw (or a bad screw—nobody was particular).

Radiomen Clyde Forbes and George Sokorski had reached that point a month before. Their attack submarine, U.S.S. *Edmond Roald Amundsen* (Skipjack class, refitted for Tomahawk cruise missiles—BGM 109s), had completed sixty days when her patrol was unexpectedly extended by twenty-one days. A fellow, Sokorski grumbled, could go right up the bulkheads in three extra weeks. And *Amundsen* wasn't exactly the flagship of "the New Navy," either. Commissioned back in 1959, she was among the second generation of nuclear subs, the sixth built since *Nautilus*. After more than two decades in service she was an arthritic old boat whose complaints multiplied without relief. You could treat her symptoms from morning until night, but you couldn't cure the disease of old age. On patrol, *Amundsen*'s electric range had failed (two weeks with cold food), her septic tanks clogged (sewage backup in the heads), her circuit breakers caused havoc in the electrical system (one washing machine for the 112-man crew). It seemed as if every valve aboard needed repacking. At the end of sixty days it was time for relief.

But that was just the trouble. Scuttlebutt said the twenty-one-day extension was caused by difficulties with Gold Crew, supposedly standing by at Holy Loch to relieve Blue Crew when *Amundsen* returned. Personnel problems or something to that effect. Anyhow, Gold wasn't ready. Judging from the lousy condition of the boat after Gold's previous patrol, that wasn't hard to believe. If the additional weeks did nothing else, they provided time to devise ingenious schemes to get even with Gold for such gross inconveniences. When Gold would finally take *Amundsen* to sea, it was in for a host of surprises.

14

Electronic beeps jolted Forbes from his thoughts. He noted a flashing green light on the control panel, unstacked his stumpy legs from the work counter, and snapped his fingers for Sokorski to activate the tape recorder. Forbes' sleeve snagged the corner of a clipboard listing transmissions monitored from Soviet surface vessels and aircraft. The log teetered and fell to the deck, scattering a dozen unfastened papers around his operations seat, and he cursed it roundly. He ignored the feeling of needles pricking his calves and glanced at the twenty-four-hour marine chronometer: 1007 hours—time for contact with Squadron at Holy Loch. Very-low-frequency (VLF) messages from Squadron were paralleled at high-frequency wave bands, usually at mid-morning when shortwave radios were busy with Russian trawler captains, lighthouse masters, and airplane pilots bantering across the Arctic distances. At one time Forbes and Sokorski enjoyed listening to this Russian jibber-jabber, but after two months it had become tedious. A message from Squadron was different, especially after eighty-one days of patrol. It had to be the expected order—*Amundsen* was finally going home.

The radio shack door slid open, emitting a murmur of voices from the control room. Behind two mugs of steaming coffee, Steven Frackmeyer stepped over the coaming into the cramped compartment. His trailing leg came down short. Brown drops splashed over the cup rims, burning his fingers and staining his dark-blue nylon coveralls below his knee. He grimaced at his clumsiness and handed the half-filled cups toward the radiomen. "Here you go. . . ."

Forbes accepted the offering silently; Sokorski's eyes barely moved from the tape recorder as he talked. "Steve, we've got a message from Squadron. Get Lieutenant Schroeder. We're going home!"

Frackmeyer looked indifferent. Everyone aboard knew why Sokorski wanted to go home. He had a beautiful reason, a red-headed little Scottish reason. But Frackmeyer didn't have anyone waiting for him in Scotland. For that matter, he didn't have anyone waiting at home in Portland, Oregon, either. Most men looked forward to leave time. For him, it was hell. "The lieutenant's probably sleeping. It's not my responsibility to wake him. Get someone who's standing watch."

"Hurry up, Steve."

For a moment the sailor hesitated, then reluctantly headed for the ladder descending to the officers' quarters on *Amundsen*'s second deck. Once the sliding door was again shut, Forbes sipped his coffee. Too much sugar for his taste, and too hot, but he gulped it down anyway, as fast as he could. As submariners went, Schroeder was a hard-nosed disciplinarian, the kind of ambitious junior officer who intended to be recognized for promotion by the efficiency of his detail. Fancied himself a disciple of Hyman Rickover from the moment he shook hands with the admiral at New London, Connecticut. Clearly, he disapproved of drinking coffee in the radio shack, though he never went so far as to forbid it. He just let everyone know that in his judgment the radio room was not a coffee shop. Those who expected "considerations" from him were guided in

16

their behavior by that "observation." Forbes hid his empty cup in the wastebasket.

"All right," the lieutenant's voice boomed out as he entered. Wrinkled shirt tails hung along his six-foot frame; uncombed light brown hair capped his low forehead. He had obviously been in his bunk. A single bound brought him to the counter to scan the communications equipment, radiotelephone, radioteletype, and facsimile, most of it seldom used. "Is this it?"

"Yes, sir . . . in Russian."

Schroeder scribbled down coordinate numbers from the tape recorder. On routine patrols nuclear ballistic submarine communications from Squadron arrived by cipher in the cryptocenter. But Patrol Polynya was so secret the normal protocol aboard *Amundsen* had been changed. An enciphered electronic communication would make the Soviets suspicious, even though they could not unscramble the meaning. To slip through Russian intelligence unnoticed, Squadron wrapped its communications in Russian-language weather reports broadcast by conventional shortwave, and at the same time sent an identical ciphered message in very low frequency (below 10 kHz) for reception under the ice. The green light stopped flashing. Schroeder extracted a tape cassette from the recorder and rose to his feet. Turning toward the door, he paused to scrutinize Forbes. "How's the coffee?" he asked.

"Wouldn't know, sir." The radioman manufactured a smile and tried to stare smartly into his superior's eyes.

"In case your sinuses are plugged, gentlemen,"

Schroeder's smile was just as artificial, "coffee smells. Furthermore, when you spill something it's only courteous to clean up." On the rubber deck runner a trail of coffee drops led from the coaming well into the tiny compartment. Frackmeyer's fault; maybe Frackmeyer's revenge. Schroeder's departing words almost whistled through his small, square teeth. "Clean it up, gentlemen."

The scent of the radio room coffee had barely left Schroeder's nostrils when he looked into the noisy wardroom. A sweet chicory aroma from stainless-steel coffee urns resisted the air conditioners. Fluorescent fixtures, mounted over a long, narrow table, bathed the compartment in bright, shadowless light. Schroeder scanned the five officers gathered around the table, but Captain Elisha Awesome was not present. He was impossible to miss.

Amundsen's new skipper had first been introduced to Blue Crew five months before on a November morning at Holy Loch, Scotland, his identity having been meticulously hidden by the commanding officer of Underwater Strategic Services, Vice Admiral Nicholas Francis Gaffy. To welcome the new skipper, Blue Crew had waited in parade formation along the quay while heavy rain clouds threatened from the northeast. Chilling winds, the forerunners of a bitter squall, gusted against the submariners, kept at attention twenty minutes beyond the announced time. When it was clear the skipper would be late, *Amundsen's* acting captain, Commander Thomas Laycook, ordered the crew to wait at ease. Cold fingers were buried in the pockets of naval pea jackets. An hour passed. Then the crew was again

18

snapped to attention; along the dock a gray Navy sedan was creeping forward, blocking the view of *Amundsen* moored to a submarine tender in the loch. Expectation rippled contagiously among the serried rows. Tyrant or benefactor, for the coming patrols *Amundsen*'s captain would be the most important person in their lives.

From the driver's seat a large black man emerged and walked briskly into full view, halting by the rear passenger's door on the sedan's near side. He seemed to place his hand on the door handle, but suddenly stiffened and swung around to face the senior officers in the front ranks. His jaw arched from left to right with military precision; his eyes gathered in the ship's company as though taking possession of foreign lands for the Crown. A whimper originated in the front and passed to the rear. Four golden strips on his shoulder boards contrasted with the navy blue of his reefer jacket. Each of the 10 officers and 102 enlisted men strained their eyes for confirmation. He was of medium height, disproportionately broad in the shoulders, but with a narrow waist and short legs, so short he appeared topheavy. Erect but not stiff, he commanded the surrounding space. His head was spherical and West African in hue. Black, that was it . . . very black.

Passenger and chauffeur were one! The black driver standing under the bleak, foreboding Scottish sky was himself *Amundsen*'s new master!

There were nervous snickers in the rear, some coughing up front. Only one possible explanation: Admiral Gaffy, an incorrigible joker, never lost an opportunity to produce the unexpected. Of course,

19

you didn't make humor about something as serious as this—that is, unless you were Nicholas Gaffy. Yes, that was it. He had presented the "new skipper" as a send-off stunt. Surely the real captain would arrive by another limousine within minutes.

Elisha Ross Awesome rotated from the waist and covered the entire submarine's complement with an in-motion salute. For several moments he stood in the north wind absorbing the benumbed silence of his white crewmen, their eyes hurt, disappointed, and mistrustful. His name had been dropped in the hopper among several candidates for commanding officer of Blue Crew, but no one seriously considered it, especially those who knew Acting Captain Laycook's credentials. Awesome was no stranger to the squadron. But as a commanding officer? Still, there he was, receiving the formal transfer of command. Where the hell was the limousine bringing the real skipper?

A guarded smile touched Awesome's lips and migrated to his cheeks. Not one inch in retreat, he planted his feet widely apart and eased into a friendly greeting. It was a brief speech, but a speech it was. The limousine wasn't going to come. They had to take this new skipper seriously. Elisha Awesome was no joke. And then the ceremony was over. Captain Awesome lifted long ebony fingers to his cheeks and wiped away the squall's first raindrops.

Schroeder was about to seek Captain Awesome elsewhere when Thomas Laycook, forty-four-year-old executive officer from Tampa, Florida, spoke above the din. "Morning, Bill. What's up?" His shining, silvery-blond hair glistened in the fluorescent light; his conventionally handsome face wore a sterner, more watchful expression than those of the other officers hunched over the table.

Schroeder didn't want to deliver the cassette to Laycook. There had been cracks about the leisure he enjoyed by virtue of his special duties—or lack of them. Communications aboard *Amundsen* were entirely one-way. She monitored Soviet broadcasts and intermittently received orders from Squadron. Transmissions, however, were strictly forbidden, since they would reveal *Amundsen*'s secret position to the Soviets. Schroeder's communications detail, therefore, had to be creative in order to stay occupied. The cassette in his fingers might be offered as proof he earned his keep, yet it was certain to produce more mileage when presented directly to the skipper.

"Out with it, Bill."

"This dispatch just arrived from Squadron." Schroeder brandished the cassette. "That's two messages in one week. For a while I thought they had forgotten us. I have to find the captain."

Conversations ended in midsentence. Good news! Everybody was expecting this directive and it had finally arrived. Laycook, a Russian textbook under his arm, pushed back from his seat and with three huge strides on spindly basketball legs blocked Schroeder's retreat to the passageway. "I'll relieve you of that, Bill."

The communications officer held the tape to his hip like a quarterback concealing a football. "I think I should deliver this directly to Captain Awesome."

"Or me. I'm authorized," Laycook's arm stretched

21

forward to snatch the cassette from his fingers. "Now, Bill, please get the skipper and ask him to meet me in the cryptocenter."

It happened too fast; Schroeder was relegated to messenger boy. No matter, he thought, *Amundsen* was soon going home. At least there were friends in Scotland to appreciate his endeavors.

Thomas Laycook scaled the ladder in a hurry. The cassette was a windfall he intended to exploit. Communications from Squadron in Scotland represented a thin link with the outside world, especially with Submarine Command above Captain Awesome. The tape held information about the patrol that the ship's skipper had yet to learn. Knowing Squadron's orders before Awesome represented, if not *Amundsen*'s actual command, then a symbol of it. For a man who had been robbed of what he rightfully deserved and had been passed over, the *symbol* of command was all he had.

Outside the cryptocenter Laycook dropped the Russian text to the deck and spun the combination lock. He had not been deaf to subtle jokes about his addiction to Russian. You didn't have to be in the Submarine Service long to understand how such humor originated from professional jealousy. Plenty of that around. After all, expertise with cruise missiles and a command of Russian had to be a winning combination in the eyes of the Pentagon, certain to be rewarded with promotion and senior command. But with Thomas Laycook it hadn't happened that way. Elisha Awesome's credentials didn't compare, yet as the admiral's protégé, he received command of *Amundsen*. The indignity of having been passed over Laycook could have handled had he believed the Submarine Service had orchestrated the injustice. The Navy was susceptible to many political pressures, not the least of which was the Black Caucus in Congress. But it wasn't the Navy or the Submarine Service that had snubbed him; it was his close friend, Nicholas Gaffy, the one man who had long stood like a mighty Gibraltar against the swirling currents of politics.

However much Laycook felt betrayed, he kept it to himself, more or less. Aching inside, he still believed in professional discipline. In no way would he allow personal feelings to interfere with his functions as an executive officer. It was only in the privacy of his tiny quarters that he grimly ticked off the days he had served on *Amundsen*. The patrol's three-week extension had been an additional punishment; still he suffered it in the belief that this nightmare would eventually end. Of that he was certain. And before departure from Holy Loch he had signed his letter of resignation from the Submarine Service. His long career had come to an end earlier than he had anticipated. The muscles around his mouth tightened when he thought of it. Retiring as commander, before reaching captain, did smell of failure, yet not entirely. Resignation from the Submarine Service had taken on a deeper significance, for, he told himself, it was a personal protest, the only kind an officer and gentleman could make in the Armed Services. One could take pride in a dignified dissent . . . and Laycook did.

And what about the future? Well, that might not be

so bleak. The expertise that the Submarine Service had spurned was bound to attract private industry servicing lucrative defense contracts, especially in the expensive Trident sub program. And with more money too, a lot more than he would receive even as captain. All the while he would enjoy a reasonable pension, medical care, PX privileges, and a host of fringe benefits that every fiber in his body told him he rightfully deserved. More than any man aboard *Amundsen* he looked forward to the end of the patrol. It was only fitting that he should be first to read the order from Squadron.

Only the skipper and the executive officer knew the combination for the lock on the cryptocenter door. Laycook's fingers fumbled nervously with the dial, and on the third attempt the lock clicked open. It was a tiny compartment, computer-filled and bathed with bluish light that cast square shadows over the ubiquitous pale green paint on the electronic equipment. Laycook shut the door behind him, slipped Schroeder's cassette into the unscrambler, and manipulated the adjacent knobs. The code changed every other day. Bad luck: A new setting was required that very morning. There was a tap on the door, but Laycook ignored it and bent over the unscrambler. Another rap, this one more forcible. Laycook concentrated in a desperate effort to win a race already lost. The third time he gave up, slipped the interior bolt along its locking channel, swung open the door. "We need another code setting, Captain Awesome."

"Got it right here, Thomas."

"Did your homework, I see." Laycook looked for a place to be out of the way. He leaned back against the closed door, buried his hands deep into his freshly pressed coverall pockets, and studied Awesome's blemishless skin and light beard, the narrow nose that suggested generational transformation from his West African ancestors, the small ears and fleshy lips that vied with heavy, penetrating eyes for dominance over his face. Except for his short legs, he was a strikingly handsome figure, especially now when the graceful curves of his torso contrasted against the square meters on the computer board. Despite his hurt over Awesome's promotion, Laycook had to acknowledge the man's leadership skills. Actually, he proved quite a surprise. Though no one commented directly, the white crew expected him to make bad mistakes. Lack of sea experience, they prophesied, would eventually test any officer's mettle. Almost from the beginning *Amundsen* experienced waves of noncritical but annoying breakdowns, first in rapid series, then in tandem. Submariners, prone to be superstitious, began to believe their boat was jinxed. Awesome took it all in stride, never lost his sense of proportion, and actually made some damned good decisions. How he came to his conclusions nobody knew, but the patrol continued without major mishap.

The delicate setting of the cryptographic machine was accomplished. There was nothing more to do but wait while crepitations in the computers punctuated the silence. An IBM Selectric ball in the teleprinter began at last to move, punching rapidly a yellow readout paper. Two sets of eyes riveted on the

25

black type:

AMUNDSEN: DUE TO INTERNATIONAL TENSIONS ON THE HORN OF AFRICA, EXTEND PATROL FOURTEEN (14) DAYS. RETURN FOR EMERGENCY AT CAPTAIN'S DISCRETION. SATELLITE PHOTOS SHOW UNANTICIPATED ICE THAW ABOVE YOU. IMPERATIVE TO REPOSITION IN WEST NOVAYA ZEMLYA TROUGH. ICE PACK OFF KOLGUYEV ISLAND APPEARS EXCELLENT: 69° 47' NORTH. 48° 59' EAST.

"Damn!" Laycook made no effort to disguise his disappointment. The crew had already been ordered to go beyond the call of duty. Now it was being asked for more sacrifice. And the thought of personally enduring additional time aboard *Amundsen* struck Laycook himself like a sledgehammer. The teleprinter kept punching letters on the readout while Awesome read aloud.

BEWARE SOVIET ICEBREAKER *ARKTIKA* AND DESTROYERS *DSKARI* AND *SVETLIVYIARE* OPERATING PRESENT LAT. 68° 25' NORTH. LONG. 40° 11' EAST. BEARING NORTH, NORTHWEST NINE (9) KNOTS. IF THIS FORCE CONTINUES IN PRESENT DIRECTION NO DANGER OF DETECTING *AMUNDSEN.* PROCEED WITH CAUTION. OUT.

*　　　*　　　*

Awesome fell silent. The message augured for enormous inconvenience . . . and more, severe danger. He seemed lost in his own thoughts until Laycook finally spoke again. "I don't like it. A lousy time to be sailing. Too much Soviet activity in the area. *Arktika* is nuclear-powered. Got an antisub helicopter aboard. She can make twenty-one knots in open water."

"No alternative, Thomas. In a week the Russians will send a pack of Golf-class subs through the Proliv Gorlo Strait, then we're trapped. Either we sail now while we have some ice cover or we sit it out here all summer."

If Awesome acknowledged the dangers even to himself there was certainly no sign in the steady eyes and expressionless lips. Was it the ebony hue of his skin that hid the feeling within . . . or the practiced art of concealment he had developed after years under public scrutiny? Laycook's voice was irritable. "I think we made a mistake by not telling the crew from the beginning that our extensions were provided in the contingency plans. Eighty-one days of patrol is pushing it. Tempers are getting strained. Nobody's going to like going on food rationing."

Awesome accepted Laycook's observation about the crew, but not his conclusion. Perhaps it had been a tactical mistake to withhold from the men the possibility of a ninety-day patrol. But at the time, they had carefully calculated the effects on morale, considering both advantages and disadvantages. Now that their luck had run sour it was no time to upbraid themselves for poor judgment. "The men are too fat anyway. They could use a little slimming before we go home."

If the skipper used that as an excuse for food rationing, Laycook thought to himself, he was going to make his first big mistake—a prospect not entirely unwelcomed. True, the crew ate too much and exercised too little. Weight was always a problem on patrol. But dieting as a justification for food rations was no answer to the stress of a ninety-day patrol. Still, shortages in the mess were hardly the most pressing of *Amundsen*'s problems. "What are we going to do about *Arktika* and her escorts? Now the Soviets have seven ships snooping around above us. Three more than Intelligence said to expect. Their navy uses Mezenskaya Bay like it's the English Channel. Something is wrong. If you ask me I'd say they've been tipped off that we're here."

Awesome cocked his head condescendingly. One couldn't discount Laycook's view, but as usual he put the bleakest interpretation on events. Increased Soviet activity above *Amundsen* presented grave dangers, but to conclude that she had already been spotted went well beyond the evidence. *Amundsen* had entered Russian waters in mid-January when most of the Soviet Arctic Fleet was frozen into northern ports. She had traveled submerged from Spitzbergen Island southward through the Barents Trough, always at safe distances from Soviet sonar that might hear the noise of her reduction gears, water turbulence, or the sound of her pumps forcing coolant through the reactor compartment. She had been hiding stationary in shallow water near the Lumbrovskiy Channel, off the Kola Peninsula, 67° 53′ North, 40° 34′ East. While using automatic hovering gear, her reduction machinery made no noise for the Soviets to hear. Detection was therefore highly improbable.

"Maybe they heard us when we sailed from Mezenskaya Bay." Laycook had been nursing that suspicion for weeks.

"We'd have heard about it by now."

"What are we going to do about the icebreaker snooping around like she's *Glomar Explorer?*"

"Our spy satellite won't orbit over this area for another week. By that time it will be too late to see if she alters course. We'll just have to pray *Arktika* keeps sailing north, northwest."

"Want me to inform the crew of our good news?"

Awesome shook his head. "No, Thomas . . . that's my responsibility. I'll break it to the officers after lunch."

"At mess, then, sir."

"The Last Lunch, Thomas." Awesome met his grimace with a playful grin.

The echo of his own words faded in the ubiquitous hum of the air blowers. Alone, Awesome flexed his fingers, numb from poor circulation. He needed some time to think. No one saw him stagger to the officers' head, where he flipped the chrome latch into its locking loop, unfastened his coveralls, and dropped onto the horseshoe toilet seat. Relief from his dizziness and knotted intestines arrived simultaneously. It was a luxury to close his eyes and for a brief moment shut out the uncertain future. What Laycook had said was absolutely correct. But however much the skipper feared the dangers ahead, he could never let the others know. A chuckle escaped his lips, taking him by surprise. There was one advantage in being black—he wouldn't blanch when telling his crew about the latest round of underwater musical chairs.

1206 hours.

Awesome slipped into the captain's seat at the wardroom table, nodded a perfunctory greeting, and signaled for the stewards to produce from a dumb-waiter four large stainless-steel serving dishes. *Amundsen's* depleted food stores had been raided to produce a special luncheon menu: canned pâté to start, followed by French bread, frozen shrimp salad without lettuce, artichoke hearts in beef stew, and a flaky pastry that almost compensated for the canned berries inside. If that wasn't enough to alert the officers that something was brewing, they had only to notice Awesome's extraordinarily slow manipulation of the silverware and his effort to keep up the banter with his favorite companion, Dr. Greerson.

One at a time the men finished their meals and sat back with anxious expressions, refraining from their normal excuses to attend to personal chores. Aware of the many eyes upon him, Awesome carefully wiped strawberry cobbler from his lips and spooned its syrupy residue from a plastic bowl. Additional coffee arrived at the moment his porcelain pipe emerged from a pouch of Boxer tobacco. With the stem clenched between his teeth, he folded the pouch and tossed it casually to the table.

Martin Rosenbaum, *Amundsen's* junior medical officer and psychiatrist, glowered at the South African trade name on the tobacco. "That doesn't

30

bother your conscience?"

Awesome waved away the enveloping smoke cloud, established his assailant's identity, and intoned, "Conscience is the prerogative of power."

"But you've got the power."

"Do I?"

Fellow officers stiffened. In the wardroom they avoided the three chief taboos: religion, women, and politics. But Rosenbaum was hardly a typical submarine officer. What did he know . . . or, for that matter, care? Raised in ethnic Brooklyn poverty, he had the unmistakable tweedy style of a poor Jewish kid who had been educated at Yale and Yale Med. A radical in his undergraduate days, he chafed equally at his three-piece suit and his three-year naval obligation. His mother called him a chronic complainer, but he preferred to think himself in touch with his own feelings. During the patrol he acted as *Amundsen's* tension barometer. Whenever there was excitement he was certain to lure somebody into an argument, but no one expected him to take on the skipper. On the other hand, nobody expected the skipper to let him get away with it. "Quite pragmatic," Rosenbaum was adding. "If you smoke South African tobacco, it's also okay to burn Arab oil and drink Soviet vodka."

"Right." Awesome displayed a flashing grin. He was quite aware that Rosenbaum was traversing the bounds of acceptable conduct, but he nevertheless felt a certain relief. How long could you expect the men to make small talk without their brains going soft? After eleven weeks at sea the traditional censorship was beginning to be oppressive. The

31

officers were bored with chitchat, spoiling for an argument, something that Awesome felt he could use himself. Besides, he personally enjoyed a heated debate, a luxury he had for too long denied himself. He smiled at Rosenbaum and settled comfortably back in his chair. "Economic boycott, Marty, doesn't change government policy."

"That's rationalizing."

"Is it? Why?"

Rosenbaum hesitated, and Awesome, suddenly tiring of the subject, shoved his pouch along the table. "Want some?"

The psychiatrist glanced at fellow officers nervously waiting for news of the dispatch from Squadron. No allies there. Under the circumstances he judged it wise to back down. But how? An oversized Meerschaum pipe emerged from his pocket. "Skipper, if you can smoke this wonderful stuff there's no reason in the world why a persecuted Jew from Brooklyn should deny himself."

Awesome slowly rose to his feet and stood behind his empty chair, pausing to gather the men's full attention. As he did when under stress, the skipper imitated the sermonic cadence his father once used from the high pulpit of the Frankfort, Kentucky, United Methodist Church. "Word travels fast. Telling you we've received a message from Squadron is like revealing the 1937 Rose Bowl score. Due to some international emergency, unknown to me, we're extended for another fourteen days."

Several seconds elapsed. No one spoke. The Submarine Service did not permit public hostility toward an order, most certainly not before the commanding officer. Lips remained motionless but resentment burned in the men's eyes, resentment, building toward rage.

"There's more." Awesome lifted his chin. "We're sailing."

"Just my luck," Lieutenant Donald Haddock, supply officer, blurted. "I've been trying to culture yogurt for four weeks now. The stuff runs like soap water. Yesterday it began to jell. We move and that's it. Back to sour milk."

Two men at Awesome's left shifted in their seats and buzzed to one another, their phrases colliding in midair—everyone suddenly talking nervously and no one listening. To be sailing was both good and bad news. Good if they were sailing toward home; bad if not.

"Sailing where, sir?" Lieutenant Commander Riley, the engineering officer, asked, on a falling note, and discovered no trace of encouragement that the skipper intended to answer.

"This isn't going to be as easy as the last move." Awesome pretended not to notice the mounting discomfort around him. "An icebreaker and two Russian tin cans are currently operating in the vicinity." A disapproving cough passed contagiously from throat to throat. Submarine officers were trained to reduce risk at all costs because with water pressure squeezing a vulnerable submarine hull there was little margin for error. Small mistakes could be fatal. Whatever the military considerations, sailing under or near a Soviet flotilla flirted with disaster.

"And gentlemen, we'll have to dash about one

hundred miles in open water without ice cover for protection."

"What happens if the Russians spot us?" Riley asked.

"We're not going to be spotted. Our objective: to reposition ourselves undetected. Nothing less. If we fail, it will amount to the worst naval incident since the *Panther* at Agadir. This little jaunt will require careful planning, gentlemen. And it's okay to pray a little, too."

Lieutenant Commander Sagi Koranson, operations chief, lumbered to his feet. There were a dozen technical points about the impending voyage to be raised. Awesome gripped the back of his chair and watched the officers around him taking over the conversation. While *Amundsen* hovered at neutral buoyancy her navigation, missile, fire control, and launch subsystems had been sedulously maintained. She was a tight ship with sufficient steam for her turbines to sail or attack the enemy at a moment's notice. Still, the order to reposition required complex coordination among her nuclear reactors, engine room, and inertial navigation. Time ran at a premium. Ohmmeters, voltmeters, ammeters, oscilloscopes, frequency generators demanded inspection. Null and phase checks had to be made. Hundreds of theodolites, autocolomators, gauges, indicators, synchros, and resolvers required adjustment. Koranson's briefing ended abruptly with officers hastily jamming the exit to begin preparations. Above the cacophony of excited voices the operations chief issued crisp commands.

Awesome followed his men to the passageway and

then returned to the wardroom table where Laycook, lost in thought, presided over abandoned coffee cups.

"At least," Awesome said, "they're likely to be too busy to get scared."

Laycook's face was dour. "Let's hope they work like hell. You'll forgive me, but prayers just aren't going to get us there."

A chair opposite Laycook groaned under the captain as he dropped with exhaustion into it. Gone from his voice was the confidence he had projected before the men. "Oh good grief, Thomas. Maybe the Good Lord will help us and maybe we'll have to do it on our own. When I speak about God, it's just a manner of speech."

"That sounds like a renunciation of faith to me."

"It isn't. Too bad, Thomas, you didn't learn faith from a pappy like the Reverend Elijah Awesome. Now, there was a man who had the Lord operating for *him*. To hear my pappy talk it was he who told God what should be done and what shouldn't."

"What happened to this great operator?"

"Well, he managed the world for a while. Brought the country out of the Depression and was just preparing to win World War II when his arteries clogged up. Got a stroke and died."

"How come God didn't help him?"

"He did—that is, for a while. But the Good Lord must have gotten tired. My pappy lay in bed paralyzed for more than a year. He always claimed a good man should die on his feet, so one morning we found him tied to a bedpost, his red-letter Bible on the floor, opened to *Revelation*. How he got himself standing up we never figured out, but my pappy died on his feet. A real tough one, he was."

Laycook deserted his coffee cups. "I'll think of Pastor Awesome while we're crossing the open water. Maybe it'll give me the urge to pray."

For a long moment Awesome regarded the handsome officer, his head far higher than the watertight door, his lint-free nylon coveralls starched, immaculately pressed, and trimly hugging his body. He was the only man aboard *Amundsen* who did not dress in dryer-wrinkled coveralls, but insisted upon inspection-quality creases running parallel over his chest and perfect pleats on his trousers. Awesome started to haul himself from his seat. "Don't bother praying, Thomas," he said, "we'll make it safely to the ice pack on the other side without your prayers."

1400 hours.

Inside *Amundsen*'s lead-insulated reactor compartment eight boron rods were slowly extracted from her uranium-238 core. The nuclei immediately captured freed neutrons, producing plutonium-239 and releasing immense energy. Heat then "cooked" highly purified water (primary water), which was passed through a "heat exchanger" and transformed into nonradioactive steam (secondary water). Driven under high pressure through the submarine's electric generators and dual propulsion turbines, the steam was routed into a condenser and reconverted to water, then pumped back to the reactor compartment for reheating. Further aft, axles from the propulsion turbines turned reduction gears, eventually spinning the drive shaft and single five-blade propeller. *Amundsen* crept forward, leaving her nest in the

Lumbrovskiy Channel.

From his periscope stand elevated twenty inches above the main deck, Awesome spun on a swivel stool, surveying the control room. Steering and diving stations to port; tactical attack center to starboard. Directly before him: cylindrical cowlings that descended from *Amundsen*'s sail overhead—two periscopes used to observe the blue-green phosphorescent underside of the ice pack. At arm's length: radar control, ship's course indicator, depth gauge, collision and diving alarms, azimuth indicators, sound-powered phone, and loudspeakers.

Awesome switched from the sound-powered phone to direct communication between himself and the sonar technician reading a visual depth indicator on the upward-pinging sonar at the depth-control panel. Terry Kamakota's crisp voice bristled back through the receiver, "Aye, aye, sir . . . ice closing in. One-zero-six above . . . three-seven below."

Under his breath Awesome cursed the Arctic ice as a mixed blessing. True, it hid *Amundsen* from Soviet surveillance while she operated close to the enemy shore, but at the same time it presented navigational problems. That, of course, was part of Nicholas Gaffy's plan. Would the Soviets expect an American submarine to be operating in such shallow waters where her propeller could easily be heard, especially in midwinter? They, better than anyone, appreciated the risks. As the easement between rafted ice above and below *Amundsen* narrowed, Awesome began to think that perhaps Admiral Gaffy had underestimated hazards known so well by the enemy. Still, it was too late for such doubts. Awesome barked a command to the diving officer behind two planesmen and a helmsman. An instant later seawater was expelled from *Amundsen*'s variable ballast tanks, elevating the submarine forty feet.

Kamakota mopped perspiration from his brow and momentarily rested weary eyes from the console before him. Three and a half hours of watch without relief. Son of a World War II submariner in the Imperial Japanese Navy, he had always wanted a career in the Submarine Service. It was more than a whim; Kamakota's father had never returned from a supply patrol in the Marianas. For the son, the sea, not the Soviets, was the primary adversary. To survive its inhospitable environment required all one's wits. A single slip, error, or inattention and the vengeful ocean would swallow its intruders, even those protected by the pressure hull of a nuclear submarine. *Amundsen*'s external skin functioned like an eggshell, designed to withstand water pressure distributed evenly over its entire surface. Her HY-80 high-tensile steel was nevertheless extremely vulnerable to puncture by a sharp object, such as a floeberg or rafted ice. A small collision hole might flood and sink the vessel in minutes. Nor was the sea without its tricks. Strong, warm-water currents under the ice pack could bend sonar waves and provide an unreal picture of what hazards lay in wait to vex the uninvited intruder.

It seemed undignified that such a powerful warship should have to probe hit-or-miss through miles of coastal ice. Yet there was no alternative . . . and no help from friendly ships. Nor was there any guarantee that once *Amundsen* finally disembrogued into open water she would not suddenly find herself boxed in again. Absolutely nothing was certain in the sea, especially the Arctic Ocean. Kamakota could have told you that before the patrol.

Beside him, C. J. Morrison was hunched over a BQS-8 Raytheon oscilloscope, monitoring its dark field with reddish sonar spikes. *Amundsen*'s passage was completely plugged. His report traveled from the sonar compartment to the skipper, who ordered the diving station "Back Full . . . Back Emergency."

"Captain, this is the diving officer: Back Full . . . Back Emergency."

"Very well," Awesome acknowledged. He ordered *Amundsen* to return via the ice passage and have another try six miles to the north. Under his buttocks the free-spinning stool turned until he faced a fathometer repeater.

"You sent for me, Skipper."

A slight shift brought Eugene Greerson, *Amundsen*'s surgeon, into view. Older by a decade than the line officers, his presence had a soothing effect upon everyone, especially during tension. Men with personal problems went to Greerson; he was the kind of fellow who was always above petty squabbling, who just seemed the natural court of final arbitration. Something of a fossil from the earliest *Nautilus* days of nuclear attack submarines, he exuded self-confidence, as if he had seen everything before. That his experience was as wide as others believed he vehemently denied, yet the myth persisted. Funny thing about Greerson, nobody but Awesome called him "Eugene" or "Gene." On his fourth patrol with Blue Crew he was still addressed as "Dr. Greerson."

"What's wrong?" he asked, standing beside the periscope mount.

"You know me pretty well, Gene." Awesome reached forward and wrapped his arm around the older man's ribs. "Your antennae are always working."

"No, Skipper," Greerson smiled in his avuncular manner, "I don't know you well at all. Don't believe anybody aboard does, either. But I know you wouldn't call me unless something was wrong."

"Nothing serious. Only I haven't had much sleep in the past twenty-four hours. Getting a little weary. Looks like it's going to be a long trip. Got something to pick me up?"

"Well, we could start with cognac, Napoleon Four-Star. . . . I'll bring you some amphetamines right away . . . enough for a week if you want. Too bad you can't let somebody else stand watch for you."

Awesome shook his head. *Amundsen's* complement had sufficient numbers to man three full shifts, more men than needed for combat. Everybody could be rotated off watch for necessary rest, everybody except the commanding officer. It was just too hazardous for the skipper to be napping.

"How long do you reckon to stay up?" the surgeon asked.

"Don't know . . . maybe another fifteen hours or so."

Greerson glanced down at his watch, mentally calculating the amphetamine dosage.

Amundsen began to slow; her propeller spun suddenly in reverse. More ice ahead. Damn it. Greerson turned to fetch the drug for the skipper. It

40

was obvious Awesome was telling the truth. The commanding officer would be awake for a long, long time.

1535 hours.

Red lights in the sonar shack cut the bright fluorescence of the control room and softened the squared casings over echo-ranging equipment. Conduits ran forward and aft from sonar displays along the bulkheads, then disappeared into adjoining compartments, eventually ending with transducers sandwiched between torpedo tubes in *Amundsen*'s bow.

C. J. Morrison massaged the crick in his neck while concentrating upon the sonar pips behind a sweeping pulse line circling a ten-inch plan-position indicator oscilloscope. For too long he had been translating the decaying red blotches into obstacles in *Amundsen*'s path and glancing at three-minute intervals to the twenty-four-hour chronometer. Relief from his watch couldn't come too soon. *Amundsen* appeared inextricably tangled in the ice and wasn't likely to escape while he was on duty. Only one hour and twenty-five minutes left to monitor the bloody screen. Then suddenly, the red blips failed to return behind the pulse line. The massive frozen obstructions that rose from the ocean floor appeared to level off and no longer block the submarine's exit from shore ice. Free to maneuver, she immediately altered course to the northeast, then debouched into deep water.

With the submarine now traveling at half speed, C.J. ignored specific orders and declared for himself

41

a momentary respite. His head aching from prolonged concentration, he tipped backward in defiance and spun 180 degrees on the swivel seat to give his watering eyes a rest. He eased the hydrophones from his ears. The crick in his neck hurt worse than ever. Koranson, monitoring the sonar display over his shoulder, spoke sharply to him, and C.J. cursed silently. He refocused his attention on the sonar pulse as it cleared the lower left quadrant. A full circle had been completed before Morrison realized something unusual had occurred. Again the pulse swept around and there it was, bearing 3 points on the port bow, 028 degrees true—two small red pips registering interference. "Two objects on the surface," he reported immediately to the operations officer.

Koranson whirled back to the hooded scope, stumbling over Glen Peebles' foot in the dull light. Peebles yelped in pain but began programming his analytic geometric computer for a fix on the objects' exact bearings. "How far . . . how fast . . . ?" Koranson growled.

In dense Arctic water sound travels slightly less than 4,800 feet per second. By calculating the time required to travel and bounce back from interference it was possible to know the absolute position and speed of the moving objects. Peebles, bowed over his analytic computer, was watching the readout. "Four point niner miles and closing . . . speed, wait a second . . . speed . . . one-five knots."

"Koos emah!" Koranson swore in the Arabic his family reserved for bad moments. "They're not whales." Following Morrison's finger over the

upper-left quadrant of the display, he phoned the skipper at the periscope stand. *Amundsen*'s turbines were immediately disengaged from the propeller and she converted to silent hovering. SQA-14 passive-mode searchlight sonar swept in 360 degrees while the sonar technicians listened carefully through hydrophones to identify the type of vessels by their propeller beats.

When Awesome opened the sonar shack door, moments later, bright light from the control room flooded the dimmed compartment. He planted himself before the console, adjusting his eyes to the light. Koranson described the sonar events, his voice raspy with tension. "Contact, sir. Two surface vessels, four point nine miles at oh-two-eight degrees true. Trouble steaming right up our ass . . . speed, one-five knots!"

Awesome focused on the red spikes, considering the possibilities—all bad. The sonar experts interpreted the beats: one very large double-screw ship, another smaller, most probably a destroyer. *Amundsen* had just made contact with two of the three surface vessels Squadron warned about. Somehow the Soviet flotilla had altered course. The large ship had to be the nuclear-powered icebreaker *Arktika;* the other, one of her escorts—either *Dskari* or *Svetlivyiare.*

Trying to keep in mind several disconnected events, Awesome concentrated on Koranson's conclusion. "On present course, they'll pass about two and a half miles ahead. We can either sit it out right here or alter our own course fifty degrees to the southeast."

43

The skipper grabbed the phone, rejecting both alternatives. At a distance of 2.5 nautical miles the Soviets could easily ping with active sonar to establish *Amundsen*'s exact bearings. But to pass ahead and outrun the force was equally dangerous, for the enemy was certain to hear *Amundsen*'s reduction gears the moment she increased speed. Their only choice was to return to the ice pack for cover. The noisy engines of the icebreaker and the destroyer had, no doubt, confounded the sonar signals heard aboard the enemy ships. With luck, *Amundsen* could sneak back under the ice before being detected.

"Officer of the deck from the captain, right full rudder, ahead two thirds."

"Captain from the officer of the deck, understand right full rudder, ahead two thirds. Aye, aye, sir."

The order was immediately executed and confirmed. "Captain, this is the officer of the deck, executed: right full rudder, ahead two thirds."

"Very well."

"Aye, aye, sir."

Amundsen banked sharply like an airplane in a turn and followed her previous course toward the ice pack. Morrison resumed his forward searching sonar. "Sir," he interrupted suddenly. *"Sir!"* His chewing gum slipped into his throat and choked him. He tried first to cough it up and then to swallow it. Neither method worked. The gum felt as though lodged in his gullet. "There's another ship ahead of us," he finally reported. "Two-three-six degrees true."

"Eight miles and closing at two-six knots,"

Peebles read the bearings from his computer.

Awesome froze. Two warships were now in *Amundsen*'s wake. And the third of the triumvirate lay in his escape route to the ice pack. *Amundsen* was trapped in open water! One ship appeared to be steaming full speed toward him, the other two forking into new positions at 45-degree angles and setting overlapping sonar grids. Retreat to the ice pack was no longer feasible. The time to run had passed; the time to hide had arrived. How he wished the Barents provided the Atlantic's deep water. Down in the depths *Amundsen* would have little difficulty in outrunning slower ships on the surface. But in the Barents' shallow 30 to 150 fathoms that wouldn't be so simple. At the moment *Amundsen* had only 40 fathoms beneath her keel. She'd need every inch of it to avoid detection by the Soviets.

"Officer of the deck from the captain. Deep submergence . . . full bubble, then all stop."

"All hands! Stand by for steep dive," a voice barked once through the squawk box.

"Captain, this is the officer of the deck. Understand, deep submergence, full bubble, then all stop. Aye, aye, sir."

Red circles replaced a series of electronic dashes on the hull opening indicator panel. Air bubbles in the variable ballast tanks were vented, allowing *Amundsen* to ingest additional seawater through flooding ports. Her descent was undramatic, for there was barely anywhere to go. All 240 feet were used. The sub was on the bottom, with 70 fathoms of water overhead. Awesome uncoiled the sound-powered phone mouthpiece and plugged its jack into the mainline circuit. His voice would now be heard by key personnel throughout the boat, his message relayed to the entire crew. "This is the captain. Rig for silent running. Rig for silent running." Throughout *Amundsen* all nonessential engines were immediately shut down. Voices stopped chattering. Men halted in their tracks.

Unaware of the Russian ships overhead, the crew had no way of knowing why *Amundsen* had stopped, turned, descended under power, then leveled off and stopped again, but the order for silent running was enough to send a chill through anyone. A terrible silence laden with unanswerable questions hung throughout the length and breadth of the submarine. Hydraulic leak? Hull flooding? Nuclear reactor problems? Or worse . . . combat. Was *Amundsen* really going to war?

Awesome peered over Morrison's shoulder at the sonar display. The tin can off *Amundsen*'s starboard bow continued to approach. The other two ships were lost from the forward-searching sonar. Time to shut that down too, for the Soviets could detect *Amundsen*'s presence from her active pinging. A sonar technician clamped his hands over his hydrophones, listening to *Amundsen*'s passive-mode sonar.

Laycook entered the compartment and halted before a dead sonar screen. His breathing was heavy, recycling the already stale air. "They've spotted us," he murmured close to Awesome's ear. "The Russians must have known all along that we were hiding under the ice pack. Somehow they got tipped off. They've been waiting for a chance to catch us in open

46

water. Now we're right where they want us."

Awesome regarded his executive skeptically. "Tipped off? That *Amundsen* was hiding under the ice pack in the Lumbrovskiy Channel? Nonsense."

Laycook was undeterred. "If the Russians don't already know, they will shortly. We're in international water now. If we get moving there's still a chance to shake them off. Time to think about ending the patrol, Captain. Once under the ice pack they won't be able to find us . . . no matter how hard they try."

Awesome listened with impatience. Laycook's naval judgment was usually sound but conservative. Yet this time he was overlooking the most important consideration, the very purpose of Patrol Polynya. The mission demanded absolute secrecy. Once detected, neither *Amundsen* nor any other American submarine could operate in the Barents. "No, Thomas. I can't risk detection. There's just too much at stake."

"And if those bastards launch their homing torpedoes?"

"That's a bit dramatic. We're in international water. They won't attack us here. Right now I'm only concerned about not being detected. I've got a responsibility to Gaffy and I'm not going to fail him."

Behind them the compartment door slid open, bringing light from the control room. It was the operations chief. A pencil slipped off the clipboard perennially at his side and from which he directed all tasks from writing to eating. It ricocheted from Glen Peebles' chair and struck the deck, coming to rest at

Laycook's feet. The exec officer froze. Like a clapper striking a bronze bell, the ring echoed in the otherwise silent air. Sensitive surveillance equipment known to exist on Soviet ships could easily hear percussion noises softer than that—even through the hull of a submarine. Fortunately, the enemy was still too far away.

"Two miles and closing, sir," the sonar technician reported.

Koranson, flushed over his clumsiness, announced excitedly in a subdued voice, "On present course the tin can is going to pass us about a half mile to starboard. It seems to be slowing down."

Awesome's legs weakened as he steadied himself against the sonarman's chair and strained to understand the Russian tactics. At first it had looked like a hunter-killer maneuver; later, a cat-and-mouse game. Were they hoping to force him to reveal his hand? Would they allow him to make the first move, then react? Or was it still possible they didn't know of *Amundsen's* presence?

Koranson spoke again. "The icebreaker's slowing down. The second can seems to be turning about!"

Awesome eased back on his heels. Suddenly a knifelike pain shot through his thighs up his spine, sharper than any of the previous attacks. His palms became wet. For days now those muscle spasms had increased in frequency and severity, to the point that he had thought of going to Greerson. But only thought of it. Even the slightest hint of poor health in the Submarine Service was guaranteed to derail a career. No matter how sick an officer was, he feigned perfect fitness, concealing from even his closest friends the smallest infirmity.

Koranson's voice was suddenly too loud for silent running. "Sir! We're in a strong current, drifting to the southeast!"

"Good. Away from the Russians."

"No, it's too fast," Koranson retorted, appalled by the new development. "We're in a basin and drifting toward submerged floebergs. We'll be over the smaller ones in three minutes. Can't make it above the peaks at this depth. We'll have to correct the course." He had a chart, which he thrust toward Awesome, who, half blind with pain, obediently turned his eyes toward it. At the moment nothing had ever looked so meaningless. His stomach knotted up. It was not enough to have ventured into open water and confronted a menacing Soviet flotilla above *Amundsen*. Now he also had to deal with a stiff current sweeping the submarine into the tops of underwater floebergs. His exec officer worried about the Russians; the operations chief worried about the bergs, and he worried about salvaging *Amundsen's* mission. And no time to evaluate the alternatives. The final decision had to be made more by instinct than by judgment. Koranson's floebergs, which had rafted together and become anchored to the ocean bed, were, after all, based on charts, not active sonar. There was still a chance the charts were wrong, or that the ice had shifted. "No . . . no . . . no engines," Awesome commanded the operations chief. "I'm not going to broadcast our position to the Russians. No matter what. No engines. We'll have to rudder through."

Koranson shook his head. There wasn't enough

water to slip over the bergs, which in some locations broke the surface. Their mass of solid ice dwarfed *Amundsen*'s 3,800 tons of displacement. Collision with such massive obstacles was like a bicycle hitting a Greyhound bus. To avoid this, *Amundsen* would have to expose her sail beyond the surface. Given the alternatives, it was better to risk detection by using the engines than to wave *Amundsen's* sail like a flag before the enemy.

Awesome was granite, as immovable as the frozen water in *Amundsen*'s course. "No. The Soviets are listening to every sound we make. No engines."

The ruddy darkness camouflaged Koranson's gesture of futility: another *Titanic*. At least on *Titanic* they got the women and children into the lifeboats. *Amundsen* had no lifeboats. "Give us something, sir. We've got to be able to see."

"The BQS-8 sonar, then. But no more!"

Koranson issued the order and the sonar was switched on for a forward sounding. Several men gasped at once; Awesome clenched his teeth. *Amundsen* was already drifting over submerged ice. Clearance under her keel was only fifty-two feet!

The skipper moved quickly from the sonar compartment into the control room, Koranson close on his heels. At the depth-detection panel Kamakota was standing a second watch. No time to find out why. He confirmed that the bergs under *Amundsen* were rising quickly. Sonar soundings bounced from the ice registered repeated patterns of wiggly lines on a calibrated cathode-ray tube. A fathometer beside it provided absolute depth on a diode digital display. Second by second the numbers decreased toward zero.

Koranson tried again. "We can rudder around the bergs. All we need is a little power. By the time the Russians pick us up, we'll be clear on the opposite side."

"No!" Awesome repeated. "No, Koranson. Positively no engines."

"We're almost on top, sir," Kamakota warned, barely masking his fear. If given an opportunity, he would have talked about distrusting the sea. As it was, he could do no more than monitor the cathode-ray screen and digital display.

Awesome snatched the phone. "Officer of the deck from the captain. Up four-zero feet."

The order was repeated and confirmed. *Amundsen* ascended.

Kamakota spun away from the fathometer. However much *Amundsen* had risen from the ice, it wasn't enough. A strong current pushing from her stern eliminated rudder control and she yawed to starboard. "We just brushed that one," Kamakota announced. The fathometer went flat. Suddenly it registered thirty feet of water and then went flat again. No sonar signal on the oscilloscope! "We're not going to make this one!" There was naked fear in his voice.

Initial impact with the ice originated three points forward on the starboard beam. The submarine ricocheted and struck again, scraping along the icy ledges, then without warning sprang free and pitched forward in the current. A second contact occurred broadside on *Amundsen*'s port, a third as her stern levitated in the water, forcing the bow down into the ice. The crewmen's cries punctuated the metallic percussions resonating throughout the boat. The electricity short-circuited in the control room but was immediately returned from emergency generators. Again *Amundsen* smashed into the unyielding bergs, drowning the men's screams under the groans of bending steel. The ice resisted the intruder, embedding its sharp teeth into her hull, crunching against the submarine's tender electric welds and valve castings.

His hands gripping a hydraulic pipe for support, Lieutenant Donald Haddock cried out without hearing himself, his mind wheeling. How long could *Amundsen* endure such punishment without puncturing? No submarine was designed to withstand it—especially not one constructed in the late 1950s. She wouldn't tolerate it much longer.

". . . up two-zero," Awesome ordered the dive officer. Higher in the water, *Amundsen* drifted in swift current, this time increasing the distance between herself and the ice. The grinding along her hull ceased, but it was only a temporary respite. Like robots, the men repositioned themselves at their duty stations. Flooding? Leaks? "Blow and go" escape procedures had been drilled into them from their fourth week at Basic Submarine School in New London, Connecticut. In theory it was quite simple, amounting to a free ascent from the sub to the surface without diving gear. But in the desolate Arctic, ascent to what? Somebody once figured out that in freezing Arctic waters a fellow could live about six minutes. Survival training had been geared to a submarine that operated in the tropics—but it was all pretty pointless. The United States didn't have many enemies near the equator.

"More ice," Kamakota exclaimed. "Bearing two-three-six degrees . . . relative."

"Up one-five feet," Awesome ordered.

New obstructions blocked and buffeted *Amundsen* angrily. From the stern a sharp blow resonated through the bulkheads, radiating aftershocks throughout the hull. Another impact—this one less severe. The submarine listed to starboard and swerved into quieter sea. Somehow she had turned her bow fully into the current and could now use the steering planes. Word arrived from several quarters that the ice was tapering off.

Awesome ordered *Amundsen* into deeper water, then turned to Laycook, who staggered toward him on straw legs that were skeptical of the firm decks below them. "Any injuries?" he asked the exec officer.

"One that I know of. Seaman Everett Young. He's unconscious in the forward torpedo room."

Awesome nodded and turned to concentrate on the reports from sonar. The ice was leveling off; unobstructed water lay ahead. The floebergs now functioned as a sonar shield between the Soviet flotilla and *Amundsen*. She was free to run her engines and hide under the ice in West Novaya Zemlya Trough. "We're through now, Thomas. God help us that the damage isn't too bad. Have Riley pack any leaks and make a damage report immediately. Resume our original course. Reduce to ten knots and remain at seven-zero depth until we know exactly how bad we're hurt. Report to me in the forward compartment."

The men in the torpedo room looked over to the skipper as he paused on the platform to survey the compartment. No one spoke, but their eyes were intent. Was everything okay? Had they, in fact, pulled through? Or was this just the beginning?

"So far, so good." Awesome made himself smile. They were kids and brand new at this kind of danger. His own experience was limited too. Nevertheless, he forced himself to meet the eyes of his crewmen—one by one. Honesty prevented him from offering false encouragement, for he didn't yet know how they really were.

Kneeling beside Dr. Greerson on the torpedo-room deck, he watched the physician's skillful hands, one feeling under Young's jaw for a pulsebeat, the other swabbing a small head wound with alcohol. The face below him belonged to a country black with ebony skin a tone lighter than his own, clean white teeth, adolescent mustache, seminatural hairstyle adapted disdainfully to Navy regulations. He and Everett Young shared a bond of sorts: unacknowledged even to themselves, a feeling that their contract to work alongside white sailors was, in the large scheme, only temporary, that the fragile alliance with those of different skin was, by nature, ephemeral.

Greerson completed his preliminary examinations as Young stirred. "Probably a mild concussion. He'll survive."

"Good," Awesome replied, and then, about to rise, he felt his own head spin and dissociate from his torso. The images before his eyes suddenly caved toward his center of vision, blurred, and faded. His chin thumped into his sternum. A final vision, amorphous though it was, looked like a giant hand rising to block his fall forward. When he regained consciousness there was a fiery flame in his nostrils, boring like a corkscrew behind his eyes into his brain. Indistinct images sharpened with painful clarity. He discovered himself pushing away a noxious agent, Greerson's hand, holding a bottle of ammonium carbonate.

The doctor flattened a palm against his chest and pushed him back to the deck. "Just be patient," he said under the din of voices around them, "or we'll have to put you in sickbay like Young." For a moment Greerson turned to direct the men lifting the black sailor into a canvas stretcher before saying conversationally, "You started to faint, Skipper." The "started to" was charitable. "Feel all right now?"

"Quite all right," Awesome replied, and made an unsuccessful attempt to scramble to his feet. His legs buckled under the sudden imposition and he toppled back toward the deck.

"Some awesome character," the doctor said, extending a hand. As they moved in tandem through the passageway, his clinical eye regarded the skipper. "He's got eighteen cruise missiles jammed into Russia's anus but can't stand a little blood." Laycook intercepted the pair outside the tactical attack center with good news. Their fears that *Amundsen*'s hull had been punctured were allayed. So far as Riley could determine, there was no immediate threat to the submarine's watertight integrity. But after the good news came the bad. The sub's ability to evacuate water from her trim tanks had been affected by a crushed hull valve and "sea chest" port on the starboard, opposite the pumps and controls. She could transfer water from her five trim tanks while submerged, but she would have a hard time remaining in trim as her buoyancy changed.

Awesome rolled his lips inward, silently evaluating *Amundsen's* predicament. From the preliminary report the damage sounded severe but not irreparable. "Anything else?" he asked. Laycook nodded. The muzzle door on torpedo tube 6 had been jammed, along with some damage incurred by the forward water round torpedo tank (WRT) drain. Considering the impact, the executive officer concluded *Amundsen* had survived remarkably well. She could not trim very neatly nor could she fire Tomahawk 6, but she was not going to sink. Her damages could be repaired at Holy Loch.

"And the ice?" Awesome inquired.

"It must have suffered worse than we. I suspect the bergs will log more downtime in dry dock than *Amundsen.*"

Awesome chuckled but he knew Laycook had meant that to hurt. In dry dock *Amundsen* was not doing what she had been designed to do. It reflected negatively upon a skipper's record when his boat sustained damages that took her out of service. Nevertheless, he flashed Laycook an infectious smile. "No, no . . . Thomas, I didn't mean that. Is there any more submerged ice ahead?"

Laycook had known what he meant. "No, sir," he reported formally. "As far as we can tell our route is now clear."

"Thank God." Sweet was the thought of having

escaped both the Russian flotilla and the submerged ice. Even sweeter was the vindication: He had been right to hide rather than run in order to salvage Patrol Polynya. "Well, Thomas?"

"Sir?"

"You see, we escaped. You thought I was afraid to run. Not true. Sometimes it's better to run rather than hide, but this wasn't one of those times. With the ice shielding us, there's no further danger of detection until we get near Kolguyev Island."

Laycook raised his chin imperiously.

"You don't look very happy, Thomas."

"In my judgment, Captain Awesome, we were just plain lucky."

"Maybe, but it doesn't really matter. When you go get your money after a horse race, it's not important whether your choice was smart or lucky. What matters is whether your horse wins. And, Thomas, we won!"

"God heard your prayers. Luck or Providence, but one of them saved us."

"You're wrong, Thomas. Maybe luck, but not Providence. I didn't say any prayers this time. So you see, God didn't have anything to do with it."

"Then what did save us?"

A wide grin expanded over Awesome's cheeks; white teeth flashed at the exec officer. Tough question. He glanced down to the black hands that he was rubbing unconsciously and immediately returned to regard Laycook, this time more seriously. A good question too, one worthy of future consideration.

*　　*　　*

Amundsen reset her course north-northeast. Her skipper stole a few moments to withdraw into himself while sitting at his station near the periscope. Laycook's question "What saved *Amundsen?*" haunted him. In his lap his long, bony fingers clenched into fists, then opened like rose petals. The skin was leathery. Day after day those hands had faithfully attended the service of his body, washed, fed, and groomed it, completing countless mundane chores. But they, he thought, had also been summoned for a loftier function, to command the Submarine Service's most daring patrol since World War II. One had to wonder whether salvation from the ice and the Soviet flotilla had really been all luck. How unfair to discount the contribution these hands had made.

What saved *Amundsen?* The answer was many things, but among them these hands . . . these black boy's hands.

Fatigued but elated, Awesome bent himself to the submarine's navigation, not, however, without interruptions. In the next hour *Amundsen's* crewmen stopped by the observation platform and proffered congratulations. Awesome didn't know whether such greetings were meant as expressions of confidence or relief, but he was pleased nevertheless. He hid his embarrassment in a gentle tilt of the head and a smile. "It was just luck," he told them. "We were just plain lucky."

2

WEST NOVAYA ZEMLYA TROUGH

(Patrol Polynya: 60th day plus 22)

Two hours and nine minutes after contact with the submerged bergs—which the crew had dubbed "the Little Andes"—Koranson threaded his way through the control room to the skipper's observation platform. "We're back in Soviet water," he said quietly. "Better get your passport ready."

"The sooner we get some ice cover the happier I'll feel."

"Brash ice above us right now. We brushed a big floe about ten minutes ago."

Awesome frowned. It had been eleven minutes, to be exact—and it hadn't been a floating floeberg. From his position directly beneath the submarine's sail, the contact had sounded more like steel striking steel than ice buffeting the hull. He put that to Koranson but the operations chief looked skeptical. "It must have been ice, sir, however it sounded. What else is there?"

"And have you ever heard, Sagi, of ice suspended at neutral buoyancy, halfway between the ocean floor and the surface? They raft together on the bottom or float on the surface, but aren't suspended in midwater."

"The bottom side of a particularly tall one, sir? That's what—"

"When all the water around it is the same temperature?"

Koranson retreated behind a question. If *Amundsen* had not struck an ice floe, then what did she hit?

Awesome was exhausted; Greerson's amphetamines were rapidly losing their effectiveness. "I'm not sure, Sagi," he said wearily. "The only thing I can think of that might be suspended in the water would be some type of Soviet listening device, say a sonar transponder, something anchored to the bottom like a mine or dangling down from the surface."

Koranson immediately dismissed the suggestion as improbable. First, Squadron had provided *Amundsen* with complete satellite photos showing the location of Soviet sonar buoys. Her course from the Lumbrovskiy Channel to Kolguyev Island had been carefully plotted to avoid known listening devices. Second, it was mathematically improbable that *Amundsen* would collide with a buoy, wherever it was. The Barents, he reminded Awesome, was a big sea, and sonar buoys were small instruments.

Awesome shook his head slowly. He could quarrel with neither objection, yet that still did not explain what *Amundsen* had struck in the water. It was characteristic of Koranson's computerlike mind to cite mathematical probability. Whenever he was uncertain about something he fell back on numbers. Fair enough . . . but what was it out there in the water?

Koranson gave up. He guessed he didn't know, but privately he still thought it was ice, about which little could be done. *Amundsen* faced so many real perils there was no wisdom in worrying over hypothetical ones. Unless, of course, the skipper thought otherwise. But after all, within an hour, the submarine would again find refuge under the ice mantle. So long as she remained quiet and motionless there was little chance the Soviets could detect her exact position.

When the operations officer excused himself to move forward toward the diving stand, Awesome scooted back a few feet and from a space beside the azimuth indicator picked up a rolled chart. *Amundsen* was soon to be hidden in the West Novaya Zemlya Trough, 69° 47′ North, 48° 59′ East, where she could rest and recover. He located the exact position on the chart, and thereafter permitted his eyes to fall south to Kolguyev Island, twenty-two statute miles away.

After eighty-two days of patrol any land, even a desolate glacier island on a map, looked inviting. Fifty-five miles wide and about sixty long, Kolguyev's only significant elevation consisted of rolling hills near her center, which tapered gradually into forestless tundra and marshy lakes around the coastline. One had only to hack a foot or so beneath her topsoil to uncover permafrost that had remained unchanged for millennia.

Strictly out of bounds to foreign visitors, Kolguyev Island possessed for Awesome an aura of mystery. He imagined her rich in ruins from Viking colonies and Teutonic fortresses, long sequestered from Western eyes, a seductive female, her unknown bounties promising sexual favors. Pleased with that imagery, he vowed to return someday and, if possible, walk on her northern shore—perhaps even tramp over the ice pack to where *Amundsen* was soon to hide.

None of what he imagined appeared on the satellite photographs. What they showed were vacant campsites of migratory hunters, a lone village called Bugrino on the southern shore, and on the north coast near *Amundsen*'s new anchorage, a weather-satellite tracking station at Kolguyevskiy Severnyy.

Direct phone communication bristled suddenly with inquiries that commanded Awesome's attention. "We're coming under the ice, sir. Depth decreasing rapidly." Before *Amundsen* arrived at her new position she had to navigate shallow water, requiring split-second adjustments to underwater topography, shifting currents, and temperature differentials. Such maneuvers were complicated by the damaged hull valve and "sea chest," affecting the submarine's trim. Back and forth, for a long, tense hour, went orders and reports, soundings and readings, near-misses and sudden dips toward safety. Awesome forgot Kolguyev, forgot Koranson's "floe-berg," forgot even his own aching tiredness. The control room around him was crowded and noisy with voices, instruments, the rattle of charts. "We're here, sir. Going down."

Cheers erupted throughout the control room as *Amundsen* tilted her diving planes and banked into deeper water. Despite minor damages the submarine was evidently very nearly her old self: Her turbine engines operated flawlessly, utilizing only a fraction of their potential power, her battery of Tomahawk missiles (less No. 6) stood ready for launch at a moment's notice, her navigation and communications options were fully open. All that remained to do was to consult the ship's inertial navigational system, readjust for errors in the computers, and position *Amundsen* under ice approximately five feet thick, exactly as ordered by Squadron. The challenge was to establish a precise location; given a known platform from which to fire Tomahawk missiles and a stationary target downrange, perfect accuracy was ensured.

Awesome had reason to feel proud. Most of *Amundsen*'s crewmen didn't know enough to appreciate the magnitude of what had been accomplished. Only Laycook, Koranson, Riley, and himself fully understood that their submarine had achieved an extraordinary naval feat: Deep in Soviet waters Underwater Strategic Services had successfully planted a secret Trojan horse!

1125 hours.

In his stateroom, Awesome leaned against a springback chair and stacked his legs over loose memoranda on his desk, relaxing from the endless paper work demanded by the Submarine Service.

Files for some of those papers were built into the opposite bulkhead, along with a tiny bunk and workbench for naval charts. Crowded though these quarters were, they were far better than those enjoyed by others aboard *Amundsen*. At least here one could be alone. Contemplating his good fortune, Awesome lowered his chin to the chest and studied his hands, palms up, palms down, doubled into fists, and finally spread open to support an imaginary globe. Silhouetted against the buff-cream bulkhead, their movements closely resembled his father's hands from the pulpit of the United Methodist Church of Frankfort, Kentucky.

In summer, an early sun used to shine through the stained-glass window above the choir loft and pass between those fingers, outstretched above his shoulders for the priestly benediction—a dramatic moment in the lives of rural black people. His hands cast a larger-than-life shadow against the western wall and contributed to the seductive power of his oration. From his lips to his hands and then beyond to the congregation, the Reverend Elijah Awesome transferred the prophetic spirit to his parishioners.

For his son, Elisha, investiture into the ministry of Christ occurred one Sunday in July when he was sixteen years old. Pappy Awesome had preached the story of Elijah passing the prophetic mantle to his protégé, Elisha. Moved by the power of his father's evangelism, Elisha walked from pew to pulpit to accept Christ's burden as his own and knelt under his father's fingers. The preacher's voice, low and sonorous, rose gradually to match an increased tempo. It no longer paused between phrases, but ran into long, unpunctuated sentences that leaped into the air like music. Higher and higher the voice soared, stronger in volume, toward a sudden, ecstatic climax. Elisha, in that indescribable moment, became infused with the prophetic power miraculously transferred from father to son.

The ordination finished, Pappy Awesome's hands fell limply from his son's head. The bellowing thunder of his voice was drained and, when he spoke again, his voice was barely audible. A proud but exhausting moment. His son, the Reverend Awesome announced to the congregation, *his son* had been ordained a lay preacher in the service of Christ. Chairs rattled behind the altar; black faces popped over the brass railing. "Hallelujah!" the alto soprano voices burst into song.

"Hallelujah!" the male baritones responded antiphonally.

Perhaps it was too intense . . . or at too young an age. No further toward a career in the ministry did Elisha progress. In fact, never once did he set foot on the campus of Union Methodist Seminary, but instead accepted an appointment to the United States Naval Academy at Annapolis. By the time Elisha received his second investiture, his father had been dead for eleven years. In one sense that was a blessing, for that second ordination was wholly different from the first—so foreign to his father's experience that the Reverend could not have understood.

On his final inspection of *Amundsen* the day before she sailed and only hours before NATO business demanded his presence in Brussels, Vice Admiral Nicholas Francis Gaffy had stood on her bridge platform alongside his newly appointed skipper. From that high loft in the Scottish loch both men looked together into the afternoon twilight, along the placid waters guarded by rugged highland hills. They heard gentle waves lap against the submarine's hull and shared a mutual reverence for the sea. Gaffy spoke first about what it meant to send a man on patrol, especially when missions were secret and two-way communication restricted. He confessed that for one as mistrustful as himself the confidence required was painful to extend. A final inspection brought his vision over *Amundsen*'s deck, full circle, to rest upon the man beside him. A long, silent moment followed. Then Gaffy snatched his skipper's black hands and rubbed them like a child's. Seconds elapsed—awkward for the captain because holding him was an admiral and for the admiral because confiding his feelings to a man of inferior rank was so difficult.

"The hands that command *Amundsen* on this patrol are my hands, Elisha," he had said. Presquall winds gusted through his silvery hair and flushed blood to his cheeks. He wasn't one to be beaten by the weather after all those years of exposure to inclemency standing watch on submarine bridges. Yet he unexpectedly suggested they go below and talk for a while longer.

Awesome uncrossed his legs and reached over his ship's desk to the library shelf for a Bible, bound in polished leather and tooled in gold. A present from Admiral Gaffy on his thirty-eighth birthday. A year later, Awesome discovered passages in the Book of

Joshua that had been underscored by Gaffy's shaky hands. On that farewell visit to *Amundsen* the admiral had spotted the Bible in Awesome's library. "Elisha," he said, his voice fatherly, "I knew you would wish to take this on patrol." Gaffy had known exactly what that particular Bible meant to its possessor. It was a touchstone, a vital and tangible link with the spirit of the man who gave it.

Awesome's first meeting with Nicholas Gaffy occurred in April 1974, at Newport News Shipyards, Virginia, at the commissioning of the U.S.S. *Los Angeles* (SSN 688), an attack submarine slated to modernize the Navy's antisubmarine fleet. On his own Awesome would never have attended such a ceremony, but it was an official duty. In a public-relations campaign to display black faces in naval uniforms, the Department of Defense assigned Awesome to a small cadre of black officers with responsibility to attend ceremonies where television cameras were expected. If the charade fooled anybody it certainly failed to impress the showpieces, particularly the Annapolis wonderboy whom, everybody acknowledged, the Navy was accelerating up the ladder toward flag rank.

In the parade atmosphere at Newport News, the naval brass relaxed. Officers gossiped about Nicholas Gaffy and his relationship with the Secretary of Defense—and, rumor had it, with the President himself. But every one of them wanted to meet him. Surrounded by a bevy of junior officers, Gaffy himself stood on the platform impeccably attired in service blue uniform, accentuated by gold lace shoulder boards with fouled silver anchors and three stars. His curling gray hair peeked from under the rim of his white cap. One by one officers mounted the steps to greet him like so many votaries ascending an altar. For Awesome, when he took his turn, the moment was a colossal disappointment. True to his reputation, Gaffy was as cold as the nippy April wind. He extended a perfunctory handshake, devoid of all friendliness or warmth.

Three months after that brief encounter Awesome was transferred from the Pentagon to Gaffy's staff in Scotland, orders accompanied by a curious, almost threatening note from the admiral: He personally had arranged for this posting and would not hesitate to exercise his full power to prevent a successful appeal against it. Maxine was furious. If nothing else, she protested passionately, the transfer of the Awesome family to Scotland would upset the children badly and interrupt their schooling. But there was more to it than that. A tour of duty in Scotland was tantamount to a career disaster. Advancement in the Navy came to those who had the opportunity to make the right contacts in Washington. Duty at Holy Loch (where was it in the foggy highlands?) amounted to banishment from the influential inner circle. Despite his training in the Submarine Service neither he nor Maxine could understand why Admiral Gaffy had selected him . . . nor why the Pentagon had concurred.

So secret were Gaffy's activities with Underwater Strategic Services that even at Holy Loch headquarters their full scope was carefully clouded. After the Awesomes' arrival, several months elapsed while the admiral traveled to Allied naval bases on the

Continent. His black officer licked his wounds behind a desk, massaging papers, most of them routine. Clearly, the Navy had forgotten its Annapolis wonderboy.

Maxine faded in the northern climate. Life in Scotland was a far cry from Washington's glamorous cocktail parties where she had sparkled among the crowds elbowing their way up the power hierarchy. There were no crowds in Scotland, no parties, not even very many people in the windswept highlands, no clamor and excitement, nobody to fawn over her beauty or admire her father's talent as a television entertainer. Nor was there any mileage to be gained by being black in a predominantly white society or, for that matter, being a crusader for women's liberation.

Awesome spent little time at home. Maxine started drinking in the afternoon, mixing cocktails before dinner and more after it. Before anyone took serious notice, it was too late. The Scottish police report stated that her automobile had swerved into the opposite lane and was sideswiped by a sheep lorry. Apparently she tried to avoid disaster by careening off the road. The roll of the car did the damage. Maxine, Randy, and Susan, all returning from a shopping trip to Edinburgh, were crushed to death before help arrived. Terry was lacerated but survived. Awesome's world fell in upon itself. Death shrouded him with a dense, impenetrable depression. He swept blame up around him with a broad hand, guilt being easier to bear than the immeasurable loss.

On the bulkhead above his desk Awesome had taped a photograph of his family, taken upon their return from a public-relations jaunt to Jamaica. Maxine was at her prime, tall and elegantly radiant, a faint smile on the sculptured lips, lips that had touched his cheeks and ears with such indescribable tenderness that he sometimes believed he felt them beyond the grave. Her beige skin and almost Caucasian features had been passed on to her children. Susan, elusive and already glowing with her mother's beauty, looked reprovingly at Randy, the younger brother, who stood in short pants and sailor's tunic, giggling mischievously. Pigeon-toed and chubby, Terry was caught glancing to the side, his face subdued by shadow.

A reminder of that Jamaican trip languished in a glass bowl near Awesome's bunk. Beside a miniature rock island, a two-inch green turtle wallowed lazily in a thumbnail of water, his reptilian eyes half closed, his snout beneath the surface. One of three turtles the Awesomes had brought home from Montego Bay, he and his mates had been locked up in the children's playroom after the car accident and abandoned until the last moment. The water in the bowl had evaporated; two of them perished. Since the children had named their pets after famous submarines (Terry was too young to remember, much less distinguish one reptile from another), Awesome rechristened the survivor Dreadnought. Master and pet recovered together; the health of one was paralleled by the health of the other.

Awesome bent over Dreadnought's bowl and babbled baby talk. The turtle promptly retracted his snout and legs under its shell—waiting for the danger to pass. It didn't. He found himself removed from the water and placed between lungworts and ferns in a terrarium beside his bowl. The new habitat wasn't unfamiliar. Cautiously, Dreadnought emerged to creep through foliage once grown in Maxine's Scottish hothouse: English hedge ferns, saffron pepper, and silver fittonia for rooting. Small round stones that had once lined the path from the Awesomes' cottage to their garden were also there. Sometimes when sadness welled up inside, Awesome would plunge his fingers into the tiny patch of earth and let it sift through them like sand in an hourglass. Submariners often tried to grow plants aboard their boats. Usually they succeeded for a week or ten days, but then their plants wilted and died. In contrast, Maxine's terrarium flourished. Several of *Amundsen*'s officers had noted the phenomenon, but Awesome didn't think it remarkable. For him, the soil was infused with Maxine's spirit.

In situations like Maxine's death, the Submarine Service typically offered sympathy but took steps to protect its own interests. When a man's emotional stability was shaken, he couldn't be entrusted with command over destructive weapons. Removal from important responsibility was routine—at least until his reactions could be observed and evaluated. Being relieved of command, one was assured, was only temporary. Of course! Still, at Awesome's age one could easily be written off permanently. The Navy had a great facility for shielding one from responsibility until eligible for early retirement and pension. Many good officers had been effectively banished in this manner.

But Nicholas Gaffy seldom did things in an

orthodox way. Almost immediately, he started to salvage Awesome's career from what had seemed irreparable wreckage. His therapy was simple: work, work, work, and more work, each step with increased responsibility. First there were short patrols in the North Sea to qualify new crews for Dolphin Wings. Next followed the toughest assignment in Awesome's career—to preside over the court-martial of seven black sailors charged with mutinous conduct. In both the American and the British press, the case received wide publicity as a racial trial despite substantial evidence against the defendants. All were convicted. Under military law any judge, white, black, brown, or polka-dot, was obliged to impose a stiff prison sentence. The press used the case as proof the Navy had not yet emerged from the nineteenth century. Hate mail arrived daily by special lorry; there were two anonymous threats against Awesome's life. Then, in the aftermath of the unpleasant trial, came his thirty-eighth birthday.

Under such circumstances one could hardly look forward to middle age, much less celebrate its arrival. Gaffys' invitation to have a drink at home with his wife, Jennifer, and thereafter motor into town for a quiet dinner, seemed just the proper touch. Awesome, moved that Gaffy had remembered his birthday at all, turned up promptly at seven, brushed and creased outside, leaden inside, intent on repaying the Gaffy's kindness by making himself pleasant, wondering how when memories of past birthdays, the children's little presents, Maxine's cake and candles, kept making a lump in his throat. The admiral's home was surrounded by cars; his living room crowded with guests. When Awesome stepped into the vestibule, a cheer went up, catching him quite satisfactorily by surprise. What the hell! Quiet drink, indeed! This was a party! The guests were people associated with Underwater Strategic Services but seldom, if ever, seen. Such an unexpected venue for the mysterious code names to materialize in the flesh! The guest list, he recognized almost at once, was no accident. Nor was it really a birthday celebration. Gaffy had moved in mysterious ways once again. The convocation could be more accurately described as an initiation rite, a formal introduction to the inner sanctum of Underwater Strategic Services.

Gaffy was in high humor. As always he clutched his glass of ginger ale and squired Awesome about, joking and laughing and telling stories. The best ones were his Katzenback tales, the story about Admiral Robert Katzenback, Chief of Naval Operations, landing his World War II Grumman Wildcat fighter on a Japanese aircraft carrier by mistake. And the one about the infamous "Katzenback supply fiasco" on Saipan, where much to the assaulting Marines' injury, combat supplies were delivered to the wrong beaches. The stories were funny and Gaffy told them well, but those who knew him understood his contempt for Katzenback. Every word clawed at his superior's competence and reputation. Some time around two o'clock Gaffy ordered his one and only alcoholic drink of the evening, his one ounce of Dewar's scotch, which signaled the party was drawing to its end. To the delight of his four remaining guests he concluded with Katzenback's foolish re-creation of the 1862 *Monitor-Merrimac* battle in the mudflats at Hampton Roads, Virginia. The party was over.

At 0740 Awesome's telephone rang sharply. Gaffy bellowed through the receiver: Awesome was to be in his office by 0820. He was there, but after only three hours' sleep he had difficulty keeping the admiral in focus, much less understanding him. His shirt and trousers unchanged from the evening's festivities, Gaffy sat saturnine and pugnacious behind his desk. It took Awesome a long while to find out why. Katzenback had struck again.

As if the Chief of Naval Operations had learned about the evening's entertainment at his expense and planned his revenge, word had arrived that he was again on the warpath against what he considered Gaffy's Private Navy. The Senate Armed Services Committee had scheduled an investigation. Katzenback could easily have forestalled or indefinitely postponed it. But he had long been eager to dismantle Underwater Strategic Services and subtly encouraged the senators. For ten minutes Gaffy growled like a bulldog, listing Katzenback's sins and stupidities, rubbed raw by the perfidy of his Annapolis classmate. They had collided over a girl in their plebe year and throughout the decades continued the combat until, "in the very *twilight* of our careers," Gaffy pronounced solemnly, Katzenback was after him again. "And he's hitting below the belt, Elisha. Anyone can see that."

Gaffy snapped his jaw shut like a shark, shoved his hands down on his desk, and jumped up. This, too, Awesome came to understand, was a ritual catharsis. Once on his feet, Gaffy was transformed. His words were carefully measured, his counterattack in hand and cunning, his eyes hungry for battle. He peered at Awesome over the rims of his spectacles: Would Commander Awesome not enjoy a trip to Washington on behalf of Underwater Strategic Services?

In security matters, congressional committees were usually deferential, perhaps more than reasonable. Still, Gaffy recognized there were likely to be questions about his squadron that dealt with means rather than ends which could easily be misunderstood. He needed Awesome, and would explain why later. Awesome nodded. He had learned that Gaffy had purposely selected men who, regardless of what others thought, would commit themselves to him personally; he had no objections to that. In Underwater Strategic Services the motto read not Duty, Honor, and Country, but Duty, Country, and Gaffy. Honor, they added, didn't figure in much.

A secretive man by nature, Gaffy seldom revealed anything before it was absolutely essential. He waited to confide his Washington strategy until Awesome had boarded the Navy transport jet. The plan was not subject to alteration, nor was Awesome's complicity solicited. It was assumed. At the last moment, Gaffy confided, he would feign illness and be confined to his room in the Hay-Adams Hotel, unfortunately unable to present himself before the Senate committee on the Hill. He gambled that the senators would be unlikely to challenge the testimony of his deputy, who was incidentally the Navy's highest-ranking black submarine commander. Certain "inaccuracies," as he called them, were essential not only for the squadron's survival, but also for America's security.

Gaffy's political acumen proved as flawless as his naval judgment. The senators were uncomfortable, even in executive session, about grilling a high-ranking black officer. The fact that New Jersey's Senator T. Wilbur Teabrook, the assistant chairman, was himself black, facilitated the ruse. Awesome led them neatly along a path of the admiral's devising, far away from the sensitive, critical issues. After two days of hearings, the senatorial investigators moved for early adjournment and a long Thanksgiving weekend. Back at the Hay-Adams, Gaffy was so ecstatic he celebrated by ordering from room service two Dewar's scotches—one for himself and one for Awesome.

Leaning over from his plane seat en route home, the admiral talked about a double victory—not only had he averted a dangerous congressional uproar, but he had also executed a perfect end run around Katzenback. It was difficult to tell which victory he prized more. What was not ambiguous was Gaffy's gratitude. Commander Awesome had been previously "frocked" as captain but had remained without a billet. Shortly after their return to Scotland the Navy's celebrated black man was given command of U.S.S. *Edmond Roald Amundsen*. With this appointment came his fourth stripe and a captain's star on his sleeve.

There was a sharp knock at the door of the skipper's stateroom. "Come in!"

Lieutenant Commander Charles Riley, his muscles bulging under his soiled coveralls, stepped over the coaming and closed the door behind him. "Reporting on our damages, sir. If it's convenient."

"Something else wrong, Riley? I went over that with Commander Laycook."

"Yes, sir. No, sir. Nothing new, I mean. But I think we can fix them ourselves." After a thorough assessment Riley had devised a plan to fix both the jammed starboard hull valve and the malfunctioning torpedo tube. It was largely a question of how much the skipper wanted to repair while on patrol and how much he was prepared to leave for what Riley unaffectionately and disdainfully called the Royal Welding Society at Holy Loch.

Awesome evaluated the determination on Riley's face. From among the Submarine Service's capable engineering officers he had been specifically requested for Patrol Polynya because he was known to accomplish at sea what required an entire division of engineers to do in dry dock. The best of his clan, he ignored the rule book and worked by sheer instinct, devising ingenious and sometimes outlandish schemes which seemed preposterous, except that invariably they worked. You couldn't say he was guilty of recklessness; that Gaffy never would have permitted. The admiral recognized in Riley another quality, something that was difficult to describe. Submariners had to be balanced personalities, yet many harbored private obsessions. And it was their obsessions that made them effective. Riley's passion was malfunctioning machines. The engineering officer, of course, denied that emphatically, but could not explain why he toiled through consecutive watches with no rest and little food until his mastery over machines had been demonstrated. During work his mood was ebullient, his cheeks almost as ruddy as his hair, his smile ingratiating. But when the job was finished his temper boiled, or worse, he slipped into morbid depression. It was seldom a chronic problem. Aboard *Amundsen* there was always a machinery malfunction to provide him therapy.

Riley's plan involved two phases: first, to pull the Tomahawk missile from tube 6 and send a welder forward to free the muzzle door and WRT drain, and second, to send a team of divers out the escape trunk to free the jammed hull valve. Both phases, he explained, presented some risk, but if successful, *Amundsen* would suffer virtually no downtime in Scotland, and Gold Crew could sail her to sea after routine provisioning.

Awesome pondered the proposal. After the collision on the Little Andes he had abandoned his hope of returning to Holy Loch with an untarnished patrol record. Riley's plan sounded not only plausible, but also worthy of any skipper who looked beyond his own needs to requirements of the Service. It was one thing to complete Patrol Polynya with Blue Crew, but what about the future? If Gaffy's plan worked for three months, it should rightfully be duplicated with Gold Crew. And that required a submarine ready to return immediately to sea. "I hate those acetylene torches, Charlie," Awesome said, more for the sake of sounding cautious than from genuine fear of welding.

"We'll take precautions," Riley answered lightly. "I'll put the circulating fans on high and pull the smoke through the carbon-dioxide scrubbers. Any particulate matter will be removed in the activated charcoal filters."

"Perhaps." Awesome unrolled a ship's plan to familiarize himself with the muzzle door and the WRT drain in the torpedo tube. The principal problems entailed in Riley's repair operation were discussed and most of the skipper's objections countered. In the end, Riley prevailed upon his duty to return the submarine in equal if not better condition than when she sailed. Yet Awesome's consent was not unconditional. The engineering officer received permission only to pull Tomahawk 6 from its tube and make repairs inside. After that had been successfully completed they would talk more about sending divers into the water to fix the damaged hull valve and sea chest.

Riley, a man who knew how to exploit his opportunities, headed for the door before Awesome had a chance to change his mind . . . or further qualify his consent. His eyes dropped momentarily over the terrarium. The English hedge ferns moved and appeared to vibrate back into place. "Hey, there's something in there . . . something alive!" he exclaimed.

"A mighty creature indeed." Silver fittonia rustled again, then Dreadnought emerged into an open patch of soil. Awesome lifted him from the miniature jungle to his palm. "Commander Riley, meet Dreadnought. Dreadnought, meet Commander Riley."

Turtles, the engineer declared, were among his least favorite pets. Nothing personal, but he just wanted the skipper to know how he felt. Such reptiles had always struck him as being singularly indolent and not at all cunning, like snakes . . . or as resourceful as their cousins, the alligators. "Besides, this little bugger doesn't like me. You see, he hides under his shell."

"He hides from everybody. Even me. He's just frightened. 'Self-contained,' you might say. Like this submarine he packs his own protection with him and pulls inside himself when he gets scared."

"*That* must be why I don't like turtles," Riley said good-humoredly. "I wouldn't know how to fix them. Submarines, on the other hand . . ." He laughed, feeling the exhilaration that overwhelmed him before a challenging repair operation.

The moment Riley left, Awesome rested his back against the door and for a moment reflected upon what he had just ordered. The engineering officer made everything sound so easy, perhaps too easy. Accepting his counsel was not without its risks, grave risks, but risks commensurate with the daring of Patrol Polynya, risks that any bold leader would have to accept. Awesome's meditations were interrupted by a sharp rap on his door.

Thomas Laycook had also come to talk about the damages. Riley's repair plan notwithstanding, he had concluded that nothing could be safely accomplished until *Amundsen*'s return to Holy Loch. The captain's surprising revelation that a repair operation had been authorized angered him. An alliance between the skipper and engineering officer served only two purposes: Awesome wanted no damages to testify against his poor judgment in battling the floebergs and Riley wanted a decoration for accomplishing the impossible. Neither officer seemed to appreciate that risks involved in a repair at sea far exceeded the benefits gained by saving downtime at base. If duty compelled Laycook to accept the captain's decision, it also dictated he express his own reservations . . . cautiously and with respect. "I don't know how much toxic gas the scrubbers can handle."

Awesome didn't seem especially concerned. Riley had assured him the fumes would not be a problem. He planned to evacuate the forward torpedo room after Tomahawk 6 was pulled from her tube and to seal off the compartment. Regardless of how much gas escaped from Riley's torches, it was just a matter of time before the scrubbers would filter it all.

"But cutting and welding in the bow is risky and we're in the eleventh hour of the patrol. It can't be long before we're recalled. Keep us out here much longer and we'll have to fish through the escape hatches."

"It will take them a month to repair that torpedo tube in Scotland, not to mention the security risk. Riley can do it in twelve hours. I have no intention of providing Gold Crew with another extended vacation. It's only fair to give Riley a chance."

"He's a bit cavalier about safety, Captain. Thrives on taking chances. . . . Riley's outgrown Erector Sets and now he's only satisfied when he can accomplish what nobody else believes is possible. The more dangerous the operation, the better it suits him. In my opinion he's tempting fate." Laycook paused before making his strongest recommendation. "If those repairs really need attention use the captain's discretion and return to Scotland."

"No, Thomas. I've had enough of that sort of talk. I'm not prepared to declare what happened on the bergs an emergency. Nor am I prepared to abort Patrol Polynya. We've done all right until now. Like any self-respecting skipper, I will persevere until we've received orders from Squadron to come home." Awesome hesitated to see whether his exec officer had fully understood the import of his words. "But I do agree with you, Thomas, on one point. Riley's somewhat overenthusiastic. Gets carried away at times."

"Any scheme to weld from inside a torpedo tube when we're returning to base in about twelve days has got to be a great risk."

"All right, Thomas. I accept what you say. We both concur about Riley. Therefore I'd like you to keep an eye on him during the repair. See he doesn't take any unnecessary chances. Be his watchdog. . . ."

"You want me to be Riley's watchdog?" Laycook balked.

"Thomas," the skipper rolled his name out fully on his lips, "you're the ideal person. You understand the missiles better than anyone aboard. You also have a good intuition about Riley. I'll feel a lot better with you overseeing."

Laycook bit his lip and stiffened almost to attention. "Yes, sir." But he was furious. Too much was being asked of him. An order to supervise a repair that he knew to be ill-advised cunningly shifted the responsibility and the possible blame to his own shoulders. It was a responsibility he did not want but could not avoid.

His eyes frozen on the black man before him,

Laycook opened the door. The fragile truce between them was in danger of fracture. Only a supreme disciplinary effort might postpone open disagreement, at least until *Amundsen* sailed home to Scotland. One could take pride in that control, even if it implied personal capitulation. "Yes, Captain Awesome," he said, like a petty officer replying to an admiral. "Aye, *aye,* sir."

Awesome returned the Bible to its place on the small shelf over his desk. What had possessed Gaffy to assign Thomas Laycook as *Amundsen's* exec officer? In the light of his disappointment, that was asking a lot of any man. But Gaffy often did things like that with a purpose: perhaps to test the man's mettle for some other assignment . . . or maybe to humble him or provide training in self-discipline. Or perhaps the answer was simpler. Thomas Laycook was, after all, the Submarine Service's only cruise missile officer. And a damn good one at that.

3

RIGA, LATVIA

(Patrol Polynya: 60th day plus 23)

0310: *Amundsen's* Russian-language translator, George Sokorski, yawned; it had been three and a half hours since the last weather report from a Soviet ship. Steven Frackmeyer in the seat beside him was slumped forward, his eyes lowered over a paperback novel. When he was into a story you couldn't interrupt him, and this one had something to do with Australians in New Guinea. For Sokorski, the time dragged by. In the early morning even the Russians stopped yakking and went to bed. "What do you say, Frackmeyer? Let's get some music."

"Can't. You know that."

"I'm going nuts. It wouldn't hurt. The Russkies broadcast music to their subs twenty-four hours a day. I know the VLF."

"Knock it off, Sokorski." Frackmeyer was halfway through the last chapter. He seemed more annoyed by the interruption than by the prospect of violating regulations. Sokorski's hand defiantly reached for the large, rubber dial on the VLF frequency modulator but withdrew in hesitation. He could hear Lieutenant Schroeder's voice warning them not to fiddle with *Amundsen*'s very-low-frequency antenna or, under threat of "capital punishment," alter the frequencies for incoming reception. The patrol had particularly stringent regulations; the lieutenant never let you forget them. "Hell, why not?" Sokorski looked to Frackmeyer for encouragement; it was not forthcoming. "Why not?" Sokorski inquired again, firmly. At 0300 Schroeder was certain to be asleep and it was highly unlikely another officer would appear. Sokorski's fingers shut down the automatic tape recorder for incoming Soviet signals and quickly spun the frequency dial counterclockwise. Three rapid adjustments and *Amundsen*'s VLF antenna rotated to the southwest.

Arctic static was heavy but there was a clearing between 10 kHz and 11 kHz. Yes indeed! Sokorski enjoyed the thought of defying the communications officer—and more, getting away with it. Reception was particularly good, better than expected: not the lively Russian folk melodies he loved most, but never mind that. Clarinet and violin music.

Frackmeyer was less impressed and looked up curiously. "What's that? Rimski-Korsakov?"

Sokorski didn't know and silenced his buddy with a hand signal. After eight staccato chords in a minor key the music stopped. He had leaned back in satisfaction to await the next selection when what he feared most suddenly happened. Both radiomen froze. Footsteps in the control room outside!

Frackmeyer jumped forward and hit the tape recorder; Sokorski's chair came down with a bang and his trembling fingers searched for the original frequency. He was reaching up to readjust the antenna when the footsteps halted outside the radio shack door. Too late: They had been caught! Sokorski's muscles went flat and left him paralyzed, his hand in midair, his eyes on the closed door. Surely it was going to slide open and show him Lieutenant Schroeder's silhouette in the oval steel frame, with his shit-eating smile in place. Nothing would please the lieutenant more than to catch you violating a regulation and justify some disciplinary action. The door did not open. The footsteps started again, but this time in retreat. Sokorski and Frackmeyer slumped into their seats until their heartbeats quieted.

An argument ensued—a heated one. Sokorski wanted to return to the music. The worst was over. Lightning never struck twice. . . . Frackmeyer thought he'd gone absolutely crazy. But frustration at dissuading the determined translator drove him back to his novel. Better to get lost in the jungles of New Guinea than to cope with a madman.

Sokorski returned immediately to the radio antenna and tape recorder, searching for Russian music. He found instead the news, read by a male announcer with a Lithuanian accent that reminded him of his father.

News wasn't worth the risk, Sokorski thought. Soviet news was always the same Communist bullshit—shoveled high and wide. Russian propaganda wasn't even clever. His fingers tightened on the frequency dial ready to change again. From the dreary, pedestrian commentary *Amundsen's* name seemed to leap like high-voltage electricity into the tiny compartment. "Must be Riga," he said aloud, increasing the volume.

. . . and American officials in the Pentagon have admitted that the nuclear attack submarine U.S.S. Edmond Roald Amundsen sank 500 kilometers off the Azores Islands in mid-January. It is believed an internal explosion parted the hull, sinking the vessel before it surfaced. According to the United States naval spokesmen, all aboard were lost in the disaster. Wreckage from the submarine has been positively identified by the Portuguese Government. Fishermen near the Mid-Atlantic Rift, 500 kilometers southwest of the Azores, have found debris with the Amundsen's imprint. A memorial service for the American sailors was held in Washington today, where the Secretary of Defense, Emilio Griffin, laid a wreath in Arlington National Cemetery. [A woman's voice followed.] The Soviet Government repeatedly has warned American allies about giving harborage to nuclear vessels. Strong protests have often been lodged with the British Government in London. The Soviet People's Government is demanding the Portuguese

make an immediate investigation.

Sokorski swore through his teeth. More Russian propaganda. Asinine shit. The Russians would have to eat that crap when *Amundsen* returned to Holy Loch.

This is Riga, the man's voice continued. *It is 0328 hours. The next news broadcast will be at 0530 hours this morning.*

His fingers closed on the dial again. Perhaps they wouldn't have to eat that crap. Anything the Pentagon said the Russians would just deny . . . or ignore. What did they suppose they gained by such a fallacious report? Did it really do much for Russian morale to believe their enemies were incompetent enough to lose a submarine? Maybe it might. He imagined steelworkers hurrying off to work with new vigor in Leningrad, ballet dancers leaping higher in Moscow rehearsal halls, East Berlin schoolboys putting out their tongues at Western tourists, Romanian garment workers sewing straighter seams—poor dopes.

Sokorski's feeling of superiority died suddenly. What if the Soviets beamed their broadcast to the West? Surely the immigrant grapevine would learn about it! His father in Chicago had a brother in Warsaw with whom he corresponded often enough. Several associates in his father's office were ham radio operators. Their businesses often took them to West Germany, Hungary, and Poland . . . less frequently, to the Soviet Union. No, Sokorski concluded, it wasn't a question of *if* that phony report reached America for his parents to hear. The only question was *when*. "FRACKMEYER!"

0807—beginning of the forenoon watch: Immediately after breakfast Sokorski entered officers' country to ambush Commander Laycook outside the wardroom. He didn't have long to wait: The exec officer appeared, in freshly laundered and pressed coveralls, at the precise moment Forbes had predicted. It was well known that Laycook was directed by some internal clock, his daily activities exactly and inflexibly scheduled. Evidently this applied to his bowels as well. In discomfort he shifted from foot to foot while his Russian-language tutor repeated what he had heard from Riga and explained how he had come to listen.

Sokorski's confession about altering the VLF antenna produced a perfunctory grunt of disapproval. The Riga broadcast was dismissed as "sloppy propaganda." To Laycook's mind propaganda was simply information with which you didn't agree; bad propaganda, inexcusable; and sloppy propaganda, beneath contempt. After a brief speech about the Soviet talent for manufacturing facts, he assured Sokorski that in America the broadcast would not be taken seriously, *if* it reached America. But when he took steps in the direction of the officers' head, Sokorski blocked his passage. The translator wasn't satisfied. Nothing had been said about the crewmen's families at home. Something had to be done to inform them. When they learned what the Russians said they wouldn't know what to believe. Most would be scared like hell!

Laycook took Sokorski's anxiety more seriously.

From the beginning of the patrol, the translator had tutored him in Russian. In the course of instruction they had developed something more than the normal relationship between an officer and an enlisted man. When they conversed in Russian they told about their personal lives, their thoughts, their aspirations . . . and their impressions of submarine life. Friendship was the inevitable result. Now Sokorski had come seeking special consideration. He had a right to expect more than a shrug of the shoulders.

"All right, George," Laycook sighed. "Report this broadcast to the skipper. He should know what the Russians are saying about us. Don't withhold any facts, and then leave it to his judgment. He'll probably decide not to say anything to Lieutenant Schroeder about the regulations, but if he does I'll intercede on your behalf." Sokorski seemed only slightly relieved. "You didn't hear what I just said, did you, George?" Laycook smiled, skipping on his toes to ease the gas mounting in his bowels. "I mean about interceding on your behalf?"

Sokorski nodded; he understood that this compromised the Navy's professionalism. Officers didn't do that kind of thing often, or openly; it was considered bad form and bad discipline. But Laycook was known to bend the rules from time to time. "Yes, sir. Thank you, sir." Sokorski headed for the captain's cabin.

Outside Captain Awesome's stateroom, Sokorski waited nervously, rehearsing the speech he intended to deliver. His first tap on the door had been timid and nothing happened. He rapped again, more forcibly, trying to remember that his mission was important to the entire crew. A moment later the black man came to the door, an unlit pipe wedged between massive white teeth, one eyebrow arched high with curiosity. Enlisted men did not often visit his cabin unannounced asking to talk with him. The translator was ordered to wait in the passageway while he returned to his desk and flipped a large naval chart upside down. Sokorski had long believed the Submarine Service's secrecy childish, but this time he was grateful for the respite, however short.

No noise from officers' country permeated into the skipper's stateroom. Awesome was leaning against his desk, waiting. In the moment of awkward silence, Sokorski felt foolish. Why on earth had he come to stand before the scrutiny of those penetrating eyes? The captain could have done more to make him feel at ease. Too late for retreat. But, damn it, he wanted to run. His first words sounded positively incoherent. "Sir, I wanted to tell Lieutenant Schroeder, but bumped into Commander Laycook first." He swallowed the falsehood, hoping Awesome would never learn otherwise. "I don't mean any disrespect to the lieutenant, but you understand . . . Commander Laycook wanted me to report this to you immediately. . . . What I mean is, you see, at the beginning, it sounded like Russian propaganda. Absurd, silly stuff, so I didn't want to wake anybody—especially Lieutenant Schroeder. You understand?"

Awesome didn't. He stood across from the translator, arms folded, one hand on his pipe, an emotionless distraction in his eyes. The idea of an enlisted

91

man jumping the hierarchy of command displeased him. But Admiral Gaffy had preached the importance of flexibility for effective leadership. In fact, Gaffy was himself a champion pole vaulter over the military echelons. Awesome decided on the spot not to discipline Sokorski for violating the rules: a reprimand, yes, but disciplinary action, no. He waited for the translator to go on. Sokorski made a hash of it, but got the story out, more or less. Only mention of the Secretary of Defense, Emilio Griffin, laying a wreath for *Amundsen*'s men in Arlington National Cemetery, near the Tomb of the Unknown Soldier, elicited a response from the black skipper. That Soviet invention struck him as quite realistic. It was the kind of patriotic gesture compatible with the Secretary's character.

Awesome thanked Sokorski for the information and asked if there was anything further.

There was. Sokorski's next remark sounded rather inane. "The Russkies said something about posthumous decorations for the crew. Wonder what they'll say when we return to Scotland?"

Awesome's expression softened with amusement. "They do have a sense of humor, as well as a vivid imagination. We'll invite the Soviet naval attaché in London to greet us at Holy Loch and he can award the medals. A special commendation for you, Sokorski."

Such lightness was a good sign. Sokorski finally brought himself nearer the point. "I was wondering, sir, whether there might be some way of notifying our families about this. Of course, I understand about radio silence. But our patrol has been extended. We're way overdue in Scotland and we haven't been able to communicate with our folks since Christmas. There's got to be some emergency procedure to cover a situation like this." Awesome looked unimpressed and Sokorski hurried on. "You see, sir, my parents will be worried stiff. They worked for the American Embassy in Moscow during World War II and when it ended Stalin shipped them to Siberia as spies, them and anybody else associated with Americans. Some way to reward your allies! You can imagine how my mother and father hate Russkies and how afraid they get about my job. It wouldn't be fair not to notify them that we're okay."

Awesome responded with professional sincerity, a certain theatrical parting of the lips and the grave, meditative tone he used with crewmen. Naturally, he could appreciate Sokorski's concern for his parents and his desire to alleviate any anxiety the Riga broadcast might produce. Yet, as a sailor, Sokorski must understand the military considerations involved, not the least of which was *Amundsen*'s order to maintain radio silence.

"I meant," Sokorski replied, not in fact knowing quite what he meant except that Awesome must do something, "that the Navy should make a public statement or, at least, contact our families privately." How Awesome was to go about achieving that Sokorski didn't know, but he felt sure *Amundsen* had some secret and special means of communicating with Squadron if it really had to, some way to get around the requirement for radio silence. Something about which only the captain knew.

Awesome settled himself in his desk chair and

pondered Sokorski's entreaty. You couldn't blame him for believing his skipper had a trick or two up his sleeve. After all, Patrol Polynya was in essence a daring bit of naval legerdemain. But even magicians must abide by natural laws. Underwater Strategic Services had not yet learned how a submarine could communicate with base without compromising her location. It was unjust to mislead the young translator: Under no condition would *Amundsen* contact Squadron or Washington. Nor was the Pentagon likely to make any statement whatsoever about *Amundsen*, for that would attract attention to what Underwater Strategic Services believed should remain inconspicuous. Awesome spoke in a calm, sympathetic voice. "I could tell you there's nothing to worry about and that the Navy will manage everything at home with consummate efficiency and tact. But in my judgment, Sokorski, that's not going to happen. The Navy won't manage anything. There's an unwritten military policy that we never respond to the enemy's propaganda and assist in disseminating false information. If we deny this lie publicly, they'll just challenge us to provide *Amundsen*'s bearings. If we did that, our cover would be lost We don't want the press to make a commotion and draw the whole world's attention to us. The only thing the Navy can do is ignore this broadcast completely."

Juding from Sokorski's troubled expression, Awesome knew he had provided little consolation. However upset the translator might be, there was still some reason for hope. Usually Soviet propaganda was directed to a Russian audience. The Soviets were sophisticated enough to know that what the Russian public would buy the American public would not. Propaganda lies could have a serious backlash.

Sokorski protested. The captain had obviously underestimated his parents. If there was something critical to know about their son, they would find out. Some ham operator in Germany would talk to a ham operator in Boston, and from there to Chicago. They'd learn—one way or the other, they'd find out.

"That's a possibility," Awesome responded, wondering if the debate would continue forever, and rose to his feet. "In my view, Sokorski, you're underestimating your parents, who may be more resourceful than you think. They know the Russians and their chicanery. They'll suspect propaganda when they hear it and also understand why the Navy cannot reply." Sokorski remained flat and unresponsive, his head cocked stiffly back, his eyes enlarged. Eighty-three days of patrol had made him susceptible to confusion. Awesome admitted that he wasn't up to form himself. "Now that I'm aware of what's being said about us, I've got a new concern. That broadcast could do damage to morale aboard. For however long we are ordered to remain on patrol I don't want this giving others the spooks. I hope you haven't mentioned the broadcast to anyone but Commander Laycook."

"No, sir. Only Frackmeyer."

"Then Frackmeyer, you, me, and Commander Laycook are the only men aboard who know about it. Sokorski, this is the way I want it to remain. Tell Frackmeyer he's under orders from me. If the story spreads around, I'll know who's responsible. Do you understand?" Awesome moved to the door and Sokorski followed, his expression of injury unchanged. He made a final effort to console the translator. "Keep this buttoned up and I'll forget about regulations. You're authorized to say that to Frackmeyer . . . and I'll also give some thought to your family situation, although I can't see now what can possibly be done. All in all, I think things will straighten out by themselves, yet I appreciate your feelings. You've got a good bargain, don't you agree?"

There wasn't time to disagree. They were distracted by voices in the passageway outside, loud and strident voices. Awesome opened the door. Laycook stood just beyond it, in heated conversation with one of Riley's engineers.

"Why aren't you with Commander Riley, Thomas?" Awesome was suddenly annoyed. The executive officer was supposed to be in the forward torpedo compartment during repairs.

Laycook's face was garnet. He gave Sokorski an icy stare and clamped his jaw shut. "One moment, Thomas," Awesome ordered. Sokorski was dismissed with a final warning to seek out Frackmeyer immediately; then Awesome led his exec officer into the stateroom. "Who's keeping an eye on Riley?"

"I am, sir. But what good it does is beyond me. Are you aware that Commander Riley is using emergency air breathers in tube 6? Using them to fight a fire is one thing, but he's not fighting a fire, he's about to start one. He's got hot torches, less than twenty-five inches away."

Awesome stared at Laycook. What the hell was

Riley thinking of? He certainly had not mentioned using the emergency air breathers, only turning up the ventilation fans to expel the toxic gases. Laycook was right; it was much too dangerous. "Did you say anything to Riley?"

"No, sir. I don't believe I was given that authority. I understood I was to report directly back to you if I felt he was doing something risky. I'm now making that report and will immediately return to the torpedo room, sir."

"That's *not* what I had in mind, Thomas! Perhaps I didn't make myself clear. I expected you to supervise the safety of Riley's work and I'm giving you authority as of this moment to intervene if and when necessary."

"Thank God. The first thing I'm going to do is get that welder out of the tube with a compressed-air tank."

"Captain! Captain Awesome, sir!" Knuckles thumped against the door. "Emergency, sir!" Laycook yanked it open as Hospital Corpsman Ted Becker, Greerson's assistant, nearly tumbled in. He was out of breath from his dash aftward through the crowded berthing compartment and officers' country to the captain's cabin. And at that instant *Amundsen*'s flooding siren sounded. Between its ear-shattering honks, Becker told them why: fire . . . forward compartment . . . explosion in torpedo tube 6!

Awesome and Laycook barked simultaneously. How *much* fire? Spreading how fast? There was enough high explosive in the spare Tomahawk missiles to blow *Amundsen* all the way to the North Pole!

"Fire's almost out, sir," Becker offered, still panting. "Commander Riley got it right away with CO_2 extinguishers. . . ." That was all Becker had time to say before the flat of the skipper's hand struck him on the upper arm and spun him around toward the torpedo room. Laycook followed close on their heels. "Sure it's under control?" Awesome bellowed.

"Yes, sir. . . . They've sealed off the forward compartment just in case."

The flooding siren stopped as suddenly as it had begun. At least they could hear themselves talk. All around them crewmen were still scurrying to their action stations, crowding the passageways. At the watertight door to the forward compartment Awesome threw another question at Becker. "Injuries?"

"Only Bert Graham . . . real bad . . . Dr. Greerson's inside with him now."

Awesome did not require an explanation. Graham was in Riley's detail, a machinist's mate with welding experience. If he had crawled forward to repair the damaged WRT drain and muzzle door and there had been an explosion, he was nearly cremated. That's all the Navy seemed to get—burns—of every permutation—burns worse than civilians could imagine. The quick-acting watertight door swung forward. An unidentified odor attacked Awesome's nostrils, yet there was surprisingly little smoke. Ventilator fans overhead growled at high volume. Riley and Everett Young were working near the breech door to torpedo tube 6, just below the platform deck. Greerson was kneeling over his patient underneath Tomahawk 6, which had been pulled from its tube and was hanging in midair by chain winches. The compartment had been cleared of all crewmen before welding had begun and only the physician had been allowed to reenter. Awesome suddenly knew what the odor was: a mixture of vaporized carbon dioxide from the extinguishers, fire foam retardant that had been sprayed over the spare Tomahawks to prevent secondary explosions, and the putrescence of burned flesh. A slippery fire-retardant film coated the deck underfoot. As he moved forward cautiously he made a guess at the damage: the dozen spare Tomahawks on automatic loading racks had been untouched, as were the tube drain manifolds, gyrospindles, and, importantly, *Amundsen*'s sonar transducers. The fire was indeed out. Everything appeared superficially in order, except near the breech door to tube 6. Fire-retardant foam everywhere. That could be cleaned up, but then there was Bertram Graham. It was difficult to look at him. Burns made some of the ugliest wounds.

Greerson was calling for help. His patient's legs had to be lifted for blood to flow into the brain and prevent shock. Water was applied to Graham's scorched lips, through which a series of groans escaped. A gauze bandage covered his eyes. Of all maladies Awesome most feared blindness. In nightmares he often experienced the terrible blackness.

Nylon tarps used by the engineering detail had been folded and laid loosely over Graham's body; Riley, his face white, glanced up at the skipper but there was no time for explanations. Graham needed a dozen immediate services to keep him out of shock. When Greerson temporarily removed the tarp for a morphine injection the full force of the explosion was apparent. Barely a place on the seaman's body had escaped the flash flame, whose heat had been trapped and magnified by the twenty-five-inch torpedo tube. What remained of the welder's service dungarees had to be cut away from the thigh to find unscorched skin for the hypodermic needle.

A stretcher team arrived to take the patient aftward to the berthing compartment Greerson had established as a sickbay. When it had departed, Awesome turned toward Laycook. The torpedo room, he ordered, had to be returned to operational status. *Amundsen* had lost the use of one launch tube, but still had five more in the event she was called to attack.

"Yes, sir, I'll see that this foam is cleaned immediately. Then we'll begin a check of the sonar and each Tomahawk. If you agree we'll pull the Tomahawks one at a time from their tubes and check them out before repeating the same with each of the spares. I don't anticipate any difficulties. That explosion was well localized in tube 6. But we should be careful just the same."

Awesome assented. He was grateful for Laycook's professionalism. In time of emergency it helped to find men cooperative . . . and efficient. No doubt Laycook was finding that vindication was sweet. Still, he would bring *Amundsen* back to operational status within hours.

With Laycook headed for the control room to organize the cleanup, the torpedo room was empty except for Machinist's Mate Everett Young, Riley's assistant. Awesome watched him check the locking mechanism on tube 6, then wipe clean an air-pressure indicator, all the while stiffly silent. The recipient of a mock Purple Heart awarded by crewmen for the concussion he had suffered during "the Battle of the Little Andes," Young had artistically re-dressed Dr. Greerson's bandage, now comically lopsided and double its original size.

Amundsen's two black men had quite consciously avoided one another. Young had never forgiven Awesome for his role in sentencing the seven black sailors to long prison terms. The captain, for his part, had been scrupulously careful not to provide his white crew with any ammunition for accusations of favoritism. It was Young who broke the long and strained silence between them by reporting, "No more damage in the tube, sir. Commander Riley got that muzzle door and the drain working. Terrible accident."

"I know what's an accident and what isn't, Seaman Young. How the hell could this kind of thing happen?"

"No, sir." Young's voice was just this side of disrespectful, his eyes defiant. "It was just an accident. They couldn't breathe forward in the tube muzzle. Had to use an emergency air breather. No other way. Could have happened to anybody."

"You were here during the accident, Young?"

"Yes, sir. Commander Riley, myself, and Bertram Graham."

"All right. Everybody will want to know what happened forward. We're going to have a full inquiry. But for the time being, I don't want you to talk with anyone. If you're asked, say you're under my orders not to comment. We hardly need wild rumors circulating. Commander Laycook should return in a minute. In the meantime, you can begin cleaning up this foam. Off the deck first—that'll make it easier to move around. I'm going aft to sickbay. Chief Kramer will make an accident report."

"I'd like to be a part of that, sir."

"You will be."

"I mean, Captain . . . I was here and saw everything. I'd like to be more than a witness. I can handle it."

Awesome strained to understand Young's request. "I know you can," he said sympathetically, "and I'm sure you'd do a good job too, but for your own protection I can't assign you this task. Chief Kramer must do it."

"But I was present. Chief Kramer wasn't. If you want to know exactly what happened ask someone who was here."

"We will. But that's exactly why I can't let you make the inquiry. Until I know what occurred I've got to hold every man in this detail responsible. You don't appoint a defendant to preside at his own trial, now do you?"

"But it was an accident, sir. I can tell you right now, it was an accident."

Awesome finally understood the implication. "Seaman Young," he answered formally, "I'm not suggesting that you are personally to blame, but somebody was. I must prevent you from exonerating yourself and letting others charge me with favoritism. I'm certain that you can understand why we need an impartial investigation."

"But it was still an accident."

"Maybe . . . but maybe, just maybe, it was a mistake. No one is responsible for an accident, but somebody surely is for a mistake. Now I know for a fact that Bertram Graham is injured and that may mean somebody wasn't doing his job. It wouldn't be right for Graham's sake not to discover who that person was. I hope you now understand why I want Chief Kramer to make this report. . . . It wouldn't be fair to ask you to put the blame on somebody else . . . if it comes down to that. Know what I mean?"

Clearly Young did not. To his mind there was no reason to blame anyone. He was still protesting under his breath as the skipper ducked through the door in the after bulkhead en route to sickbay. Awesome's stubbornness, Young knew, was certain to compound the tragedy. You had to expect that from him. Had he not demonstrated his dedication to military justice during the "Trial of the Seven"? Booker Anderson, one of the unfortunate mutineers, had been a distant aquaintance, not close enough to call a friend, but certainly an acquaintance. For three months Young had silently rehearsed a defense plea for the imprisoned black seamen, a speech he imagined himself delivering at some future occasion to Elisha Awesome. The opportunity had unexpectedly presented itself and before it could be seized was lost. When the moment had arrived, Young found himself unprepared . . . perhaps, even worse, afraid.

The CO_2 fire extinguishers had presented even a better opportunity. He should have aimed the cone-shaped barrel of one at Awesome's face and blasted it with a coat of white "snow." In training, they said

CO₂ produced temporary blindness . . . and worse, painful blisters. Good, Young thought, as he lifted an extinguisher from the deck and fondled its triggering lever. The more he thought about the black skipper, the more he yearned to blanket him with CO_2 foam. His fingers squeezed the lever. A swish of gas oozed from the cone muzzle, but no CO_2 snow. Commander Riley had emptied the chemical cylinder fighting fire in tube 6.

1230 hours.

Amundsen's mess filled a thirty-foot-square compartment, seating forty men at a time. Hungry submariners clustered in small groups near the closed chow window to wait for the noon meal. An aroma of roasted chicken, mild onion, and oregano filled the air. After eighty-three days of patrol, food, once so abundant, had begun to appear in smaller quantities and then to disappear altogether. No meal was any longer complete. Every day there was speculation about what would be missing next. There was a brisk and lucrative trade among the men assigned to the first sitting and those on the second and third. And there were rumors about hidden food: Squadron had all along planned for an extended patrol with food reserves that the crew had not begun to tap—though no one could figure out where in the crowded submarine they might be. Submariners who had never tasted C rations began to take them seriously. There was also a rash of bad jokes about the Navy's proverbial hardtack.

Talk hushed suddenly as Everett Young entered the mess. A heavy-set fire-control technician, sporting a pointed Edwardian beard, spoke first. "We heard that Bert Graham is hurt bad and that if he doesn't make it to a hospital soon, he isn't gonna make it anyplace."

A frozen moment passed. "How should I know?" Young replied, trying to look unconcerned.

"You were with Graham when it happened and you're friendly with Commander Riley."

"I don't know any more than you. All I know is that Bert's burned bad. He looked like a burned log in a fireplace. Sickbay's out of bounds. The official word is Bert's recovering. I don't believe it."

The food-service window rolled open with a sharp crack and the men scrambled for position in line, the technician and Young among them. But Sokorski grabbed the black sailor's arm, pulling him from his advantageous place. "Come here. I've got something to tell you."

Young opened his mouth to object; Sokorski was going to make him lose lunch altogether. Too late. The men behind had already surged ahead. Young reluctantly followed the translator to a table and sat down on the vinyl seat opposite him. Sokorski leaned forward to whisper, "You know I tutor Commander Laycook in Russian. We spend a lot of time together and have gotten to be pretty good friends. He hinted to me—off the record, of course—that Bert's dying. There's no chance he'll make it unless he gets intensive care in a hospital burn center."

"I knew those cats were lying. Where do they expect to find a burn center? If there's no sub tender nearby, he won't get treatment. They'll let Bert die before he gets intensive care."

"Who's *they*, Everett?" Sokorski asked.

"Superstar . . . black wonderboy and his con men."

"Not Laycook," Sokorski interrupted. "He never said it in so many words, but I know he's no fan of your wonderboy."

Young's nostrils flared. "Not *my* wonderboy. Stepping on black brothers ain't my way of going up the ladder. He's started to put his footprint on me too."

Clyde Forbes appeared, tray in hand, his plate scantily filled with a rationed portion of roast chicken blanketed by a corn starch gravy that slopped over canned potatoes. The usual peas were missing. He sat down beside Sokorski, listening attentively. Son of a Baltimore longshoreman, Forbes had grown up near the Northwest Harbor and was no stranger to race issues. Midway into Young's condemnation of the skipper for his participation in the Trial of the Seven, he interrupted. "You don't believe such drivel, do you, Everett? I followed that mutiny trial on television and your little black friends got caught with their hands in the cookie jar. I don't have anything personal against them—but they were stupid. Proved nothing . . . and now they have to pay for nothing by years in the brig. Awesome was just the presiding judge, not the prosecutor. He was only doing his job. Frankly, I thought he did all right. Musta been hard not to be biased and take it easy on fellow black men."

"Life in prison? That was just doing his job? A white boy tried to blow up a whole aircraft carrier in the Mediterranean last year and got only

106

seven years.''

Sokorski dropped his hand over Forbes' arm. "I've been thinking a lot about this," he intervened. "You see, I figure we have at least twelve more days of patrol—maybe a few less. We gotta go home soon anyway, so why not move now and help save Bert's life? There's got to be some emergency provision for this. At the beginning of a patrol, you don't head home because somebody's hurt. But we've put in our time. Food's almost gone. Christ, Gold Crew's got to be ready by now. Seems to me that with Bert injured we have reason to sail home right away."

"Sure," Young answered. "Dream on."

Sokorski was undaunted. "It could happen. If we did something. Like, how about writing a letter to the captain asking him to help save Graham's life? We don't have to say it in so many words, but that means getting him to a hospital."

Young's expression was skeptical. He pushed back to uncross his legs. "Man, you gotta be kidding! That's a joke. You Polacks really are as stupid as they say. Black wonderboy is more Navy than Hyman Rickover. He'll cut off your balls for a letter like that. You saw what he did to the Seven."

Forbes grinned. "But they were black," he said.

Sokorski shot him an impatient look. To Young he said, "I agree with you, Everett, but maybe all Awesome needs is some encouragement. What would happen if we get the officers to go along with us and sign that letter?"

"It won't work. You can't get officers to sign stuff like that."

"Suppose I told you I could get Commander

107

Laycook to support it?"

"I wouldn't believe you."

"Leave that to me. I know the commander thinks Awesome has mismanaged the patrol—he thinks he's responsible for the collision on the Little Andes and ultimately for Bert's accident. I can convince him to help. I know I can." First, Sokorski explained further, they should draft a good letter. That was the key because the wording had to be perfect—not just good, but perfect. No hint of disrespect or insubordination or, God forbid, mutiny. Not a trace, not even a suggestion of such things. Once the letter was written a committee could be formed to approach other individuals. When a respectable list had been compiled, Sokorski himself would approach Commander Laycook for his help.

"You're just nuts. Nuts." Young angled his legs from the booth and slipped sideways along to the aisle. He picked up an aluminum tray and headed for the chow window.

By the time Young got there, nothing was left in the roasting pan but a desiccated chicken wing. The commissaryman ladled brown gravy over a roll, allowing some of it to slop onto the tray. Young stared in dismay. He didn't have much appetite; after what had happened to Bert Graham he didn't really feel like eating, but he had more appetite than *that*. He opened his mouth to protest but the commissaryman gave him his sweetest, deadliest smile and Young gave up. By then there were empty seats, as well as a free table. Time to be alone . . . or so he originally thought! A bad choice of places. The fire control technician was sitting at the next table. As if there had been no break, he continued right where he had left off before mess service. Was it true, he persisted, that Captain Awesome was on the warpath against Riley's engineering detail? Had he really ordered a full investigation? Was Commander Riley's head on the chopping block?

Young kept his eyes on the chicken wing, his knife poking for the tendon. Despite a queasy stomach, he stuffed the soggy roll into his cheeks, chewing slowly, forcing himself to swallow. Only once did he lift his eyes to Sokorski's table, where others had begun to gather. The technician finally departed with a hostile remark. Frackmeyer tried to catch Young's eye but he refused to acknowledge the gesture. Open opposition to command was not only foolish but also dangerous. More roll got stuffed into his mouth and ground up methodically. Something as innocuous as Sokorski's letter was not likely to change Awesome's mind but was guaranteed to cause trouble. Good for the skipper; bad for Sokorski. Awesome would see to it, just as he did at the Trial of the Seven. No doubt about him—an arrogant, power-hungry man. Why couldn't the others see that?

Young wiped his mouth on the napkin and started to rise. No longer was it possible to ignore Sokorski and Company, now openly conspiring. You had to admit they had guts. Lots of guts. Young felt confused, almost ashamed. His resistance was waning. Maybe Sokorski could carry it off and show Awesome up for what he was. And maybe the time had come to deliver that speech he had been rehearsing, the one he had failed to deliver in the torpedo room. Only now there was some help—white boys who were a lot more difficult to discipline than black boys. Young began to like the idea. He was certain Booker Anderson would too.

1940 hours.

On *Amundsen*'s lower level two stablization gyroscopes spun inside metal cowlings with a whirling hum. The dull monotonous white paint of the compartment was broken only by two red fire extinguishers beside the watertight door and black numbers stencil-sprayed on the conduits running overhead and along the bulkheads. In the packed space Sokorski's ad hoc committee gathered for its second meeting. A buzz from the spinning gyroscopes homogenized the crewmen's voices, cushioning their strident debate. Sokorski clung to the exterior gimbal for support, often shouting over the din. Despite *Amundsen*'s progress since the collision on the Little Andes, her list to port proved she had been injured. Why had Captain Awesome not been honest with the crew? After all, their lives were as much at stake as his. Because he feared telling the truth. And why had he feared telling the truth? Because it affected them all, not just Bertram Graham.

Sokorski shifted his balance for a better view of the men clustered behind him. Several attempts, he continued, to learn about Bertram Graham's condition had been unsuccessful. Directly after the accident there was a medical report indicating he was in critical condition, then nothing more was said. Nobody in authority would talk. Silence itself was a sort of confession, since there was no reason to keep good news secret. And why was bad news a secret? Because the key to Graham's condition was intensive care in a hospital burn center . . . therapy he wasn't going to get.

So what were they going to do about it? They had a letter. A beautiful letter. Carefully drafted. But it needed signing. Despite the cautious, deferential wording, all but a handful had refused to take a stand and plead for a shipmate in perilous need. That was sickening, Sokorski commented. The movement floundered. Success was limited; brave men were always scarce. A few men, it was true, had re-examined their consciences and added their signatures. Every name made the following ones easier to obtain.

But 43 signatures from a 112-man crew was little more effective than the original 4. Nothing less than 100 percent, or perhaps only slightly less, would encourage the captain to take action and save Graham's life. Moreover, once the movement had been launched, if the others did not throw in their lot, those who had signed could be singled out and disciplined.

Young, sporting a new dressing creatively molded to his head, had thrown his energies behind the solicitation campaign. Fruitless exhortations had driven him to the conclusion that an enforcement team was required to influence his well-meaning but timid shipmates. In the first test of his leadership, Sokorski energetically attacked the idea. Under no conditions was personal intimidation advisable. Men who did not wish to help save Graham's life would have to deal with their own consciences. That opinion was based on more than a persuasion for democracy. Once Awesome learned that some men had been forced against their wills, he would reject the letter outright and label its drafters as trouble-makers . . . or worse. But Young had some supporters. Those who had signed were feeling antagonistic against the holdouts. Sensing the mood shift, Sokorski ventured to share a very personal feeling. No longer the defender of the injured and the advocate of free choice, he spoke in a tremulous voice, a man facing circumstances that mystified him. "Something's strange about this patrol and I'm not the only one who knows it. I mean Captain Awesome's appointment, and the long patrol, and all these mishaps, the Little Andes, and now Bert." He carefully omitted the Riga broadcast which the skipper had specifically forbidden mentioning. Obedient to this command, he vowed not to go beyond the general sense, but the broadcast remained uppermost in his mind. Awesome almost told him his folks would just have to get used to the idea of their son's death. They would have to be "resourceful," live with grief and fear until the Navy, in its almighty wisdom, chose to enlighten them. Just how cold could one man be? And to smile while he said it! Sokorski fought down a new wave of fury as he spoke. "No one's heard from us since Christmas, four months ago. And we still don't know for certain when we'll return. Nobody's talking. Could be a long, long time. They might even have us rendezvous with a tender, get provisioned, and return to patrol. Our families are probably worried stiff. You, Larry,

112

your wife and kids might be crying, 'Daddy's not coming home . . . ever.' What does that feel like? And Brian,'' he spun to port theatrically, "what's your girl friend's name? Sally? She's probably thinking of who to shack up with about now.''

Sokorski had gone too far and was assailed from all quarters. "Speak for yourself, buddy. . . . Cut the dramatics. . . . *I'll* be home. . . . Don't give me that Cassandra shit. . . .'' Brian's agitated defense of his girl friend (Polly was her correct name) hung loudly in the sudden hush. The purring of the gyroscopes usurped the momentary silence. Commander Laycook stood in the open doorway. His eyes ranged widely to establish the company and ended on Sokorski. Puzzled by the strange assortment of men, he waited for the translator to enlighten him.

"It's all right . . . it's all right,'' Sokorski mollified both the executive officer and his committeemen simultaneously. "I've asked Commander Laycook to attend this meeting as a special favor to me. There hasn't been time to consult with him, so he's probably as confused as you are about why I asked him to come.'' While the commander made his way through the path that opened for him, Sokorski displayed a black folder in which he had placed the original typewritten letter with forty-three signatures affixed below it. Fanning the folio above his head, he spoke directly to the executive officer. "We've written a letter to Captain Awesome asking him to do everything in his power to help save Bertram Graham's life. It would be much more effective if the officers signed it too.''

The men watched Laycook accept Sokorski's

document with reluctance and were suddenly aware of the translator's bravado. He had led them to believe Laycook was already committed when, in fact, he had not even been consulted. However much some wanted to dissociate themselves immediately, they were stuck. Too late to flee; too late to protest. Laycook scanned the letter, and then carefully perused the signature list as if punching the names into a computer for later retrieval. The delay tested everyone's nerves. As the seconds ticked by, the hostility toward Sokorski mounted. He had obviously promised far more than he could deliver.

Laycook closed the folder. "George, this letter suggests that Captain Awesome is not doing all he can to help Bertram Graham."

"That's right, sir." Young pushed forward. "Those officers who agree with us should add their names up front. They're either with us and Bert, or they're not."

Sokorski waved Young to silence. His argument was tactful and well-rehearsed, the climax of long efforts. It was a fact that the men felt more could be done to help Graham. Since *Amundsen* was damaged and long overdue she should return immediately to Scotland. Everyone was convinced that Laycook was the key person to influence Captain Awesome. The men had faith in their exec and depended on his understanding. If he were to support the letter, the entire crew would follow suit. If he chose to withhold that support, others would be reluctant, and Graham would surely die an excruciating, ugly death aboard ship.

A long, tense silence followed. Laycook simply

stared at Sokorski. His surprise, almost bewilderment, he could not have disguised had he intended to do so. His chin jerked high, his eyes scrutinized the rebels one at a time. "I think there are some basic things you men have misunderstood about the captain, about me, and obviously about how the Navy operates. Let me correct these notions right now, before this goes too far. What this letter doesn't say is more important than what it does. If Captain Awesome misunderstands your intentions, you're wasting your time, but if he understands, which I have no doubt he will, this is patent insubordination or worse. Under the circumstances of this patrol, I wouldn't want to add to our difficulties. Nor would I wish to test the captain's patience with a document like this." Laycook listened to the echo of his words to judge whether they had expressed his views. They had—and with unmistakable clarity. "However . . ." he raised his voice to mark the contrast with what else he intended to say, "however, I want you to know that I share your concern for a fellow seaman. No human being would be against the *sense* of your petition. . . ."

"Letter," someone corrected.

"Okay, call it a letter. Even Captain Awesome wouldn't be against the *sense* of it. And I can assure you he wants as much as any of you to save Bertram Graham's life—contrary to the implication of this petition . . . or letter. But . . . there are priorities that must be respected. We're not here now because Captain Awesome has personally ordained we should be, nor has our patrol been extended because of his fancy. He follows orders as we expect you to. Now

115

this brings me to my final point. The Navy doesn't work this way; it can't. Whatever officers feel privately, they won't subvert a commanding officer. The system has been tested for a long time. True, there are conflicts between private opinions and official positions. But no officer will undermine the authority of his CO. I can promise you no officers will sign this. Most certainly not me."

"Lieutenant Rosenbaum said he would." Forbes sprang his trap on the exec officer. "He said he'd sign if you would."

Laycook exploded with indignation. "Rosenbaum! Rosenbaum! You're going to rest your case on him? He's a doctor, a psychiatrist. Not a line officer, an outsider who got transferred to the Submarine Service from the surface Navy . . . from the Reserves, no less!"

"He promised to sign."

"Then let him," Laycook growled, "but his support doesn't inspire me."

Young started for the door. "Come on, brothers. Sokorski made a mistake. This guy is against us, otherwise he'd sign right now. Graham ain't got no time to spare. A brother is dying, a white brother. I'm disgusted you cats can't make up your minds. We can still get this letter finished without Commander Laycook, only we've got to get going. Don't waste any more time on him."

The executive officer watched Young bulldog his shipmates toward the door, then glanced toward Sokorski. The translator was letting the revolt slip through his fingers. Evidently he didn't know what to do about it. Without hesitation Laycook jumped to the gyrogimbal and thundered over the dispersing submariners. "Now everybody stop right where you are!" His own volume impressed him, especially with its reverberation in the crowded compartment. "Get this clear and try to see the whole picture." The men following Young buckled under his authority and reversed directions. "Which one of us—you, me, or the skipper—ever thought the Submarine Service would cut short an important patrol if he became injured . . . or was about to die? That's something each of us understood the moment he came aboard. Sure it's easy for me to say this because I'm not in sickbay like Bertram Graham. But if I were in Graham's position, I'd expect somebody to stand up and give the same speech. Of course, I wouldn't like it, but that's what it means to serve in the Submarine Service. This isn't news to anyone. You wouldn't be here now if you didn't believe this deep inside. The bottom line, gentlemen, is sacrifice, not only of time, but also of health, and, if necessary, life. Bert's sacrifice could have been yours, may still be"— Laycook paused—"and you know that."

"Is Bert really going to die, Commander?" an unidentified voice beseeched, causing Laycook to groan inside.

"I don't know, I'm not a doctor. I hope not."

Young abandoned caution: "Don't believe him! What's left of Bert ain't worth living for. I saw him in sickbay—charred to a stump."

"Commander Laycook . . ." Sokorski pleaded, his voice urgent. And at last Laycook realized what was really going on. "This letter is *our* only chance, for Graham and for ourselves. The submarine is dam-

117

aged. The Russkies must have learned this. Don't ask me how, but I know they're aware of what's happened. If we don't return soon, there may not be another chance. We gotta let the world know we're still afloat!''

That ludicrous Riga broadcast again! Precisely the intent of the Big Lie: dissension, misunderstanding, controversy. The purpose of the Soviet propaganda machine was suddenly quite clear. Awesome had understood it from the outset and had commanded that nothing more about the broadcast be mentioned. An exec officer who knew his job would put a lid on it immediately—before it got out of control and caused some real damage. "You're exceeding your authorization, Sokorski," Laycook snapped.

"See what I told you," Young called from the passageway back into the gyro compartment. "We've got two kinds aboard: those who sign and those who don't.''

Laycook spoke directly to the men beside Young, his tone neither indecisive nor ambiguous. "All right, gentlemen. This has gone quite far enough. The meeting's over. I strongly advise you not to continue with this letter any further . . . at least not until we get a new medical report from Dr. Greerson. If Graham's improved, this letter may be entirely unnecessary. Let's hope he is.''

"They won't tell us about Bert's condition,'' Forbes objected.

"I'll take responsibility for that." The executive officer refused to be lured into further debate. "Leave the next move to me. Just put a stop to this nonsense now and I'll see that you get a full and accurate report on Graham's medical condition. No lies, no bullshit . . . just straight facts. We'll report it exactly as it is . . . good . . . or bad. Let's hope for the best. If not, we'll meet again and talk about the future. But for everyone's sake, don't circulate this petition . . . or letter . . . among yourselves or to Captain Awesome before you hear from me again." He looked directly to Sokorski for his pledge. The translator was wilted against the gyromount, the defeat on his face revealing a history of distrust for government authorities. The Siberian labor camps of his youth had done little to inspire trust. Enlistment in the Navy and then the Submarine Service represented a major leap of trust for him. But one didn't erase one's past conditioning so easily. "Well, Sokorski?" Laycook asked firmly.

"I'm just sure, sir, that if we don't go back now, we never will. We'll never get out from under this ice. You know what I mean."

"Nonsense. Stay calm and act responsibly and we'll pull through this together. We're almost at the end now. It would be a damn shame to jeopardize everything by a little impatience. A letter like this would create just the disaster we're all hoping to prevent. We have enough real problems aboard without having to fabricate new ones."

Laycook was greatly surprised by his own powers of persuasion, for the men with Young were seizing the opportunity to disperse. Those near the gyroscope edged cautiously toward the door. Sokorski alone remained motionless, his eyes downcast over the black folder. So much hope had been invested in it only to have it crushed at a critical moment. But how were the others to know about the Riga broadcast? And even if they had, no doubt everyone would have rejected it as absurd. It was absurd, wasn't it? Sokorski kept asking himself that question. Of course, it was absurd; still the broadcast continued to haunt him.

An odor resembling burned sugar permeated the passageway, less nauseating than the stench of charred flesh Laycook was soon to encounter in Greerson's improvised sickbay. The fetid smell tenaciously resisted recycling through the sub's CO_2 scrubbers and air regenerators. Laycook's stomach churned; sweat coated his palms. He had always hated hospital visits. His mother had languished for many months in a Florida hospital before succumbing to breast cancer that metastasized to her lungs. His father had been in and out of almost every clinic in the Sunshine State with a variety of ailments, sufficiently complicated to delight scores of young doctors eager to test their medical expertise. Breathing through his mouth, Laycook yanked at a thick, lead-weighted curtain. He was met in the doorway by an excruciating moan from Bertram Graham, followed by a series of pitiful cries in rapid succession that rooted the commander where he stood. Martin Rosenbaum was crouched over the bunk, adjusting the flow from three intravenous bottles. Two hung from a chrome stand beside the patient; the third, from the berth overhead. Clear albumin, saline, and antibiotic solutions dripped through plastic catheters inserted into Graham's veins, replacing body fluids at the same rapid rate as moisture exuded from exposed muscle tissue. The psychiatrist, in sterile gown, mask, and cap, finished with the bottles, donned his surgical gloves, and started swabbing antibiotic ointment over his patient's wounds.

Usually garrulous in the wardroom, Rosenbaum freely confessed that the M.D. behind his name was more a permit to practice psychiatry than a testimony to his knowledge of physical medicine. In Yale Medical School he had dutifully memorized the polysyllabic Latin names of muscles and bones and eventually reproduced them on the general medicine boards, but then had happily forgotten them. Most memorable from the "black years," as he called them, had been a rotation through surgery in which he was forced to witness the unholy trespass into bellies and chests, made more insufferable by ritual scrub-ins and the surgeons' irreverent banter about their anesthetized victims. "Cognitive dissonance," his own psychiatrist suggested. Perhaps, Rosenbaum responded, but that did not make it any easier. Fortunately, he developed symptoms of infectious mononucleosis—only symptoms, because his private doctor could find no hematological evidence of the disease in repeated blood specimens. But symptoms were enough to get Rosenbaum excused from further surgical rotations and that, quite curiously, was enough to eliminate the symptoms.

He had been an unlikely candidate to answer the Navy's recruitment advertisement in *Resident and Staff Physician*. But he'd needed a stint in the Navy to help diminish the mounting debts for his education. Actually, the recruiters were quite co-operative. It was agreed he would complete his psychiatric residency at New York Hospital in conjunction with Cornell University. It was also clearly agreed that once on active duty he would function only as a psychiatrist: clear at least to him, if not the Navy. The reality of his service drew him inexorably from the original intent. When he re-examined the recruitment papers he found them cleverly vague.

As backup to Dr. Greerson, Rosenbaum was obliged to help with the round-the-clock care of Graham. His medical ignorance notwithstanding, he was surprised at what trivia he remembered from medical school and even more encouraged by his ability to improvise for what he didn't recall. Graham's tragedy vindicated his father's often repeated adage that there was no ill wind that didn't blow somebody some good. In his new medical chores Rosenbaum found unexpected relief from his counseling duties. He was the first to admit that aboard *Amundsen* nobody needed a shrink more than the ship's psychiatrist. Aboard a tight boat depressions were as infectious as viruses. Men were expected to function normally under the most abnormal conditions, and contrary to a psychiatric axiom that belittled sex and sunshine as universal elixirs, there was little bothering the men that a good screw and twelve hours on a sunny beach would not help cure. Empathy was a poor substitute for what was patently unavailable. No wonder the therapist had become as frustrated as his patients. After all, he too needed a sunny beach and some screwing. And then out of the blue came Graham's accident and a new role as healer. Rosenbaum liked it so well that on several occasions he entertained the fantasy of leaving psychiatry and retraining for a medical specialty.

Thomas Laycook avoided looking at the grotesque body before him in the bunk. "Marty"—he pretended to be unaffected by the horrible sight—"I've come to learn how Graham's doing."

The patient writhed away from Rosenbaum and emitted an excruciating yelp as he rolled onto an exposed hip muscle where the skin had been entirely destroyed. The IV stand swayed, its half-filled bottles shaking. Trying to settle his patient with one hand, Rosenbaum steadied the teetering apparatus and inspected the needle at the other end. "Under the circumstances, he's holding on."

"Does that mean he's got a chance?"

Rosenbaum paused to consider the extent of Graham's sedation before openly discussing his condition. "He's got a chance," he replied, "but not aboard ship."

"You mean no chance at all? There's got to be some small percentage . . . 1 or 2 percent . . . but some outside chance. I can't tell Graham's friends he has *no* chance."

"Commander, look for yourself. Does it look to you like Graham can survive without special burn facilities? There's a slim possibility of saving this man's life if he gets intensive care. We're way overdue at base now. Sooner or later we've got to return. What's a few more days? There have to be emergency regulations that would permit us to return—especially after all we've been through."

"You sound like Sokorski."

"Bert sacrificed himself for our society. I believe we

123

owe him the best chance available."

"So do I, Marty. But this isn't a student demonstration. Navy officers don't encourage or sign petitions to abort missions. When these men approached you with this, you should have notified me immediately."

Rosenbaum absorbed the reproach, holding himself under tight rein. He hated lectures. More important, he loathed having to defend himself. "I made it clear I'd never sign until the senior officers did. I told them if you signed then I would too. Lord knows, Graham needs more than we can provide aboard this boat. I understand Navy protocol, but it doesn't change medical facts."

Graham twisted again and came to rest on the exposed side of his thigh. Four staccato shrieks curdled in the compartment. The slack segment of plastic tubing connected to his foot lightly rubbed the upper leg, a hideously painful touch against his draining calf wounds. In a desperate fit he struggled to sit up. But having risen to his highest position, there was no place to go except back to the pus-soiled sheets. He coiled in agony, each new movement exacerbating the pain.

"Jesus, Marty," Laycook implored, feeling even more helpless, "how about giving him some morphine?"

"I can't give him more now. It will kill him. He's already had fifty milligrams in the past half hour."

Graham's third thrust forward overwhelmed Rosenbaum's attempt to restrain him. Far larger than the psychiatrist, the wounded sailor lurched upward, partially disengaging his catheters. One bottle unhooked and came crashing to the deck. The other two swayed precariously. "Give me a hand," Rosenbaum called over his shoulder to the executive officer. "Grab a new bottle of saline from the shelf."

For a frozen second Laycook's feet remained anchored to the deck. His eyes were fixed on serum oozing from Graham's shoulder and back. Large pustules were suspended on mutilated cartilage near what remained of the sailor's ear. He wished fervently that he hadn't come.

"Give me a hand!" Rosenbaum repeated, more urgently than before.

Laycook jumped to a medical locker and produced a second saline bottle. At least he hoped it was saline; he was too shaken to read the label.

Whooping outbursts preceded Graham's new lunge to sit up. In response the psychiatrist threw himself without reserve against his patient. Both men scuffled for leverage. Rosenbaum's feet lifted from the deck. A moment later he was prone beside Graham. Between new groans Laycook implored again, "Can't you do something for him, Marty?"

"There's nothing more I can do. . . . It's now up to you and Captain Awesome. If you want to help, get him to a hospital quick!"

Cautiously, Rosenbaum released his embrace and eased himself back to the deck, his white gown, gloves, mask, and glasses smeared with topical antibiotic and body secretions. "I'll give him more morphine in fifteen minutes."

Graham took advantage of his temporary freedom and lurched up with a howl.

Laycook prepared himself to endure another set of

ear-shattering shrieks. "Can't we give him a little morphine now, Marty?"

There was no time to reply. More nimble than before, the psychiatrist sprung back to his patient and pressed his weight gently over him. Graham's surge upward was short-lived, a final, desperate flutter before semiconsciousness.

In a quiet moment Rosenbaum slipped from the bunk. "You can help me prepare the syringe," he said. "I'll give him something when I can. Graham might not remain still much longer; we'd better get it ready now."

His eyes constantly upon his patient, the psychiatrist explained that he wanted to keep his hands sterile in case of emergency. In Graham's condition infection was as dangerous as loss of body fluid. Laycook took the keys to the narcotics locker from Rosenbaum's hip pocket, uncapped a morphine bottle, and prepared a syringe. A slight pressure on the plunger expelled onto his wrist .5 cc excess from the needle tip. He put the syringe and capped needle on a stainless-steel tray beside Graham's bunk. "What can I tell the men about his condition, Marty?"

Rosenbaum peered through his smudged spectacles, delaying his reply. "The truth?"

"I can't do that. Can I say that Graham's 'holding his own'?"

"That's up to you. I expect you'd better be honest about it."

"They'll mutiny."

"Then keep them too busy to worry about it."

Good advice, the executive officer thought, but hard to implement. Now that he was free to leave he was reluctant to desert the physician . . . at least before Greerson or the hospital corpsman returned. More help might be required. Laycook fell back to the curtain and there watched the psychiatrist at his work. His round, unathletic shoulders narrowed imperceptibly into a bull neck and pumpkin-shaped head. How his Semitic features contrasted with the Hellenic ideal that had come to be associated with Navy tradition. Before the patrol Laycook had been suspicious of Rosenbaum. Men like him had seemed to invade the new, technological Navy. Relying upon intellectual achievements rather than nautical experience, they rose rapidly in the ranks, subtly altering values that had been unquestioned a decade before. Noncareer men, they introduced innovations that threatened the established way of doing things. But Laycook himself had also come to question many axioms of naval behavior. Fresh blood was healthy. You had to respect Rosenbaum. Perhaps a little out of his element in the Submarine Service, he was, nevertheless, an honest man. And you had to like him too.

"So, Commander?" Rosenbaum looked over his shoulder. "What are you going to say?"

It was difficult to smile under the circumstances, yet Laycook sensed he had established an understanding with the psychiatrist. "What else?" he grinned. "I'll make up a work roster."

2043 hours.
Not all submarine skippers made daily tours of their boats. Several were notorious for their aloofness, allowing their XO's to make primary contact

127

with the crewmen. Awesome had, in contrast, recognized the uniqueness of his captaincy and no matter how occupied he squeezed in a quick daily tour. During the patrol's extension morale became a critical issue and he lengthened those tours, calling everyone by name, paying out compliments where he could. But after Graham's injury the good will had vanished. The crewmen were respectful but unfriendly. The cheerful badinage that characterized the pre-Andes atmosphere was gone. When Awesome asked a question he received a proper answer . . . but that was all. The exchange was over and dead. Something was brewing, of that Awesome was certain: something beyond the normal disappointment of an extended patrol, something that exceeded the crewmen's anxiety for an injured shipmate. Awesome had just made a mental note to tap the chief of the boat, Waldo Kramer, for a reading, when Thomas Laycook found him. "May I speak with you, sir? It's fairly urgent."

"Then we'll go to my quarters, Thomas."

They turned in unison. Laycook followed a few paces behind, wondering whether he had made the right decision. Graham's condition was deteriorating. Sokorski and his cohorts were likely to send their letter to Captain Awesome. Better to prepare him in advance so he could make a judicious response or, better yet, take some steps to prevent trouble before it erupted. But outside the captain's stateroom both men were hailed by Claude Diller, *Amundsen's* sole Marine.

Sergeant Diller, with a bulldog chin and scintillating emerald eyes that had dazzled recruits during his drillmaster days, had been assigned to Patrol Polynya as a cold-weather combat specialist. Throughout the patrol he had held himself apart from what he considered the sloppy, lackadaisical submariners. One suspected that his tough armor protected a brittle human mechanism within—if that were true, he was as much an oddity in the Marines as the Navy—but no one knew him well enough to say for sure. At the moment he stood before them stiffly, thrusting a white paper toward the skipper. Its handwriting was unmistakably Eugene Greerson's, written in haste. The final syllable of each word dissipated into a snakelike squiggle until a bold and fresh updraft began a new word. There were few words to read.

GRAHAM COMMITTED SUICIDE . . . ADVISE, GENE.

Awesome crumpled the note into a ball. "Tell Commander Greerson I'll be right there." He turned to face the bulkhead, lifting his hand to the sealed conduits overhead.

Dr. Greerson was waiting in the narrow passage outside his sickbay. He launched immediately into an orderly, dispassionate narrative, the kind of summary Awesome appreciated: Graham died from an overdose of morphine that he shot into his own body. Corpsman Ted Becker was taking a break while Martin Rosenbaum covered for him. Thinking Graham well sedated, Rosenbaum went to relieve himself. Upon returning he discovered the syringe on Graham's mattress. Apparently the agonizing sailor reached over to the bedstand, snatched the syringe, and injected himself with enough morphine to stun a rhino. In his weakened condition the overdose killed him instantly.

Awesome accepted the report without a question and then entered the berthing compartment to see Graham's body. Rosenbaum was waiting beside the bunk, his cheeks gaunt, his eyes almost hidden behind the thickly smudged glasses. He started to speak but was silenced by the skipper, who drew back the polyester sheet from Graham's face. It was singed black, but there was a ghostly pallor on the temples and forehead where his welder's helmet had shielded him from the flash flames. For a long moment, Awesome riveted his eyes on the grotesque countenance, trying to remember what he had looked like before the accident. His memory would not produce an image; Graham's face blended into a collage of anonymous seamen, all blurred and unrecognizable. "His pain must have been excruciating," Awesome said. His throat ached from the lump in it.

Rosenbaum inched closer. "I left the syringe filled with morphine out on the bedstand, intending to inject Bert when his tolerance was higher. It never occurred to me that he could reach the damn thing. When I went to the head, I just forgot the syringe was there."

His eyes still on the dead man, Awesome ignored Rosenbaum's confession and slowly removed the bedsheet, exposing the torso and legs. Only Graham's feet, covered with thick rubber shoes, and the parts of the head protected by the welder's helmet had escaped the flash. Skin and muscle tissue, cremated while Graham was alive, bore no resemblance to their original form. Burned into a crusty black residue and caked with creamy white antibiotic ointment, the body emitted a sweet, pungent stench. For a long moment, Awesome remained immobile, then slowly ran his eyes back and forth over Graham's remains—testing his tolerance. Though nausea churned in his stomach and his head whirled with lightness, he refused to hurry. The least one could do for Graham was to regard the horrible tragedy, to witness with one's own eyes the extent of the disfiguration and to fix it in memory. It was a painful penitence. The minutes dragged slowly until Awesome judged nothing more could be gained, then he replaced the bedsheet, gently smoothed down an untidy wrinkle in one corner, and turned toward Laycook. "For the time being, until we all have a chance to put this into perspective, let's call this an act of God. We'll bury Graham at sea with honor and dignity."

"No, you don't understand," Rosenbaum interrupted. "I should never have left the morphine out. It happened because . . ."

Awesome hushed him with an uplifted, firm hand. Black fingers returned to the white sheet, tracing a divine cross over the dead man's head, chest, and stomach. "In the name of the Father, Son, and Holy Spirit." He raised his voice. "Bertram never had a chance. It's a terrible thing to say, but each of us knows it's true. He's better off now; at least, he's out of pain. I would have done anything I could, but it just wasn't in my power to save him. I know he

131

understood that and I hope all of you do too. He's in peace now, whatever small consolation that might be."

"I feel implicated in this," Laycook said, still battling with the thought that by preparing the syringe he had aided Graham's self-destruction.

"An . . . act . . . of God." Awesome pronounced each word separately and with grave emphasis. Refusing to be nettled by either Laycook or Rosenbaum, he spoke with measured phrases. "As far as I'm concerned Bertram Graham died from burns sustained in an accident while he was repairing this boat. I don't like the idea of covering up the truth, but in matters of suicide it's done all the time, for the immediate family . . . and for the soul of the deceased. Besides, at this point in the patrol, the truth could only do further damage. I personally have doubts about Graham's motivations, doubts that cannot be substantiated. It isn't possible to know whether he intended to kill himself. We'll never know that, and if we did, so what? It's no longer important and won't change anything. Let his soul rest in peace.

"Gene"—he suddenly glanced over his shoulder to Greerson—"prepare Graham's body for burial as soon as possible. We'll shoot it out a torpedo tube. Weight it down good so he doesn't float to the surface."

Near the sickbay curtain he turned again to those within. "Maybe Graham was just tortured with pain that he could not tolerate. The present meant insufferable agony; the future, if he lived, disfiguration. Or maybe he understood that injured in the way

132

he was he had become a liability to the patrol. And to save others dragging his anchor he deliberately cut himself loose so they could complete their assigned mission. If he intended that, his sacrifice will make an immeasurable contribution."

"It was pain," Rosenbaum said. "Sheer, unadulterated, insufferable pain, not sacrifice. No heroics. No patriotism, but pain, just pain. Make him into a hero if expedient. But that's not why it happened."

"All great men experience pain, Lieutenant Rosenbaum. That's what makes them great. The deeper the suffering the greater the man. Gene, in half an hour, I want this funeral in progress. I want it quick, dignified . . . and over. We'll convert Graham into a hero before the crew makes him a martyr. Make sure it's dignified. I'll have Sergeant Diller arrange an honor procession. This is one sailor I don't want anyone to forget."

2130 hours.

An American flag, creased from storage folds, lay loosely over Graham's body, its flows of red and white stripes broken by his hips and feet. Claude Diller adjusted two thick leather straps to hold the corpse securely against a stretcher—snug but not so tight as to cause Graham "pain." Diller knew, of course, that the seaman was quite dead, but he also knew that millions of individual cells in the body remained alive. The biology of death was of no interest to him. Even less had he interest in matters of the occult. But there had been that time in Vietnam. . . .

Cay-San had been designated at the battlefield to

update the tired image of the Marines assaulting Mount Suribachi on Iwo Jima. Jeff Cushman arrived by chopper with a photographic team to take pictures of combat-weary Marines defending the flag. With his square jaw and blond hair he should have been before the lens rather than behind it. While they waited for a good light in which to take the photographs, Diller passed a half-smoked Virginia cigar across to Cushman. Somewhere in the distance an enemy rifle fired, its crack barely perceptible amid heavy artillery counterfire. Cushman slumped backward into the semitropical scrub like a heavy overcoat dropped to the floor. A bullet had entered his cheek and exited through the larynx, severing the head from its body. No pulse, no heartbeat. Yet when Diller introduced the cigar into the dead man's mouth for a final puff the tobacco embers brightened and a cloud of smoke escaped from his etiolated lips. Didn't that prove that the dead retained some feeling . . . at least for several minutes after death? Too bad that Dr. Greerson prohibited smoking in sickbay. It would have been a good time to test his theory and offer Graham a contraband Havana.

The surgeon stepped alongside Graham's bier and tightened the leather straps loosely buckled by Diller. He obviously had not witnessed the same phenomenon in dying men in Vietnam. His attention was distracted when Commander Riley entered the sickbay and, without greeting, assumed a pallbearer's position at Graham's head.

"Becker is going to take that end," Greerson said.

The engineering officer looked determined. "It's my personal obligation."

Greerson regarded Riley with an uplift of his eyebrows. Normally he was the supreme authority in medical matters and the skipper had deputized him to organize the funeral. Yet guilt was not something a sensitive man overlooked. Greerson gave in. If the Irishman needed to carry Graham's remains, so be it.

The bier had to be maneuvered into the passageway. Riley led; Diller followed. The stretcher bumped clumsily toward the companionway, with the four designated pallbearers helping wherever there was space. A pretaped snare drum roll droned through the loudspeakers. Graham's funeral procession crept slowly forward from the engine room through the auxiliary machinery room, the reactor tunnel, into the control center, past men stationed at their posts.

A shipmate was sobbing openly as the bier passed. "I promise never to forget you, Bert. A promise . . ."

"I'll write your folks for sure."

"Poor sonuvabitch." Another raised his voice for the benefit of the officers. "Blew himself up for nothing. In the eleventh hour, when we were going home anyway. Goddamn nothing. Nothing."

The cortege paused briefly for prayers from Graham's close buddies, then descended to *Amundsen's* second level. In the mess, on the way to the forward torpedo compartment, Clyde Forbes stepped directly into Riley's path and brought the procession to a halt. Everett Young and George Sokorski presented themselves beside Forbes. From his position at the foot of the bier, Diller shoved the stretcher gently into Riley's hip, urging him to proceed. The

135

engineering officer scuffled several small steps forward, but Forbes didn't budge.

In the rear, Awesome and Laycook were trying to see what had occurred ahead. Sokorski stepped past Riley and stopped beside the stretcher. Even those who had never set eyes upon his black folder with its letter and signature list sensed in the gesture something provocative. Sokorski held it high for all to observe. Then slowly it was dramatically lowered over the dead man's eyes for Graham's perusal. When Sokorski finally spoke his voice projected through the mess. "This letter is for you, Bert. We wanted to get you home for treatment to save your life. Sixty-one men signed it. If you had lived just a bit longer everybody on this boat would have signed for you."

The mess was silent with shock. Everett Young was looking at the senior officers. "Everyone will sign now," he announced belligerently. "The secret is out. We all know the Russians are aware of us. They're telling the world that we sank three months ago." He spoke louder, over the sudden murmur of puzzled voices around him. Awesome clenched his teeth. Damn Sokorski! "You ain't alone, Bert. We're all gonna be dead if we don't get out of here. You're just a few miles ahead of us."

Diller tried again to urge the stretcher into Riley's spine and said softly. "Move, Commander." But Riley was determined not to be coerced by anyone, especially Diller. He craned his head toward the Marine just at the moment Diller's patience shattered. "This is a disgrace," he bellowed in stentorian voice, calling upon the full power of his drillmaster's authority. "Bertram Graham deserves a solemn funeral without disruption. This demonstration is disgusting. In the Marines we wouldn't tolerate it. Not for one moment. Even lowly rats exhibit more respect for a dead man. Now let this procession proceed forward . . . NOW!"

"That's enough, Diller." Awesome pushed through the pack of bodies. His eyes were stern. "I'll take that petition, Sokorski."

When he finished, Awesome studied the faces of the provocateurs: Sokorski, a victim of upsetting Soviet propaganda; Young, a hostile black resentful of Navy discipline; Forbes, a reformed street hood whose reflexes brought him wherever there was a fight. They were hardly a formidable triumvirate and yet the three submariners had publicly challenged his authority. In drafting and presenting their petition (the temerity to call it a "letter"!) they had failed to appreciate his own narrow range of choices. As *Amundsen*'s commanding officer he had to regard the petition as unpardonable; insubordination demanded disciplinary action, if not on his own account then symbolically for military authority.

Yet try as Awesome did to conjure up righteous indignation, it did not flow. How could one feel resentful of youths whom the Navy required to act with the full maturity of adulthood well before their numerical years? What sinister motive drove them other than fatigue and fear? Did he really believe that their petition threatened naval command? Until the moment he spoke, his brain was scrambled with unanswered questions. And the words, when they came, were not his own but those of the Reverend Elijah Awesome. How eloquent they were! Pappy

Awesome's orations were always eloquent.

"Death and Misunderstanding sleep together. . . . Suffering is for those who serve the Lord. Bertram Graham died to save our lives. Not my life or yours, but *our* lives collectively." Like waves tumbling toward the shore, his father's phrases continued on his lips. "Lord, whither shall I go from Thy spirit? Or whither shall I flee from Thy presence? . . ." When Awesome at last looked at Sokorski, the translator motioned for Young and Forbes to step aside and make room for the cortege to pass. Whether they had been touched or shamed by what was said the skipper did not know—but his father's words could humble the mightiest.

In lethargic undulations, the cortege crept into motion and weaved its final steps toward the torpedo room. Inside the compartment Laycook locked the watertight door. There was a brief consultation with Riley, who affirmed that tube 6 was indeed operational. To eject Graham's remains through it into the sea made practical sense: a good time to test the muzzle door and WRT drain and, while it was small consolation, prove that Graham's life had not been sacrificed for nothing. Awesome had reservations about the ethical propriety of using tube 6 in this manner but relented. There was something to be said, he agreed, for demonstrating a useful result from Graham's sacrifice.

Three officers transferred the dead man's body to the torpedo rack, and when all was ready, Awesome removed the American flag from the shrouded remains. Four points of the Holy Cross were traced upon the chest. Riley, Laycook, and Diller worked the body forward into the tube. The breach door clamped shut; its interlocking mechanism slipped into position. Gauges indicated when the air pressure inside was equal to the ambient water pressure. Then the muzzle door opened flawlessly. So far, Riley was right. They would know about the WRT drain after the seaman's remains were ejected to an ocean grave.

Awesome nodded his head. A surge of air pressure suddenly fired Graham into the Arctic waters. Surrounded by a coffin of air, the body traveled thirty feet from *Amundsen*'s bow until, dragged by lead weights, it separated from the gaseous bubble and began a final descent to the ocean floor. Behind it, the muzzle door clamped shut. Seawater in the tube was evacuated into the WRT tank, and from there was pumped back into the ocean.

Riley mopped his brow. He had always believed the tube would operate properly, but then you could never tell with absolute certainty until there had been a test. "Thank God," he exclaimed. Awesome and Laycook both looked at him with puzzlement, uncertain whether he referred to Graham's burial or the repaired torpedo tube.

Outside the forward compartment, Awesome's anguish, now that the funeral was over, threatened to engulf him: the first sailor lost under his command. Lives were rarely lost on submarine patrol, although a death at sea was not altogether unknown. Still, Graham's death should not have happened, even under emergency conditions. If nothing else it confirmed what the Submarine Service had long since known: Sixty days of patrol was enough. After that period men lost their efficiency and made mistakes . . . tempers erupted . . . the finely honed balance between men and machinery essential to a nuclear submarine became upset. For that Awesome was not responsible. It was Squadron that had ordered the extensions. En route to his quarters he questioned Admiral Gaffy's judgment. An old, experienced submariner like the admiral should have known: Sixty days was really quite enough!

4

HOLY LOCH, SCOTLAND

(Patrol Polynya: 60th day plus 24)

1145 hours.

The steady purr from the ventilators in the captain's cabin was interrupted by a husky yawn as Awesome luxuriated in the first true moments of peace since *Amundsen*'s departure from Lumbrovskiy Channel. Despite everything, there was much for which to be grateful—most important, the continuation of Patrol Polynya. Awesome's stocking feet lifted over his desk and descended upon Sokorski's black folder. It had been there all night and all morning, untouched and unread. Now that *Amundsen*'s routine had been re-established he could ignore it no longer. Though he appreciated that extraordinary tension aboard *Amundsen* had led to the drafting of Sokorski's letter, and to the translator's disobedience about the Riga broadcast, naval conduct had, nevertheless, been breached. Some response had to be made. One inner voice counseled him to discipline the offenders with such severity that future acts of insubordination would be unthinkable. But another voice, one he believed originated from Nicholas Gaffy, warned against administering harsh punishment. Above all, Gaffy had taught that judicious use of authority is the signature of successful leadership. How did he phrase it?

From the inside cover of Gaffy's Bible, Awesome extracted an envelope imprinted with the seal of the 12th Submarine Squadron, Holy Loch, Scotland. It had been delivered by the admiral personally just as he was about to leave *Amundsen*. His executive, Rear Admiral Donovan Billings, who had come aboard with Gaffy's party, had suddenly arrived at Awesome's cabin to say farewell before departing by launch for the dock. It was an unfortunate interruption, for Gaffy had just begun to relax. Normally he scheduled his activities to the minute. Many a bewildered visitor found himself deposited with Gaffy's secretary the moment his official business with the admiral was finished. But on that day aboard *Amundsen* the Admiral showed no signs of haste. Quite the contrary, that is, until Billings was ready to disembark. Gaffy stood then, withdrew the khaki envelope from his breast pocket and handed it to Awesome. "I wrote this for you last night, Elisha," he said, "but don't read it until you're at sea. It doesn't require a reply and once under way you won't be tempted."

At the very spot where Gaffy's letter had been delivered Awesome perused the words, written in longhand by arthritic fingers that the admiral feared would eventually compel his retirement from the Submarine Service. If necessary he would have accepted retirement, but only after Robert Katzenback was gone from the Navy. And so far Katzenback showed no signs of budging. Gaffy hid his arthritis by not writing in longhand. Difficult as the almost illegible script was to decipher, the handwriting shared the author's greatest secret, his failing health. Awesome treasured it as a sign of the admiral's trust.

Dear Elisha,

Now that you are under sail, I want you to know what lies heavily upon my heart. Several times I tried to reveal my thoughts, but transformed into words they sounded trite. This confirmed my long-held suspicion that important ideas do not require communication. Rather, they are understood and preserved by men who have no need to disclose them. We enjoy such sharing. Words are only encumbrances between us. In essence, that is why I wanted you to command *Amundsen* when she sails beyond my reach. You, Elisha, more than any man, are my heart and mind. I rest easy with your judgment.

You should know that during this patrol many things can happen at home. A change in government and Bob Katzenback will hit my Achilles heel, bringing down "Gaffy's Petit Empire" like a deck of cards. Lord knows, he's been trying long enough. All these years each of us has been waiting for the other to weary. Both our careers are approaching the final round, but neither wants to quit without a knockout. My enemies hover like vultures waiting for the beast to expire so they can pick his bones, and each year the buzzard's circular flight gets smaller and closer to earth. Gaffy hasn't many friends. Some respect him, more fear him. He wanted it that way. But if Katzy succeeds, your name will be high on the extermination list. The Service will have another in command. There'll be no one to protect you.

As you know, Underwater Strategic Services developed in a haphazard fashion, following the ebb and flow in the Pentagon and Department of Defense. *Détente* promises even more drastic alterations in our Service. Looking back now, I realize what special men we have attracted. We live lonely lives. Rewards? Certainly not financial. Fame? Who is permitted to talk of his achievements? All we gain from our work is a tacit understanding, a common experience, a shared perspective. Those who have done it, know . . . and that knowing alone is their total sustenance.

Patrol Polynya's secrecy will place you in rough leadership crosscurrents. You know too well that one's authority is proportional to his resolve. If anything, Elisha, you err by being too severe. Don't make my mistake—the opposition is often worth placating. I never learned how to make my men love and respect me at the same time, so I chose the path of respect. Near my career's end, I have doubts it was the correct route.

When we are old, I want to return with you to Holy Loch. We'll sit together in the Tipsy Cleric Pub and I'll drink my scotch in honor of Forgotten Polynya. Let's walk along the dock and look out over the loch where *Amundsen* anchored beside the tenders. I'll light a candle and for the first time you'll hear old Nick recite a thanksgiving prayer.

I shall be a very sentimental, nostalgic sailor.

Your trusted friend,
Nicholas

Awesome folded the letter and replaced it inside the Bible cover. Next, he opened Sokorski's folder. Sixty-one signatures had been alphabetically arranged to give each name equal value, conjuring up for Awesome a sense of *déjà vu*. While climbing up the Navy's hierarchy he himself had contemplated subtle schemes to oppose superior officers. More symbolic than real, these petty acts of insubordination were natural results of naval rigidity and shipboard tensions. A good skipper always provided his crew with ways to let off steam. Gaffy put it a little differently: "If anything, Elisha, you err by being too severe . . . the opposition is worth placating."

There were times when Awesome knew it was crucial that he defend Navy discipline. A black captain had to run an especially tight ship. But this was an extraordinary operation. With the worst now past, Awesome feared internal discord as the greatest danger to the successful completion of Patrol Polynya. Thus appeasement seemed a pragmatic as well as a psychologically compatible policy. To put it another way—Awesome smiled—it was time to exercise Christian forgiveness. He clicked open the toggle switch to *Amundsen*'s loudspeaker system. After a quick volume adjustment, he cleared his throat and began in a rich baritone.

"Now hear this . . . now hear this. Captain Awesome speaking. I've got an important announcement for you. Gentlemen, I wish I could tell you how long we will be extended for this patrol, but I'm not at liberty to disclose this information. Obviously Squadron knows we're overdue and ready for relief. The moment that's practicable, I'm sure we'll be heading home. I also wish to share with you my sadness about Bertram Graham's death. A fellow shipmate has died, a brave and self-sacrificing sailor. That's a tragedy whenever and wherever it occurs. I'm sure all of you fully understand that such an accident was not the first time an American sailor lost his life, nor will it, unfortunately, be the last. With the kind of machinery we're called upon to use, it doesn't seem we're able to eliminate all accidents— no matter how hard we try.

"Gentlemen, whatever time remains for this patrol, it's important to set the record straight on several issues that I know concern us all. First, I want to correct mistaken rumors about damages incurred on the Little Andes. So there's no misunderstanding, I want you to know we are sustaining a trim problem due to a damaged sea chest and hull valve. But in no way is the integrity of our pressure hull endangered.

146

We'll be sending divers into the water to clear the jam before returning to Holy Loch. By the time we reach Scotland *Amundsen* will be fully repaired—all eighteen Tomahawks will also be fully operational. *Amundsen* will be as strong as she was when we departed, less, of course, one fine seaman and several thousand pounds of food.

"Some of you may still have concerns or complaints. That's only natural on a long patrol. I fully appreciate that tensions build up. If you feel this way, I am asking you to come and tell me what's on your mind. Maybe I can do something to alleviate the problems, maybe I can't. But I'll try. There's no need for more secrecy, innuendoes, or childish games. For twenty-four hours I shall be available to talk with each and every man on this submarine. There will be no reprisal or punishment for anything you might say directly to my face, and, you have my pledge, what is said will remain confidential."

Awesome pressed the receiver close to his lips, altered his voice, and began a different subject.

"Despite Seaman Graham's death . . . it's our duty to see that life goes on. For the welfare of everyone, we cannot afford to become depressed or let morale sag. I know Graham would want us to go on and to finish with pride what we set out to do. We've all earned some recreation. Therefore, tonight I've planned a special dinner with some fun to lift our spirits. Contrary to public opinion, we're not at the bottom of our food stores just yet. In honor of this dinner we're dipping into the reserves to prepare the best that's available in underwater *haute cuisine*. We'll wash it down with sparkling cider . . . and have some good entertainment too. Following that I've planned a major athletic competition involving every man aboard.

"Please remember what I just said about talking directly with me. Take advantage of this invitation. That's all. See you at mess tonight. . . . Out."

His first step toward *rapprochement* taken, Awesome relaxed, fully confident he had made the right decision. Delighted with the prospects of closing the gap between himself and his men, he climbed to his feet and approached Dreadnought's bowl. The turtle, taking the air atop his island sanctuary, hastily retracted under his scalloped shell. A moment later he extended his snout with caution and peered at his master from a tiny slit between double eyelids. Awesome reached for him; Dreadnought pushed off with his feet and plunged into the shallow water. A moment later he was in the skipper's palm. Dark everted lips touched his shell collar just over his withdrawn head. "You're an old friend, Dreadnought," an affectionate voice whispered. "My oldest and my best."

1800 hours.

Awesome called his dinner "a Little Andes bash" and more than one submariner applauded the play on words. Announcements were posted around the sub, cranked out hastily on the *Amundsen's* old duplicating machine. Three separate sittings in the mess were planned for the 111-man crew. Red, yellow, and aqua crepe-paper streamers, plus clusters of fat balloons, hung from the stanchions and beams. Calder-inspired mobiles circulated in drafts from the air ducts. Additional tables supplemented the fixed furniture to accommodate the officers, who normally ate in their wardroom. Arranged in narrow rows as the configuration of the messroom permitted, the tables were festively decorated and laid with white tablecloths. At every second place there was a five-by-seven-inch typed card:

THIS LITTLE THOUGHT, JUST FOR YOU
D.H.

It was supply officer Lieutenant Donald Haddock's way of introducing a gastronomic surprise. From stores hidden among the dried fruits in *Amundsen*'s food lockers, he had produced three cases of Catawba sparkling grape juice, originally traded from a British supply officer in Scotland. True, it wasn't real booze, but it was the closest they could get, given the Submarine Service's strict rule against alcohol. You couldn't get drunk on it, but provided the ambience was conducive and the company infectious, men had testified that they experienced a psychological high. Given the recent psychological low, that wasn't an unattractive prospect.

A hunter and storer, a finder and hider, Haddock could almost have taken the wolverine's place as mascot at the University of Michigan, where he had taken the Reserve Officer Training Course before transferring into the Submarine Service. Both his forehead and his chin sloped back sharply from a beakish nose with flared nostrils; when he talked he had a way of smacking his lips. Even his teeth seemed smaller and sharper than most men's. At the bash he sat to starboard, his eyes bright with satisfaction over the grape juice and enjoying the gossip about pirated goods and the men who procured the finer amenities for shipboard life. Stories about the Navy's wild, horse-trading supply officers were legend, but 99 percent was pure fantasy: Since World War II the Navy had cracked down on "unrecorded" sales of government property. All exchanges had to be documented and ledgered, then photostated in quadruplicate and sent by Squadron to accounting offices in the bureaucracy beyond. This was not to say that supply officers had no latitude for personal discretion. Between the cogs of the unwieldy bureaucracy they carved for themselves some autonomy. Top brass conveniently overlooked their bribery, cheating, and thievery because, beyond the marketplace and out at sea, supply officers made shipboard life more comfortable than it would normally be. And in so doing they improved the general morale.

"Look what the lieutenant stole from a Russian vodka party!" Haddock saw a sailor flaunt a four-ounce can of Caspian caviar. "Tapioca, black engine grease, and five pounds of salt."

Directing his comment to starboard, an engineman answered. "Next time, Lieutenant, how about some real eggs? Surrounded by ovaries and big tits."

Clyde Forbes was wearing a sanctimonious look. "A helluva lot easier to get caviar than women in Russian territory. You guys are blind. A million clues and you just don't want to believe how deep we are in Russian waters."

"Right, smart man. So put your money where your

mouth is." Hendrick Phearson sounded impatient. For many sailors defending their commanding officer was a cultivated art, practiced with finesse, usually to obtain special privileges. But Phearson just disliked racism, or thought he did. Challenging it, at any rate, gave him a good conscience, especially when he was suspicious of Awesome's critics. "There's six hundred dollars betting we're in the Norwegian Sea off the Soviet coast, under two hundred dollars betting we're in the Barents. This is your chance to make a mint."

Everett Young looked up. "You didn't sign the letter for Bert Graham, did you? One of those friggin' kissasses . . ."

Phearson opened his mouth angrily but he was interrupted by Waldo Kramer. When the chief spoke nobody kept talking. Seldom did he raise his voice or exert the physical power he possessed in his muscular frame. One look at him and you couldn't forget the strength he held in reserve. To become the target of his displeasure was unthinkable. He rose from the head table and rapped his half-filled glass with a teaspoon. Somebody augmented his signal by striking a Catawba bottle. "Speech . . . speech!" Kramer beamed. "Let's hear a few words from the skipper," he proclaimed in his raspy voice. "You men may not know that Captain Awesome came in second only to Fidel Castro in the International Havana Filibuster. I reckon he's earned a chance to harangue this august body on the virtues of a good cigar."

The sparkling Catawba had lulled Awesome into other thoughts, and he hadn't really been listening. Rosenbaum leaned to the left and nudged the stem of a Meerschaum against his arm. Kramer's introduction registered. Awesome rose in some distraction to scan the faces before him, his unprepared mind reaching for something to say. Public speaking terrified many men, particularly those without experience, but not Awesome. He had been trained for public oration in his father's church, where words of inspiration were never prepared in advance. Someone once quipped that since all such testimony was extemporaneous every word originated directly from the Almighty. To Awesome's mind that was going too far. The phenomenon was better explained by simple training. Once on his feet before a congregation, a speaker simply drew upon a reservoir of anecdotes that had been purposely stored in his memory for just such an occasion. A good smile was a good beginning; his smile was warmly infectious. "Well, gentlemen," he drained the Catawba glass in a salute, "to the successful conclusion of our patrol!"

Mild applause from the officers' table was obviously more obligatory than spontaneous. He continued, "I reckon the biggest floeberg in the Little Andes isn't quite as big as she used to be." A faint chuckle rippled from the front row and spread aftward throughout the mess. "But then again, I guess the mightiest attack submarine in the ocean isn't quite as strong as she used to be either." Freer approval, stimulated by Chief Kramer's hearty applause, encouraged Awesome. "You'll all be interested to learn that yesterday I received a message from Captain Nicholai Borishelov on the Soviet icebreaker above, inviting us up for vodka cocktails.

Naturally, I was forced to decline. Captain Borishelov, a poor victim of Marxist-Leninist propaganda, apparently thinks that American sailors enjoy cocktails." Awesome paused to hand his glass for a refresher and was pleased by the laughter that reached the head table. "Then, gentlemen, the Russian captain radioed again that my men might be particularly interested since his ship was filled with female athletes en route to a competition in East Germany. *Natürlich*, I was forced by circumstances beyond my control to refuse again."

"Awwwww . . . Skipper, why'd you do that?"

"Since you asked, sailor—I told Borishelov that American seamen, especially those in the Submarine Service, weren't interested in . . . athletics." Laughter roared throughout the mess. Awesome waited for the noise to abate, then raised the refilled glass for attention. "Once a century I generate a brilliant idea. . . . When we left Scotland I asked Joe Crackleberry to get some special films for important occasions like this. Not his usual repertoire . . . I know what you guys have been watching. . . ." There was interrupting laughter from those who patronized Crackleberry's porno films. "But let's say this has some socially redeeming value." Laughter from those who disapproved of the porno. "Frankly I can't judge the quality because I haven't seen this myself. All I can say is it has not been shown before and, after our recent spate of reruns, that's got to be a hit." Applause and cheers; Awesome sank back into his chair. The lights immediately dimmed. Clapping punctuated the darkness and continued for several seconds undiminished. He listened, his heart pumping in overload, his fingers clasped together between his legs. In that dark, private moment, Awesome knew he had carried it off. Against tremendous odds, he had won back the crew's confidence. Despite all that transpired, he still possessed their trust.

The commotion suddenly stopped in anticipation. Koranson had sworn Joe Crackleberry to secrecy so that no one knew what film would be shown. An advertisement on the mess bulletin board proclaimed its manufacture in Denmark, and since Crackleberry was *Amundsen*'s unofficial porno king, the sailors exchanged ribald comments. It was certain to be a shocker.

Celluloid chattered through a projector, noisily eating up the lead. 04 . . . 03 . . . 02 . . . 01 . . . a metallic mixture of sounds evolved into marching band music.

ARMY-NAVY GAME

The moment Awesome saw that he expected a mass exodus. Aside from Laycook and himself, none of *Amundsen*'s crew was a graduate of the United States Naval Academy. A pro game would have been better, or even a college bowl engagement. But the Naval Academy? That would appeal only to a very select cadre in the Navy, only certain high officers in the Submarine Service. Awesome waited to hear feet scuffling on the deck, an uproar of disappointment. He overheard a couple of disparaging remarks as one man headed for the aft door. But the rest remained. Either they were in a good mood or exceedingly bored by the movie reruns. No matter, they stayed.

"Jesus Christ!" Awesome jerked to his right and tapped Koranson's arm. "I didn't know we had this film! Saw that game myself when I was in Washington for a briefing before this patrol!"

"The Army-Navy game . . . fans," the announcer's voice drowned out the captain's, "that rivalry, perhaps the oldest and strongest in athletic competition, will be played out again today! The nation's military academies are set to battle each other on the gridiron as they have done every year since 1890. This year, Navy enters as the underdog, with five wins and seven losses, to the Army's eleven-and-one record. But Navy has won its last four games by lopsided margins, upsetting Michigan last week by an astonishing twenty-eight points. And Maryland by ten the week before."

The movie projector, housed behind a panel at the rear of the compartment, balked and sputtered. Horizontal black lines obscured the images on the screen.

"Damn it, Crackleberry," Schroeder cried as the lights went on, "what's wrong with that projector? Runs perfectly well when you show your pornies!"

"Got any new ones, Crackleberry?"

"You guys need some variety." The projectionist was tinkering with film near the machine's gate. "Novelty's the essence of sex. The only thing that'll get you guys up. Trust me." Amid a spate of jeers, the lights faded for a second time and the sound came back on. Awesome settled back, staring at the introductory footage on the screen and listening to Koranson's nasal breathing in the darkness beside him. That particular Army-Navy game had been played only five months before, but it seemed like a decade.

It was a cool Saturday morning in late November when Awesome and Admiral Gaffy met for breakfast in Washington and left by Navy limousine for the football game in Philadelphia. The evening before, Gaffy had briefed Awesome about *Amundsen*'s top-secret mission, Patrol Polynya, named after a Russian word for a surface break in the polar ice pack. Being selected for this important patrol more than compensated for Awesome's transfer from the Pentagon to Holy Loch and redeemed his naval career from permanent derailment. His years of training and service, many of which seemed unappreciated, at last made sense. His gnawing, debilitating fear of failure evaporated. Like a Roman candle bursting in a darkened sky, he experienced the euphoria of rebirth. Even Maxine's and the children's deaths fit into perspective.

And yet, whatever the thrill and pride, it was only a part of Awesome's rapture. The other was the cementing of his friendship with Nicholas Gaffy, the man who had not abandoned him in his bereavement, who had trusted his naval competency and, when others were prepared to banish him behind a desk, had provided the tools for recovery. His appointment as commanding officer of Patrol Polynya testified to the confidence Gaffy had in his new black captain, but more important, it proved to Awesome that he had been worthy of the man whose judgment he valued more than any in the world.

Why particularly Nicholas Gaffy? Because his

trust had been extended at a critical hour when Awesome doubted he would survive the loss of Maxine and the children. That explained the friendship, but not the profound respect he held for the man. Respect had to do with what Gaffy represented in the Submarine Service. The Navy, Awesome had come to learn, was staffed with cautious men who advanced through the ranks by appeasing their superiors, not by virtue of their talents. Intelligent, reasonably competent, ethical men, they nevertheless lacked imagination. They were sharp in the ways of bureaucracy; they sparkled at Navy politics, but were thick-headed in matters of defense. Those with professional acumen got out while they were still young enough to retrain for another career. There had to be better ways to spend a lifetime than to stick around in the Navy, collect a meager salary, and then as a loyal civil servant retire to the golf course and eventually to the cardiovascular ward of the National Naval Hospital, Bethesda, Maryland, or the local Veterans Administration hospital.

Gaffy was refreshingly different. Unlike most who had achieved flag rank by cautious navigation through the minefields of the hierarchy, he was an outspoken critic of his superiors. It was a rare officer who did not subordinate national defense to Navy politics and his personal career. That Gaffy had not been ambushed somewhere along the line was a credit to his keen perception of the dangers around him. By his wits he had bulldogged his way up to vice admiral, but there his advancement was solidly blocked by Admiral Robert Katzenback. Gaffy's career-long feud with his superior was the delight of the press, which elevated it from a personal conflict into a matter of national defense. Despite Gaffy's precarious future, you had to be awed by how he survived the Navy's pulverizer. Even his enemies respected his creative thinking. God, how the Navy needed it!

The collision course between Gaffy and Katzenback, begun at Annapolis, materialized in open conflict by the mid-1950s when young Captain Nicholas Francis Gaffy championed the concept of the single-screw nuclear submarine. Too risky, his superiors argued. While a single-propeller vessel reduced underwater noise, it subjected its crew to the mercy of the sea. Gaffy's indiscreet comment to the press that it was better to be subjected to the mercy of the sea than to the blockheads in the Department of Defense did little to enhance the Pentagon's affection for him. Two years later the Navy ordered its first single-screw nuclear submarine. His enemies took credit for the innovation.

Twenty years after that, Gaffy's hair had turned silvery, but he was still scrappy. The Chiefs of Staff were no more impressed than they had been the first time by his proposal for another high-risk, high-gain weapons system. Tempers boiled. Gaffy showed he knew how to punch in the corner, yet this time he violated a cardinal rule of military decorum: He jumped the hierarchy and went directly to the Commander-in-Chief. In the White House he found a man who understood submarines, but, more important, saw how Gaffy's plan might minimize the hopeless overkill inherited from the Nixon administration's counterforce strategy. Knocking out Soviet ICBM silos one by one with a combination of American Minutemen, Poseidon, and Polaris nuclear missiles and B-52-delivered bombs had little to commend it, except as a deterrent to Soviet aggression. In actual warfare the counterforce strategy was certain to be a disaster both for the United States and Western civilization.

Gaffy was far less interested in deterrents than in effective combat strategy. An avid reader of history, he pondered what would happen *when* war broke out rather than *if* it did. The key to America's defense, he had not the slightest doubt, was in Western Europe. To survive a conflict with the Soviet Union the United States had to repeat what it had successfully accomplished in two previous wars— restrict the battlefield to Europe. According to American military intelligence the Soviets were likely to strike America's NATO allies with their SS-20 mobile-platform intermediate-range ballistic missiles. So lethal were these weapons that in the first hours of combat Western European armies would be effectively annihilated. The United States would have no alternative but to retaliate with its blockbusting nuclear arsenal, forcing the Russians into a counterstrike against the American continent. The scenario sounded gruesome for both defeated and victor alike. How much better an alternative to blunt the Soviets in Europe and let their NATO allies defend themselves against the "barbarians" from the East, as they had done since the establishment of the Holy Roman Empire. The question was: Could the United States Navy help to immobilize the Soviet intermediate-range ballistic missiles? Gaffy argued it could—and moreover he showed the Commander-in-Chief how this could be accomplished *without* recourse to nuclear weapons.

His plan required no new technology, only the combination of two separate weapons systems, one already long in service, the other in its final phases of development: a nuclear attack submarine capable of operating for several months under the polar ice pack, and the Navy's version of the tactical cruise missile, Tomahawk—BGM-l09.

The first stage of the Soviet SS-20 ballistic missiles, he explained, was dependent upon radiation sensing for its trajectory. Naval Intelligence had learned that this guidance was supplied from a ground station at Nar'ian Mar on the Mezen River, south of the Kanin Peninsula. If, according to this thinking, the ground facility at Nar'ian Mar could be destroyed in a pre-emptive strike with Tomahawk missiles, there was a good chance the NATO allies could not only blunt a Warsaw Pact assault, but also mount their own counterattack.

What sold the President was not the prospect of allowing the Europeans to chew each other up but that of aiding American allies and delivering a critical blow to the enemy without reliance upon nuclear weapons. Gaffy argued that in America counterforce strategy nuclear warheads substituted for missile accuracy. The more accurately a missile could be delivered to target, the smaller the payload required. In the Tomahawk he found a weapon with so accurate a delivery system it needed no more than a conventional 1,000-pound high-explosive warhead.

He reckoned an attack submarine could launch eighteen Tomahawks from standard twenty-five-inch torpedo tubes and deliver them all dead on the money—that is, within ten feet of their designated target. That amounted to 18,000 pounds of high-yield explosive bull's-eyed on the Soviet missile guidance facility at Nar'ian Mar. The Tomahawk had yet other characteristics unknown to Polaris, Poseidon, Trident, and Minutemen ballistic missiles. Though its turbojet engine propelled it at a relatively slow subsonic velocity, its trajectory followed the contour of the land—well underneath Soviet surveillance radar. Tomahawk was the ideal weapon for a preemptive strike. The enemy couldn't destroy what it could not first see. Their initial contact with Tomahawks would occur when they exploded on target.

But the best feature of all was the cruise missile's price tag. Unlike its multimillion-dollar big cousins, the Poseidon and the Trident, a Tomahawk could cost as little as $50,000—a veritable steal at the current inflated prices for weapons.

It all sounded too perfect, and the President was wary. Gaffy was the last one to believe that his, or any other, plan was failsafe. There had to be a risk in so imaginative a scheme. And so there was in Patrol Polynya. In order to deliver nine tons of high explosive on Nar'ian Mar, Underwater Strategic Services would have to establish the Tomahawk launch platform (a nuclear attack submarine) within 450 miles of its target, somewhere north of the Kanin Peninsula. Guided by terrain-comparison digital maps (TERCOM) in the Tomahawks, the "birds" would then follow the peninsula's land contour until they arrived at the Nar'ian Mar guidance center. The trick, Gaffy admitted, was to position a nuclear submarine in Soviet water without getting caught. But with proper training and caution he had little doubt the objective could be achieved.

Did the President really have a choice? In the remote event that Gaffy's scheme failed the United States still had the full power of its submarine, ICBM, and B-52 nuclear counterforce. If it was possible to hide the missile platform, there was nothing to lose. The Commander-in-Chief, once a military man himself, enjoyed tactics as much as strategy. What kind of a nuclear submarine did Gaffy have in mind?

The admiral smiled: an old one, not a sub of the Sturgeon class, with torpedo tubes amidship, but an older Skipjack-class boat with the tubes in the bow, like the World War II fleet-type submarines. He had the ideal vessel for the mission. Of course, she would require overhaul, but no structural work—nothing expensive.

As expected, the Chiefs of Staff raised innumerable objections, but they couldn't shake the basic soundness of Gaffy's proposal, and in the end he won. Hundreds of technical details had to be worked out, but those, the admiral announced, were what he liked to think of as mere plumbing. With their careers at stake, the Joint Chiefs buckled under the President's enthusiasm, just as Gaffy had predicted they would.

The admiral was by nature a cautious man who took nothing for granted, especially his personal security. To get what he wanted he had stepped on many toes, committing the unpardonable sin of jumping the chain of command. Those who disliked him before had now new ammunition for their guns: His isolation in the Submarine Service, not to mention the Navy, was now complete. Underwater Strategic Services could look to no branch of the armed services for help.

At Gaffy's side in the alumni section during the Army-Navy warmup, Awesome felt the man's energy radiate beyond his physical presence. On the job the admiral assumed project after project, toiling indefatigably. His daily schedule paid no homage either to the clock or the calendar. But when Gaffy was finally finished, he relaxed with equal intensity. It was perhaps his undistracted concentration that distinguished him—the unique way he walloped a golf ball, shook hands, or, presumably, screwed his devoted wife, Jennifer. One and only one interest at a time riveted his attention. And that brisk afternoon in Philadelphia it was, not Underwater Strategic Services or Patrol Polynya or Admiral Katzenback, but football. Gaffy himself had become a legend at the Naval Academy in his midshipman days. He played middle linebacker, a position from which he inflicted terrible punishment on the opposition's backfield and upset its passing offense. His blitzing technique was so formidable it had come to stand for an offensive maneuver: In naval combat an attack in which a destroyer squadron breached the enemy's flank and made a penetrating torpedo run on its capital ships became known as a "gaffy."

By the end of the third quarter the score was Army 14, Navy 0. Army had made the first touchdown and conversion, followed by another. Navy pursued, but each time surrendered the ball inches short of the critical first down. Gaffy's patience collapsed. "Gustafson!" he yelled from his seat, twenty-six rows up almost dead center on the fifty-yard line. "Take your bloody Gross out. Put in Peabody. We want Peabody!"

In *Amundsen*'s darkened mess, Awesome smiled. The sailors around him were waiting anxiously for the fourth quarter, warmed by the sparkling Catawba and swept into a festive mood. Everyone knew the game's outcome, but it was easy to pretend to be in Philadelphia for the first time.

The camera panned to the Navy rooters. "We want Peabody! We want Peabody!" The crowd had taken up Gaffy's demand. The chanting spread laterally through the alumni section to the midshipmen, their families, and finally the entire Navy side. "We want Peabody! We want Peabody!"

Awesome tugged at Gaffy's sleeve. "Who the hell's Peabody? Have I missed the Messiah?"

The admiral looked shocked. "Peabody? He's the second-string quarterback. Transferred from West Point the year before last—first time ever. The Army was mad as hell. A real coup for us. He's a great passer, but Gustafson only plays Gross, so Peabody never gets a chance to throw the ball."

Still, Gustafson did start him at the beginning of the fourth quarter. Gaffy was beside himself with glee. "Go get 'em, Peabody!" he screamed. "Show 'em the stuff of the Navy!"

The admiral was on his feet as Peabody engineered Navy's first TD. The second would have been as easy had the halfback not fumbled on his own nine. Army's colorless but methodical offense took charge. Her backs, at will, slashed through the center of Navy's line for five and six yards at a time, escalating the score to 20–7. Peabody played for two turnovers until Carl Gustafson returned quarterback Gross to pilot Navy's certain loss.

Gaffy's enthusiasm soured. "We want Peabody! Peabody! Peabody!" he howled. The lesser-ranking officers nearby backed him up. "Peabody . . . Peabody . . . Peabody!"

Meanwhile, Gustafson paced the bench. With twelve minutes to go, Peabody was standing at his side and taking final instructions before re-entering. Navy returned a punt to its own forty-five.

"Go . . . go Peabody!" Gaffy jumped up. "Now we're going to win." Gaffy's jaw was set tight, his eyes burned like lasers. A snap from center sent the young midshipman back to pass. Navy's line held like a fortress while Peabody watched the right end and left halfback crisscross. The pass went thirty-five yards through the air, and as it fell the Navy rooting section rose to guide it into the receiver's outstretched arms. In the excitement, Gaffy dropped and permanently damaged his binoculars. Next play: The fullback battered nine yards over Army's goal.

There were some calls of "Down in front," but nobody, least of all Gaffy, cared. In the final moments the entire Navy section was on its feet. At 20–14, Army tried to kill time on the ground. When Navy finally received the punt there were only two minutes and ten seconds to play. Gustafson was a wreck. He returned his first-string line and called a time-out. As play resumed, Gross ran out to quarterback the final sequence. Gaffy rose furiously from his seat. "Goddamn Gustafson. He'll renew his contract at the Academy over my dead body!"

Awesome was chilled by the admiral's public proclamation. Nicholas Gaffy never made idle threats even at a football game. Carl Gustafson was coaching for the last time at the U.S. Naval Academy.

Navy's first play was a pitchout to the right halfback, who lobbed a high pass out of bounds. As the linemen rose near scrimmage, a Navy back lay sprawled on the green. It looked like a stratagem often used at game's end to stop the clock, but Gross was actually carried off the field, holding his shoulder.

"Peabody! Peabody!" Gaffy sprang to his feet, not the least bit concerned with the quarterback's injury. "Victory! Victory!"

Pass down the center. Caught! The receiver was tackled on Army's thirty-yard line, but the clock was running. With only fifty seconds left, Peabody ordered a pitchout around Army's flank to the sidelines. Seven-yard gain!

"Peabody! Peabody, pass it down the middle!" Gaffy's voice boomed over the roaring crowd. "Hard! Pitch it down the middle!"

Alexander Peabody took the snap; the halfbacks flanked; the ends crisscrossed. Navy's line held until an Army linebacker crashed through the right tackle and pursued Peabody to his left.

"Pass it, Peabody! Throw it!" Gaffy almost

166

climbed over the full admiral in front of him.

Peabody paused, cocked his arm, then tucked the ball tightly into his midsection. He dodged tacklers to his right, zigzagged forward through Army linemen, and cut diagonally left toward the goal, crossing the seven to the five-yard line, where a defensive end hit him from the side. With hips still shifting and thighs grinding in a desperate surge for the goal, Alexander Peabody crashed down on the four. "No! No!" The crowd moaned helplessly. The clock advanced. Navy couldn't pick itself from the Astroturf in time for another play before the final gun.

Lights switched on in the mess and around him Awesome heard the harsh complaints about Coach Gustafson and Midshipman Peabody: No mercy for the defeated; no substitute for victory.

After the game in Philadelphia, the admiral had invited Awesome to a dinner party attended by the Navy's top brass, and during cocktails they inadvertently found themselves in Coach Gustafson's company. As introductions were being made, Gaffy strategically turned 180 degrees toward the hors d'oeuvres tray, just as Gustafson held out his hand. The hand was left dangling in the air. "Were you at the game this afternoon, Admiral?" The coach barely covered his embarrassment.

A long awkward silence elapsed while everyone looked to Gaffy for a reply. The admiral let the seconds pass; it was clear he had heard the question and was purposely ignoring it. With deliberation he waved a greeting to a distant acquaintance far across the living room and turned back to the hors d'oeuvres. "Pretty good pickings for a defeat party." He scooped a whole shrimp into his mouth, ground it up, and speared another from the corner of the departing tray. "The chef prepared for victory today, but look what he got. In my days at the Academy, gentlemen, we put our best men on the field. Didn't keep them on the bench as reserves. That's how we sank the entire Jap navy in the last war. They kept their big guns at home, but we put our capital ships out in the Pacific where they could do some damage."

Gustafson blanched but managed a reply, his voice perceptibly wounded. "I don't think you understand, Admiral."

From another waiter, Gaffy reached for a crab canape. "I'd hate to think the Navy's lost its fighting spirit. I was ashamed today. You know, it starts here at the Academy. What you see on the gridiron sets the mood for the entire service. Cowardice on the field permeates every boat, every ship, every flotilla. We should look for men to represent us in the stadium who can exemplify what we want at sea. And those who are weak and limp, I say, get rid of them."

"I'd hate to be Alexander Peabody now," someone ventured. "Did you call that final play, Coach?"

Gustafson, the full specter of defeat reflected in his eyes, shook his head. "Never. It certainly was not what I instructed Peabody. I wanted an up-and-out flood play with two options. But Alex panicked. He just hadn't enough experience under pressure. Made his own decision at the last moment. A big, big mistake, but nothing I could do about it."

Gaffy's scowl vanished utterly. He stared at the coach. "Is that why you didn't play Peabody earlier?"

"Yes. You see, I had a good idea what Peabody would do under pressure. That's just when Gross is at his best. Imagine how helpless I was with Gross hurt and the inexperienced Peabody calling the play. After I instructed him, all I could do was stand with my hands in my pockets. Once the ball is snapped there isn't a goddamn thing you can do except play with yourself in your pants. I told Peabody what I wanted but he got confused and called the wrong play from the beginning."

"Gentlemen, dinner is served," a voice announced from the rear.

Gaffy followed the others toward the dining room, hands buried deep in his trousers, causing his sleeves to buckle inelegantly over the forearms and cover the three gold admiral's stripes. Like the coach, how many times had he stood on the quay watching submariners sail from Holy Loch beyond his control? He had trained and coached his skippers, then entrusted the game to them, his proxies at sea. When a submarine disappeared from sight he was always rent by doubt and mistrust, followed by hours of hell. It was his custom to absent himself from everybody until the mood passed. Over the years he had developed a ritual that began when he locked himself in his office and closed the blinds. As long as it took, he sat submerged in darkness. If the depression became severe he belted down a single jigger (never two, never three) of Dewar's scotch.

During these isolated and terrible moments after departure, Gaffy languished in impotence. He had schooled his commanders to think and react like himself, and as skippers of their submarines to be clones of his own spirit. And yet deep within he understood the deception. When all went well they were admirable proxies. But in crises like that which faced Alexander Peabody, a human being was certain to bolt from his master, to revolt against indoctrination and training. The ultimate act of defiance is independence, the exercise of individual, sovereign judgment.

Gaffy saw himself pacing before the Navy football bench, the clock racing unmercifully toward defeat. Through pants pockets his fingertips fondled his testicles. Peabody took the snap from center and ran back into position. From that moment Gaffy knew the play was wrong . . . more, it was disobedient . . . a terrible error of judgment. They were bound to lose. Gaffy squeezed on his own testes, howling over the anguished din of the spectators, his voice lost in the cacophony. Peabody's error was his error; Peabody's shame, his shame.

All but a few guests had gravitated to the dining room when Gaffy discovered his hands buried in his pockets, his fingertips on his genitals. He snatched them away, flooded with embarrassment, and glanced belligerently around. The room was nearly empty and no one appeared to have noticed. Gustafson was still engaged in a dispirited postmortem of the game with a young aviator. A mischievous twinkle flickered in Gaffy's eyes. He stepped in front of Gustafson's lone respondent and silenced him by shoving a gold-embroidered admiral's sleeve toward the coach.

Whatever Gaffy did, he seldom made excuses and never apologized. "I don't believe we've formally met, Coach," he said. Gustafson's bewilderment was almost comical. "I'm Nick Gaffy. I was hoping to have a private word with you. With some luck our hostess has put us together at the dinner table. Shall we go in?"

The men were on their feet; Crackleberry was rewinding the film through the clattering projector. In the postgame arguments that circulated around the mess, Awesome, for reasons he did not understand, found himself defending Midshipman Peabody, but his excuses fell on deaf ears. It was not a night for underdogs. After a while Awesome gave up and headed for his stateroom. At the door someone tugged at his sleeve, very tentatively. Missile Technician Phearson wore his usual nervous smile, but his eyes looked anxious. The technician's hair was dusty blond, clipped so close to the scalp that he looked out of place, like a ghost sailor left aboard from the 1950s. His pale blue eyes only momentarily met the captain's, then fell somewhere to the plane of his cheeks. He wanted, he said, to speak privately with the skipper. "Not just me, sir. A buddy and me."

Awesome arched his eyebrows in genuine concern. "Is it urgent?"

"Not exactly," Phearson replied in an undertone. "If there's a more convenient time."

Awesome seized the chance to postpone it. He was worn out. He suggested an appointment the following day at 1100 hours, providing neither man was standing watch. Phearson did some mental arithmetic before responding that 1100 sounded good to him.

"Who's the other man?"

"Warren Glass, sir."

"All right, then, Phearson . . . 1100, in my state-room." Only when the skipper was stretched out on his bunk did it occur to him that he had forgotten to ask why the two submariners wanted to see him. No matter; he would learn in the morning.

5

BARENTS SEA

(Patrol Polynya: 60th day plus 25)

At 1100 Quartermaster Glass stood beside Phearson
in officers' country outside the skipper's stateroom.
They adjusted their blue Navy coveralls and looked
to one another, as though neither wanted to knock.
Phearson was the shy one; Glass, merely diffident.
Though he was unexpectedly strong for his slight
frame, Glass's skin clung to his bones like unpadded
upholstery, accentuating the skeletal structure beneath. His complexion was blemishless except for a
single mole that punctuated his left cheek. A thin,
gooselike neck sank loosely under a wrinkled collar
and an equally crumpled undergarment. Well liked
aboard *Amundsen,* he showed no sign of discomfort
at the prospect of talking with his commanding

officer, nor did it concern him that someone might see him waiting outside the captain's door. Phearson, on the other hand, looked apprehensive. He glanced nervously to his right and left, then quickly knocked. No answer. Someone was certain to spot them entering the skipper's cabin. More knocks. Again there was no answer. "Sir," he called, "we have an appointment at 1100."

When he finally appeared, Awesome's eyes were watery. A headache pulsated through his temples, made worse when he stood up. He had forgotten about his appointment with the two submariners. The twenty-four-hour period designated for personal conferences with the crew was nearing its end; the two men at Awesome's door were the only ones who had sought him out. He recovered his wits as quickly as he could and invited them inside, pointing to the desk and conference chairs. For himself there was the bunk. An apology was in order: the headache had robbed him of his memory, but he was now ready to hear what they had to say. In fact, he was most eager to learn what was on their minds.

Phearson had hoped he wouldn't be plunged so quickly into the purpose of their visit, but the captain wasn't inclined toward small talk. Like most shy people, Phearson came, almost too bluntly, to the point. "We want you to know you're not alone aboard." Awesome, in spite of himself, looked a little startled. "I mean, sir, we didn't sign the letter for Graham because we feel you've gotten a raw deal. Some men just don't like having a black skipper and it doesn't matter what you do or don't do, it's always going to be wrong. Know what I mean? We just want you to understand that we're certain what happened to Bert Graham wasn't your fault."

Awesome relaxed against the bunk railing and asked himself if he heard correctly, or had his headache scrambled his comprehension. On guard, he sifted his thoughts before responding with a cautious smile. "Well, Phearson, that's not quite what I expected when you asked to speak with me last night. But praise is the kind of thing a fellow likes to hear whatever the occasion, and it is nice to have some friends aboard. Your support is appreciated and welcomed." Awesome hesitated, suddenly concerned that he might have said too much. The faces opposite him were unrevealing and he concluded they were either nervous or intimidated.

"Sir," Glass filled the awkward hiatus in the conversation. "Despite what you said on the squawk box yesterday about damage to our boat, there are some heavy rumors floating around. Some fellows believe we're hurt real bad."

So that was it! And were Phearson and Glass some of the fellows in question? Were they just the front men? Awesome thought they probably were, but if they wanted to play the game this way he could see no harm in it. More civilized than Sokorski's method. Awesome's smile was disarming. "Thanks for being honest with me. Likewise, I'd like to be totally forthright with you too. Everything I said on the squawk box was absolutely correct. There was damage to a muzzle door and WRT drain on tube 6, but that's apparently corrected now. A sea chest and hull valve still need to be repaired. Other than that there's only one further detail: to check out Tomahawk 6 completely. That's the full picture." Awesome paused and the two seamen stared at him, round-eyed and solemn.

"The repairs don't particularly worry me, but something else does," he went on. He suspected that he knew the rest of what was bothering them. "Here you two gentlemen could do us all a great service. For reasons I don't fully comprehend, a touch of fear seems to have laid hold of this boat. I know it sometimes happens on a long patrol, when men are exhausted and have been under water too long. I also know there's no foundation for the pessimism. This afternoon Commander Riley will send a scuba team out the escape scuttle to free that jammed hull valve. Later, Commander Laycook will begin work on Tomahawk 6. When both details are finished, there will hardly be evidence of our contact on the Little Andes. I'd be appreciative if you would start setting the record straight. Nothing can cripple a submarine worse than the spooks based on unfounded rumors. They're hard to stop once they get into the ventilation system, and you can't get rid of them in the scrubbers, know what I mean?"

Glass sank deeper into his chair, released an audible sigh, and looked greatly relieved. His final question was more for reassurance than information. "Is that all?"

"A few minor leaks, nothing serious."

"When they collected signatures for that letter, they said it was much worse and that the Russians knew our bearings and our condition."

Damn Sokorski! "No, we have no evidence to suggest anything of the kind. I've told you all there is, straight and uncensored." Glass nodded his head freely; Phearson changed positions, obviously more relaxed, yet still skeptical. Several seconds elapsed while Awesome evaluated the wisdom of taking both submariners into his confidence. He began again cautiously, prepared to withdraw if they became uncooperative. "Since I've leveled with you, gentlemen, I'd be grateful for your help. A fellow can't help wondering about why so many men signed that petition for Bert Graham. Sokorski felt pretty strongly about his buddy; Young is a hothead; Forbes may be a little too streetwise for his own good. But I don't want them scaring my crew, even if they meant well. Was there any intimidation?"

Glass and Phearson stirred uneasily, deferring to each other. Phearson cleared his throat and uttered an unconvincing answer in the negative. "Not to speak of," Glass augmented, but immediately felt himself under the skipper's penetrating scrutiny. "Well"—he shook his hands to simulate a physical scuffle—"there might have been a little persuasion, but even the signers wound up afraid of Commander Laycook." Phearson cleared his throat a second time to warn his buddy against revealing too much, but the younger submariner had already committed himself. "Commander Laycook put the quietus on them at that meeting."

"What did he say?" Awesome climbed to his feet and wheeled around, trying to seem merely interested. Thomas Laycook implicated? It was the first thing he had heard about the executive officer's involvement! Nothing had been reported.

"We weren't at the meeting," Glass continued,

fearful he had already erred in mentioning Laycook's name. "But the way I heard it, Commander Laycook was pretty angry about that letter. He didn't want it circulating around."

Awesome sensed the submariners' discomfort and eased up on his questioning. "I'm glad Commander Laycook was able to head off a confrontation. It's tough enough for men to be hovering in a submarine for months without having to contend with foolish rumors. I guess we're all a little on edge. Thank God some of you fellows kept your heads screwed on right." Awesome brought his hands together in a decisive clap to signal the discussion closed.

The noise awakened Dreadnought from his lethargy. He scrambled to the edge of his rock island and ungracefully plopped into the water with a splash. Ripples ricocheted from the circular interior of his bowl.

"We didn't know there was a stowaway aboard. Has that little bugger got a ticket?" Glass inquired, with his usual infectious smile.

"Now would the Navy permit travel without a ticket?" Awesome fished the turtle out. "What this little creature doesn't have is a passport—a passport for the Garden of Eden. You see, every day I let him walk around in this terrarium." He reached back to his desk for Sokorski's black folder, balanced it between Dreadnought's bowl and the terrarium, and placed the reptile on it. For a moment the turtle just sat there, a lifeless hulk. Then, quite unexpectedly, four paws emerged from the little shell, and Dreadnought made a short but inspired dash across the improvised bridge. His energy spent before

178

reaching the terrarium, he stopped in his tracks and recommitted himself to his shell.

"Bravo!" Glass laughed approvingly. "When in doubt, stop! Forbes should have met this turtle."

"How so?" Awesome asked, aware that beside him Phearson was clearing his throat again and frowning prodigiously. But Glass gave him a bland look.

"That little scuffle in the mess. Over the letter for Bert Graham, of course. Forbes lunged at Crackleberry but it was a bad decision. Joe's a karate black belt, you know. At least, everybody thinks he's a black belt. Flattened two guys with chops to the chest, then flung a kick at somebody, I won't mention any more names, sir, charging from his rear. Only Crackleberry struck low and caught him in the balls. Poor bastard doubled up like a potato bug; thought he'd puke his nuts right out his throat. Then McFarland turfed some guy across the mess like a log in a Scottish tattoo." He glanced up at Awesome. "I hope you won't need to follow up on this, sir. No real damage done. Imagine I shouldn't have mentioned it."

Awesome merely grinned. "It sounds as if my 'royalists' can handle things for themselves," he said. And then made himself look a little less entertained. "Brawling is a punishable crime in the Navy, you know. But I believe you said this was just a scuffle?"

"That's right, sir," Glass appeared encouraged by the skipper's understatement, "so small you'd hardly notice. The worst is over now. With Bert's death the movement against those who refused to sign that letter kind of lost steam. And then your sermon at the funeral was pretty good too." Glass's eager eyes failed to conceal his curiosity. "Some fellows said your father was a parson or minister or deacon or something like that in Mississippi."

Inwardly Awesome cringed. Glass hadn't meant that as an insult, but it was. The crew automatically located his origins in the Deep South, suggesting he was an immediate descendant of illiterate back-country slaves. Old stereotypes die hard. "Not quite, gentlemen. My father was a Methodist preacher in Frankfort, Kentucky. That's not quite Mississippi. As a matter of fact, white people in my county fought the Civil War on the Union side. Preaching, I guess, comes natural to me. I disappointed my father by not entering the ministry myself."

Phearson seemed to relax a little. He confessed that his father also had wanted him to enter the ministry, but not the Methodist Church. They were strict Lutherans, too strict for Phearson's tastes. That's what scared him away from the Church, a certain evangelical fanaticism. Suddenly embarrassed by the conversation, he shoved his hands in his coverall pockets. A piece of folded paper crackled under his fingertips; a pained expression crossed his face. "Oh yeah," he exclaimed, drawing the paper before the skipper's eyes.

The cartoon, mimeographed on $8\frac{1}{2}$-by-11-inch paper, stopped Awesome cold. It was drawn by a skilled cartoonist whose figures were instantly recognizable. Crouching under the wide-spread legs of a large white man was a black naval officer, naked except for captain's boards and sleeve stripes. The man above him was equally nude but hirsute, with admiral's boards tacked to bare shoulders. In the black man's hand was a tape measure, which he was stretching over the admiral's dangling member from scrotum to foreskin. "You see, Nick," the caption read, "I told you I'm a bigger prick than you."

Awesome studied the drawing, marshaling his full powers of control. The cartoonist's pen had craftily captured his own physique by capitalizing on the comic imbalance between short beagle legs and schnauzer torso. Less skillful were the stereotyped negroid lips and prognathous jaw. Because the artist could consult his model aboard *Amundsen,* the black man was more convincing than Admiral Gaffy whom, Awesome concluded, the artist had seen only once—if ever. What little he had remembered was represented with particular malice: A bulging stomach replaced Gaffy's iron gut tightened by one hundred situps every morning at 0500; thin, hair-flecked feminine legs caricatured his thick calves and bull thighs firmed by hard jogging along mountain sheep trails; a gnarled, knotty penis dangled grotesquely past the knees. Awesome granted artistic prerogative for such extravagances. But no license would excuse the expression of shame, mortification, and defeat drawn into Gaffy's eyes. No interpretation of that unpardonable desecration was valid. Whatever Gaffy was, even as the object of humor, he was never pathetic . . . and never weak . . . most assuredly never defeated.

"Can I keep this?" Awesome's voice crackled with dislike.

"Sure, it's yours." Phearson moved toward the door. "There are hundreds in circulation."

"There *were* hundreds. I'm enlisting two volunteers—a Navy of two, you might say—to collect every one of these cartoons and deliver them to me personally. If you can get the stencil, all the better, but be careful and don't get yourselves into any trouble with your buddies." He touched Glass's shoulder. "Can I count on you?"

"Sure," Glass responded. Phearson nodded.

"We can try, I guess. They're all over."

"Try." Awesome unclenched his fists. "Thank you for coming, gentlemen." He regarded them both in turn. "And remember, if there is any new harassment and help is required, you know where to come. We needn't say any more about this otherwise."

When the submariners departed, Awesome locked his stateroom door and immediately unfolded the cartoon to restudy its details. Once again, his eyes confirmed the malicious misrepresentation of Nicholas Gaffy. He was finding it oddly hard to breathe, and a dizziness, like that he'd had after contact with the Little Andes, scrambled his vision. The spell lasted only a few seconds before the constriction eased from his throat and his legs steadied. When it was over, Awesome displayed the yellow paper before Dreadnought's blinking eyes. At last he refolded the drawing and stored it beside Gaffy's letter, inside the Bible cover—a weed, he sighed, overshadowed by a majestic rose.

Was it for Gaffy's sake or his own that punishment of the cartoonist was so important? Or was it a matter of naval discipline? As Awesome pondered the question he stood before a tiny mirror beside his bunk and studied his own image. Moved by his instinct to defend his commanding officer, he took his service cap with its gold embroidery and eagle insignia over fouled anchors from the locker and set it upon his head. It made him feel better, though it might have had the opposite effect. The caricature of Admiral Gaffy had been an insult to the authority that cap represented, just as it showed profound disrespect for his emissary at sea.

Awesome manufactured a fierce expression. Crow's-feet wrinkled around his diminished eyes, and his lips thinned. He showed his teeth. That caused him to laugh aloud. The truth was that Elisha Awesome was not a very formidable disciplinarian, not even sufficiently ferocious to scare himself. Awesome laughed again and vowed not to lose his sense of humor. Above all, not that. With it, he and the sub were all better off.

1455 hours.
Depth: seventy feet. *Amundsen*'s sail was ten feet beneath the underside of the ice pack to reduce sea pressure and to make it easier on the two divers working on the jammed hull valve and sea chest. Their egress into the 31° F water had been achieved by means of an escape trunk below *Amundsen*'s forward access hatch over the torpedo room. Used by underwater demolition teams, the trunk could hold five or six men when sealed off from the compartment below. A storage space for perishable foods, potatoes, and onions during the first month of the patrol, it had long been emptied and now served as one of two such exits. Divers were evacuated by equalization of air pressure inside with the ambient water pressure. Once the trunk was permitted to fill

with seawater, those inside paddled through a scuttle into the ocean. They returned to the submarine by reversing the procedure.

Below the escape trunk Awesome paced in a circle, glancing repeatedly at his watch—not that any of them could tell exactly how long the divers' air would last. That depended not only upon the depth at which they worked but also upon their rates of exertion.

Riley had presented his repair plan with his usual optimism (Laycook called it bluster). Right after Graham's death there had been a predictable back-lash among the crew, a tendency to be skeptical of anything the engineering officer proposed. Despite Riley's tight-lipped fury, Chief Kramer completed an investigation into the circumstances surrounding Graham's accident. Young had been a prime witness whose interpretation of events greatly influenced the final judgment. If Riley's exculpation surprised anyone it was certainly not the star witness. He could have saved everyone the trouble. Hadn't he called it from the beginning? Accident . . . that's what it was, an accident.

How much Awesome was convinced it was difficult to tell. Laycook, on the other hand, made no effort to conceal his skepticism. The report on Graham's accident he was prepared to let slip—but not Riley's plan for repairing the hull valve and sea chest. There were at least a dozen reasons why the operation was inadvisable, not the least of which were questions of safety. Awesome weighed these objections judiciously but depended upon the wise counsel of his operations officer. Koranson had complete faith that with proper precautions the repair presented no inordinate dangers, nothing with which trained divers could not cope. After all, he argued, what was their training for if they feared to use their skills when necessary? There was a prolonged verbal scrap between Laycook on one side and the operations officer on the other. In the end Awesome intervened. Not without some reluctance he authorized "Operation Bertram," as Riley referred to his plan, because the reputation of Blue Crew was at stake. Good submariners took it as axiomatic that difficulties incurred at sea should be solved at sea. A good crew didn't bring its troubles home. If that became necessary it reflected on the ingenuity of the submarine's leadership and on the skill and courage of its crew.

Men crowded under the escape trunk (more than the skipper believed necessary), chatting garrulously in expectation of the divers' return. But doubts had a way of lingering with Awesome and he wondered how it was possible for them to be so confident. Waldo Kramer announced the elapsed dive time as forty-three minutes, which meant that the compressed air in the self-contained Emerson breathing rigs was running short. Awesome caught himself holding his own breath, as if that could somehow help the divers in the water. He shivered. Not a bad underwater swimmer, he trapped a lungful of air and held it for thirty-seven seconds while upbraiding himself for not accepting Laycook's counsel. Time was certainly running out for the divers. They were no longer within view of the periscopes mounted on *Amundsen*'s bridge and for some reason they weren't near the escape scuttle either.

At forty-seven minutes, twenty-two seconds into the dive, a technician on the top rung of the ladder, peering through a small circular window in the entry hatch, saw the first set of black diving fins slip into the trunk. Once the diver had entered fully he paddled back to assist his partner. "Commander Riley," the seaman announced, identifying the fire-orange strip on his thermal hood. "They're both in." Awesome heaved a sigh of relief and mopped perspiration from his brow.

No one was surprised when Riley had volunteered to lead the expedition into the water. He best understood the mechanical difficulties, but more, Graham's death had had a profound effect upon him. Rosenbaum's comment that he suffered from "survivor guilt" fueled much speculation among the crew. And once again, unfounded rumors ran wild. Some said that Riley and Graham had made a sacred compact: If one man perished, so the story flourished, the other was duty-bound to persevere in the name of the dead man's ghost. To that point the gossip was innocuous. But it escalated further into quite irrational speculation. Riley and Graham knew something which no one else did; they had premonitions about undefined dangers lurking in the waters beyond *Amundsen*'s hull. Both Awesome and Laycook tried to disparage the theory, but fighting rumors was like swatting mosquitoes. The moment you rid yourself of one you were attacked by two more.

After the second diver was safely inside the trunk Riley secured the scuttle by a hand wheel, then dropped to the platform and signaled through the window. Compressed air stored in high-pressure tanks immediately flooded the trunk, purging seawater into an auxiliary tank and back into the ocean. Within seconds the waterline dropped past the divers' shoulders to the level of the platform. Chief Kramer mounted to unfasten the lower hatch. Black flipperless booties dropped over the open coaming and felt for the ladder. Riley stabilized himself on the top rung and then began descending, packing a tank of MAPP gas and a welding torch with Fox Sierra tip on his chest, his scuba rig on his back. Thirty pounds of lead weights had been left inside the trunk. Off came his underwater welding goggles and hood, followed by an exclamation about the eerie phosphorescent glow refracted from the canopy above and the warm current traveling beneath the ice.

Sidney Killerman, the second diver, accepted help from those unstrapping his emergency cutting rig, equipped with two tanks, one oxygen, the other hydrogen. All the while he chattered with excitement. Riley, with a boyish grin, let him tell the story. After having paddled aftward past *Amundsen*'s sail to the auxiliary machinery room, about 110 feet, they had descended along the starboard. There was no time to lose. Riley located the jammed hull valve. His gloved finger showed where he intended to make kerfs in the steel collar. Killerman nodded, but was certain Riley had made a mistake. Valuable time was expended marking off the cut zone since a small error could cause a leak and threaten *Amundsen*'s watertight integrity. A single burn severed the obstruction and, to Killerman's surprise, almost freed the jam.

Unfortunately, time was working against them. Riley could probably have pried the remaining steel away with his bar but elected to return rather than risk getting decompression sickness. What remained to be finished was far less than what had already been accomplished. "The commander knew exactly where to cut," Killerman summarized proudly. "He was right on target!"

Everett Young read from scuba diving charts the time required for excess nitrogen to leave Riley's and Killerman's bloodstreams before re-entry into the water. Fifty-two minutes. Riley shivered, too cold to glory in praise.

Awesome swabbed at the icy water on the engineering officer's back with a polyester towel. It didn't absorb much water but it also didn't leave much lint to clog *Amundsen*'s air regeneration system. As Awesome listened to a detailed report, he felt vindicated by the operation's success. After all, he had been right at the Little Andes, right about the mood of the crew, and right about repair of the hull valve and sea chest. His voice resonated with the old pre-Andes confidence as he spoke with Riley out of earshot of the crew. "I don't like your going out there again for a second time, Charlie. If it's so easy now, let somebody else take your place. You're just too valuable to us. How about sending Everett Young?"

The Irishman's expression was half appreciative, half suspicious. "I started the job and I should finish it."

"But you've already made your point."

"To the men, maybe, but not to Bert Graham." The moment he said that, Riley knew he had revealed more than necessary. He did not expect the skipper to understand his feelings about Graham, nor was it appropriate to explain them. "There's something strange up near the control plane on the sail," he changed the subject. "When I was swimming back, I think I saw some free lines near the bridge, a whole bunch of things I don't understand. Couldn't take time to paddle up and look around. And my Tekna lamp wasn't strong enough to penetrate far. We've only got fifteen or so minutes of work on the hull. I'd like to go back up and check it out on the second dive."

Awesome threw the damp towel to a seaman. Riley's story was obviously an invention to justify his mysterious conduct about Bertram Graham. One thing was clear, there were no free lines dangling from *Amundsen's* bridge. The submarine's fair-water, atop its sail, housed radio loop and whip antennae, attack and radar periscopes, search radar and snorkel, yet all were retractable under a metal shield when *Amundsen* dived below the surface. From the fairwater observation platform Awesome had personally seen these instruments safely housed before *Amundsen* submerged below the waves, three miles beyond the entrance to Holy Loch. The bridge was absolutely clean. If Riley's story were not fabricated, it could only have been a hallucination. Such phenomena weren't all that uncommon in dull, refracted light from the ice mantle.

"Captain!" Clyde Forbes bolted through the compartment door and scrambled forward toward the skipper. "Lieutenant Schroeder needs you in the cryptocenter. We've got a message from Squadron."

189

Awesome turned to follow him. "Listen, Charlie," he said, patting Riley on the shoulder, "get some rest and warm up. We'll talk about that second dive when I return."

"Captain!" Riley jumped up in protest and promptly fell over a spare set of lead diving weights in his path. "Damn it!" he yelled. "Captain!" And grabbed his toes. "Oh, God, that hurts!" Awesome was already gone. Nothing to do but stand there, desolate and aching, to vilify both the crewman who left the weight in his path and his own stupidity for not completing the repair on the first dive. Leaving a job unfinished was not Riley's style; and damned if he was going to let another man clean up the tag ends for him. *That* wouldn't be the kind of tribute to Bert Graham's memory he'd wanted to make at all.

When Killerman, dried, warmed, and cradling a mug of coffee, came in to inquire about the equipment for the next dive, he was surprised by the engineering officer's temper. There wasn't going to be a next dive, Riley growled like a bulldog, at least not for him. The skipper had gone to the crypto-center without giving permission to finish the job. Nor did he say when he would authorize the completion.

"What? What the hell!" Killerman didn't know whether to be bewildered or shocked. It was an affront. Their successful work on the first dive had gone unappreciated. He grabbed for explanations. Was the captain's hesitance a punishment for not having finished on a single dive? Was he worried what they might find if they investigated further the unexplained shapes near *Amundsen*'s bridge? Riley shrugged his shoulders and withdrew into his thoughts. Did the skipper say that he "would" talk about a forthcoming dive or that they "could" talk about it? In both cases it was just a question of time. Sooner or later divers would have to go back and finish up.

"What do you think is up on the sail?" Killerman inquired. When Riley didn't answer, he repeated the question a second time. "Commander?"

Riley was jarred from his thoughts. "Oh hell, who knows? Bert Graham's ghost," he barked angrily. "That's what's out there. Bert Graham's ghost!"

Killerman backed off. He had never seen the good-natured engineering officer in such a foul mood. "Funny-looking ghost," he replied half humorously from a safe distance, and blew on his coffee. "All lines."

Outside the cryptocenter Schroeder paced an oval pattern over the deck. Between his fingers he turned an unlighted cigarette. Not that he intended to light up right there in a no-smoking area. But as soon as the captain arrived and deciphered the message, he meant to beat it to the wardroom. The cigarette could be considered as a celebration. The entire crew was waiting for this communication ordering *Amundsen* home. About time, too. Command had been treating Blue Crew like an experiment; somebody was curious to see how long men could endure an extended patrol without going bonkers. Then an ambitious smart-ass would write a position paper on it and get a promotion. Meanwhile Blue Crew suffered and Gold languished. Schroeder pointed the cigarette at the compartment door as Awesome approached, doubletime, from the control room. "Commander Laycook's already inside."

Awesome pounded on the locked door. No answer. He gritted his teeth. "Thomas!" The door slid open. For a brief moment Laycook's silhouette was framed by the doorjamb. The second he turned into the fluorescent light the pallor of his face revealed that something was wrong. Awesome caught his breath. "What, Thomas?" He bulled his way past the commander, who slammed the door shut behind him.

The cryptographic machine was still clattering away, unscrambling the last of the message. "The Russians are closing in on us," Laycook reported. "We're trapped!" Awesome ripped the yellow readout from the teleprinter and read it aloud, his voice emotionless, his speech slow and methodical.

AMUNDSEN: SATELLITE REPORTS SOVIET ICEBREAKER AND TWO CORVETTES ENTERING ICE PACK 69° 46′ NORTH, 44° 31′ EAST. ICEBREAKER *ARKTIKA* DESTROYERS *DSKARI* AND *SVETLIVYIARE* CURRENTLY SAILING SOUTHEAST TOWARD KOLGUYEV. TWO PATROL ICEBREAKERS FROM SEVERODVINSK HAVE EXITED WHITE SEA AND ARE HEADED IN YOUR DIRECTION. TWO POTI-CLASS SUBMARINE CHASERS AND ONE UNIDENTIFIED GOLF-CLASS SUBMARINE ON COURSE TO BUGRINO FROM AMDERMA. DESPITE ALARMING NAVAL AC-

TIVITY WE HAVE NO INDICATION OF YOUR DETECTION. BELIEVE DUE TO NEW MISSILE GUIDANCE NETWORK BEING CONSTRUCTED IN CENTRAL KOLGUYEV, USE DISCRETION. UTMOST CAUTION. OUT.

Laycook knew what he would have done. If it was his command he would already have been sailing. But Awesome just stood there, thinking. It made Laycook impatient. For himself the situation looked like a disaster: The Soviets were tightening the noose. There was still time for *Amundsen* to escape the trap, but she had to move . . . and fast. It suddenly worried him that perhaps Captain Awesome did not appreciate the urgency. After all, he had failed to understand at the Little Andes, an error in judgment that eventually claimed one man's life. Laycook inhaled gustily, unable to restrain himself further. "With respect, Captain . . . we've got to move immediately."

Awesome angled his head, examining his exec officer. "I just can't believe, Thomas, that we could have been detected. Squadron doesn't think so either."

"They're nuts. How else explain what's going on around here?"

Awesome wagged his head slowly. "Perhaps a new missile guidance center on Kolguyev. Perhaps routine naval maneuvers. Who knows, Thomas? But there's also no way they could have found us. That just doesn't make sense. It's easy to panic."

"I'm *not* panicking. It's time to go home, anyway.

Admiral Gaffy has already provided you with discretionary powers to end the patrol. This looks like an emergency to me and even if it's not at the moment it will be shortly. They're converging upon us from three directions. A few hours and we won't be able to sail without certain detection. This quiet, remote corner of the Arctic is getting to look like the Straits of Gibraltar. The longer we postpone it the harder it's going to be to run the gauntlet. And this time it won't be like the Little Andes. First, there are now four times as many ships, and second, we're no longer in international waters. They can do whatever they please to us here. They don't have to call it an 'attack,' just target practice in their own back yard.''

Awesome knew Laycook wanted to say far more than he actually did. He was too good a submariner, too proud a naval officer to be insubordinate. Yet the battle lines between them had long been drawn. However much Laycook muzzled himself, their ways were probably about to part for good over this decision. A pity, because you couldn't fault his logic. Things seemed to be collapsing around *Amundsen*. Nine out of ten skippers would do exactly what Laycook advised and run. But nine out of ten skippers could be wrong. *Could* be, Awesome repeated wryly to himself. Was that being responsible . . . or arrogant? But somebody had to look after their mission. And Squadron—Gaffy—almost ordered him to stick tight. "Our position is precarious, Thomas," Awesome admitted, "but I don't think the time is propitious to run. Squadron did not order us to leave. On the contrary, this message states clearly that there is no hard evidence we've been discovered.

If we sail we increase the chances we'll be picked up by sonar. We won't make it through the sonar buoys and the fleet radar without somebody hearing us. That means Patrol Polynya is over. No American submarine will be able to operate in these waters for a long time. Admiral Gaffy's Tomahawk punch will be lost and we're back facing nuclear disaster. That gloomy prospect must be worth some risk."

"We've been through this station before, Captain," Laycook snapped.

"Right, Thomas. We have been through this station before. But we're going to dive back to the bottom to sit it out again. It worked for us at the Little Andes and it will work here. I don't care how long it takes. The Russians will eventually move away. When we decide to leave the Barents it should be on our schedule and not theirs."

Laycook glared at him. The captain's words were brave, fine, simplistic words. Run! He wanted to yell. Run, you dope! The Russians are coming for us in swarms, and what if they know we're here? Then what are the odds? But he had already said all he could. In the hour of peril, *Amundsen* hardly needed an open fight between her top-ranking officers. With supreme discipline Laycook voiced the words "Yes, sir," then composed himself with thoughts of escape. Riley's repair operation on the submarine's hull suddenly possessed a new dimension. "If we are forced to take evasive action, we're going to need that jammed hull valve." His mouth went dry. For the first time the trick of feeling self-righteous through obedience to duty seemed thin living indeed.

"Riley's almost finished," Awesome reported.

"One more quick dive and we'll have some insurance in case our Russian friends decide to poke around even closer. We'll have our maneuverability, Thomas. And very soon, too."

Laycook followed him to the tactical attack center, where Awesome reached for a phone to the forward torpedo room. "Commander Riley, this is the captain. . . . Commander Riley, this is the captain. . . ." He spoke calmly into the speaker. Communications from the skipper normally elicited an immediate response. Yet this time an answer was slow in coming. Awesome repeated himself impatiently.

"No, sir. . . ." The voice that finally answered wasn't Riley's at all. It was Everett Young. "The commander is in the water, sir."

"What? He didn't ask for permission to leave the boat. How long has he been gone?" Awesome made no attempt to conceal his alarm.

"They left five minutes ago, sir."

Awesome slammed the phone back onto its chrome hook and whirled around to face the XO, eyes enraged. "Riley's started his second dive in direct defiance of my orders, Thomas. I specifically told him to wait until we had a chance to talk before re-entering the water. I've got a good mind to dive to the bottom without him. It would serve him right."

Laycook luxuriated in the momentary pleasure of Riley's disobedience. All along he had counseled the skipper about the engineer's bravado. He allowed himself to smile, just a little smile. "Well, Captain, I guess he'll have to be taken down a notch or two. Who'd have thought?"

Awesome's face was stony. "That's enough, Thomas."

"Aye, aye . . . sir." It was petty and Laycook knew it. He drew himself erect. If this were indeed his last tour of duty and if they ever got out of here, he didn't want to have to remember such things about himself. But, damn it, the black man had a talent for bringing out the worst in him.

Awesome endeavored to reconstruct his parting words with the Irishman, to remember the exact phrasing of his order to wait, yet could recall only the general sense of the conversation. "I'm going to the escape trunk, Thomas. The minute the divers are back, we'll drop to the bottom. Have Sagi make preparations." He headed for the door but suddenly turned to face the exec officer. For the first time since the Lumbrovskiy Channel he felt glad that Laycook was his executive officer rather than some obsequious simpleton who always agreed.

"I owe you an apology, Thomas. You were right about Riley. Thank you." He touched Laycook's arm. "I'll settle with that Irishman privately, as soon as he finishes."

1741 hours.

Huddled below the single escape trunk twenty crewmen, each ready with an argument for the necessity of his presence, shared the ominous feeling that something had gone wrong with the divers in the water. Koranson at the periscope stand had been monitoring their progress through the scope, but had lost visual contact. He spun the lens around 360 degrees and focused at different distances. Report:

negative. It had been nine minutes since *Amundsen's* sonar stopped collecting signals from the divers, and no one could explain why it required more than five to paddle the 110 feet forward to the escape scuttle near the bow. On the previous trip the divers had tapped on the submarine's hull to mark their progress. The same procedure was repeated on their second dive, but the tapping had ceased near *Amundsen's* sail and did not resume. Kramer assured everyone that Riley and Killerman had waited their required surface time before going out. True, they hadn't left time to spare, but provided they were back soon they could avoid decompressing.

The space under the trunk became more crowded as additional men arrived to stand vigil. Thoughts of the icy waters beyond *Amundsen's* controlled 72° F temperature sent chills through those who waited with hands buried in their pockets. Most of the crewmen, highly skilled technicians, were comfortable with numbers. They conversed about water pressure and its effect upon the gases in the scuba tanks, lungs, and bloodstream. The purpose, nobody wanted to admit, was to kill time—time that was working against the divers. You could calculate the figures several ways, but you couldn't avoid the conclusion that the compressed air supply the divers carried in their Emerson rigs was perilously near exhaustion. Forty-eight minutes had elapsed. Why hadn't *Amundsen's* sonar picked them up?

Chief Kramer waved his hands for silence. "Their air is exhausted," he announced. "I've kept an accurate time and there's no way they could still have any air left. They're overdue now by five or six minutes."

Young looked toward the others in Riley's detail, expecting a buddy to protest on his behalf. There wasn't a man who didn't admire the engineer's courage . . . and his skill. But there was also something even more commendable about him. Unlike the other officers, he openly fraternized with anyone, regardless of rank. That had to injure his career, though none of the brass wanted to draw attention to their own élitism. At least the enlisted men appreciated in Riley what the officers did not. But oddly, none defended Riley against Kramer's remark. Young filled the void. "That's got to be impossible. They've got plenty of air. Commander Riley wouldn't wait till the last minute."

Kramer's reply had to wait: A report from the sonar compartment claimed that signals were again being received. Good news, indeed. Then came the bad news: The signals were weak, very weak. No visual sighting by periscope.

Awesome stood on the platform beside the entry port window, partially mesmerized by the gentle swirl of the water inside the trunk. So far had his thoughts drifted from the immediate events around him that he failed to notice a pair of black fins slip into the chamber, followed by legs and a torso. He caught himself immediately and announced that a diver had returned. Cheers erupted spontaneously from all sides. Someone asked if the hood stripe was orange or blue. He couldn't tell in the turbulence. When the diver turned the color was clearly visible. Blue.

"That's Killerman, sir."

What happened inside was obscured by bubbles. Awesome presumed that Riley had followed Killerman into the trunk and closed the scuttle behind him. What actually occurred was quite different. When the water cleared the scuttle was sealed but Riley was not inside. Killerman had dropped to the bottom near the access hatch and was peering directly at Awesome outside. "Hey," the skipper screamed through the circular glass, "open the hatch for Riley! Damn it, open it up for Riley!"

Killerman shook his head, flailing his arms in frantic gestures. Over and over he struck the window with the palm of his gloved hand. His face again disappeared behind water turbulence. When it cleared the diver's mask was flat against the window, his owlish eyes magnified by terror and three layers of glass. A hand slashed across his throat signaling air hunger. The signal was repeated in frantic gestures, obscuring Killerman's face in turbulence.

"Where's Riley?" Awesome shouted. "Where's Riley?"

Killerman's bulbous eyes rolled back and were lost from view. A stream of carbon-dioxide bubbles escaped from the second stage of his regulator and trickled upward. Four orphan bubbles chased their predecessors. There was no further response to the skipper's entreaties. Killerman sank to his knees, his head slumped into the collarbone. Gas bubbles thinned into a narrow column and then ceased.

"Purge it," Awesome commanded to those below him. "Purge the trunk."

Below Awesome, Young howled. "We gotta go get the commander! Let me swim out and get him! I'm

200

qualified with scuba."

Awesome ignored Young, concentrating on Killerman inside the chamber. His body had contracted into an amorphous hulk, anchored to the interior platform by thirty pounds of lead weights strapped to his belt. His gas tanks for underwater cutting had evidently been jettisoned before his re-entry into the trunk. Alongside the skipper, two submariners crowded the tight work area at the access hatch. As the water level descended over the diver's head they were already working the hand wheel. Seconds later a swoosh of freezing air escaped from the trunk. Kramer squeezed through the pack of them into the evacuated chamber to rescue the collapsed diver.

"Let me get Riley," Young's voice bellowed over the din of excited voices. "Riley's out in the water. Somebody's got to get him back."

They carried Killerman down the ladder toward the torpedo-room deck. No one had thought to unstrap his breathing tanks, which banged on the railing. The bulky weight belt dropped to the deck with a loud clang. Too many hands and not enough leverage; too many feet and not enough room to maneuver. Awesome ordered the spectators to general quarters and quickly appointed an emergency detail.

Killerman was stretched out on the deck below the escape trunk. Dr. Greerson applied a face mask and pressure bag, hooked to a tank of pure oxygen, and started manual pumping. Nothing happened. He squeezed more firmly, uttered some Latin expletives, and then cursed roundly in street English. Under the thick wet suit Killerman's chest expanded slightly but caved in. More curses and more pumping. The diver's chest expanded again, sagged, expanded, and sagged in small increments. Each expansion appeared larger and more sustained than the one before. Aided by Greerson's pressure pump the lungs filled and emptied, sending oxygenated blood throughout Killerman's body. The doctor's fingers monitored his pulse; his stethoscope listened to the heartbeat. Two minutes later color began to return into the patient's face. Breathing became more regular. Greerson left the oxygen mask in place, but stopped pumping. The bag was now filling and emptying by itself.

"Where's Riley?" Awesome cried.

Killerman was barely able to breathe, let alone talk. He whispered a phrase that was lost in the torpedo-room noise. Awesome placed his ear near the diver's mouth. "Up there . . . near the control planes . . . Riley's dead."

After a few moments Killerman struggled to sit up. Greerson and Awesome propped him against the bulkhead. "I tried to work Commander Riley free . . . too tangled . . . used up his air fighting to get out. . . . We shared my tank; maybe six or seven minutes." Killerman's eyes closed, not from fatigue but from horror. "We were breathing . . . on the same tank . . . down to forty pounds of air. . . . I couldn't free him . . . tried to cut the commander off with my cutting torch. . . . He looked at me through his mask, saw my air gauge, and signaled for me to swim back." Killerman met the skipper's unsympathetic look. "I returned to the escape scuttle without air. Nothing left. Look!" He dipped his head toward his Emerson rig and regulator. "No air . . . nothing!"

202

Awesome sat back on his heels. He still didn't know what Riley had gotten tangled *in* but he thought he knew and he felt sick. For the first time since Little Andes he remembered that short, loud bang of metal against metal, that inexplicable but unnerving sound heard just once. He remembered his exhaustion and the argument he'd had with Koranson, who said it was caused by collision with an ice floe. That wasn't plausible then and Awesome knew it, yet he had permitted himself the luxury of postponing judgment, judgment he didn't want to make because of the implications.

"The sea chest is clear now," Killerman was saying. "Commander Riley got it freed just as he promised. The hull valve is okay too."

Awesome could visualize the Irishman's eager face, smiling with youthful vigor. He was always saying, "I can do it. . . . Let's have a go." A brave man. Killerman too. Awesome felt as though he were swimming beside both divers—fifty pounds of water pressure per square inch squeezing them. Air precious, almost gone. All three were suffocating. "Greerson"—he turned toward the physician—"get the men out of here!"

Greerson turned on his heels. "Back to work," he snapped with unusual severity. "Sid doesn't need any more help. He'll be all right."

Laycook pushed through the dispersing men and knelt beside the skipper, studying his face and waiting for orders he knew would follow. *Amundsen* had even more pressing business than Riley's death.

"All right, Thomas," Awesome said, a knot of uncertainty in his stomach, "pull the plug. On the way down test that hull valve to see if Riley was as good as I think he was."

"Yes, sir." And Laycook was gone, issuing orders as he went, headed for the phone.

"Let me go get Riley!" a voice wailed over the captain's shoulder.

Awesome pivoted and looked up at the black sailor. "Too late, Young." He hoisted himself to his feet and put his hand on the seaman's shoulders. "Believe me, Young. It's too late."

"We can't let him die without at least a try." He wrenched free.

"Riley's been dead a long time now. Now get out of here, son."

Laycook was taking *Amundsen* down. Variable ballast tanks were vented. Seawater flooded the tanks, reducing the air bubble. Vertical descent began almost immediately. The submarine's list to port corrected, evidence that Riley and Killerman had successfully freed the jammed sea chest and manipulated the hull valve. Behind Awesome there were muffled comments of approval . . . a couple of subdued cheers.

He returned to Killerman, who was still resting in place, no longer dependent upon Dr. Greerson's oxygen mask. "I want you to see Lieutenant Rosenbaum. That's an order, not a request." The diver looked at him blankly, but Awesome didn't elaborate. Killerman was too near shock to understand that it was one thing to have survived a close brush with death, quite another to have succeeded at the expense of a fellow shipmate.

"Now, Killerman." Awesome's patience was gone, his voice harsh. "What really happened to Commander Riley out there? I know there are no free lines for him to get tangled in. This isn't *Cutty Sark;* we don't drag lines in the water."

"Yes, sir . . . that's right. There are no lines near the after hull valves. But the commander got caught up on the bridge."

"Everything's retractable on the bridge, nothing up there either."

"There were lines caught in the starboard control plane," Killerman insisted. "When we finished with the hull valve, we started to swim forward to the access scuttle. Commander Riley pointed to a line that seemed to be dangling from the control plane. We paddled up to look. I know this sounds strange but it was there. A line was tangled between the plane and sail where it retracts vertically for breaking through the ice pack. One line was attached to a buoy-shaped device with Russian writing on it. Commander Riley signaled for me to help him untangle the damn thing. He wanted to clear it from *Amundsen* in the worst way."

Awesome took a deep breath and held it in his lungs. Then it was true what he feared to believe! After the Little Andes *Amundsen* made contact with something. It wasn't ice, was it, Koranson? Just as he had suspected . . . a sonar buoy . . . a damnable Russian sonar device. Had it given away *Amundsen*'s position? Of course it had! That made Laycook right; the enemy knew their bearings. Russian surface ships were listening for the smallest sound to checkmate *Amundsen*. No, not checkmate . . . just check. *Amundsen*'s move. Run or hide? *Which?* "With Russian writing?" He expelled the lungful of carbon dioxide.

"That's right."

"Go on."

"It was empty, sir. It was a decoy."

"How do you know that, Killerman?"

The youngster grimaced painfully. "It scared the hell out of us when we saw it. Commander Riley died trying to make sure that sonar buoy couldn't operate. At first he thought it was a real buoy, maybe sending signals to the enemy. There was no question about what he wanted to do. In order to free the lines, he had to pull the damn thing down over us. I think he wanted to get inside and destroy the mechanism. That's how he became tangled himself. The joke was on both of us, a terrible joke. He shined his light inside for me to see. He wanted me to know so that I could tell you. The buoy was empty. It was a decoy. A damn decoy!"

Killerman paused to rest for a moment, his chest heaving. Awesome waited without comment for him to continue. "You see, the exterior was genuine, all right, but it couldn't have operated. It's just a shell—totally hollow and round, constructed to ride upright in the water or sit there on the ice. Both Commander Riley and I shined our lights right into the empty cavity. I entered partway when I was trying to cut him free with my Airco torch. I tell you, it was a shell only, nothing more. It just couldn't be doing anything but sitting there. I don't understand what it was for."

Awesome did. It made good sense for the Soviets to plant dummy sonar buoys in the Barents. Like operating buoys, they appeared on enemy sonar and could easily be mistaken for the real thing. On aerial photographs taken by spy satellites dummy and genuine buoys were indistinguishable. In either case, they served an important function—to discourage American submarines from navigating waters near Soviet installations. Dummy buoys were almost as good for deterring the enemy as were real ones—at a fraction of the cost. They were also damn good at frightening American skippers!

Awesome settled back upon his heels and momentarily closed his eyes. His heart was still pounding and blood throbbed against his temples. A knot in his stomach ached like an aggravated peptic ulcer. Several minutes elapsed before the pain eased. In that span of time he had traveled all the way to hell, but he was now on the return journey. *Amundsen* was safe, after all.

6

KANIN PENINSULA

(Patrol Polynya: 60th day plus 26)

The radio-shack chronometer read 1036 hours, Greenwich Mean Time. Both radio operators heard the door slip along on its grooves, and Laycook's size 12 shoe hit the radio room's hard rubber deck runner. Sokorski glanced momentarily over his shoulder, then without greeting dropped his eyes to the work counter, concentrating on what was coming through his earphones. Forbes said nothing. The executive officer leaned over the translator and stared at the daily log listing Soviet ship communications. Under the date, April 10, there followed two pages of polysyllabic Russian names and their serial numbers. Laycook raised his eyebrows. Not that he was surprised at the proliferation of ships in the vicinity—he had been grimly certain he would find more Russian warships than usual operating in the Barents, massing to hunt the intruder. He was, however, distracted by Sokorski's unusual diligence.

"What do you make of this, Sokorski?"

"Nothing special, sir," he replied curtly.

"Come off it, George. You radiomen never bother to log more than a half-dozen messages from the Russians on any given watch. This morning you've got two full pages of communications. Tell me what you think is going on."

"I really couldn't say, sir." Sokorski had resolved not to confide any further in Thomas Laycook. He felt betrayed. In the privacy of their Russian lessons the executive officer had now and then dropped hints, albeit veiled ones, that he disapproved of Captain Awesome, but in public, when it counted, he had taken the captain's side. It had occurred to Sokorski that perhaps he had allowed himself to be deceived, perhaps even heard words that had not existed. But either way, his friendship with the XO was over.

"Come on now, George, spill it out."

Forbes pivoted in his seat. "Yeah. Come on, George." After all, *Amundsen* was in trouble. Her best chance for escape resided in Laycook, however reticent he was to buck the captain's authority.

Sokorski looked stiffly from one to the other and then caved in. "All I can say is that"—he pushed his earphones back on his neck—"more Soviet ships are operating on the surface beyond the ice pack. Seem to be routine communications that don't acknowledge us. I've tried to discover some code word for our boat. But there's nothing exceptional." Then, looking at Laycook and in a tone heavy with significance, he added, "The Russkies are good at tricks. Nobody, not even the enemy, seems to admit we're really here, yet we are—or at least I think we are." He hadn't told Forbes about the Riga broadcast; he hadn't told anyone but Young, and even then his words had been cloaked with mystery.

Laycook made an impatient gesture. He intended to say that he was getting pretty fed up with the translator's fixation on that propaganda but just then his eye fell over something on the work counter, a piece of pink mimeograph paper decorated with medieval calligraphy and an elaborate filigree border. "What's this?" He traded the transmission log for the pink paper.

Forbes wore a smirk on his face. "Chief Kramer just delivered it from Captain Awesome."

PROCLAMATION:
THE FIRST SUBMARINE OLYMPICS

IT IS HEREBY PROCLAIMED THAT *U.S.S. EDMOND ROALD AMUNDSEN* WILL CONDUCT THE FIRST OLYMPIC COMPETITION UNDERWATER BEGINNING WEDNESDAY APRIL 11. THE CONTESTS WILL CONTINUE UNTIL GOLD, SILVER, AND BRONZE MEDALS ARE AWARDED IN THE FOLLOWING EVENTS:

WEIGHT LIFTING
WRESTLING
BOXING

                    DECATHLON
                    SPRINT
                    ENDURANCE RACING ON GYM
                      BICYCLES
                    CHESS
                      BRIDGE
                        GYMNASTICS
                        HOP, SKIP, AND JUMP
                        MIME
                          DRAMATIC READING
                          COMEDY ACTING

OTHER EVENTS WILL BE SCHEDULED
LATER. THE TORCH FOR THE FIRST
SUBMARINE OLYMPIAD WILL BE LIT IN
THE MESS TONIGHT: 1800. ALL CREW-
MEN ARE EXPECTED TO PARTICIPATE
IN AT LEAST ONE EVENT. THERE WILL
BE NO LIMIT TO THE NUMBER OF EN-
TRIES PER MAN. YOU WILL BE CON-
TACTED PERSONALLY ABOUT SIGNUPS.
PRELIMINARY COMPETITION TO BE-
GIN WEDNESDAY 1600.
                    CAPTAIN ELISHA AWESOME,
                            COMMISSIONER
                    CHIEF WALDO KRAMER,
                            COORDINATOR

Laycook dropped the proclamation to the work
counter in disgust. He remembered suddenly that the
captain had mentioned something on the squawk
box about an athletic competition, but circumstances had changed—drastically! With Riley's body

floating about over their heads and the Soviets searching the Barents for them, Awesome's timing was abysmal.

Sokorski stared glumly at the announcement. "You'd think," he said, "that the skipper would have canceled or at least postponed that till we're on our way home."

"Did Chief Kramer really deliver this proclamation?" Laycook asked. "I can't believe it."

"Yes, sir, with his own clammy hands."

"Then it isn't a joke. Kramer would never forge the skipper's name to something, even in jest. He's too square. Besides, the chief's got a good sense of humor, and this isn't funny."

"We . . ." Sokorski suddenly whirled back to the work counter. A message . . . in Russian. He repositioned his earphones. By the rapid movement of his pen over a memo pad it was clear he heard something extraordinary. "They're talking about aircraft," he reported as he wrote.

"Military planes?"

"No, not exactly. I think they're supply aircraft from Arkhangelsk. You can listen if you want." Sokorski pointed to the auxiliary earphones. "Good practice for your Russian."

Laycook adjusted the phones over his ears and strained to comprehend the rapid speech, broken by static and communication formalities. Two years of intense Russian grammar did not qualify him to understand Russian conversations, especially those amplified from VLF signals under the ice pack. In frustration he abandoned the earphones and concentrated on Sokorski's transcription:

... DUE TO INFLUENZA EPIDEMIC ON THE KANIN PENINSULA ALL AIRFIELDS IN THE REGION ARE CLOSED TO AIR TRAFFIC AND REROUTED THROUGH ARKHANGELSK. UNTIL FURTHER NOTICE FROM THE HEALTH PRESIDIUM ZONES 65°–67° NORTH AND 43°–47° EAST WILL REMAIN OUT OF BOUNDS TO ALL GROUND, AIR, AND SEA TRANSPORT. ...

For Laycook the message was startling. Of all the land masses in the Soviet Arctic, the Kanin Peninsula had special significance for Patrol Polynya. *Amundsen's* battery of Tomahawk missiles had been preprogrammed to guide themselves along its 175-mile north-south axis following in-flight digital maps of the peninsula's terrain, maps obtained from spy-satellite overflights. Moreover, *Amundsen's* target, the Soviet guidance center at Nar'ian Mar, was located in the zone designated out of bounds. If this announcement was true, then a simple flu virus had succeeded in doing what *Amundsen*, for all her trouble and danger, had not—put Nar'ian Mar out of commission . . . at least temporarily.

"Does this mean something special?" Sokorski inquired. "Weird message, if you ask me."

Laycook was lost in thought. "I don't know what this means," he answered automatically. "Could suggest a lot of things."

"Think it's true? After all"—a meaningful note returned to Sokorski's voice—"you can't trust the Russkies; they manufacture all kinds of things to suit

213

their needs. Could be a trick."

Laycook scowled. "Could be," he commented, unwilling to divulge the truth about *Amundsen's* mission. "Look, George, see if you can pick up some confirmation of this. I need to learn more, especially from another source." He glanced over to Forbes and spoke in an official tone. "For the time being everything you've heard here in the radio shack is top secret. I don't want this circulating around the boat. Meanwhile, I'm going to consult with our Olympics commissioner."

Just as Laycook opened the door, Young and Frackmeyer arrived evidently in a hurry. Young came to a sudden stop behind the coaming, his eyes flashing. Frackmeyer nearly crashed into him. Ordinarily Laycook would have sent them packing; they hadn't any business being in the radio room. But he had more urgent things on his mind. "Excuse me, gentlemen," he said, angling around the black submariner.

Young stayed put. "We didn't expect you here, Commander," he snapped, "but this is a good chance to find out about this ridiculous Olympics. Graham and Commander Riley are dead, and everybody aboard knows the Russians are all over us. Why else are we hovering near the bottom again? This ain't no time for sports."

Laycook's reply was flat and unresponsive. "I've got much more important things to do, Seaman Young, if you men will permit me to pass."

"No, sir, we won't." Young stepped over the coaming. Frackmeyer squeezed into the tight space beside him and slid the door closed. "We've formed an action committee," Young proclaimed, "and we ain't gonna play in these Olympics games."

Frackmeyer seemed to be in something of a panic and abandoned his customary reticence. "That's not exactly why we're here. We know the Russians have us trapped. We haven't been told all the details but we've got a damn good general picture. We know all about that sonar buoy. We figured it out. Killerman claims it was empty, but how do we know that for sure? The captain would have made him say that, wouldn't he? It wasn't empty; it was calling the Russians. Unless we do something *now*, we'll all end up like Graham and Riley. At least some of us are not going to be led to the slaughter. Somebody aboard this death trap has got to protect us."

"Are you scared, Frackmeyer?" Laycook's voice was contemptuous. He scrutinized the two crewmen. "Some tough submariners!"

Sokorski was on his feet, near the executive officer. A sonar buoy! He had pledged not to trust Laycook any further, yet Frackmeyer and Young had given him no alternative. "We need you, sir. We need you to radio Scotland and tell Squadron what's happened. The captain will never do it in a million years. Please, sir!"

"No more bullshit. No more sweet talk," Young added. "No games."

Laycook jockeyed for space in the crowded compartment. Limbs touched each other; body odors intermingled. But that was the least of his problems. He needed mental space. On every count the situation was deplorable, the kind guaranteed to escalate into gross misunderstanding . . . or worse.

There were too many private motives to untangle and much too much emotion. What the hell had happened to *Amundsen's* discipline? He himself was responsible for part of its loss . . . but only part. What he wanted to say was that he would have nothing to do with any scheme to bypass Captain Awesome's authority. More, he absolutely despised the mood of panic which had taken hold of certain crewmen. But what he actually said was less assertive: If the men didn't wish to participate in Awesome's Olympic games that was their own business. And Awesome's. The warning against sedition (he purposely didn't mention the word "mutiny") was feeble, designed more as an appeal to reason than as a threat. "Now *get out of my way*, Young!" He brushed past the sailor just as the door slid open. Captain Awesome stepped in.

Awesome stood tall, shoulders cocked back, chin high. A friendly smile faded from his face as he pivoted on the deck. "Am I interrupting something? Obviously! A familiar caucus! I see Mr. Young . . . Mr. Sokorski . . . Mr. Forbes . . . Mr. Frackmeyer. Very familiar, indeed. And Commander Laycook . . ." Awesome wasn't smiling at all now. His eyes were very black. "Gentlemen, your presence here confuses me. I have no idea what you're doing at this moment. But I'm sure the commander can enlighten me at a later time." He glanced sharply at his executive officer. "Frankly I didn't expect to find all of you here together, but since you are, there's something I wish to announce." He was carrying a clipboard and a copy of the Olympic proclamation. "I'm personally taking the names of participants for

216

the games." Young's uninhibited grunt of disgust sounded like a fart. The skipper pretended not to notice. "Everybody must compete. Officers and crewmen alike. Now, Sokorski, I understand you're a fair wrestler. I wasn't so bad myself while at the Academy. This is your chance to give the old man a tumble, a legitimate way to get off some of your aggressions. You could become a hero overnight, gold medal and all—sort of represent certain members of the crew, if you know what I mean."

"I'm not in the mood for sports . . . sir." The translator's reply was surly.

"Like everyone else on this boat, Sokorski, you'll get in the mood."

"My back has been giving me trouble."

"You'll have eight hours to eliminate the trouble . . . or choose some less strenuous event. I will expect you in my quarters at 1900. I need to know for scheduling which and how many events you intend to enter. Now, how about you, Seaman Young? You look like a sprinter or boxer to me. I certainly expect to see your name on several lists, and I'll be disappointed if you don't win some medals."

Without waiting for a reply, Awesome pivoted toward the executive officer, who avoided his eyes. "And Commander, I think you should take time from your busy schedule to play a little bridge. By reputation you're the best bridge player in the Submarine Service, maybe the entire Navy. I've included a bridge tournament especially for your benefit."

"Captain Awesome, I'd like to see you privately, please." Laycook waited for the skipper to lead him into the control room.

"In a minute, Commander."

"It's an urgent communiqué, sir."

It was difficult for Awesome to disengage himself from the confrontation, for there was obviously more going on than met the eye and he wanted to get to the bottom of it. Yet an urgent communiqué could not be ignored. The skipper turned and headed for the navigation center. They came to a halt under a ship's inertial navigation binnacle, suspended from the rafters overhead. A navigational data assimilation computer emitted crepitation, masking their voices from nearby crewmen.

"We've intercepted something of interest," Laycook reported.

"Curious," Awesome muttered as he read Sokorski's translation to himself, "curious. What do you make of this, Thomas?"

"I don't really know."

"Sounds like something's going on in the Barents. And we're right smack in the middle of it."

"You don't believe there's an influenza epidemic?"

"Could be. But the important thing is what's going on at Nar'ian Mar. It might be related to the naval buildup around us."

"Or *because* of us. This could be a preliminary move before closing the noose around our necks."

Awesome sighed. Would Laycook never give up? "That could be so, Thomas. If we were detected. I still don't believe we were." He reread the message, slowly. "First thing we should do is get some confirmation. That shouldn't be too difficult. Maybe we'll also pick up new clues. I'd like you to stay on this for me. Keep in touch with the translators; show me anything that looks suspicious. While we're waiting I'm going ahead with plans for the Olympics. I know, Thomas, that you're not enthusiastic about these games, but I hope you'll nevertheless take them seriously. Despite your skepticism, I think you understand why they're so important to me.''

Laycook swept his blond hair back from his forehead. ''It's only fair to tell you, sir, that the crew's in a foul mood. The men are angry and frightened. They know about the sonar buoy and the Soviets upstairs and they think we should pull out. Some of them believe their captain has lost touch with reality. The Olympics will become their *casus belli.* You can't expect much enthusiasm. These games could have a boomerang effect and cause more trouble than they solve.''

Awesome listened intently, but responded with assurance. ''Possible—but we're going ahead with the games anyway. We'll watch carefully what the Soviets do around Kolguyev. I can't tell you the reason they're here. But we're right in the middle of whatever it is, where, as Admiral Gaffy says, we can do the most damage. Exactly what it means I honestly don't know, and I don't think you do either. But at some point—tomorrow, the next day, perhaps in a week, sometime down the road—we're going to have to react. And when that moment arrives I need a disciplined crew, not our current rabble. I can appreciate the extraordinary tensions, but this crew has degenerated into a naval scandal. While I'm waiting for clues to what's going on, I plan to restore discipline, then morale." He smiled that trusting smile Laycook found so aggravating. "The idea of an underwater Olympics does sound bizarre. I'm the first to admit that. But I've given it a lot of thought and I'm convinced that athletic competition will retarget the frustrations and defuse the hostilities. This kind of rivalry usually has that result. All I need now is a little support—especially from you, Thomas. You're a key man. The men have confidence in your judgment. If you help me sell the concept the Olympics themselves will do the rest."

"No salesman in the world could sell Young and that bunch."

Awesome sighed. "Poor Young. He is so very righteous. Well, wait and see, Thomas. I know the Olympics sound impossible now but don't overlook how fast moods can change. The closer men herd together the faster their feelings can be altered. If your message about Nar'ian Mar is genuine, then we might have something to rejoice about: Sick men can't fire ballistic missiles. Our luck may have finally turned for the better. If our primary target is incapacitated, Admiral Gaffy will order this patrol terminated and, as soon as the Soviet task force disperses, we'll be headed home." The idea of an honorable end to Patrol Polynya inspired Awesome with such hope that he took a long shot at enlisting Laycook's support. "Thomas, I'm prepared to make you a genuine offer, one I want you to consider very seriously. . . . Help me make these Olympic games a success and I'll forget about certain activities that have recently occurred on this boat. That's a sincere offer which I want you to extend to Young,

Frackmeyer . . . and Sokorski.''

Laycook received the invitation with a mixture of insult and shame. He resented having to bargain for exoneration from a conspiracy in which he had not participated. Walking the tightrope between Awesome and his crew had become impossible. The honest broker was destined to be mistrusted by both sides, fated to end his mission of good will in failure and disgrace. No, Laycook remained adamantly silent; he would not throw more than his official duty into the Olympics. His enthusiasm, that part of him not subject to naval duty, he vowed to withhold.

Awesome waited a moment, then his face dimmed with disappointment. "I'd still like you to give it some thought, not only for your own sake, Thomas, but also for the welfare of the crew. Whatever our differences, you can't avoid the fact that discipline couldn't be worse. Officially we're *both* responsible for morale. I can't promise these Olympics will work, but at least I'm not sitting on my hands without a plan. That's something I learned from Riley.'' Awesome paused, searching for a sign that Laycook would compromise. He could discern none. "Right after Charles Riley's memorial service I'll need an answer. Don't just dismiss the idea without thinking through its merits. Put your influence behind these games and the men will become enthusiastic. Withhold it and I'm going to have trouble. I won't deny that. Thomas, I don't believe you'd renege on your duty and maliciously undermine what's good for all of us.'' For several moments Awesome said nothing. He studied Laycook's features, in every way contrasting with his own. Different though they were both physically and philosophically, Awesome believed they ultimately shared a common concern for the safety of the crew. He wanted to say that he needed Thomas Laycook, but his pride prevented him from voicing the words. The nearest he could come was, "Everybody aboard is depending on you, Thomas."

Laycook was not ungrateful for that admission. He swallowed hard, fortifying his earlier resolve. The trust the men had in him was a double-edged sword. Didn't Awesome know that?

0200 hours.

The portable furniture had been removed from *Amundsen*'s mess to make room for Charles Riley's memorial service. A single table had been centered in the forward section, and on it was a lectern covered by an indigo velvet mantle used for divine worship on Sunday mornings. Behind the pulpit stood Dr. Greerson, who had been specifically requested by the crew to share chaplain's duties with the skipper. By virtue of his professed agnosticism he was something of an anomaly as a religious leader; still, he balanced Awesome's evangelism. In a strong voice he read Psalms 118 and 120, one for faith in the Divine Father, the other for the soul's immortal delivery. Surprisingly, he found himself moved by the poetry, if not the theology. He shut Awesome's leather-bound Bible and lifted his bespectacled eyes to Sidney Killerman.

The diver advanced toward the pulpit with trepidation. The faces in the congregation were, for the most part, hostile, though some compassionate ones were sprinkled among the accusing stares. The lectern creaked under Killerman's weight as he bent over it. He was grateful that Dr. Greerson didn't abandon him; it was comforting to know he lingered nearby, just behind his left shoulder.

The physician understood about survivor guilt. It had been upon his recommendation that the skipper granted Killerman permission to talk about Charles Riley's final moments. Such a maudlin subject wasn't likely to promote high morale, yet Greerson believed that censoring the truth would be counterproductive. What everybody needed was time for quiet, reasonable reflection, a period that could be attained only after the men understood the truth. And who could better explain that than the person who was with Charles Riley in his final moments?

Killerman spoke without preamble. "The commander and I were breathing off my tank. We couldn't talk but I read his thoughts. I was giving him all the life I could; he knew it and took it. He was very calm. Once, near the end, he smiled at me. Over and over we shared what little air was left. That couldn't continue—two men breathing from a single supply. He was hopelessly tangled in the lines, but I think I was more frightened than he. The thought of leaving him to die terrified me. God be my witness, I didn't want to leave him. I didn't even think I had enough air to swim back myself. By the second the situation was getting worse. The commander looked at my air-pressure gauge and finally refused to accept my octopus mouthpiece. He shoved me away, pointing toward the bow. 'Go back,' I thought I could hear his voice, though I know you can't hear words in the water. Still, I thought I heard his. He was gasping for air. I passed my mouthpiece to him for one final breath and closed my eyes. . . .

"I can't remember what happened during the time I swam back to the scuttle. All I can recall is dropping into the escape trunk, my lungs ready to burst. Know what it's like to think you're going to drown? The hatch battened down over me like a giant manta with enormous black wings. It was dark . . . really dark. A feeling of being crushed . . ." The diver stopped to compose himself. "That was happening to Commander Riley too, up on the sail. I wish I could have cut him free. I tried but I just couldn't."

Abruptly Killerman turned away from the lectern and headed for his seat. His eyes were full of tears. Some lowered their own in embarrassment, for the moment was too intimate. Greerson, his hand on Killerman's waist, gently guided him from the pulpit to the professional care of Martin Rosenbaum.

The moment Awesome rose, a series of disapproving coughs erupted from the congregation. He held his breath, muzzling the disgust he felt for those who would defile the moment when the living and the dead touch for a final time. Funerals were privileged events; the Reverend Elijah Awesome had always regarded them with the utmost solemnity. Before Bertram Graham's demise it had never occurred to his son that even his severest critics might desecrate such a moment. However much he understood the tensions he still suffered from that insult. Nevertheless, this must continue to be the crew's time with Riley. He closed his eyes and bowed his head briefly, as if in prayer. A spate of coughs trailed away uncertainly. Awesome sensed his father's presence beside him. "Commander Riley," he lifted his head, "our Charles Riley, was a man with uncanny ability to repair what lesser men believed to be irreparable. Think what it means to salvage what others have abandoned, to fix what others have discarded, to restore what others have jettisoned. Some people are teachers, others scientists, managers, philosophers, merchants, but Charles Riley was a mender . . . yes, a mender . . . a man who put things together and kept them operating. For him tinkering was more than a craft; it was an art. Riley's passion, his creed . . ."

"Riley shouldn't have died," an unidentified voice called suddenly from the port side.

"Right on," from the starboard.

Awesome knew it was Young but held his breath, pretending to ignore the remarks. For many seconds the crowded mess was perfectly silent. Somebody's move—but whose? The skipper continued, as though nothing had been said, "It seems so terribly unjust, perhaps a bit paradoxical, that such an expert technician should have died in an accident that . . ."

"It wasn't an accident," the voice interrupted again.

"Right!" others encouraged the provocateur.

"Gentlemen," Awesome left the pulpit and strode fiercely around the table past the first row of officers, "remember that we're here to eulogize the deceased. I will not permit any disrespect to Charles Riley."

The same southern voice: "And *we're* not gonna permit you to dish out this bullshit about his death."

Awesome heard several gasps and a sharp rustle as most of the men shifted their footing. No one spoke, but one by one everybody identified the voice as belonging to Everett Young. The atmosphere was thick with anticipation for the skipper's response. Awesome knew what he was going to say, yet even in his fury he ached over the necessity of saying it. Since he had assumed command of *Amundsen* his skin color had been de-emphasized, but he knew that suddenly, and irrationally, everyone was thinking of it—officers and crewmen alike. Was their captain capable of detaching himself from his own blackness to discipline publicly and impartially a fellow black—the only black crewman?

Well, of course he could! But what caused him to hesitate was the anticipated reaction from the men. However they disguised their pleasure, white men would enjoy seeing black man pitted against black man. To be the agent of such entertainment was repugnant. Still, discipline was at stake and he knew what he must do. "Seaman Young, you are on report." His voice bellowed over the din of anxious voices. "Will Sergeant Diller please escort Mr. Young from divine service!"

To port a small group around the black submariner fought against his flailing fists. "Bullshit!" Young was yelling. "Don't let this Uncle Tom get away with that crap!" He broke from his captors in a maelstrom of flying elbows and lunged in the direction of the skipper until stopped by a phalanx of officers in the second row. Above the tumult, his voice howled, "I was at the escape trunk when Riley got tangled in the Russian sonar buoy we've been dragging along on the sail. I wanted to swim out and rescue him but Captain Awesome didn't want any of us to know about the buoy. It was him who allowed

Riley to die in the water. The Russians know exactly where we are and if we don't do something this monkey will get us all killed, just like Graham and Riley." Young's buddies grabbed him under the armpits and lifted him off the deck, temporarily halting his forward thrust.

"You're on report, Seaman Young. Take him out of here and confine him to his bunk," the captain's voice boomed out.

"You going to lock me up like you did those seven black brothers in Scotland?" Young retorted.

"That's exactly what I'm going to do. Even you must learn some respect for authority. You're a disgrace . . ." Awesome had begun to say "to our race" but at the last second substituted, "to the Submarine Service."

Young wrenched free from his new captors. He chopped furiously at a fire-control technician in his path and caught him on the side of the neck. The technician reeled to the deck, leaving a small space in the human chain. Little more was needed. Young lunged through the breach to the cordon of officers. A halfback slicing through an opposing football line, he veered to the right and pierced the interwoven arms. More men swarmed around him as he angled suddenly, charging head-on into Lieutenant Haddock. The supply officer had just recovered from the initial onslaught when he saw the black seaman drive toward him. Fellow officers converged to help, but were too late. Haddock saw but could not prevent the knee that advanced into his groin. Contact drove his testicles into the pelvis. Pain exploded in his lower intestines, and he cried out. Wounded, he slumped from the ranks guarding the captain. Young exploited the temporary opening and bull-dogged his way past the broken resistance toward Awesome. A final lunge brought him onto the skipper's shoulders.

Both men tumbled backward against Greerson's pulpit. Many hands reached out to stop the assault but none could get a grip. Awesome's first blow staggered the enraged sailor and sent him reeling. The second struck his ear. As a boy in Frankfort he was no stranger to brawling. Neither preachers' kids nor black kids ever were. In those days frustrated black adolescents, who were prevented from challenging their white counterparts in school or in sports, refocused their hostilities on equally frustrated black surrogates. A ritual dance to the goddess Impotence, they clawed and scratched, beat and knifed each other until they saw their opponent's blood flow. Small consolation but it was red—the same as they imagined streaming from the wounds of white enemies. It had been many years since Awesome had felt the touch of black skin in combat, the sting of black fists. Still, he reacted instinctively to it.

Both combatants tussled for position and renewed the attack. A ferocious blow aimed at Awesome's neck was deflected, then a well-directed punch struck Young hard in the eye. A wide gash opened, spurting blood over the eyelid and partially blinding him. But Young lunged again, and they toppled to the deck. Somewhere on the way down Young dug his incisor teeth deep into the skipper's neck. Awesome's shock, humiliation, and hurt merged into outrage; he bellowed a truculent war cry. His knee thrust into Young's lower belly, and with his next breath he screamed at Koranson, "Get this savage off me!"

It was hard to say what crippled Young—Awesome's knee to the belly or his choice of name. When Young had neither wind in his lungs nor spirit in his heart the battle ceased. Many hands did what they had failed to accomplish before—they dragged the black seaman from the captain and pulled him to his feet. For Awesome it was a far longer journey to stand upright. Several pairs of hands reached forward to assist but were waved off. First, he balanced on his knees, where he paused to catch his breath. Finally, he hoisted himself the distance and swayed precariously. His legs were wobbly and his head swirled. Greerson, deaf to his protest, moved quickly to steady his patient and examine a set of teeth wounds now oozing a thin trickle of blood.

"Commander Riley . . . Commander Riley," Awesome tried to rally his audience, as though Young's assault had been a fiction. But his voice had as little power as his legs and refused to conspire in the charade. "Charles Riley . . ." His volume was pathetically weak.

"Let things settle down here," Greerson whispered. "You can't reason with men when they're in this mood."

Against this advice, Awesome again attempted to speak but was interrupted by rude caterwauling. There were also cheers for Young, who was being hauled from the mess by Sergeant Diller and his ad hoc detail. Somehow the hoots and cheers hurt more than all Young's punches. Like the irate sailor,

Awesome had lost his will to persevere and yielded to Greerson's gentle tugging. Once beyond the steel door he wrested himself from the doctor's guiding hand and listened to the cacophony behind him. Voices rose in angry accusation and then in rebuttal. As the din grew louder he could no longer distinguish who was talking. It didn't matter. Accusation and defense merged. He heard only a simple indictment of inadequacy and failure.

When Awesome opened his eyes he was lying on his bunk with a gauze dressing wrapped around his neck. There was minimal pain, only a faint throbbing where the left hip had struck Greerson's pulpit and a dull ache in the right buttock, the result of an intramuscular injection. Had he authorized the shot? Perhaps Greerson had administered a narcotic.

It was easy enough to find out. The doctor was sitting at the desk chair, peering over his plastic-rimmed Navy-issue glasses, a definite twinkle in his eyes, anticipating the question. The injection contained no analgesic and was nothing more than an antibiotic to prevent infection from the neck wound. Then, true to character, Greerson recited a litany of terrible-sounding diseases that one could contract from human bites. Awesome grimaced: Evidently it would have been better had he taken on anything from a weasel to a wild boar.

Greerson lingered in the stateroom longer than necessary, providing his own brand of comfort. He elected that moment to talk about his own private battle with the bottle and his ultimate victory. Men could be cruel about such things; on shore leave fellow submariners watched him like hawks for a hint of alcoholism. He made certain none got that pleasure. On patrol he wasn't tempted to drink. The temptation diminished where spirits were almost unavailable and drinking severely punished. At sea he was shielded from everything but bad jokes which persisted behind his back.

Awesome was touched by the doctor's confidence. A quarter hour of listening to him confirmed what he had long known: Thank God for Gene Greerson.

1720 hours.

When Laycook entered Awesome's cabin, the skipper was huddled over the desk, intent on writing a report, his neck encircled by the gauze dressing, his fingers clenching a mechanical pencil. During the lonely hours aboard *Amundsen* he had taken to doodling calligraphy, ornate montages of arrows, letters, and occasionally stick drawings that looked suspiciously like maps of famous naval battles. Several pages were scattered across the desk. Designs filled them, extending from the center to the four corners, gradually covering the free space until it became necessary to begin afresh on a clean sheet. More often than not Awesome balled the blackened papers into a tight wad and looped them toward his wastebasket with a hook shot which, according to his mental tally, succeeded 60 percent of the time.

Laycook eyed the drawings while waiting for the skipper to address him. When it appeared as though he had forgotten about the executive officer for whom he had sent, Laycook opened the conversation. "I guess you blame Everett Young entirely for that display in the mess."

Adhesive tape pinched Awesome's skin as he craned his neck to regard the XO. "I wouldn't call what occurred at Riley's memorial service a 'display,' Thomas. And since it was Young who mauled me like a predatory panther I can't think of anyone more suitable to blame—that is, unless you're suggesting that it was I who jumped him and dug my teeth into *his* neck." Awesome returned to the two-page document he had just drafted and inserted new punctuation.

"No, sir, I wasn't suggesting anything of the kind. I was only indicating that what you had to field in the mess is just the top of the iceberg. As I said this morning, there's a lot of hostility aboard. Some of it's justifiable; most of it, not. But it's not just one black sailor that's all stirred up."

Awesome spun around, snatching the papers in his hand and jumping to his feet. "I understand all right, Thomas," he said. "But there are also many things that have been happening that I don't understand. And I'm not sure why. Somehow I'm out of touch, and it's my job to be in touch. Somebody's been fanning the flames of dissension from the moment I took command. The troublemakers are getting support despite what I do to counter them."

"Are you implying that I'm involved in this?"

"I'm not implying anything. Only it's not clear to me about your role with Sokorski's clique and what you were doing with them in the radio shack."

"You'll remember, sir, that I didn't sign that letter. Yes, I was approached to sign, but I tried to squash it before the silly thing escalated into a full mutiny. If you don't believe me check the signature list."

232

"Damn it, Thomas, I know you wouldn't sign a letter like that, and I also know you've been trying to keep the lid on this misunderstanding until we get back to Holy Loch. But everywhere there's fire you seem to be present. Since the Lumbrovskiy Channel I don't seem to be doing anything but putting out fires. Where's all this conspiracy originating from, Thomas?"

Laycook shrugged. "Where do jokes come from? Or the wind? Sokorski and Young, originally, but it spread. A lot of little things. The men are frightened, not because they're scared of the Soviets or because they don't trust *Amundsen's* pressure hull. They're petrified because they think their skipper's behavior is inexplicably erratic. Somebody told Young how you fainted beside him when he was hurt at the Little Andes. He's a kid and just spoiling for a cause; he'll distort anything and yammer about it to anybody. Then somehow they learned the general outline of that Riga broadcast . . . just enough to confuse them. Scuttlebutt has it that *Amundsen* is a phantom boat, that even the Pentagon has stricken her from the roster. Now they know about the buildup of Russian ships in the Barents and the sonar buoy and, to top it off, they're asked to participate in an athletic extravaganza. They don't *know* anything for certain, but they have plenty of mysteries to ponder. The truth is our crew is bored, tired, and just plain frightened. *Amundsen* is careening toward a mutiny. It may be a blundering, half-assed mutiny, not the *Bounty* or the *Caine,* but a mutiny just as tragic. Almost anything could ignite the fuse. At the moment it's a black kid from Memphis who was naïve enough to be used by his shipmates."

During a long moment of silence, Awesome studied his executive officer. However much Laycook might wish to discredit him, however much he longed to show Gaffy he'd made a mistake, he was a Navy man to the core, the best and the ablest in the Submarine Service. He might not go out of his way to douse the coals of discontent, but he himself would never abet or support a mutiny. The idea was unthinkable. "I don't believe you'd encourage sedition, Thomas," he said, his chin cocked high but with unnatural angularity. "Not you. Of course, you'd enjoy seeing me squirm. But in the end you'll support me because you don't believe in mutiny, even against Little Black Sambo here."

Laycook swallowed the insult . . . or was it a compliment? He would have gladly discussed his own duty with anyone else in the Navy but not with Elisha Awesome. Duty was something he did not take lightly. Until that very moment he had fulfilled it to the best of his ability. Only it was no longer clear exactly what it was. Aboard *Amundsen* many of his earlier certainties had begun to fog, the sterling principle of service to one's country, tarnish. The man standing before him was not responsible for this fall from grace, yet he was the cause of it. Only one thing was sure: Laycook would not debate the question of duty with Captain Awesome. "What are you going to do with Everett Young?" he asked, changing the subject.

"There are two pages of formal charges, Thomas. There's no alternative. I have to throw the book at him. Uniform Code of Military Justice, Articles 91,

92, 93, 94 . . . 98, 99 . . . insubordination, striking an officer, incitement to mutiny . . . and that's only the beginning. I've got to show some teeth to this rabble of a crew. They'll get the message soon enough. You saw the whole sordid affair in the messroom, didn't you, Thomas?"

"Yes, sir." Laycook looked annoyed. "With respect, sir . . . Young is only a symbol here. Make him into a martyr and we'll have mutiny for certain."

"I've already given some thought to that. You're right. That's the last thing we need now. So, Thomas . . ." Awesome paused in a final reflection, "I'm asking you to sign these charges. If you sign, this insurrection will be defused in an instant. The moment the white boys see you're not supporting blackie they'll abandon Young and watch him burn."

Laycook could hardly believe his ears. His face flushed red with rage; his eyes burned with resentment. Now what was he going to do? Awesome had very neatly cut him off, not from the group, but from the position of independence he'd been intent on maintaining. "Sorry," he said at last, aware that it sounded feeble, "I'm afraid I didn't get a good look at that scuffle."

"You just admitted you did. I'm honestly sorry, I wish I could make this a simple request, but I'm afraid that it must be an official order. In my opinion it's essential, Thomas, that you sign."

"You can't order that, Captain Awesome. It just isn't fair to ask another man to bring charges against a seaman!"

"Not ordinarily. I quite agree. But as you've

explained so convincingly, we're not operating under ordinary conditions. I can't let Young get away with what he did without compromising my authority. But you're right, it would be dangerous to make him into a martyr. Still, what I can't do, you can, Thomas. And you must. We're way beyond the point of worrying about fairness. If you refuse to sign, I'll just go ahead and write your name here at the bottom of these articles anyway."

"That's a forgery and I strongly protest, sir," Laycook snapped.

"You can protest all you like, when we get back to Holy Loch. Right now you're out of luck. And I warn you, Thomas, if you do have the gall to try complaining when we get home, I shall recommend a general court-martial and charge you with insubordination. Given the critical situation of *Amundsen*, the court will be on my side. First, because any one of the judges would have done exactly what I'm proposing to do. Second, because military courts almost invariably affirm the authority of the captain. It's too dangerous to set a contrary precedent. Ever hear of a court-martial not supporting command authority in combat, Thomas? It is only necessary to convince the court that discipline aboard *Amundsen* was absolutely critical to her safety. Furthermore, when we return, Nick Gaffy will support me one hundred percent."

"I may not get the opportunity to protest," Laycook interrupted bitterly. "The Russians have enough power in the Barents to trap and destroy us any time they please."

Awesome dropped back into his desk chair and

casually draped his leg over the armrest. He wasn't particularly worried about being destroyed. To begin with, the Russians would have to find *Amundsen*. Next, they'd have to know that she wasn't carrying a battery of Polaris or Poseidon missiles that could make the Barents uninhabitable. They might be caught; they might blow the mission; they might spend a lot of time in a Russian prison; they might ruin Gaffy's career, and they might create an international incident. But they *would* return.

"And if you manage to keep Young quiet what do you have up your sleeve for the rest of the men?" Laycook's voice was sarcastic.

"I'm going to see that every man is busy, very, very busy—on and off duty. And I'm going to restrict your duties entirely to the forward torpedo room. I want Tomahawk 6 fully checked out, and ready to fire by the time we start for Holy Loch. There's no reason why Gold Crew should have to load another Tomahawk and assume an additional security risk. The less movement of cruise missiles the better." Awesome stopped and waited for another burst of outrage. To his surprise, something like interest passed through Laycook's eyes.

For a long moment the executive officer considered the skipper's directive. No doubt, banishment to the forward torpedo room was Awesome's way of separating him from the men, a cunning strategy to sever the intimacy he enjoyed with the troublemakers. But however detestable that transparency, the thought of breaking contact with the crew was not altogether distasteful. On the contrary, Laycook relished being relieved of his onerous personnel

237

responsibilities. Anything to be free from the impossible crossfire. Riley was right: It was easier to deal with machines than with people. Laycook nodded his acceptance. "What about Seaman Young?" he asked as an afterthought.

"He's going to be disciplined. Once others are involved in the Olympics, they'll forget everything but his punishment."

"Your Olympics won't fool anybody."

"Believe it or not, Thomas," Awesome spoke with imperturbable certainty, "I'm not trying to 'fool' anybody. I only want to take the men's minds off ridiculous petitions, Russian propaganda broadcasts, and clandestine meetings. Mostly, I want my men to regain some confidence. From now on, Thomas, I manage the morale aboard and you take care of the birds."

"I still won't sign these charges."

"Why not, Thomas?"

Laycook hesitated. How could he possibly explain? Six months before he would have signed them readily, even authored them. But now he felt certain that they were a private vendetta of one black man against another. Under the circumstances, Young was the result, not the cause, of the problem: He had been first to intuit that Elisha Ross Awesome was no leader. The captain's judgments had been dictated by his overwhelming desire to shine in Gaffy's eyes. What was right for the patrol had, in Awesome's mind, become hopelessly confused with what was good for its skipper, who could no longer distinguish the two agendas. Young had sensed that before the others and had unwittingly permitted himself to become the spokesman for the white crew, the mouthpiece of its anger.

"I can't sir . . . I won't."

Making no effort to conceal his hurt, the skipper dropped the document on the blotter. At the very moment when Awesome needed him the most, when he depended upon his personal and professional support, it was denied. Just as he picked up his pen there was a knock on the door. It was Waldo Kramer, and Laycook seized the opportunity to take his leave.

"Captain Awesome . . . I think we should reschedule the Olympics." Kramer said "reschedule" instead of what he wanted to say, "cancel." "The men won't sign up. I've done everything I could to encourage them. I even . . ." he hesitated. "I even offered some . . . some incentives. Nothing substantial, a few greenbacks, just enough to generate enthusiasm. I'm afraid that didn't work."

Awesome knew that Kramer had exposed himself to ridicule for supporting a patently unpopular cause. "I know you tried, Waldo, and I appreciate it very much. It's a vicious circle: We can't have our Olympics because morale is so low, and we can't raise morale without our Olympics. I wish I knew what else I could do."

"Nothing short of producing a miracle, sir. The problem is built into our situation. The men won't participate so long as they believe they're in danger. They're just bloody frightened—that's all."

"Well, then, suppose we give them some good news."

"It would have to be awfully good news. At this moment, our Olympic contestants include you, me, and a couple of guys who'll do anything for a few bucks."

Awesome looked somber while he reflected. Something had to be done to save his Olympics . . . something bold and something quick. He lifted the phone from its hook and dialed for open circuit throughout the sub. "By tomorrow, Waldo, you'll have more entries than you can handle.

"Now hear this. . . . Now hear this. . . . Captain Awesome speaking. . . . I have some very good news I want to announce. I expect this will significantly relieve many of your anxieties about our current situation. We have just learned that *Amundsen*'s primary target in the Soviet Union is temporarily dysfunctional. All we know for certain is that the news has been sent to Soviet air and naval units in the area. Our impression is that for a week or two she couldn't be a threat to American security. Let me remind you that at this moment the information is still preliminary and has not been confirmed. But if it is true, and gentlemen, I must emphasize the 'iffiness' of this, then *Amundsen* will be given a respite—a chance to return to base and change crews. I have reason to believe we'll be ordered home the moment Squadron has this information confirmed. Generally, it is not my policy to disseminate such unsubstantiated information, but I know all of you have been under enormous stress and I believe you will accept this news for what it is and nothing more. I will keep you posted as soon as there are any new developments. . . ." Awesome glanced up, evaluating his chief's skeptical reaction. "Gentlemen, while we're waiting, we'll stage the biggest and best

Olympic games ever conducted under the ocean. To raise the level of competition I will permit those actively engaged in training for their respective events to practice whenever not standing watch. Meanwhile, start thinking about events in which you'll want to compete. Chief Kramer will handle the signups. . . . I look forward to seeing all of you at the torch-lighting ceremonies tonight . . . 1800 hours . . . Out."

Awesome switched off the squawk box and whirled around to learn the chief's reaction. "Think that will do?" he inquired.

Kramer was smiling. "I don't know, sir, but it certainly is a good start. What we need now is for the bookies to start taking bets on the Olympic events."

Awesome grinned. "Between bookmaking operations and your petty officer's pay, you guys make more money than I do."

Kramer was uncomfortable, not knowing whether to reply officially or unofficially. He hedged for a moment, then answered without committing himself. "Gambling is against regulations, sir."

"A matter of definition. Right now, staging these Olympics is my overriding priority. If one chief petty officer happens to make a few extra bucks on the side that's hardly my main concern. All I ask is that you use a little discretion and, for a man of your talents, that's not difficult. Now can you think of anything else that might stand in the way of our Olympics?"

Kramer studied the captain's face. "I think we're on the right track. My guess is that the only stumbling block will be Commander Laycook. If I may take the liberty, sir . . ." he hesitated before continuing, "Commander Laycook has been acting kind of strange. He's been snooping all around this boat, from bow to stern, as if hunting for something that was lost. Real tight-lipped too. Can't get a word out of him. He's not going to be in favor of the new training schedule. For reasons I don't understand he's enforcing every possible regulation. The exec has a reputation for driving his men, but in all deference, sir, I think he's being a bit excessive."

"Have any ideas what he's looking for?"

"No, sir. And nobody else does either."

"Well then, I'll handle the commander," Awesome promised. "What goes for the crew as a whole goes for men directly under his authority. He's going to be working full time in the forward torpedo room from now on. Missile technicians will break for the Olympics like everybody else."

"Well then"—Kramer started for the door—"you'd better get out your checkbook. We'll be taking bets first thing in the morning."

7

MID-ATLANTIC RIFT

(Patrol Polynya: 60th day plus 27)

Below the forward compartment platform near torpedo tube 6, Laycook looked once more at his nonradium dial Seiko watch while continuing to pace a figure eight. His technicians were already twelve minutes late for duty, four minutes later than the previous watch, and a full ten minutes later than the watch before that. The villain, he was certain, was the festive mood of Olympic competition and its resulting relaxation of discipline. Checking out a Tomahawk at sea required a rigorous schedule and coordinated planning, both of which were being interrupted constantly by athletic training and special accommodations announced periodically by the skipper. To compound the difficulties the technicians reported to work exhausted. Their performance while standing watch dipped below standard efficiency and then some. They had neither the strength nor the patience to perform their assignments with the precision required of them.

"Good morning, gentlemen and fellow Olympians," Glen Peebles' shrill voice bristled suddenly through the squawk box. "This is your own Howard No-sell speaking from the warm Tahitian waters and bringing you today's Olympic play-by-play action. But first a brief commercial. Do you know that I cut my throat today shaving with my Gillette razor? I want a word with you pretty ladies who use the other brand razor on your long, voluptuous legs. You're needlessly scratching yourself and your boyfriend. Use our blades and you'll enjoy a feel you've never had before. Better yet, spread your legs wide apart and let your boyfriend do the shaving and I can guarantee a feel you'll really enjoy. After that neither you nor your boyfriend will even care if you've got hairy legs or not. Howard No-sell again . . . I'm looking forward to seeing everyone at Olympic Stadium. Today's schedules are posted in the mess."

Laycook growled disapproval and again consulted his watch: 0814—and still no technicians! Even Lieutenant Curtis was late. Rather than restoring discipline as Awesome had planned, the Olympics had disrupted the normal routine and created a new kind of anarchy. A wise skipper should have evaluated the tradeoffs. Awesome couldn't expect both his Olympic games and a repaired Tomahawk—one or the other, but not both. Laycook shoved open the watertight door and headed for the mess.

Inside, the chairs were sloppily rearranged after the evening training session; ashtrays and cigar butts were strewn over the tables; litter was uncollected on the deck; confettied remains of *Pravda, Amundsen's* Olympics newspaper, were gathered like autumn leaves in uncollected piles. Announcements for the bookmakers' odds, ladders, and poop sheets decorated the bulkheads. Around a single table eight crewmen sat at breakfast, conversing in subdued voices. "Where is everybody this morning?" Laycook asked, glowering at them from the doorway.

Andy Jacobs rotated mechanically in his chair and glanced over his shoulder to identify the voice. At the same lethargic pace, he swiveled back and dropped his eyes over the plate. Sokorski, opposite him, followed less spontaneously, his eyes lingering somewhat longer on Laycook's tall frame before he also returned to his chow.

"Damn it," Laycook's control slipped several notches, "where is everybody this morning? What is this . . . Christmas? What the hell's going on here?" He glared at the translator. "Come on, George, what's this royal snub all about?"

Sokorski took his time about answering. "I don't know, sir," he said at last, his tone brittle. "You might ask Everett Young. He has lots of time to think about it."

"Oh, hang Young," Laycook growled, sorry he said it. Rapidly he crossed the mess to the bulletin board and the Olympics schedules. They might tell him where his men were, even if Sokorski wouldn't. The schedules were there, and next to them, prominently displayed among the jungle of papers, was something else: Awesome's articles against Young. Two long, closely written sheets of charges, just as Laycook had seen them in the captain's cabin. He lifted the top and looked at the signature. "Commander Thomas Laycook, U.S.N.," in Awesome's hand. So he'd done it, just as he'd promised! At least that explained Sokorski's and Jacobs' insolence. "Damn Awesome," he muttered under his breath.

Lieutenant Curtis craned his neck through the mess-room door. "The men are waiting for you, sir," he announced, sounding innocent. "They're all in the torpedo room. Will you be coming forward soon? They've been waiting quite a while."

Laycook whirled around to face the lieutenant. Damn him too!

0910 hours.

Eighty-seven days of patrol . . . long, wearing days . . . but only forty-eight hours more and *Amundsen* was going home! The order had finally arrived from Squadron. A yellow teleprinter readout lay on Awesome's desk. He had read and reread the command confirming what was already known about the epidemic on the Kanin Peninsula. He'd expected Squadron to make use of that situation; with Nar'ian Mar out of commission, it was a good time to change *Amundsen*'s crews—a windfall, in fact. Gaffy never failed to exploit the windfalls that came his way. Awesome visualized *Amundsen*'s sail and control planes high in the water as she proudly pulled alongside a nest of submarines and tenders at

Holy Loch—Patrol Polynya accomplished.

A successful end of the mission meant more to Awesome than relief from the oppressive events that had plagued his boat since collision on the Little Andes. It vindicated his previous judgments, beginning with the decision to hide from the Soviet task force and ending with the signing of Laycook's name to charges against Everett Young. The fact that he had grappled with delicate distinctions and wavered before reaching his conclusions did not diminish their ultimate verdicts. On the contrary, it validated them. Admiral Gaffy had often said the best decisions were always the hardest to make, not because they were intrinsically correct, but because in the act of judgment one acquired tools for better opinions in the future. History, he observed, had a way of vindicating a good decision and obliterating a bad one.

One could also feel an additional measure of pride for the difficult process by which victory had been achieved. In the worst moments, Awesome's critics had counseled him to capitulate. Several times he himself had dipped into their despair and neared failure. The defeatists were not wrong, for had he been in their shoes he might have counseled similarly. Spies that Moses had sent into the Promised Land were only honest in their evaluations of the enemy's strength beyond the Jordan River. On the contrary, it was Joshua and Caleb who were wrong . . . wrong, but inspired! During the bleakest hours of *Amundsen's* ordeal, when others were overcome with gloom, a spark of hope had refused to die inside Awesome and he experienced a strange, recurring physical symptom. When the heart was filled with despondency and the brain with confusion, his fingers tingled with a peculiar but pleasant sensation resembling a faint electric current. Voltage it was—a mysterious but quite perceptible voltage!

As he had done repeatedly, Awesome examined the hands before him, curling his fingers and thumbs into fists and slowly extending them, palms up, to the light. If the truth be known, they had occasionally trembled, but when the moment of decision had finally arrived, they possessed the steadiness of a surgeon. Paradoxically, the hands appeared familiar and unfamiliar at the same time: familiar, he thought, as they attended to routine, and unfamiliar as they exerted independent energy. When Awesome asked for the source of that power he remembered Admiral Gaffy standing on *Amundsen*'s bridge during his final visit to the submarine. The wind had been gusting from the loch when Gaffy reached across the platform and seized Awesome's hands in his own. In that moment a phenomenal transfer of power had occurred, for it was Gaffy's spirit that had steered *Amundsen* through perilous waters. "The hands that command *Amundsen* on this patrol are my hands," he had said. He might also have said, "The heart that commands her is my heart."

When Awesome's hands performed with strength and resolution they were, indeed, deputized by Nicholas Gaffy, but they served still another master. When those same hands reached forth with healing and deliverance they were his father's—fingers that

248

contrasted against stained-glass windows over the choir loft in the United Methodist Church of Frankfort. Two complementary powers had been instilled in him; in the hour of trial neither had failed. Toil had been rewarded and suffering had been retributed. In the hour of need Awesome's hands had been worthy of the proxies entrusted to them.

He had just folded the yellow sheet and unlocked his desk (he felt more like framing it than locking it away) when *Amundsen* rose from below and abruptly shifted aft. His arms sailed beyond his bewildered face an instant before an uplifting force elevated him in his chair and hurled both together across the cabin. In midair, he and the chair parted company. Awesome felt his legs and torso curl into a pike—hips bent, knees straight—as he was flung the remaining distance to the opposite bulkhead. His feet cushioned the initial impact against the bunk, but his shoulder took the brunt of the rebounding collision against the starboard partition. His flight ended with a limp and graceless tumble to the deck, where for several seconds he lay stunned in the sudden darkness.

A second, less powerful explosion rocked the submarine, rippling her bulkheads: Steel grated against steel, stanchions creaked in resistance, spot welds snapped from tension. Awesome groaned aloud and crawled over the deck, which still vibrated with aftershock. One sharp, pulsating pain immobilized his right shoulder, while another stabbed into his ribs and central back. In the pitch blackness, his fingers pawed over a familiar object displaced by the explosion—something round and moist like a wet chestnut—Dreadnought! The turtle had been flipped upside down, onto its shell, its tiny feet flailing to right itself. Awesome tucked the hapless creature into his coverall pocket.

He crawled across the deck, grabbed the bunk, and hauled himself painfully to his feet. A vision of the Reverend Awesome strapped to a bedpost with his red-letter Bible open on the floor crossed his mind. You had to admit that Pappy Awesome was grandiose—even at the moment of death . . . particularly at the moment of death. "A man should die on his feet," the Reverend's rich, stentorian voice admonished, as though criticizing the Divine Maker for a flaw in His creation. Pappy Awesome never wavered, never doubted; he established a challenging model for his son to emulate. Small consolation, Awesome thought to himself, but he too was now upright. "Look at me, Pappy . . . look!" he cried out in anguish. "I'm on my feet."

EEEEEEEEEEP . . . EEEEEEEEP . . . EEEEEEEEP . . . EEEEEEEP, the alert Klaxon wailed, penetrating and shrill. Awesome's mind cleared: The Soviets had somehow penetrated *Amundsen*'s sonar and fired a homing torpedo at her under the ice. Laycook had been correct from the beginning. How stupid to have permitted their attack, like turkeys awaiting a slaughter!

The skipper stumbled toward the sound-powered phone, snatching the receiver. It was not subject to power failure, and through it men could communicate, even if their ship had not a volt of electricity. Just as Awesome plugged into the jackbox, however, an emergency generator suddenly flooded his quarters with bright light. Blinking, he fumbled for the loudspeaker to rally his crew. For what? To receive more torpedoes? To resist being rammed by a Soviet submarine? To defend the sub? Impossible . . . *Amundsen* was designed as a cruise missile platform and carried no torpedoes, guided or otherwise. Her Mark Forty fish had been removed to make room for the Tomahawks.

"You all right?" a quivering voice called through the cabin door. "It's me, Tom."

Awesome staggered to the door and pulled at the latch. Not everyone had been killed. A voice . . . any voice . . . even Laycook's . . . especially Laycook's! The face opposite him was coated with brown sludge. "Explosion in Tomahawk 6 . . . a bad one . . . we were pulling it from the capsule sleeve when the booster rocket fired . . . don't think it punctured the hull."

"Thank God. I thought it was the Russians."

"It may become the Russians."

Their movement forward through the submarine was obstructed by men recovering from shock: Some crawled to general quarters, others remained where they had been pitched to the deck. Beyond terror, their eyes were dazed, their expressions flat. Awesome and Laycook pushed through them, heedless of the questions that met them at every hand. In their dash they vaulted over outstretched legs, spurring each other to find new corridors through the cluttered passageway.

Closer to the explosion site the crewmen were better organized. Inside the sealed torpedo room, firefighters were already smothering the highly flammable cruise missiles with fire retardant protection. To evade the clouds of billowing smoke they had positioned themselves between the automatic torpedo racks and chain winches; some were screaming for volunteers to help haul the forward Tomahawks from areas of intense heat. Awesome took immediate command, weaving among the men and calling orders to those on the front line. Unventilated smoke clogged the lungs; firefighters hacked for breath. "Keep that fire away from tube 5! . . . Douse the starboard bulkheads! . . . Bring forward auxiliary pumps! . . . We've got some leaking from the forward muzzle. . . . Slow down the ventilators, yes, down. . . . More nitrogen. . . . We'll breathe somehow . . . smother the fire if we have to." More men rushed forward to assist the firefighters, some with emergency air breathers and asbestos jackets. But there were not enough for everybody. One man near asphyxiation crawled aftward from the flames and collapsed at Laycook's feet.

"Quick, over here!" Awesome cried, dragging him into a vacant space between Tomahawks 14 and 15. The smoke became insufferable. Firefighters without emergency breathing equipment began to collapse. "All right, Harrison," the skipper ordered, "we'll have to turn up the fans and clear some of this smoke through the scrubbers. Just a little . . . and slow too." Awesome turned to Lieutenant Howard, who was pulling an injured seaman to safety. "How many men hurt?"

"Five, Captain, hurt or dead . . . maybe one or two more."

Awesome stared at him: So many more good men gone. When new clouds of smoke forced him to move he nearly stumbled over two missile technicians who lay dead like charred and discarded equipment on the platform. Despite the furious heat, his body was racked with chills. The pain in his shoulder had succumbed to a dull senselessness. "All right," Awesome howled over the din of voices . . . "let's move in closer." A commissaryman surrendered his CO_2 extinguisher into Awesome's hands. Without an air breather, the skipper led a fresh assault, disappearing momentarily into the smoke.

When he finally withdrew from the forward tubes, his coveralls were brown and a thick sludge coated his face. He couldn't stop coughing. Particulate matter burned his eyes and clogged the nasal passages. But the worst was over in tube 6. They had kept the fire from spreading to other Tomahawks, averting certain destruction by minutes. Awesome staggered to a torpedo-tube indicator box and lifted a nearby phone. "Officer of the deck from the captain: Bring us up to the ice-pack canopy as far as she'll go. Depth: six, eight feet. Keep the oxygen as low as possible. We'll manage to breathe somehow. We've got to reduce water pressure up here and stop the leak in tube 6."

"Captain, this is the officer of the deck. Understand ascend to the ice pack. Aye, aye, sir."

"Very well."

"Depth . . . six, eight feet, sir."

"Very well."

While the skipper clung to the phone and pumped commands to the OOD, a half-dozen men from the

253

reactor compartment rushed forward to help carry the wounded to sickbay. "Let's get some engineers up here," Awesome continued. "Damn it, we need Riley now. Where's Waldo Kramer? Have him bring some torches. Get every engineer forward."

"Kramer's over here, Captain," a torpedoman called from behind. "He's dead."

"Damn it, Kramer! We need you to repair this mess!" Awesome winced as pain suddenly lanced through his injured shoulder: Needlelike jabs assaulted him from the neck to the armpit. "Wait!" He climbed over some debris to a stretcher team on its way out. "Who's that there?"

"It's Doc Greerson, Captain. He was forward helping one of the wounded and got trapped by the fire." The report was blandly matter-of-fact.

"Get him to the berthing compartment immediately."

"Too late, sir. He's dead."

Awesome's legs buckled and for a moment his head swirled with the same dizziness he had experienced when a Scottish policeman came to his apartment with the news that Maxine and the children had been killed on the road from Edinburgh: once again the compassionless Angel of Death. The Stokes litter bearing his chief medical officer sidled forward, struck him in the hip, and he stood aside. For several feet, he followed behind it mindlessly.

Amidship, Awesome left the cortege and slowly mounted a narrow companionway to the control room. The line officers turned toward him, their faces flat and professional, masking their fear, more or less. "It could have been worse," he reported. "A miracle we didn't sink. I think our condition has stabilized. Given the force of the explosion, God only knows why the other Tomahawks didn't blow and fracture the hull."

Koranson called over from the phone. "It's Rosenbaum in sickbay. Wants to see you immediately."

"I'll talk to him." The captain seized the receiver from the operations officer. "Marty, Awesome here. How's it going? . . . No . . . no . . . I can't make it down there right now. I'll be in sickbay as soon as I can. . . . Just hold on. . . . Yes . . . I know you're swamped. We all are. No, goddamn it. . . . I can't come right now. You'll just have to wait. . . ." He slammed the phone onto the chrome hook and rested his aching back against the bulkhead.

"Now let's figure out what happened."

The preliminary reports were soon coordinated into a comprehensive picture of *Amundsen*'s injury. In order to work on Tomahawk 6 in the confining space of the torpedo room the technicians under Laycook's direction had begun to slip the missile from its protective launch capsule, pulling it aftward from the tube. With part exposed they disconnected the turbojet engine from its 385-pound solid-propellant jet fuel and, as well, the 1,000-pound high-explosive warhead. They then resumed pulling the Tomahawk farther from her capsule, when the booster rocket and 390-pound fuel tank exploded. Had deactivization precautions not been taken, more than 1,000 pounds of explosives would have detonated in *Amundsen*'s bow, igniting Tomahawk after Tomahawk in a deadly reaction. As it was, the explosion had been largely contained near the breech door to tube 6. Flooding through the muzzle hatch had been prevented by some unidentified torpedo-man who managed to shove the burning hulk of the Tomahawk forward and lock the breech door behind her. The lack of oxygen inside the tube smothered the flames.

In summation, Awesome reported with a cautious measure of relief, *Amundsen's* pressure hull had not been fractured and there was no immediate threat to her watertight integrity. Yet however well the submarine had survived mortal injury, she had still been badly maimed. Sandwiched between the torpedo tubes were sensitive sonar transducers for broadcasting and receiving sound impulses. So important to an attack submarine's navigation and enemy tracking were these transducers that beginning with Sturgeon-class submarines the entire bow compartment was reserved for sonar equipment, and the forward torpedo tubes were moved amidships. Unfortunately, on the older *Amundsen* the tubes were—like World War II fleet subs—still in the bow. The damaged sonar transducers had left her blinded and unable to navigate in shallow water under the ice pack. Paramount attention would have to be devoted to the dysfunctional apparatus. Technicians were immediately ordered to make at least part of the impaired system serviceable.

"What about the Russians?" Schroeder inquired with obvious apprehension. "If they hadn't discovered us before, they will now. It shouldn't take them long to pinpoint our exact position from the blast and come hunting."

256

"That's right, Schroeder." There was only a narrow chance the enemy had mistaken the explosion for volcanic activity, not uncommon in polar regions. And there was a slimmer possibility that they had failed to register the echoes. Under normal circumstances prudence would have demanded that *Amundsen* make a dash for safety—even without sonar eyes. But conditions were far from normal. First, *Amundsen* was operating in extremely shallow water where charts could not be used to identify shifting ice. Her periscope was totally blind under the keel where contact with the bottom was likely. Escape with full sonar was hazardous enough; without it, impossible. Second, the Soviet fleet would be listening for the reduction gears of a nuclear submarine in motion. Better, then, to take what time was required to make the necessary repairs on the sonar—if it could be repaired.

Awesome accompanied the sonar technicians back into the forward torpedo compartment. Laycook arrived a half hour later to receive their preliminary report. Bad news. Repair of one transducer required cannibalizing others and then building a new unit almost from scratch. The operation was theoretically feasible but would take time, a minimum of several days. How many exactly, nobody knew. En route aftward, Awesome and Laycook came to their first agreement: Patrol Polynya was effectively over. *Amundsen* could not afford to wait for her sonar to be repaired. It was time to implement an emergency plan of rescue, leave the Barents, and head for Holy Loch.

When *Amundsen* had entered the Barents, Admiral Gaffy ordered U.S.S. *Yellowtail* Sturgeon-class nuclear attack submarine to patrol in the Norwegian Sea, off the Finmark coast. In the unlikely event *Amundsen* required assistance, *Yellowtail* could rendezvous within thirty hours. Awesome abhorred the thought of exposing her to the Soviet fleet, yet any vessel in Underwater Strategic Services would have willingly assumed the danger to assist a sister submarine. *Yellowtail*'s sonar would guide *Amundsen* safely through the narrow ice into international water. Gaffy had thought of everything—even rescue.

Neither Awesome nor Laycook spoke as they entered the radio shack to extract from its safe a brass-shanked key to unlock *Amundsen*'s radio for outgoing transmission. A second key was collected from the ship's vault before the two officers parted company.

In his cabin, Awesome regarded the two keys, each shaped like a Y, with jagged teeth that pricked his leathery skin. No greater symbols of defeat existed in the Submarine Service, and no greater humiliation could be conceived than to transmit an SOS. He started to work, grimly, trying not to think of its effect on Gaffy. Surely Admiral Katzenback would capitalize upon the accident to dismantle Underwater Strategic Services and destroy the man who had so admirably built and directed their squadron.

Awesome imagined reception of the SOS at Holy Loch. Admiral Gaffy is seated at his desk with technical papers piled high like medieval parapets over which he usually peers into three conference chairs before him. This afternoon he is alone reviewing memoranda that have accumulated during a secret trip to the Aleutian Islands. A knock at the door interrupts his concentration. He adjusts bifocals on his nose, and raises his eyes over Navy-issue plastic rims to one of the precocious young submarine officers he collects around him like art objects. The lieutenant delivers *Amundsen*'s SOS in a sealed envelope. During a sixty-second interval Gaffy ponders the news, providing his junior not the slightest hint of his reaction. Better than anyone, the architect of Patrol Polynya understands that its risks are commensurate with its objectives. Every fiber, every sinew of the admiral's body abhors failure, yet he also comprehends the magnitude of the ineluctable forces about him. Stoically, he accepts the inevitable. On the telephone with Admiral Donovan Billings, Gaffy activates the contingency plan for sending *Yellowtail* to act as *Amundsen*'s eyes and guide her through the shallow waters of the Barents.

Awesome's hands were surprisingly steady as he reread the SOS. Yes, it confessed impotence and asked for help. Its words said much about *Amundsen*'s misfortune, but nothing about the long history of events that vexed her, not one word of excuse for what had transpired. He wondered what Gaffy would make of it, and if he would understand.

EXPLOSION TORPEDO ROOM. BUOYANCY POSITIVE. SONAR IRREPARABLE AT SEA. EXPECT IMMEDIATE SOVIET RESPONSE. REQUEST *YELLOWTAIL* RENDEZVOUS AT CURRENT POSITION TO GUIDE *AMUNDSEN* FROM ICE PACK.

Awesome slipped it into a khaki envelope and sealed the flap. In his career as a skipper he had never broken radio silence to transmit a communication. When absolutely necessary other captains had done it. Custom dictated that the skipper personally supervise the transmission, but he had other duties. Lieutenant Schroeder would serve as his deputy.

"All right, Bill," he unlatched his door and called to the communications officer, who had been ordered to wait in the passageway along with Sergeant Diller. "Here it is. Send this *yourself*. Immediately. Top Secret . . . I repeat, Top Secret. No one is to know, especially George Sokorski. Do it yourself, understand?"

"Yes, Cap'n, right away." Schroeder took the transmission keys. They were heavier than he remembered when the locks were finally sealed and the keys delivered personally by Donovan Billings after his visit to *Amundsen* in Holy Loch. Unannounced, the admiral had arrived with two technicians to replace the auxiliary transmitter with a late-model radar jammer for which Schroeder still had not discovered a practical use. All the last-minute urgency, the comings and goings of the admiral, had struck Schroeder as bizarre, but then everything about the patrol had been odd, starting with the extraordinary appointment of Elisha Awesome as skipper.

"And Bill," the captain followed him several feet into the passageway and whispered, "when you receive confirmation from Holy Loch, meet me immediately in sickbay."

He watched Schroeder depart, then turned to Diller. "Please come in." The Marine had been pacing along the passageway for an hour and made no effort to disguise his pique. One of the things that annoyed him most about the Navy was its lack of punctuality. However maligned his own Marine Corps was in the post-Vietnam era, members of *that* service were taught to show proper respect for another man's time.

Awesome waved Diller to a seat and, once settled himself, regarded the Marine. "What I'm going to say, Claude, is Top Secret. You're officially our security officer and I need you for something very important. This is entirely between you and me."

Diller wanted to qualify the job description as "security officer," but the skipper did not provide the opportunity and kept talking.

"Before the Olympics training began this morning Commander Laycook worked alone in the forward torpedo room. I want a report on exactly what he did and who, if anybody, visited him."

"A report about the commander's work shouldn't be difficult. Lieutenant Curtis keeps good records."

"That's not what I mean. I'm not interested in the official reports, Diller, I want to know exactly when the commander was alone, or nearly alone, in the forward torpedo room—say before his technicians arrived at forenoon watch or when they broke for Olympic training. Do you understand what I mean?"

"Everybody not standing watch was jammed into the mess. I can personally vouch for that."

"Not everybody," Awesome corrected him. "Commander Laycook refused to attend the torch-lighting ceremony. He was the only man aboard who didn't sign up for a single event, which means he had no training schedule."

Diller puckered his lips in a perplexed expression and only slowly accepted the skipper's implication. He was not a man to mince words; nor was he afraid to ask for clarification . . . or help. "Are you suggesting sabotage, sir?"

"No, Diller . . . not exactly. I'm not suggesting sabotage because I don't believe an officer of the United States Navy would do such a thing, especially Commander Laycook. But I must be thorough. I just don't know what happened in the torpedo room . . . that's why I need you to find out. I need some eyes and some ears. And there isn't much time, either. This is urgent. Two hours—that's all. So you're going to be under a lot of pressure. I wish I had more time to give you, but I don't."

The thought of sniffing out a would-be saboteur pleased Diller. It was a job tailored precisely to his skills. The limited time allotted enhanced the challenge. "Then I can't waste time now," he said while rising. "I'll have to work damn fast . . . this afternoon at 1430."

"Thirteen-thirty, Claude."

"Just thought I had an hour's credit, sir . . . for the one I spent waiting in the passageway."

"You've got it, Claude, only payable in ale at the Tipsy Cleric in Holy Loch."

Forty feet from sickbay Awesome could hear the injured seamen's cries, punctuated by a steady flow of

262

medical instructions from Lieutenant Rosenbaum to Ted Becker and another corpsman. In the passageway hammocks had been hung to accommodate the less severely burned, and below them, sitting stiff and distracted, their legs interlaced along the deck, those with superficial wounds. Wafting from behind the sickbay curtain came a nauseous stench of burned flesh, vomitus, and disinfectants. Breathing through the mouth relieved some of the unpleasantness. As Awesome passed beyond the sickbay curtain he forced his eyes over one bunk at a time. The sight was far worse than the malodorous air.

Four wounded and deformed men filled the crowded berthing compartment. Awesome visited each, though only one was conscious enough to acknowledge his presence. Words of encouragement snagged in his throat; the reservoir of facile phrases was dry. For their adolescent eagerness young submariners had paid a dear price. Innocent? Not exactly. From the outset they understood the secrecy of *Amundsen*'s mission, and from the five-hundred-mile range of her Tomahawks they could have no illusions about how distantly she operated from the designated targets. And yet, there was so much about Patrol Polynya that they didn't know. They didn't know exactly *where*, or exactly *why*. So the conditions of their service were still a mystery. Compensations? Besides a small pay increment for hazardous duty, the men of Blue Crew received no rewards except involvement in something more exciting than what they might have expected in civilian life. In sum, sacrifice was great and recognition meager.

Awesome repeated a favorite scriptural passage,

wondering as he spoke how much was for the injured and how much for himself. "If I ascend into the Heavens, Thou art there. And if I descend into the netherworld, behold Thou art there also. . . ." He had to stop himself. He was turning statements into questions.

"Captain." Martin Rosenbaum emerged from the space he had established as an operating theater and searched for a place to confer in private with the skipper.

"Over here, Marty." Awesome motioned him behind dispensary lockers filled with open medication bottles.

Rosenbaum's white gown was stained from the chest to the knees with fresh blood and human secretions. His eyes were red with fatigue; his voice, brittle. "It's a mess here. We've got three emergency cases. Joe Crackleberry just died. Six dead now. Two more are so badly burned they can't hold on much longer. Others won't live without immediate treatment. Amputations, right now . . . God help me, maybe I can handle a couple."

"Well, Marty," Awesome affected a tone of confidence, "go ahead and operate. We'll give you all the support you need."

"That's not the point. I'm no surgeon and haven't had any training in this kind of medicine. I fainted when I had to do my surgical rotation in medical school. Greerson was the only surgeon here; Band-Aid stuff is all I'm good for. I just can't perform the surgery. I was afraid something like this might happen when I let the Submarine Service talk me into this patrol. The Navy thinks every M.D. is qualified from dermatology to proctology. You've got to understand, Captain, that I'm not the only M.D. who couldn't do this."

Rosenbaum was trying to wipe his hands clean on his blood-soaked gown; Awesome wished he would stop. "That's not accurate, Marty," he said in a calming voice. "The Submarine Service knows full well that you're a psychiatrist . . . and so do I. Do what you can. Nobody's asking from you more than you can deliver. Just remember: Without Gene, you're the best we've got. Your patients will be grateful for whatever you can do for them."

"Cap'n . . . sir," a familiar voice called from the passageway.

Awesome whirled around. Schroeder's urgent hand signal distracted him from commending the psychiatrist's courage. "Take care of them," he repeated, but there was a sudden constriction in his chest. Something was wrong. It was too early for the communications officer's return.

Schroeder started talking the moment Awesome stepped outside the sickbay curtain. "You won't believe this!" he gasped, out of breath from the race down two decks and almost half the length of the submarine. "You just won't believe this!"

Awesome turned him about-face, almost dragging him through the passageway and away from the injured seamen. "Believe what?" he asked as soon as they reached the privacy of the gyrocompartment.

"The keys you gave me . . . I inserted them . . . took off the transmitter panel and began adjusting to send your message. But the radio was dead. I mean really *dead. DEAD!*" Schroeder's usual sardonic expression was wiped utterly away; in the back of his mind Awesome noted that it made him look years younger. "At first I thought we didn't have any juice, but I tested the current and it flowed perfectly. So I took off the inner cowling to find out what was wrong. Everything looked all right, then I saw it. There's a big fucking hole where the modulator circuit should be. It's gone!"

"That's impossible. We're getting messages in every day. Hell, we've got so many communication gadgets aboard we can tell when a toilet is flushed anywhere in Russia."

"Right, Cap'n. Coming *in*. But we haven't anything going *out*. No functioning transmission— absolutely nothing. We've been under a broadcast blackout since Holy Loch so how would anybody know?"

"For Christ's sake, Schroeder, why the hell didn't you check the equipment?"

"I couldn't check it. You and Commander Laycook alone had access to the keys. If you wanted the transmitter inspected, you should have given them to me sooner."

Awesome winced. Schroeder was absolutely correct. Gaffy had specified that *Amundsen* remain totally silent even in Scottish coastal waters and had ordered that Admiral Billings himself lock the transmitter before delivering its only two keys. One was deposited in the radio-room safe, the other in the ship's vault, which only the skipper and executive officer could open. "What about the spare parts, Bill? You've got spares for everything. I read the manifest myself. There's got to be at least two spare modulator

266

circuits aboard."

"First thing I did. There's a check list for every spare circuit we might need on patrol." He removed a crumpled list from his coverall pocket and pointed to a serial number in the left-hand column. "Look here: Every transistor has a serial number. This is for the modulator circuit. There should be two, it says so right here, Cap'n."

"Well?"

"But they're not in the spare-parts locker. Gone! Disappeared. I searched everywhere."

Awesome shouted, ignoring the wounded in the passageway. "Who has access to that locker?"

"The men in communications. Everyone who works in the radio room knows where we have the combination written down."

"Sokorski too?"

"Certainly. He often stands watch at night. He'd have to know how to get at the spares if necessary."

"What about the auxiliary transmitter?"

Schroeder snapped back. "What auxiliary? Admiral Billings' men replaced it with a C-1113 jammer before the patrol. Remember—when he came aboard with Admiral Gaffy for the final inspection?"

Awesome wilted. "How in God's name are we going to send this SOS?"

"Fact is, we can't send a blasted word." Schroeder produced the khaki envelope and returned it to Awesome. "Here's your message, Cap'n. Maybe we can walk it over to a Russian icebreaker and let them send it for you."

"Damn it, Schroeder. I don't believe you. I'm going to have a look for myself."

The communications officer knew better than to protest for the captain would understand only when he had seen it with his own eyes. After all, it was hard to believe, absolutely incredible.

The two officers clambered up the companionway to the main deck. As they passed the wardroom Awesome read the faces of those waiting in line to donate blood for their wounded shipmates. Their eyes were glazed with bewilderment. They stared at him, too frightened to ask what was going to happen; either they feared the answer, or worse, they reckoned their skipper himself did not know. Awesome hurried by. For the first time he felt that the power of salvation had begun to slip from his fingers.

Both radiomen jumped from their chairs to greet the lieutenant . . . and the skipper. As far as either one could remember, the captain had never before entered the radio shack. But Schroeder didn't allow them to enjoy it; he was ordering them out as he came through the door. Ever since he had opened the transmitter and quickly closed it down again he had acted bizarrely . . . very bizarrely. Whatever was causing this behavior, the skipper seemed fully apprised. He looked bizarre too.

"Where's that modulator circuit, Schroeder?" Awesome barked the moment the door slid shut behind the radiomen.

"Back here, Cap'n." He was already unhinging the transmitter cowling with a Phillips-head screwdriver and hex key. Schroeder pictured the crated auxiliary transmitter as men from Billings' detail maneuvered it through the supply scuttle to a sub tender's loading crane. Somehow those stupid technicians had taken the modulator circuits along with the other bits of equipment they removed from the submarine. Chalk up another fiasco for the Navy.

A last screw slipped free from the cowling and fell to the deck. Schroeder removed the sheet-metal plate and pointed a conical penlight beam into a jungle of electronic circuitry. The light described a figure eight and finally targeted on the modulator's location. Awesome bent over Schroeder's shoulder to inspect the vacancy, then grabbed the flashlight and poked his nose close to the electronic maze. The gap that the communications officer had spotted loomed larger than he had expected and reminded Awesome of an old man's toothless mouth. Centered in the spot of light were exposed leads and disconnected terminals. No mistake: The modulator circuit had been removed. "Christ, Schroeder, can't you improvise something to work here?"

The communications officer was leaning against the operator's seat, enjoying his temporary vindication. "I could have cannibalized parts and concocted something for the old transmitter, but not for this *new* model. Two weeks before departure we had a change of equipment and I can't find the specifications for this baby anywhere aboard."

Awesome resisted an urge to jam his fist into the circuitry and *make* it work. The missing modulator circuits and the disappearance of the specifications suggested more than ineptitude. Much more! He turned abruptly to face Schroeder. "That modulator and the spares have got to be aboard this boat. Circuits don't just disappear. Somebody took them and I think I know who did. Bill, check every man who had access to the spare-parts locker. I don't care how you do it, just get those circuits back . . . and fast! Start with Sokorski . . . I don't think you're going to have to go much farther than him."

Schroeder disagreed. Maybe someone in communications was guilty, but there was more to it than that. Anybody in the communications detail, he explained, could have used the combination to open the spare-parts locker, but only two men had access to the two transmitter keys: Commander Laycook . . . and Captain Awesome. Without either of those two keys nobody could have stolen the original modulator circuit from the transmitter.

Awesome considered Schroeder's observation without rejoinder. The flashlight beam shot up toward the young officer's eyes, momentarily blinding him. "For the time being, Bill, I want you to forget *how* those circuits were stolen and concentrate on getting them back. Look everywhere. Do what's necessary with Sokorski. Use every man you can find. I'm giving you *carte blanche*. This is absolutely urgent. Use any means, but get them back. Report to me in an hour, Bill. No later."

In the control room outside the radio shack Schroeder glanced about, searching for the two radiomen, who were nowhere in sight. Now what? How could he leave to find them? The radio room had not been left unattended since *Amundsen*'s departure from Holy Loch. What would happen if an important communication arrived while there was no one standing watch to receive it? Damn Paul Kimble and David Drew. Schroeder made a mental note to discipline them severely for leaving their post. He had never meant for them to ramble off somewhere. Then Schroeder recalled that both were close buddies of Sokorski. Having seen the skipper in the radio shack they had probably hurried off to warn him. Or perhaps they themselves were a part of the conspiracy? If so, they would try to destroy the evidence that linked them with their crime. That thought set Schroeder off at a dash.

1232 hours.

Sergeant Diller, flushed with excitement, presented himself at Awesome's quarters an hour before the prearranged time. He paced the tight passageway, like a hunting dog ready to pounce into a pheasant field. Originally he had believed that his extraordinary posting aboard *Amundsen* had to do with a previous double tour of duty as a cold-weather combat specialist in Fairbanks, Alaska. But when he learned there would be no opportunity to exit onto the ice, much less train submariners for combat, he abandoned that thought and decided he must merely be a window dressing for the Marines. How the heroes of Guadalcanal, Iwo Jima, and Okinawa had to scrounge for an authentic role in the post-Vietnam era! Diller's personal contribution to Patrol Polynya had yet to be made as the patrol entered its final hours. Then, quite unexpectedly, came Awesome's secret assignment and an opportunity to salvage his pride and justify at least part of the wasted months. Indeed, it proved to be more than that. Diller found himself investigating the most urgent security question. Through a strange confluence of events he was no longer an outsider among Blue Crew. On the contrary, he was running the inside track and sharing intimacies with *Amundsen*'s skipper.

"Keep in mind, sir, that I haven't had much time," he said. Nevertheless, he had drawn up a comprehensive picture of Thomas Laycook's activities during the Olympics. His detail in the forward torpedo room worked around the clock, "six and six," six hours on watch and six hours off, a schedule that allowed little rest—especially during Olympic competition. Not that it seemed to bother the executive officer. At least half the time he was gallivanting around the sub, sometimes in the auxiliary machinery room, sometimes in the reactor compartment or engine room. He had also been seen snooping around the crew's and the officers' quarters. Lieutenant Haddock reported his presence in the food storage lockers. What he had been doing no one seemed to know.

Awesome kept shaking his head and on one occasion mumbled that Laycook's behavior baffled him. "Was it possible for him to be alone in the torpedo room?" he inquired, returning to the original question.

Diller had compared records of when the missile technicians arrived in the mess for the Olympics and concluded that it *might* have been possible.

"Wouldn't that have attracted attention?"

"No, sir. The mess was jammed to the gills. Almost everybody was at training, so his presence wouldn't be missed, especially since he hadn't been to any previous practices." Diller added, hurriedly, "And there's something else. I don't know if this is significant but I learned that before the Olympics there were two secret meetings organized by George Sokorski and Everett Young."

"What about?"

"I'm not certain. But I know they were in contact with Commander Laycook." Diller fished into his pocket for a folded paper and opened it on his knee. "I thought I might try to find out, so I entered his quarters just a few minutes ago to look around." Awesome grimaced at the trespass but said nothing. The sketch he presented had been removed from Laycook's bunk. There was more that he did not take: a spool of thread, some empty aluminum cigar cylinders, and some felt marker pens. "I don't know what it represents," the Marine concluded. "Any ideas?"

Awesome adjusted the sketch before his eyes and studied it, then suddenly leaning against the spring back of his chair and staring overhead, he repeated aloud the list of articles that Diller had seen on the exec officer's bunk. Once again he scrutinized the drawing. No, he could not be certain . . . but . . . felt marker pens could be inserted into the aluminum cigar cylinders, much like Tomahawks slipped into *Amundsen*'s torpedo tubes. The drawing was rough, but might represent the compressed aerodynamic cruciform fins that stabilize the Tomahawk in flight as well as the booster rocket that propels it to the surface of the water and then into the air.

Watching him, Diller grinned. "I gather that sketch *is* important. Just the kind of thing you wanted, isn't it?"

"Only hypothetical, Diller," Awesome warned. "First, the implications of this are terrible, well beyond what I expected from Commander Laycook's motives. Second, if this sketch is significant, I wouldn't expect him to be so foolish as to leave it lying around. That's not exactly the stealth of a saboteur. Remember, this is only a hunch. What we've got here may be meaningless."

"Shall I continue with my investigation, sir?"

"By all means. But for the time being I want you to find Laycook and stick with him. Inconspicuously. I urgently need to know what he's up to."

1300 hours.

The wardroom was almost vacant except for Koranson, who was seated midway along its central table, and Awesome, who was talking in a subdued voice with Schroeder. The communications officer rolled himself a cigarette but had difficulty sealing the gummed edge with his dry tongue. Tobacco strands straggled loose from the paper seam and scattered over the Formica tabletop. His eyes were lowered over the cigarette while he spoke. An admission of failure was inordinately painful for one who believed in his own powers with such conviction. But failed he had. *Amundsen's* modular circuits were still missing. Physical persuasion, a bit excessive even in the light of Awesome's *carte blanche*, had produced nothing from George Sokorski.

"Captain Awesome from Sergeant Diller. Captain Awesome from Sergeant Diller in the forward torpedo compartment," a familiar voice blared through the loudspeaker.

Awesome bounded from his chair to the bulkhead phone to receive the Marine's report on a private circuit.

"Captain, I found Commander Laycook in the bow. He's pressurized tube 6 with an auxiliary compressor and has opened the breech door. Damned if he hasn't pulled some of that wrecked Tomahawk back into the torpedo room!"

"What the hell's he doing that for?"

"I don't know, sir . . . he seems to be tinkering with something on the inside . . . and he's got with him those cigar cylinders and felt pens."

"Well, get him to shove that bird back into the tube and close the breech door right away. I can't chance any more flooding. Bring him immediately to the wardroom. And don't let him out of your sight—not for one minute, understand, Diller? Not for one instant." The phone slammed down on its receiver; Awesome whirled back toward the table and slammed a fist into his open palm. Laycook was caught in some new infamy . . . or covering up the evidence that would link him with the explosion in tube 6. Damn good thing Diller was monitoring his activities before he caused any more damage.

When the sergeant and his charge arrived, Awesome thanked and dismissed Diller. Freshly laundered coveralls, no doubt returned to the steward many times until perfect creases were achieved, fit snugly to Laycook's chest and waist. His sleeves were rolled to his elbows and his fingers were coated with hydrocarbon fuel from the damaged Tomahawk. He quickly acknowledged Koranson, then Schroeder, and assumed his customary seat at the foot of the table. Two empty cigar cylinders, two felt-tipped pens, and a spool of thread emerged from his pocket.

"I've been doing some investigating," Laycook said, glancing again at Koranson and Schroeder, "and I think I'd better speak with you alone, Skipper."

Awesome ignored him. His chair screeched over the deck as he stood up. "Gentlemen," he addressed Koranson and Schroeder, "this is the saddest moment one can have in the Navy, but I want you to witness that I'm relieving Commander Laycook of all duties aboard this boat." Both Schroeder and Koranson stiffened with astonishment: Laycook could be difficult, but he was a competent exec officer, one needed in an emergency. "This is damn hard for me," Awesome continued, "because all the evidence for what I'm going to say is circumstantial. I don't want to believe what I've seen and heard. But I can't ignore facts either. I have a responsibility for this crew as well as a lot of other people. Doubts? I've got more than I can handle at this moment. Still, the truth is that since I assumed command Thomas Laycook has undermined my authority. At every juncture he has counseled me to terminate the patrol, head home, and admit defeat. An early end to this operation would prove beyond a shadow of a doubt that Admiral Gaffy had made a terrible mistake by appointing me over him as skipper of this submarine. But in response to this defeatist counsel I made it patently clear that I would not abort Patrol Polynya without the admiral's explicit command. So long as we have operational status it's our obligation to stay on patrol, extensions or no extensions."

"With deference, Captain Awesome," Laycook interrupted, but Awesome continued undeterred. After Bertram Graham's death, he said, the comman-

276

der was involved with certain crewmen who circulated a petition designed to discredit him. Sokorski was the ringleader and it was well known he and Laycook were friends. If the exec officer intended no sinister result from such contacts they were nevertheless so poorly managed that everybody eventually suffered.

Laycook smacked the table with his palms and leaped to his feet. "Captain Awesome, now wait just a minute! We've already been through this farce before. You know perfectly well that I didn't sign that letter."

"Sit down, Commander. Control yourself. I am talking now and will not tolerate interruptions . . . and it didn't stop there, gentlemen. I was saying that Laycook believed the extension of this patrol excessive and that Admiral Gaffy would push us to our limits. Then suddenly, somebody aboard this boat stole the modulator circuits for our transmitter and hid the spare parts. Whoever it was reckoned that I was weakening and that if I couldn't communicate with Squadron I'd exercise my own discretion to terminate the patrol. Thomas Laycook and I are the only men aboard who had access to *both* transmitter keys. And I didn't take them!"

Koranson's eyes were wide, and for an instant his mouth hung open. Schroeder seemed more fascinated than shocked. Laycook was on his feet again, transfixed, his eyes glued to Awesome's. "What!"

"Thomas," the skipper lifted his chin, looking injured "I honestly don't understand it all and I confess my confusion. But for the safety of this crew and for the security of the nation . . . I cannot permit this dangerous game to continue. I want those circuits and I want them now . . . this very minute. Before the Russians get here. Do you understand? We have run out of time; there is no more time."

Laycook was leaning far over the table toward the skipper. "*What* are you saying about the modulator circuits? Say that again, please, Captain. Please!"

"The modulator circuit is missing from the radio." Schroeder spoke for the captain. "Spares are missing from the spare-parts locker. Without them we can't send for help."

"Is that true? Is everybody sure?"

"Everybody's sure," Awesome answered.

Laycook straightened up, his eyes flashing. "I'm not surprised. I should have known . . . it fits like a glove . . . those bastards . . . I should have known all along what those bastards would do."

Awesome was unmoved. "Come off it, Thomas. You wanted to make sure I'd return to Scotland a failure. You wanted everyone to see the damage sustained and tried to reverse Riley's superb repair of torpedo tube 6. With a fouled muzzle door and a faulty WRT drain we'd go straight to dry dock. To my shame. Only while you were messing with it a Tomahawk accidentally blew its booster rocket and five seamen were killed along with Eugene Greerson. Seven more were badly injured. That's how I see it and I call that treason."

"Bullshit!"

"Don't deny you were just tampering with Tomahawk 6. Diller just saw you with the breech door open, destroying the evidence that links you, Sokorski, and I don't know how many others with this sabotage." Awesome unfolded Laycook's sketch and exhibited it before Koranson and Schroeder. "This is the commander's own diagram. It shows how he intended to foul the muzzle door and drain that Riley and Graham fixed."

"You idiots! Listen to me! *Amundsen* was sabotaged, all right, but not by George Sokorski, or me, or anybody else aboard. I certainly was in the forward torpedo room. And I drew that sketch to figure out what caused the Tomahawk to explode. The booster rockets on these cruise missiles are specially designed to ignite only when the bird is forty feet beyond the muzzle door. The turbojet engine cannot function until after the rocket has been fired and the missile is airborne. It has solid-propellant fuel that won't burn without electric ignition. And the thousand-pound high-explosive warhead cannot explode without an electronic signal from the TERCOM guidance system. So . . . I couldn't have caused that explosion even if I had wanted to." Laycook quickly moved his thread, cigar cylinders, and pens into position on the tabletop. "Look here, Captain. Suppose Tomahawk 6 had been rigged before we left Scotland . . . we would never know the difference, would we?"

"Ridiculous . . . what the hell does that mean?" Koranson barked.

Laycook held up an empty cigar cylinder. "Look." He stretched a length of thread alongside the felt-tipped pen and stuffed it inside the cylinder. "When we're ready to fire a Tomahawk we must first flood the torpedo tube, but pressurize the protective capsule around the missile itself." He twisted the pen inside its aluminum cylinder to demonstrate. "After

279

alignment, the missile is ejected by our hydraulic system. As it leaves the muzzle door into the water it draws out upon a forty-foot lanyard"—he drew the thread from the cylinder—"and when it comes to the end the lanyard triggers the booster rocket to fire. Now suppose somebody at Holy Loch shortened the lanyard down to twelve inches, like here on the butt of this pen. What would happen? Tell me what would happen when we fired the Tomahawk?"

"That's ludicrous."

"No, it isn't. Just tell me what would happen if the lanyard were shortened from forty feet to twelve inches."

"It would blow the booster rocket, all three hundred and ninety pounds of its hydrocarbon fuel."

"Precisely! And that's exactly what did happen. When we started to check the Tomahawk we didn't have enough room to remove the missile and her protective capsule from the tube so we left the capsule inside and slipped the Tomahawk aftward. First thing we did was to disconnect the electric solid-fuel ignitor and deactivate the warhead detonator. Good thing too, because they would have blown up with the booster rocket and sunk *Amundsen*. But the one thing we didn't do was detach the lanyard because we figured we had forty feet. It never occurred to us that it had been shortened."

"That's all crap," Koranson said. "You're describing how you monkeyed with the bird. Clever, but we won't buy it."

"You'd better buy it, Sagi, otherwise we continue to be the idiots we've been all along. Suppose it became necessary to fire the birds. Squadron would only have to tell us to pull Tomahawk 6 from its tube, fire Tomahawks 1 through 5, then load and fire the additional twelve birds. But on the other hand, suppose for some reason our presence was discovered and we were given an order to fire Tomahawk 6 alone. As soon as we used the hydraulic ejector and the twelve inches of lanyard ran out—the booster pops, then the turbojet fuel, and seconds later the high-explosive warhead. What Tomahawk 6 doesn't do to finish *Amundsen* the rest of the missiles in the torpedo room will. Bang . . . there goes *Amundsen* without a sign. No evidence of our nefarious position in Soviet water and no blame for Underwater Strategic Services. Admiral Gaffy, with his inimitable sleight of hand, wiggles off the hook. All the evidence of what he's done is permanently destroyed.''

Awesome fumed with exasperation. ''That's absurd, Thomas!''

''Why?''

''Because if Tomahawk 6 was sabotaged, it had to be somebody aboard this submarine. If Squadron had done it, Admiral Gaffy would know. He'd have to know. He knows everything that occurs at Holy Loch. He told me personally that he and Donovan Billings inspected every inch of this vessel before we sailed.''

''Right, Captain Awesome, and has it ever occurred to you that the great, mighty, and wonderful Admiral Nicholas Francis Gaffy and has ass-licking Donovan Billings could have shortened that lanyard themselves?''

Awesome's voice thundered in rage. ''We're not

281

judging Admiral Gaffy here, just you, Thomas Laycook. Now goddamn it, return that modulator circuit. We haven't got time for your wild imagination. Can't you understand that?"

"I don't have your circuits, nor does Sokorski or anybody else aboard," Laycook replied. "Captain Awesome, *you're* the one who doesn't understand. You've got one enormous blind spot, dead ahead. You just refuse to admit that your admiral is screwing you."

"That's enough! Stop slandering Admiral Gaffy. You're accusing one of the Navy's finest officers and don't know what the hell you're talking about. He would no more sabotage one of his submarines than screw his own mother. He just wouldn't do it, not in a thousand years. It doesn't make any sense. Gaffy has no reason for doing what you said and he wouldn't do it even if he had one."

"He has a reason." Laycook slumped in his chair. "He can't rescue *Amundsen*. Look at us—a nuclear submarine without sonar, deep in enemy water, now infested with a dozen Soviet warships. To dispatch *Yellowtail* into the Barents would be foolish, a tactical error. No naval commander in his right mind would sacrifice a good ship to save a bad one. Nor should he. Putting *Yellowtail* in the Barents would vastly increase the danger of detection and ultimately risk nuclear war. This old tub just isn't worth it."

Awesome was calmed by an expression his father often used: The ultimate decision rested not within the province of mortals but through the providence of God. Only the Almighty would not rescue *Amundsen* directly, but through the agency of

Nicholas Gaffy. Sure, Awesome admitted to his officers, rescue was dangerous. But the decision to accept such risk lay solely with the admiral. What his verdict would be there could be no doubt. If the task was remotely possible, Gaffy would accomplish it. That's what made him so different from the others in the Submarine Service: When others were timorous he was brave, and when others were weak he was strong. But his response depended upon having the correct information. Contact with Squadron was essential. Nothing could be done until Gaffy received an SOS.

"He's powerful, all right," Laycook interrupted. "But he's already made his decision. The judgment was made in Scotland before our patrol began. As long as we remain undetected and safe, Gaffy can afford to wait proudly on the quay at Holy Loch and welcome home his warriors. But once we get in trouble, this old 1959 submarine is expendable. She was ready for the scrap heap a long time ago, only she was too valuable for Admiral Gaffy. Now he won't have to make that terrible decision whether to rescue us. He's already seen to it that he'll never receive our Mayday. Ask yourselves, if you were in his position, how would you ensure we couldn't send an SOS and inadvertently reveal our position? How could Gaffy guarantee that we would never divulge our bearings— even accidentally? Suppose he were to remove an essential component from the radio transmitter . . . a modulator circuit, something that couldn't be replaced. Then suppose he also managed to remove the spare modulators, even though the manifest still lists them. If the radio is locked away under strict orders

283

not to be used, by the time we discover the duplicity it's too late."

"Thomas, your estimate of Gaffy's power with Underwater Strategic Services is all wrong. He doesn't act in a vacuum. Admiral Katzenback and the Department of Defense are always breathing down his neck. Every move he makes is carefully scrutinized."

"Right, and he has to cover his own ass. He's got to, especially if it becomes necessary and expedient to destroy his own submarine. In fact, that's what I couldn't figure out until just a while ago. Gaffy never moves one inch without securing against every eventuality. I asked myself over and over how I would cover my own ass if I were him. How would I avoid handing Katzenback and the Joint Chiefs a reason to dismantle Underwater Strategic Services? Gaffy once privately admitted to me how he feared the very success of Underwater Strategic Services. The Pentagon boys were always ready to pounce upon him. Great peacetime warriors, they don't want Congress to learn how well the nation is defended. Americans must always live with the big scare that in the event of war the military will not be adequately armed or prepared. That means more money, more guns, more men, and more power. But Gaffy learned long ago that the best defense isn't always equivalent to the biggest weapon, but to the cleverest one. And for a decade he was doing what the other services could only talk about—taking risks they were incapable of and unwilling to assume. Still, he had to prepare public opinion for the worst, well in advance of any potential disaster. He left clues to what he was doing, only nobody seemed to pick them up. But Sokorski heard one . . . the word Azores, the Azores Islands."

Koranson and Schroeder looked bewildered. Awesome didn't speak.

"Anyone know, offhand, how many subs were produced in Skipjack class?"

Koranson began enumerating: *Skipjack, Scamp, Sculpin, Snook . . . Shark*. He stopped after five. There was one more, wasn't there?

"Right," Laycook answered, turning to Awesome for the final answer.

"Amundsen."

"Amundsen," Laycook repeated, and Koranson flushed with embarrassment. "But what about *Scorpion* SSB-589? Everybody has forgotten *Scorpion*, which sunk with ninety-nine men aboard in 1968."

"That makes seven," Schroeder remarked. "I thought you said six."

"Seven, officially. My guess is there never were more than six boats in Skipjack class."

"What kind of nonsense is that?" Awesome snapped.

"I mean that according to the commissioning papers on the bulkheads over there," he pointed to the starboard bulkhead, "the U.S.S. *Edmond Roald Amundsen* was launched in December 1959 at Mare Island Naval Shipyard in San Francisco Bay. Lots of pictures there of dignitaries at the launching. Pretty official-looking papers too. But that word 'Azores' made me suspicious, and I decided to give this boat a good search. I didn't know exactly what I was looking for and didn't know where to poke my nose.

We're all aware that *Amundsen* has been completely overhauled, especially in the forward torpedo room and tactical attack center. So I didn't expect to find anything there. I searched the older equipment—the reactor compartment, auxiliary machinery room, and engine room. Eventually I found what I was looking for. On the electric motor shaft behind our reduction gears there are mounts to the transverse frame—structural steel that can't be replaced. Painted over many times in white, tucked into a corner, I could barely make out the stamped initials 'EBD.'"

"Electric Boat Division," Schroeder interpreted.

"Precisely. But *Amundsen* was purportedly built at Mare Island, three thousand miles distant from the Electric Boat Division of General Dynamics at Groton, Connecticut."

"So?" Koranson asked.

"If *Amundsen* wasn't built in Groton, *Scorpion* was. According to *Jane's Fighting Ships*, she was commissioned in July 1960 right there in Groton. That caused me to wonder where in hell Nicholas Gaffy found a submarine to refit secretly for Tomahawk missiles. Why didn't he want a more modern boat, Sturgeon or Narwhal class, one with the torpedo tubes amidship and with better sonar up in the bow? Of over fifty available attack submarines he specifically chose this old battlewagon. Why? . . . Why a submarine at the end of her life, one destined to become a reserve trainer?"

"Because *Amundsen* was already in his squadron," Awesome answered. "She was available for refitting when Underwater Strategic Services got the go-ahead for this patrol from the Pentagon."

"That's right. She was 'available.' But she was available because Gaffy got her back from the Mid-Atlantic Rift. That's where she came from . . . the Mid-Atlantic Rift!"

"Preposterous." Awesome looked annoyed.

"Not if you believe Admiral Moorer's report, which designated *Scorpion* as lost in the Mid-Atlantic Rift sometime in April–May 1968. Wasn't that just about the time Nicholas Gaffy was starting his Underwater Strategic Services? What he needed then was identical with what he needs today, ten years later—a submarine that the Soviets don't know about, one secret to all but a handful of top people . . . just one boat that he can employ as he chooses without Department of Defense meddling and congressional interference. But where would he find such an unaccounted-for submarine? . . . My guess is that he created it.

"In April–May 1968 he fictitiously sank *Scorpion* in the Mid-Atlantic Rift. She was stricken from the naval roster and quickly forgotten. Then she reappeared among the squadron of Underwater Strategic Services, only reincarnated under a new name, *Amundsen.* Gaffy shuffled her around five giant oceans on various secret patrols in a submarine shell game, carefully keeping her submerged for more than 95 percent of her life and under radio blackout, virtually out of communication with the world. He used the clandestine expertise of Underwater Strategic Services to provide crews and provisions, mostly at special rendezvous with submarine tenders on the high seas. Since all who served aboard *Amundsen* were forbidden to mention their boat outside the

Service, her identity was never questioned."

"That's absolutely preposterous," Awesome roared.

Laycook agreed. At first it seemed preposterous to him as well. But Gaffy tipped his hand. What had worked so flawlessly in 1968 he tried to duplicate a decade later. The Riga broadcast heard by Sokorski sounded so outlandish that it was almost overlooked. Nobody took it seriously and yet it was intended to be dead serious. Losing a phantom submarine at sea is one thing, but how would one account for the disappearance of its crew? With a similar stratagem used by *Scorpion* a decade before. Gaffy planted phony debris in the Atlantic for Portuguese fishermen to discover, debris with *Amundsen*'s name for identification. Then he leaked information to the press that *Amundsen* had sunk accidentally on routine patrol near the Azores in the Mid-Atlantic Rift, the deepest hole in the Atlantic, where the depth precludes further investigation. So the cause of the mishap was left unknown.

"Even the Department of Defense blundered into the act at home, most probably without being fully apprised. Nobody understands the sewers of government better than Nicholas Gaffy, and no one in the military is more adept at exploiting the travelers who frequent them. All Gaffy had to do was sit back and wait for Secretary of Defense Griffin to suggest a public memorial in Arlington National Cemetery. The Secretary was a ham at heart who loved telling the American people what sacrifices were being made in its name by the armed services of the United States. Once he 'buried' *Amundsen*'s crew in public, Gaffy was covered from all sides."

"I don't see how," Koranson said. "Suppose we came back."

"He expects us to come back. If we return on schedule without mishap the press will laud Gaffy's little stratagem as the ruse of the century. They'll love it. 'A mission so secret that the Navy had to "sink" its own ship.' Secretary Griffin will have no alternative but to claim he understood from the very outset. Gaffy would never have to reveal anything about the self-destruct lanyard because as soon as the crew disembarks he can personally board *Amundsen* to remove it. But he's always got the other alternative if our presence in Soviet water becomes a liability. All he has to do is order us to fire Tomahawk 6. We eject the bird and *kabloom*, *Amundsen* disappears. No evidence. No record. No witnesses. As far as the public and the Department of Defense are concerned we have already sunk in the Mid-Atlantic Rift."

Laycook turned back toward the skipper. "Believe this scheme is mad and you underestimate Gaffy's genius. For all intents and purposes *Amundsen* is a ghost ship, one that was lost near the Azores three months ago. Would the Russians search for a phantom submarine that doesn't exist, three thousand miles from where it sank? Until now I was convinced they had actually detected us. But I was wrong, and you, Captain Awesome, were right. They couldn't have known we were here unless they picked us up on their sonar and, even if they did, they couldn't identify us. As far as Soviet Intelligence knows the United States is currently operating with one less nuclear attack submarine from its base in Scotland." He paused. "A cheap gamble too. Only one hundred and twelve men and a single second-generation nuclear sub, almost obsolete by modern standards, one stricken from the naval roster a decade before. Don't you see what he's done? We're the ultimate weapon—a Cold War kamikaze!"

Awesome sat without movement, his eyes cast over his hands, and breathing through his mouth in long, heavy breaths. When he finally lifted his eyes to regard the executive officer his voice was assured, but lacking its usual resonance. "No, Thomas. No. This might sound plausible, but it's wrong. Too much depends upon your perception of Nicholas Gaffy. However shrewd he is, I don't believe he's capable of such deception. No, that's not the Nicholas Gaffy I know. He wouldn't prevent us from transmitting an SOS for help. No officer in the Navy would do that."

"Lieutenant Schroeder . . . Lieutenant Schroeder," an unfamiliar sound reverberated from the squawk box and startled everyone. "Lieutenant Schroeder . . . this is the radio room." Schroeder went to the phone. "What's up?"

"There's a message from Squadron coming in, sir."

The skipper immediately shoved his chair back along the linoleum deck and flew to his feet in a surge of energy. The moment for debate was over; the movement for action imminent. Anything was better than Laycook's speculations. "Bill," he snapped at the communications officer, "get that tape and meet me in the cryptocenter." Schroeder was already at the door; Koranson also had pushed back his chair.

Only Laycook remained seated, nonplused by the rejection of his disclosure. "Wait!" he implored as the triumvirate began to exit.

Awesome hesitated, then reluctantly deposited his name sourly into the air. "Commander Laycook . . . you are ordered to remain in hack. Stay in your quarters. As of this moment you are relieved of all your duties."

Laycook slumped in his seat, threw his head back, and stared into the rafters.

A steady computer hum in the cryptocenter was punctuated by the nervous tapping of Koranson's fingers. There was nothing to do but watch Awesome while he skillfully manipulated the complex controls. Several long seconds elapsed before the teleprinter's Selectric ball began punching at the readout tape. Koranson leaned over Awesome's shoulder. What he saw struck terror into his heart:

RED ALERT . . . REPEAT . . . RED ALERT.

Between thirty and forty American ballistic submarines were currently prowling the Atlantic and Pacific oceans. Behind them were a thousand Titan, Minuteman II ICBM's, plus squadrons of B-52 long-range jet bombers armed with nuclear ordnance. Was America's entire deterrent force being transformed into an offensive power? Or was *Amundsen* alone receiving the order? However preemptive her attack was designed to be, the moment her first salvo of birds hit targets at Nar'ian Mar, war was certain to follow.

Awesome struck the readout tape from the teleprinter and handed it across to Koranson for his confirmation.

YOUR PRESENCE DISCOVERED. RE-
PEAT: YOUR PRESENCE DISCOVERED. SO-
VIET ULTIMATUM AND MOBILIZATION.
DURING DIPLOMATIC CRISIS ACHIEVE
CONDITION 1SQ. MAINTAIN PREPRO-
GRAMED TARGET ACHIEVE CONDITION
1SQ AND HOLD FOR ORDERS. REPEAT:
HOLD FOR ORDERS. OUT.

Koranson's stomach plummeted into his bowels.
"All right, Sagi," Awesome commanded, "we've
got five Tomahawks in their tubes, another twelve in
automatic loading racks ready to fire. Spin them all
up to Status 1SQ immediately. Get the permission-
to-fire key from the ship's vault and meet me in the
tactical attack center."

Koranson hurried away, his complexion blanched.
Awesome walked forward to the ballast control panel
and unhooked an intercom phone. He reached under
a clear Plexiglas protection guard and pressed the
vermilion-colored alert button beneath. An instant
later—all hell broke loose.

EEEEEP . . . EEEEP . . . EEEEP. A shrill, nerve-
wracking alarm penetrated the sub, pervading every
space, even the berthing compartments where men
rested in their bunks. Scramble . . . scramble. Bodies
lunged toward battle stations. Feet scampered over
the deck. The captain's voice bristled through the
squawk box: "Now hear this. . . . Now hear this.
Captain Awesome speaking. Man battle stations,
missile. . . . Man battle stations, missile. . . . All

292

hands. This is a red alert. . . . Repeat: This is a red alert. Set Condition 1SQ. . . . Repeat: Set Condition 1SQ."

The Klaxon's wail sent echo waves jumbling together in the tight passageways. For the skipper it was a moment of exhilaration. He shouldered his way among the scrambling seamen, half running himself. Since the Little Andes, *Amundsen* had only reacted to events, but suddenly she was literally going on the attack, doing what she had been trained to do. He had nearly reached his stateroom when Laycook fell into step beside him.

"Is this a drill?"

"No. And you're confined to quarters."

"Not a drill?" Laycook's handsome face wore a peculiar look. "Do you mean you're going to fire?"

"If ordered." Awesome would not be stopped. Men racing through the passageway cut between the two officers. Laycook was forced to fall in behind.

"Then you're going to kill us all."

"I know that, Thomas." Awesome kept moving.

"They'll find us, you know, once we've surfaced to launch. They'll discover the break in the ice. Hiding won't help. Without sonar we can't escape."

"I know that, Thomas." Awesome came to a halt before his cabin door. "Now report to your quarters, please." He slammed the door in the executive officer's face.

The captain's safe was built into the starboard bulkhead beside a small bookshelf. In it was deposited the second of two permission-to-fire keys required in the fire-control console before launching the Tomahawks. Awesome's steady fingers turned the combination lock and freed the key from where it was taped to the inner wall of the vault. Once the brass instrument was in his hand, his exhilaration drained away. A cold chill shot from his spine to the extremities of his limbs. Laycook was, after all, absolutely correct: The destruction that *Amundsen* had barely avoided on the Little Andes was drawing near. Everett Young was also correct: The entire crew was following in Bertram Graham's footsteps—only a few miles behind. So it had finally come to the ultimate sacrifice that the Navy had so long honored in its past heroes. If war between superpowers became inevitable, *Amundsen* alone could prevent escalation into nuclear holocaust. Given the proportions of World War III, loss of an early-vintage, over-the-hill, second-generation nuclear submarine was, indeed, a small price to pay for deliverance.

Quite unexpectedly Awesome felt himself rising toward a new and sublime achievement. He alone stood in the path of apocalypse. A preacher's son had been promoted through the ranks of the Submarine Service until he took command of a strategic mission. He was not meant to maim and destroy, but to heal and save. Heal and save he would! After all, wasn't that what Patrol Polynya was all about?

His mind raced with his feet as they carried him double-time up the companionway toward the tactical attack center. Biblical stories flooded his mind, stories of military men—Jephthah, the bastard son of Gilead, who had delivered his people from Ammonite incursions; David, the son of Levi, who had fought the Philistines; Joshua, the warrior son of

Nun, who subdued the myriads of Canaan. The second Isaiah had spoken about the coming savior— a man despised and forsaken, one knowing trouble and disease. God's servants were meant to suffer. With that recognition the cosmic scales shift into balance. Personal travail was not without its purpose. However great his predecessors' accomplishments, Elisha, son of the Reverend Elijah Awesome, could save more. The Reverend Elijah Awesome had saved hundreds, but his son, millions!

1320 hours.
Status 1SQ. Sagi Koranson, shirttails out, forehead flecked with sweat, reported to Awesome in the tactical attack center. "We've got five feet of ice in the pack above us. Not bad. We can break through at zero bubble—flat up."

"Officer of the deck from the captain," Awesome spoke into a phone to the observation platform in the control room. "Let's prepare for breakthrough. Keep our identical posture—south-southwest. Two-one-six true. Watch for any drift and don't blow the ballasts until I give the order."

"Captain from officer of the deck, understand prepare for breakthrough. Maintain identical posture—south-southwest, two-one-six true. Understand: Hold for further orders."

"Very well," Awesome confirmed and replaced the phone. He drew Koranson aside. "Sagi," Awesome spoke with a poise that surprised himself, "we must assume we'll receive a command to fire our birds. To save this crew we're going to have to take some daring steps. I'm prepared. I think you are too. There's only one alternative: The moment *Amundsen* surfaces I want to disembark the men and march them over the ice pack to Kolguyev Island. Once at Kolguyevskiy Severnyy we'll storm the Soviet satellite tracking and weather station, then use the transmitter there to contact Gaffy and arrange a rendezvous with *Yellowtail*. One of us will remain aboard *Amundsen* to fire the first salvo, operate the automatic loaders, fire the second and third salvos, then scuttle the boat."

"What can we do with the wounded?" Koranson's voice was a note higher than usual.

"We'll take them on litters along with whatever else we can salvage from the boat."

"The minute the Russians see *Amundsen* on the surface they'll jump us like wolves."

Awesome concurred. Yet he was not one to underestimate the element of surprise. Never before in modern naval warfare had an entire crew abandoned ship to take refuge on enemy soil. The Soviets would naturally assume *Amundsen*'s crewmen went down with their ship. Before they realized the truth and mobilized a response, *Yellowtail* would have time to rendezvous with *Amundsen*'s crew and then disappear again beneath the ice. "Look, Sagi . . . I recognize the enormous dangers, but it's the only chance. If negotiations between Washington and Moscow are successful, God willing, we'll be ordered to surrender peacefully and the Soviets will make an accommodation for us in their final settlement. But if the negotiations fail and we're ordered to launch, there is going to be chaos in the Baltic and the Barents; the Russians will have neither time nor

296

inclination to bother about a boatload of sailors on a glacier island. In either case, one thing is clear: We can't permit the enemy to capture this vessel. Regardless of what happens, we're going to have to scuttle the boat. It's just a question of time. Better to move now with the element of surprise than later without it. Get the men prepared for a two- or three-day trek on the ice. Strip the sub. Take everything you can carry . . . and see that the wounded are made as comfortable as possible."

"How much time have I got, sir?"

Awesome thought for a moment. "Well, I guess that depends upon if and when we get the order to fire. Technically, I'm supposed to be on the surface for Condition 1SQ. Every second could be important. But I'll take another chance. I'm going to bend the rules a little. We'll delay the actual breakthrough until we're ready to move out on the ice. I'm going to put Sergeant Diller in charge of the assault operation; Haddock, assembling the supplies, food, maps, weapons; Rosenbaum, the wounded. It'll be hell out there, but God help me to save these men."

When Koranson had gone, Awesome went to the phone and flipped the toggle switch for open circuit throughout the sub. "Now hear this. . . . Now hear this. . . . Captain Awesome speaking. . . . Men of the *Amundsen*, please listen carefully. This message will not be repeated. Washington has ordered us to Condition 1SQ. This is not a drill. Repeat: This is not a drill. I know each one of you has always dreaded this moment as I have, but as Navy men, we have been called to protect the United States and cannot back down. Whether or not we shall be commanded to launch our birds, I cannot say. But we must be ready should that order arrive. . . . Our Tomahawks will be one hundred percent effective because we are deep in Soviet water and very close to the targets, perhaps closer than many of you realize. To be exact, we're three hundred and forty statute miles north of our target, only twenty-two miles off the coast of Kolguyev Island. . . ."

Behind the skipper a lone voice proclaimed victory. "I called it! Everybody said I was crazy for grabbing the low number, but I knew we were in Russian territory all the blasted time . . . four hundred smackers!"

"Everyone knows that *Amundsen* has been seriously damaged," Awesome continued. "Neither our sonar nor our radio is operational. We can, however, still launch our birds. If we are ordered to do that, and I must plan as if we will be, it won't take the Soviet Air Force long to locate and attack us. Even if we abort the missile launch, we're still trapped in shallow water. Therefore we have one chance and one chance only. . . . The Russians have a weather satellite tracking station on the north shore of Kolguyev Island about twenty miles from here. As far as we know, it is occupied by only thirty scientists. We are going to capture it, use the radio there to contact *Yellowtail*, now on patrol off the Finmark coast, and expedite a contingency plan for rescue. If we're lucky this nightmare will be over in about fifty hours, but until then things are going to be rough and dangerous. It will be a terrible trek over the ice. I am putting Commander Koranson in charge of the patrol once it leaves the submarine. Sergeant Diller is hereby given a combat commission and will co-ordinate the assault on the ice station. I'm going to remain aboard to fire the Tomahawks once everybody has disembarked and hopefully covered good distance from the submarine. I will rendezvous with you on Kolguyev Island, at Kolguyevskiy Severnyy."

With stupefied expressions the men around him were staring at Awesome. How was it possible to abandon the submarine in subzero temperatures? Nobody said anything about cold-weather combat when volunteers were solicited. Operation Polynya was billed as just another Arctic patrol. Who would have volunteered for an outright invasion of the Soviet Union? It was one thing to trespass in Soviet waters, quite another to violate the sovereignty of Russian land. Trouble with the squawk box was you couldn't reply to it . . . ask questions. And God, there were a thousand questions. Captain Awesome's voice kept coming through the loudspeakers.

"I wish I had time to explain more fully what has happened. All of you have a right to be informed. Yet each second is precious. When we are safe again, I promise to explain everything in detail. For now, we must make immediate preparations for departure to the ice pack. At the last moment we'll break to the surface and disembark. Stand by for further orders." Awesome hesitated. "I want to say, gentlemen, that despite our adversities, *Amundsen* could not have a better crew nor could our country have known braver defenders. God bless each and every one of you. Out."

His head momentarily rested against the bulkhead. Awesome closed his eyes and listened as the crewmen recoiled from the shock. There was much frantic talk, most of it loud and angry. Voices were frightened; a few were full of swagger . . . all were confused.

With so many things to do, there was no time for Awesome to deal with all that personally. He opened his eyes and saw a fire-control technician—a skinny kid, not long out of high school—blinking away tears as he went through his gear to see what he would take with him. Too naïvely and too completely the youth had entrusted his welfare to his superiors. That trust, Awesome remarked to himself, would soon be tested in the freezing polar wind.

Sergeant Diller thrived on crisis. Weren't Marines trained to meet it? The key was discipline and clearly defined purpose. Both he possessed in surplus. With drillmaster's precision, he organized a dozen ten-man squads and conducted minibriefings on weaponry, Arctic survival, and combat tactics. Meanwhile, Rosenbaum assigned his hospital corpsmen to the construction of supplementary litters from the latticed panels in the wardroom. Blankets, gloves, caps, boots, and gray-green insulated nylon parkas with fur collars were piled in the mess. There weren't enough for the whole crew, a fact which produced a few bad jokes and many shivers. Lieutenant Haddock's supply teams transporting food and weapons clogged the submarine's narrow passageways. Chief Kramer's skill at coordinating different jobs was greatly missed.

At 1420 hours Lieutenant O'Connor reported to the skipper that the submarine was standing by for breakthrough. The cold-weather gear had been parceled out. Stretchers and stretcher bearers were waiting in the forward torpedo and aft engine rooms, under the access hatches, ready to move. Beside them were the teams of submariners, each with his backpack of C rations and blankets. Such weapons as were available had been divided among them.

An uncommon quiet had fallen over *Amundsen* when Awesome, Haddock, and O'Connor made their final tour. The decks rang hollowly under their boots; the compartments echoed in the silence. Seamen's quarters were a jumble of turned-out seabags; there was a tangle of clothes underfoot, a hodgepodge of books, letters, and an occasional framed picture of some sailor's family looking up at the ceiling. In the galley, cabinets and lockers remained open, nearly empty; in the mess the papers on the bulletin board fluttered in a draft from the air conditioners; in the control center, computers continued their crepitations. Electronic signals flashed across oscilloscopes with no one to see . . . or care.

Near the periscope stand Awesome turned on the intercom: "Now hear this. . . . Now hear this. . . . Captain Awesome speaking. We are ready for breakthrough. If there's a problem remaining at any station this is your last chance to speak up." Twenty seconds elapsed. When there was nothing but radio crackle, he continued. "Once the submarine surfaces, you must move out fast because the boat will be fully exposed. . . . All right, read out the subsystems."

"Engine room . . . go."

"Fire control . . . on the money . . . green go."

"Launch control . . . green go."

"Reactor compartment . . . noncritical . . . all radiation shielding in place . . . all permanent seals fixed in position . . . green go."

"Integrated monitoring panel . . . check . . . positive."

"Steering station . . . control planes rotated vertical . . . ready."

"All systems go," Koranson repeated. "Ready, Skipper, we're standing by."

Awesome spoke into the phone: "Now hear this. . . . We're ready. Countdown for breakthrough will commence in six-zero seconds. Everybody hold on. . . . We're going up. . . . Then we're all going home." He took a deep breath. "Surface. . . . Surface. . . . Surface. . . ."

The diving Klaxon sounded three times to signal *Amundsen's* ascent. Venting valves closed; flooding valves opened. Compressed air surged into the forward and after ballasts, expelling seawater. *Amundsen* shifted from neutral to positive buoyancy as air bubbles in her main and variable ballasts expanded. Her vertical ascent began slowly but accelerated in proportion to the loss of tonnage. Bulkheads rattled; decks creaked. *Amundsen,* that grand old prowler of the depths, was making her final ascent.

Awesome released the phone and jumped into his observation seat, from where he could see the planesmen and dive officer. "Hold on . . . four . . . three . . . two . . . one . . ."

Men braced themselves against impact. The crunch occurred a second later than expected and was accompanied by a blunt, ear-shattering thud. *Amundsen* listed sharply to starboard but immediately shifted back to port. Overhead, her eighteen-foot sail hammered into the frozen canopy until the ice cracked in a thundering roar, diagonal to her keel. All 3,800 tons of steel slammed mercilessly into the weakened ice, splintering it into huge floes and smaller brash. *Amundsen*'s sail and vertically rotated control planes knifed upward into the Arctic air; fore and aft the 251-foot cylindrical hull battered open an oblong polynya. Far astern the vertical steering plane punched a second hole. With her topside deck, except for the teardrop bow, fully exposed above the ice, the submarine's upward motion ceased.

Awesome was at the attack periscope, his eye pressed against its rubber eyepiece. Weather favorable, he reported—clouds driven by what appeared to be strong winds, good protection against aerial surveillance. He adjusted the focal length of the 8-B periscope lens by twisting its horizontal handles, then walked the scope 360 degrees for a complete sweep of the icescape. Ice and patina snow, but nothing more. "All right, gentlemen. On your way." Sergeant Diller and five seamen scrambled through the forward escape trunk and out the access hatch onto *Amundsen*'s deck over the torpedo room; another half-dozen men exited through the after hatch over the engine room. A confirming weather report was relayed back: a thick medium ceiling of altostratus clouds. A seven-knot wind was blowing from the northeast. The men on the afterdeck screamed for someone inside to pass along a line to establish a footing on the slippery topside.

Two sailors had ascended the twenty-five-inch trunk through *Amundsen*'s sail and exited on the fairwater observation platform called back for others below to give them a hand—an odd request, but no one had time to argue. More boots clambered up the ladder. Those outside were climbing on the starboard control plane. Suddenly a black object appeared in the access scuttle and excited voices instructed those near the top of the ladder. Many hands reached up to help. The object was lowered gently from rung to rung. On the control room deck a technician wailed. "God, it's Commander Riley!"

Rolled onto his back, the engineering officer peered open-eyed into the clear water trapped inside his underwater welding goggles. His frozen lips were still sealed over the Emerson mouthpiece. Icy water ran along the cheeks and neck as Awesome gently unfastened the rubber strap and removed the goggles. Riley's skin, once ruddy and mottled with acne, was blanched, marble cold. His eyes were grotesquely enlarged. Mourners in the control room stood with heads lowered in silence. Awesome recited a short, quick prayer, only vaguely aware that Sidney Killerman was hovering mutely in the doorway behind him. There was nothing immediately available with which to cover the body. Someone improvised with a chart from the navigation center. As he laid it across Riley's face, the skipper sighed. It was a chart of the Lumbrovskiy Channel, where all their troubles had begun.

"Sergeant Diller's already on the ice pack," a voice called down from the bridge. A nod from the skipper signaled for the departure of the first supply and reconnaissance teams. The long line of men and equipment bunched up near the forward scuttle inched closer toward the Arctic air.

*   *   *

1500 hours.

Despite eighty-seven days of patrol neither sunlight nor warm air welcomed *Amundsen*'s crew to the outside world. The temperature was 26° F; the wind-chill factor made it –18° F. A squalling wind peppered frozen hail over ten-foot-tall ice hummocks and whistled around *Amundsen*'s steel hull. The clouds were low, the sky gray except for a single shaft of iridescent light that rose like a rainbow from the horizon and arched toward the northwestern sky. Wind penetrated the crewmen's insufficient clothing and froze the moisture that clung to their beards. A hoar-frosted crust provided poor footing for a small vanguard that ventured from the submarine to reconnoiter the route toward Kolguyev.

Three details, commanded by Lieutenant Haddock, hauled bundles of equipment through the forward and aft scuttles, then along the deck, where they were dropped eight feet to the ice pack below. After a brief probe, Terry Kamakota and two scouts reported that the pack was anything but flat. Pressure against the ice had molded ridges of five to thirty-five feet in height. Wind erosion had cut sharp, irregular sastrugi in the frosted mantle. Brash ice floated in the water leads that crisscrossed the pack. But terrain certain to frustrate the twenty-two-mile journey to Kolguyev would also camouflage *Amundsen*'s crew against detection from the air.

Beside the stretchers waiting to be lifted through the access hatch, Rosenbaum, his pockets bulging with medications, attended his patients. Framed by the forward-compartment watertight door, his silhouette appeared comically top-heavy. He finished adjusting a seaman's blankets and signaled for another stretcher to move out. Red-rimmed eyes, weary with exhaustion, peered through spectacles still smudged with ointment at Awesome, who approached with final instructions. "Marty, if you can't make it with these men, bivouac on the trail. We'll return to get you. If we manage this thing at all, it shouldn't be too long."

"We'll make it," Rosenbaum said. When the last stretcher team left he zipped his parka, shivering suddenly in a draft from the open hatch. "You know," he grinned, "my father used to say that old saw there's no ill wind that doesn't blow some good. We ought to give that one a real good testing today." Scrambling quick-step behind the final stretcher, he paused below the escape trunk and turned for a final glance at Awesome, with a mischievous smile reminiscent of Greerson. "Don't let it bother you too much, but my father was nearly always wrong."

He climbed onto the deck, worked his way to starboard, and jumped overboard. Landing on the frozen ice mantle was harder than he expected. Bottles of medicine rattled against each other in his overloaded pockets. At least one shattered, spilling its contents into the parka seams. When he rose to his feet the full force of the gale attacked his cheeks. Rosenbaum stood erect, suddenly sobered. Already his father's saw was discredited: No good could possibly come from such a compassionless wind.

A sign, hastily painted on cardboard in block letters and decorated with fouled naval anchors, greeted Awesome on his return to the control room. The crew's farewell gift.

OUT OF CONTROL ROOM

Its satire he could accept but not the humor. It was not the least bit funny because it was tragically true. In other times and different circumstances he would have burned with indignation against such callous crewmen. But after all they had suffered you really could not blame them. *Amundsen*'s control room was, in fact, quite out of control.

From the main deck Awesome descended to the lower level and made his way abaft to the reactor compartment. If there were a way to destroy the uranium in *Amundsen*'s nuclear piles he would have done it. But the truth was that nothing could be done to the radioactive fuel other than ensure it would remain noncritical and unlikely to enter a nuclear chain reaction. The control boron rods had already been locked into their reactor cores, emergency shields had been sealed around the inner compartment, and all pressure-resistant watertight doors surrounding the external lead insulation had been welded permanently shut. From the reactor tunnel Awesome read, through a round observation window of lead glass, a Geiger counter inside the compartment. For the final time he turned an observation mirror to inspect the interior, bathed in an artificial emerald light. His last check was on the external Geiger counter and the seals to the insulation doors. *Amundsen* would leak no radiation into the Barents Sea.

Farther abaft in the engine room he rendezvoused

with Lieutenant Howard, who was connecting the final wires on explosive charges in *Amundsen*'s bow, midship, and stern: a textbook procedure, the lieutenant explained, one he had practiced innumerable times at Class "A" Submarine School, San Diego. The detonator, an eight-inch, olive-colored, Army-issue device, battery-operated, was connected by a spool of radio wire to the three charges. Howard demonstrated how to unwind the wire upon departure from *Amundsen* and then how to detonate the explosives. "*Amundsen* deserved a better end," he said ruefully.

"We all did," Awesome replied. Immediately he wished he had kept his mouth shut. Not only was it trite but also it was his first public expression of doubt.

Beside the companionway to the control room, Schroeder met Awesome and handed him a transceiver in a black vinyl case. "Here it is, Cap'n. . . . I just put in fresh batteries so we can expect good reception in the dry air outside. To save power we should coordinate our watches and agree on an exact time to make contact."

Awesome read out the Greenwich Mean Time from his Rolex. "Let's say we'll communicate with each other at precisely five minutes past each hour, starting at 1805. That way we'll be in continuous communication. And, Bill, remind Koranson again not to commence his attack on the tracking station without a confirming order from me. You understand that?"

"Yes, Cap'n . . . I'll tell him. We tested these walkie-talkies outside and they work fine, but don't expect to hear anything inside the boat. Once I'm on the ice pack I'll remain with the crew. . . . I guess I'll see you at Kolguyevskiy Severnyy."

At the escape trunk, at the last moment, Awesome stopped Schroeder. "Bill, I'm sorry about what occurred with Sokorski—for you and for him. I still don't understand what happened to those circuits. Maybe George didn't take them after all. I can't believe someone would do something as cruel as that." He hesitated as though considering whether to say more. The winds howled outside and whistled through the open scuttle. Men were freezing on the ice pack; it no longer mattered who stole the circuits. "Bill, do me a personal favor. I haven't had a chance to speak with Sokorski. Give him my apology."

Schroeder did not understand. When the history of Patrol Polynya was written, Sokorski's name would be featured prominently, if not as a saboteur then certainly as a troublemaker and a contributor to *Amundsen's* tragedy. Schroeder's nod was ambiguous, committing him to nothing. It was clear that the skipper had extended a request, not an order. "Hit 'em hard, Cap'n," he encouraged, changing the subject. "And don't worry about us. . . . I'll get through to Holy Loch on the Kolguyev radio."

"God speed, Bill." Schroeder climbed the last rungs onto the deck. The moment he stood in the lee of the wind he bundled into his parka and took hold of the guideline strung by Sergeant Diller's men. His parting words to Awesome haunted him in the final seconds beside the jumpoff position. How could he have been so confident about the Soviet radio in Kolguyevskiy Severnyy? Who knew what equipment the Russians used, or what condition it would be in after Diller's assault? Arctic winds tore into the exposed skin around Schroeder's cheeks and forehead, ending his speculations.

Awesome turned to survey *Amundsen*'s deserted control room. Until moments before it had been crowded and busy, twenty-four hours a day. Now there was no one but him. Except in the privacy of his stateroom he had been surrounded by other men and had become fully conditioned to their physical closeness: voices, odors, breathing, even the subtle sexuality transmitted by their bodies as they touched in passage. Solitude tempted him to rush topside and order a few men to stay behind. Without voices, the hum of ventilation fans, the crepitation of computers, the buzz of SINS binnacles hummed louder by many decibels.

An unexpected sound sent Awesome whirling about in surprise. It wasn't a mechanical sound—of that he was certain. He had given explicit orders for all hands to disembark; yet somebody was still aboard! Anger at having been disobeyed was dissipated quickly by a genuine sense of relief, for the stowaway's presence eased his acute loneliness. "Who's there?" Awesome advanced on the hydraulic manifold. "Who's there?" His ears had been tricked by an echo in the deserted control room. A sharp turn athwartship compensated for the original error in direction. A figure crossed before fluorescent lighting and threw a momentary shadow over the hull opening panel. Another quick correction brought Awesome on target. The stowaway and the skipper almost collided. But Thomas Laycook stood his ground and refused to budge. "Elisha," he addressed Awesome for the first time in five months by his given name, "you go to Kolguyev. They'll need you there. I can fire the birds."

Awesome made no effort to conceal his contempt. "You'd never push the buttons."

"I can and I will. I can fight as well as you. You're the one who always avoided combat. Now it's my turn. Give me a chance."

"You, Thomas, are responsible for much of this mess. Now get out on the ice before I have you shot. Damn you, men are freezing out there! They can't afford to wait. . . . NOW MOVE!"

"No. My kids have been brainwashed to think their father is a killer because he's a submarine officer. They're right. I *can* kill when necessary to protect them. I want to do what I was trained for, so damn it, let me fight. It's my job. . . . I know more about these Tomahawks than you do. I'm the right man to remain aboard, not you. If you won't let me remain alone, let me stay with you. You'll need help with the automatic loaders."

Awesome shoved Laycook toward the bow. "Get going, Thomas. If you want to fight, do it with Sergeant Diller. But I'd watch he doesn't shoot you in the back. Every man here has reason to detest you. And the colder they get the more they're going to think about those modulator circuits. You'd better watch which way the rifles are aimed."

Laycook pivoted about and strode beyond the skipper's reach. "Did you ever think up a reason why I couldn't manage to return them?"

311

"You'll explain that to me one day . . . after your court-martial." Awesome's voice trembled with indignation. "Now get your ass out on that ice!"

Laycook resisted a second shove by planting his feet firmly on the deck, and when he spoke, the bitter tone of earlier confrontations was gone. The inferno of jealous hatred no longer raged. What had occurred in the wardroom before Koranson and Schroeder was, after all, quite impersonal. He would have left it there had not Awesome threatened a court-martial. That went beyond the impersonal—indeed, struck at the last dignity Laycook preserved of his officer's commission. "It took me a long time, Captain Awesome, to understand why Nick Gaffy chose you rather than me to command this patrol. From the moment we left Holy Loch I've been haunted by the patent injustice of it. I could have handled the insult from anyone else but Nick because Nick I considered my close friend—I'm ashamed to say my closest. That's why the wound he inflicted was so painful—it came from an unexpected quarter where I had no armor for protection. I put myself on trial a hundred times, examined all the facts because I was certain that I had done something to offend my friend. He was beyond betrayal so it had to be I who had erred. Then you put me in hack. I had just explained the mysteries of this patrol and I was right. Still, you didn't want to hear. You were pigheaded and obstinate, simply refusing to listen to the truth. And *that* was my clue! Until that moment I couldn't see the forest for the trees. It was so simple, yet I was blinded by jealousy and by hurt. . . . You see, Captain Awesome, Nick didn't reject *me* . . . he selected *you*. And when I realized that, then I began to ask the right questions: Why among all the possible candidates in the Submarine Service, why from all the experienced skippers available—why did Nicholas Gaffy want *you?* It couldn't have been your technical expertise. Sure, you're well trained. You've passed Rickover's courses like the rest of us. But your special forte is public relations. Nor could it have been your previous experience, because there are officers with more patrol duty than you. So it had to be something else, something that fitted Gaffy's scheme."

Awesome raised his fist but Laycook swept it aside. "Listen to me, Captain. It's important." He put a chair between himself and the captain and gripped the back of it. "To make his nefarious plan work, Nick needed someone in command who was constitutionally incapable of questioning him, someone with such total allegiance that he would be blind to the evidence of deception. I made a mental list of all the possible candidates in the Submarine Service who could have been appointed as commanding officer. There was only one man who fit that profile perfectly—the son of a domineering, almost despotic father, an eloquent, spellbinding preacher, the very deputy of God Himself. You've been trained all your life for this role. Gaffy hand-picked a man who had suffered such personal tragedy that he almost came unglued . . . a man who hungered for even the smallest gesture of human kindness . . . a man who owed his entire career to him. You're the biblical expert, Captain, but I couldn't help thinking of Isaac blindly following his father, Abraham, to be slaughtered.

"But you, Captain Awesome, weren't Nick's only

victim. You see, he didn't trust his own judgment . . . and that's where I fit into this sordid drama. Remember what you did when you needed Riley to repair torpedo tube 6 and didn't trust him? You appointed me to be his watchdog. Nick did the same thing; he assigned me to be *your* executive officer to keep an eye on *you*. This may come as a surprise, but I'm the only man aboard, besides Rosenbaum and Diller, who did not train with Blue Crew. Nor did I volunteer. Gaffy appointed me and when I protested he promised to make it up when we returned. By that time I no longer hungered for his favors. It seems the laugh is on Gaffy, for I had as little influence over you as I did over Riley.

"In one final way, Captain, you were perfect for Nick's plan, and he exploited you as he does everyone else. I wasn't the only commander in the Submarine Service who was outraged when you were promoted. Everybody balked at the reverse discrimination. Nick expected that, though he couldn't care less about compensating for past injustices done to America's blacks. The criticism he could endure because having a black skipper paid dividends. He knew that should *Amundsen* get in trouble and cause an international incident, the public would hold *you* and not *him* to blame. Sure, he'd have to answer to Congress, but he relied upon good old-fashioned American bigotry for support. He understood that white Americans would believe a black man just wasn't up to the responsibility of command. And, what's more, he also knew that black Americans would hide their heads in shame."

"Shame! You think they would be *ashamed?*" Awesome was nearly blind with rage. "At this

314

moment I am still captain of this vessel and I am ordering you to GET OFF THIS BOAT! Tell your crap to the court-martial. God help me to reach that day of justice. NOW GET OUT!"

"God help us both, Captain," Laycook answered. He supposed he never really expected the skipper to understand. Awesome was right in one thing: They could not continue to argue the merits of his interpretation while good men were freezing on the ice pack. Besides, it really made no difference anyway. There was little purpose in laboring to comprehend the past when the future was so forbidding. Donning the hooded parka, Laycook stepped through the watertight door and jumped the first rungs of the ladder to the access hatch. Moments later he had dropped from the submarine's topside to the ice pack below.

Awesome gave the control room a final inspection. He too donned his parka and hoisted himself up the ladder through the sail to the fairwater on *Amundsen*'s bridge. Strong winds greeted him the moment he climbed through the hatch to the platform. Small particles of ice gusted against his skin and peppered the submarine's black hull. Forward and aft the colorless icescape stretched monotonously toward the horizon. It was impossible to discern precisely where the ice stopped and the dull, grayish sky began. Near the black ship, crewmen huddled between pressure ridges to protect themselves against powerful winds. Hail flurries interrupted Sergeant Diller, who barked Marine drill commands to keep his men in tight formation. His orders were obeyed so long as the sailors faced leeward, but when the wind shifted suddenly, they readily abandoned their squads to find shelter among the hummocks. A single sailor glanced up toward *Amundsen*'s bridge and waved both hands: Hendrick Phearson.

Awesome grinned and signaled for Phearson to alert Koranson. The operations chief trudged over the ice to a position below *Amundsen*'s control planes. "On your way, Koranson," Awesome called. "We're ready now."

"Yes, sir. Good-by, sir." Koranson saluted and turned away.

Near the stern, Terry Kamakota marched forward, slowly activating the column behind him. Like a caterpillar, the ship's company bunched and separated over the slick crust, staggering the first small steps toward Kolguyevskiy Severnyy. Stretcher bearers lifted their loads and struggled for traction in and around footholds established by those already lost from sight.

"See you at Kolguyev . . . God speed," Awesome yelled into the wind, knowing that only syllables, not words, reached those on the ice pack below. He squinted into the fading afternoon light to read the large black initials inked on the parkas of men bent forward into the wind. U. . . . S. . . . S. In America the initials were read "United States Ship," but in Scotland as "Underwater Strategic Services." The sailor assigned to bring up the rear pivoted with a final salute. When he turned to follow the last stretcher, Awesome noted the other three initials that his eyes had unconsciously avoided: E. . . . R. . . . A. . . . He repeated the letters very distinctly and very slowly: "E. . . . R. . . . A.—*Edmond Roald Amund-*

sen.'' As the rear guard dwindled into the landscape, he watched until he could no longer tell if he was seeing men out there or only blowing snow. "Good-by, *Edmond Roald Amundsen.''* He had long been conscious that his personal initials were identical with those of his submarine. An ominous coincidence; Good-by, Elisha Ross Awesome.

For the last time he scanned the skies for Russian aircraft. Soon, very soon, sleek, silvery jets would dip low beneath the cloud layer, their wings blazing with fiery rockets aimed at *Amundsen's* unprotected hull. In sortie after sortie, the murderous birds would swoop down over the ice pack, dispatch their deadly ordnance, and rise again through the clouds to the bright sunshine high above. His eyes fell again to the desolate icescape, which had swallowed his crew like uninvited intruders, as if their presence was never destined for more than a brief, uncomfortable stay. A deep sadness overwhelmed him as he descended below.

Amundsen had been reduced into a ghost ship indeed, a mere skeleton of steel and machinery, its vital organs eviscerated, its bloodstream dry. Awesome ignored the gnawing loneliness by concentrating on the integrated monitoring panel in the tactical attack center. When he was certain the Tomahawks were prepared for launch, he moved aft to the fire-control console, which synthesized the ship's speed, missile alignment, trajectory data, Tomahawk's guidance package (inertial guidance systems composed of accelerators and gyroscopes), and all interlocks. Two rows of launch buttons, three on each side, fluoresced eerily as if challenging him

317

to depress them. With *Amundsen* on the surface nothing prevented actual launch but interlocking mechanisms operated by the two permission-to-fire keys. One Commander Koranson had inserted in the lock for Tomahawk 1, the other remained in Awesome's pocket until inserted into a second lock. Both keys turned in unison. An ivory NO GO switch changed to brilliant emerald-green GO. Awesome repeated the procedure for Tomahawks 2 through 5.

The switch for Tomahawk 6 he dusted with his fingertips, ignoring their trembling. He needed only enough strength to press five buttons, then activate the automatic loaders for the second and third salvos. After that there was nothing to do but scuttle *Amundsen* and follow the path Sergeant Diller had been instructed to leave behind en route to Kolguyevskiy Severnyy.

How long he would have to wait before hearing from Squadron he had no idea. It could not be too long, for Gaffy had ordered him to Status 1SQ and knew that *Amundsen* was awaiting orders on the surface—exposed to Soviet surveillance. But what the admiral did not know was that the longer she waited before beginning an attack, the better chance her crew had for reaching Kolguyev Island undetected.

TA-DEEP . . . TA-DEEP . . . TA-DEEP . . .

Awesome spun toward the cryptocenter. Despite all his mental preparation for a communication from Squadron he was still unnerved. As he expected, Squadron was bypassing the radio camouflage and, in the interest of saving time, was transmitting directly through the cryptographic machine. Commence attack . . . or abort? Would there be some other change? Targets? No, that was impossible. . . . *Amundsen*'s Tomahawks carried only two TER-COM digital map systems, and with no crew it was too late to change from Nar'ian Mar. Awesome's mind was flooded with hypothetical situations, his eyes blurred over the IBM Selectric ball as it began transcribing a message to the readout paper. Behind the lightning-quick printer he devoured the words:

AMUNDSEN: RED ALERT CANCELED. REPEAT: RED ALERT CANCELED. ABORT ALL MISSILES. REPEAT: ABORT ALL MISSILES. DOWNGRADE TO CONDITION 2SQ IMMEDIATELY AND HOLD. DIPLO-MATIC ACTIVITY SUCCESSFUL. UNITED STATES ANSWERS RUSSIAN ULTIMA-TUM BY DENYING SUBMARINE PRES-ENCE IN SOVIET WATERS. CONTINUED SECRECY URGENT. MAINTAIN RADIO SILENCE. DO NOT ALTER POSITION. REPEAT: DO NOT ALTER POSITION. HOLD FOR FURTHER ORDERS. OUT.

He ripped the yellow paper from the teleprinter and reread each word as instant euphoria circulated from his head to the extremities of his body. The marvelous news was a narcotic to his brain, a tranquilizer for his raw nerves. From the scanty evidence provided in the messages from Holy Loch he proposed a scenario: After the explosion had revealed *Amundsen*'s presence in Soviet waters, the enemy mobilized. As they had done in Cuba and on several occasions in the Middle East, the Russians unsheathed their sabers and like wild Cossacks twirled them in the air hoping to frighten their adversaries into capitulation. But Gaffy had nerves of forged steel. He acted with infinite patience and caution, knowing the deterrent power of forty-one Polaris and Poseidon submarines held in reserve. Unable to intimidate him, the Russians would end their war dance. There was nothing the enemy could do but return its lethal weapons to its scabbards and accept Gaffy's terms.

Awesome pivoted on his toes and surveyed the vacant attack center. The Tomahawks at Status 1SQ were primed like dynamite to explode. During the moments of waiting, he himself had come to believe that attack was inevitable, that in due course he would become the spearhead of America's assault. History had hung in the balance, its future in the hands of a few men. Never had he thought that a black boy from the farmlands of Kentucky could share in a deed of such human magnitude. It was as if sentence had been pronounced and then at the last moment mercifully commuted. Millions of human beings spared. Squinting through moist eyes he read the chronometer: Greenwich Mean Time: 1618.

"With these tired, tormented black hands," he mumbled, the message rotating in his fingers. When he raised his eyes he saw his own image in the glass panels alongside six Tomahawk launch buttons. From the outset Patrol Polynya had been plagued by misfortune, but in its darkest moments when he had lost all but the faint spark of hope he heard Gaffy's voice admonishing him from across the ocean.

Though separated by great distance the two men had exchanged unspoken messages in private intercourse. "Words," the admiral had written, "are only encumbrances between us."

The face in the glass opposite him had eyes glazed with fatigue, lips cracked from gnawing, cheeks drawn by tension. Thomas Laycook could not bear to accept the truth that Nicholas Gaffy had selected a black man to stand with him at the most crucial juncture in modern times. He had ordained him to be his own proxy at history's vortex, where no human had stood before: no emperor, king, president, scientist, philanthropist, no writer, scholar, humanitarian, or statesman. . . .

TA-DEEP . . . TA-DEEP . . . TA-DEEP. The cryptographic machine sputtered again. Awesome was jolted by the unexpected noise and involuntarily sprang to his toes. His eyes followed the wake of the printing ball:

AMUNDSEN: NEW RED ALERT. REPEAT: NEW RED ALERT. DISREGARD PREVIOUS COMMUNICATION. REINSTATE CONDITION 1SQ. FIRE TOMAHAWK 6 A-LONE. REPEAT: FIRE TOMAHAWK 6 A-LONE. EXECUTE ORDER IMMEDIATELY AND RETURN TO INTERNATIONAL WATERS. OUT.

Awesome reread the instructions aloud, aware of a contradiction, though not clear what it was. The Soviets had discovered *Amundsen's* presence in the Barents, saber-rattled, and then backed down. Now

Squadron had ordered a single 1,000-pound high-explosive warhead dispatched toward the enemy guidance center at Nar'ian Mar. But a single Tomahawk did not pack enough fire power to destroy it. Perhaps it was intended as a warning probe, the Navy's symbolic shot across the bow. Was it in response to a flare-up on the Horn of Africa . . . in the Persian Gulf . . . or Korea? No way of knowing. Nor with respect to *Amundsen* was the reason important.

But Tomahawk 6 couldn't fire! There had been leakage through the muzzle door; its WRT drain had been damaged. Had he forgotten to notify Admiral Gaffy about that? No . . . it was impossible to inform him because the modulator circuits were missing from the transmitter. And then the booster rocket had blown up . . . that was right, wasn't it? Yes. He remembered. Six men had been killed.

FIRE TOMAHAWK 6 ALONE. REPEAT: FIRE TOMAHAWK 6 ALONE.

The words resonated and finally clanged together in a wild, internal echo that ricocheted from the walls of his cerebral cortex. There had to be some mistake! Tomahawk 6 had a short lanyard. To fire it would ignite 390 pounds of booster-rocket fuel, followed by 385 pounds of solid-propellant turbojet fuel, and finally 1,000 pounds of chemical high explosive. There had to be some mistake. . . . It was impossible to fire Tomahawk 6!

Awesome fell on his knees and searched for the previous yellow readout he had dropped to the deck.

Certain it had fallen over the rubber deck runner, he crawled on all fours. At last he saw it, half hidden between the computers. He held it in trembling fingers before his eyes; all but the essential phrases blurred. By contrast, those he remembered as pertinent appeared suspended in relief:

UNITED STATES ANSWERS RUSSIAN ULTIMATUM BY DENYING SUBMARINE PRESENCE IN SOVIET WATERS. . . .

ULTIMATUM . . . an American submarine had trespassed into Soviet waters. A dangerous cancer, she had to be excised from the body of Mother Russia . . . rejected . . . irradiated . . . destroyed . . . utterly obliterated. If the United States failed to perform the essential surgery the Soviet Navy would . . . and that ultimately meant nuclear war. Gaffy's denial that an American submarine had penetrated Soviet defenses was a mere diplomatic formality . . . a face-saving falsehood that served the interests of both superpowers. Well before *Amundsen* had been detected, Admiral Gaffy considered this contingency. He had shortened the lanyard in Tomahawk 6 to perform for the Soviets what they could not do for themselves without perpetrating a nuclear holocaust!

FIRE TOMAHAWK 6 ALONE. REPEAT: FIRE TOMAHAWK 6 ALONE. EXECUTE ORDER IMMEDIATELY AND RETURN TO INTERNATIONAL WATERS. OUT.

*　　*　　*

Awesome dragged himself toward the fire-control console and stared at the single launch he had purposely failed to activate with his permission-to-fire keys. Thomas Laycook had been right from the beginning: the loss of *Scorpion* in 1968 . . . the Riga broadcast announcing *Amundsen*'s demise a decade later . . . the missing modulator circuits . . . and finally the order to self-destruct. From the moment *Scorpion* had been fraudulently "recommissioned" as *Edmond Roald Amundsen* and had departed from Holy Loch on Patrol Polynya she was no more than a nautical kamikaze. With cunning dissimulation she had been written off a decade before near the Azores, then once again two days after *Amundsen*'s departure from Scotland. Finally, in an act of unconscionable duplicity, she had been ordered to her grave.

In the reflecting glass of the console Awesome saw the real Elisha Awesome—no longer the Navy's wonderboy who had survived personal tragedy to emerge at the vortex of modern history, no longer proxy for the men who cushioned Western civilization from nuclear holocaust, no longer the savior of millions. He saw himself turned inside out, the human being he had tried so desperately to avoid. Before him was the face of a black man home from menial labor, weary from toil that had sapped his health, humiliated by work that made other men rich and himself poor. He scorned the image, loathing himself as the victim of human deception as much as the man who perpetrated it. Beyond even that: He would have traded roles with the scoundrel to have escaped the desolation of the fool.

"Goddamn you, Nicholas Gaffy!" The echo of

Awesome's voice thundered against the tight bulkheads. "A hundred and twelve lives—as though they didn't exist . . . to cover up what you had no business starting in the first place. You treacherous, perfidious sonofabitch . . . Goddamn you! You engineered this whole sordid scheme. You planned to use me from the moment we met in Newport News. Then you had me transferred from Washington to carry out your scheme."

As his fingers ranged over the launch buttons primed to fire the first salvo of Tomahawks at Nar'ian Mar, Awesome visualized the emerald GO lights switching to scarlet FIRE and one by one the missiles blasting into the polar sky. There was sweet revenge in the imagined specter of Nicholas Gaffy, sitting in his control room at Holy Loch and monitoring the missiles as they lifted into the air. The massive holocaust he had so meticulously schemed to prevent was unfolding before his very eyes. Each daring step he had taken, each clever ruse he had invented, each fail-safe precaution he had engineered had worked . . . admirably . . . every one . . . except one. Gaffy had fatally miscalculated Elisha Awesome's fidelity. However desolate within there were limits beyond which his black boy would not and could not be pushed. In that moment of realization Nicholas Gaffy would experience the utter powerlessness he had never known. The man who exploited human frailty would come to recognize impotence in himself. There could be no more fitting retribution for betrayal, no better punishment for the father's abuse of his son.

Black fingers continued to hover over the emerald

buttons, waiting for instructions to right the scales of justice. Green lights did not change to scarlet, but instead blended into a kaleidoscopic maze of crimson, yellow, and blue shining from the windows behind the choir loft in the United Methodist Church of Frankfort. The summer sunlight filtered through stained-glass panels and passed between his father's fingertips spread in blessing over the heads of the congregation. Giant larger-than-life shadows of those hands were cast against the western wall an instant before his fingers rested upon Elisha's head and charged him with the responsibility to heal. The transfer of power electrified his body, infusing it with well-being and strength. His childhood memory of the moment endured until the crimson, yellow, and blue colors faded from his vision. Once again, the emerald buttons shone bright on the fire-control console before him. Steady fingers dusted each of the launch buttons without fear; no rebellious nerve would cause them to fire a Tomahawk accidentally. The symbolic gesture of revenge was swift but complete. A moment later he triggered the ABORT LAUNCH switch and then with the permission-to-fire keys closed down each missile system in turn. Hundreds of electronic impulses were automatically wiped clean from the computer memory banks, and the crew's laborious work of spinning up the missiles for launch was instantaneously erased.

Crepitations from the computers suddenly ceased, leaving only the swish of the air conditioners in the background. How long the Soviets would delay their inevitable attack on *Amundsen* depended upon Moscow's patience in waiting for a response to its ultimatum. When Awesome had permanently closed down *Amundsen's* missile system he ended his role in the drama. Thank God, he had given Koranson strict orders not to attack the Soviet tracking station without confirmation. It was clear *Amundsen's* crew could now do no better than surrender peacefully to the Soviets on Kolguyev and hope for an agreement of repatriation. At least there would be no more loss of life.

Awesome glanced at his watch: 1700 hours. If he hurried, he could be on the ice pack in time to be in touch with Schroeder and Koranson at 1805. If he hurried. A dash down the companionway to the second deck and through officers' country brought him to his cabin.

An M14 rifle, three clips of 7.62mm ammunition, a Xeroxed map, a compass, some matches in a watertight canister, canned foods, and Sterno were left on his bunk by Lieutenant Haddock. Schroeder's transceiver and Howard's scuttling detonator were on his desk. Awesome quickly rummaged through his clothing locker for thin undergarments and proceeded to cover himself with three layers of nylon coveralls. Sergeant Diller had stressed repeatedly that many layers of thin clothing produced better insulation against cold than a few layers of thick clothes. Three pairs of socks cramped his toes inside thick combat boots, and one pair had to be removed. British-issue Wellingtons fit snugly over the boots after determined pulling. Next came the knapsack. Photos of Maxine and the children were packed near the bottom; above them, the food, Sterno, walkie-talkie, and Howard's detonator.

Awesome quickly wiggled into his cold-weather parka, shouldered the knapsack, and slung the M14 beside it. As he passed the bunk his eyes dropped over Dreadnought's bowl. The turtle languished serenely on his island sanctuary, mesmerized by a reflection in the glassy water. There was small comfort in the thought that the reptile's species had survived from the Paleozoic Era, virtually unaffected by natural selection and evolution. It would, no doubt, continue long after *Homo sapiens* had extinguished itself from the earth. Perhaps, Awesome wondered, Charles Riley was wrong after all, and Dreadnought was right: Survival was vouchsafed not for those who fixed what was wrong but for those who hid and waited.

Once before Awesome had inadvertently abandoned the reptile to die and once before his own health had been linked with its survival. He scooped the turtle into his hand and quickly tucked him into his breast pocket. Tiny spiked claws scratched through the nylon undergarment against his chest. "No more strolls in the Garden of Eden, little one."

There was one thing more—the leather-bound Bible, gift from Gaffy, but only the book itself. The admiral had nothing to do with the words inside, or with what memories they evoked, those idyllic, dreamy Sundays in church. The Bible, Pappy always taught, was a bulwark for lives on the verge of collapse. His son weighed the 2½-pound volume in his hands. It was really too heavy to take . . . but he wanted it; he needed it. The fat tome found a place in his knapsack beside Howard's detonator.

Once again in the control room, he stood before

the hull opening panel. Affectionately referred to as the "Christmas tree," it possessed rows of red circles and green bars to indicate the disposition of hull and backup valves for venting and flooding the ballast tanks. One last job: to light up the Christmas tree with red circles, open the vents, and flood the ballast tanks, scuttling the ship—fast and without ceremony. In that brief moment, he imagined the control room filled with crewmen; voices were chattering and there was the chink of coffee mugs near the radio shack. An epitaph for the submariners who never returned from World War II came to mind. It was engraved on an old Mark Thirteen torpedo at the Naval Academy: "Still on Patrol." *Amundsen* was soon to begin her eternal patrol in the deep.

TA-DEEP . . . TA-DEEP . . . TA-DEEP . . . a familiar beep distracted him from the open door of the cryptocenter. Damn it, he had forgotten to turn the blasted instrument off. No more chicanery. No more messages from Gaffy. Not now. Not ever. It was too late to worry about anything but saving *Amundsen*'s crew. His only concern was to salvage 104 lives from the wreckage of Patrol Polynya.

TA-DEEP . . . TA-DEEP . . . TA-DEEP . . . Awesome headed for the cryptographic machine, determined to put an end to the infernal noise. An inner voice told him not to look, but at the last minute he couldn't help it.

AMUNDSEN: WASHINGTON: NICK GAFFY . . .

Gaffy in Washington? That startled him. All

previous communications had originated from Scotland. As a matter of principle, Gaffy traveled to Washington only when absolutely necessary, demonstrating his independence by his physical distance from the Pentagon. He feared the President's power, detested the Chiefs of Staff, and with visceral animosity abhorred Robert Katzenback. Gaffy would go to almost any lengths to avoid submitting himself to their jurisdiction, but there he was, wallowing in the Potomac muck, cajoling and beguiling the brass to avoid fouling himself.

ELISHA: URGENT. SOVIET DEADLINE FOR ULTIMATUM IMMINENT. IN GOD'S NAME FIRE TOMAHAWK 6. LAST CHANCE. THROW THE BALL, PEABODY. PEABODY, PEABODY, THROW THE BALL OR ALL IS LOST. NICHOLAS. OUT.

"Up your ass, Nick! Peabody's on his own now. Even if I could, I wouldn't throw the ball. Peabody's not throwing your ball!"

A moment later, red circles on the Christmas tree panel replaced green bars. Vents opened; flooding commenced. There was a slight shift beneath his feet. *Amundsen* had begun her final dive.

8

KOLGUYEV ISLAND

(Patrol Polynya: 60th day plus 28)

Bitter winds gusted from the northeast. Awesome poked his head through the access hatch on the aft deck, then for a final second ducked back to enjoy the submarine's warmth. The luxury was short-lived; *Amundsen* was sinking below the ice pack. Already her forward deck was fully submerged. Amidship, port and starboard of the sail, dark green-blue water could be seen where her hull parted from the ice. A crying groan of steel and ice in friction hastened Awesome's departure. He unfastened the reel of detonator wire, freeing it to unwind as he made his way over the ice pack. The knapsack and rifle preceded him to the white mantle. A moment later, he followed with an arching leap.

The ice under Awesome's feet absorbed little impact as he struck the hard surface and toppled forward, braking his fall with his gloved hands. The M14 served as a walking stick to assist his balance on the slippery surface. For a hundred yards he followed along an ice rill, feeding out the detonator wire. On a seven-foot pressure ridge he paused to glance back. *Amundsen*'s radar periscope, search radar and VLF antenna alone were visible atop the fairwater.

Whisking away ice flakes that the wind had blown up into his face, Awesome stood at attention for a formal salute. His eyes became watery and a frozen crust formed upon his cheeks. Last to submerge, the submarine's VLF antenna slipped from sight beneath the polynya. The detonator spool ran out wildly and then stopped. A few more steps over the hummocky ice consumed the remainder of the lead wire.

No article of clothing seemed sufficient to protect his body against the billowing wind. He turned against it and huddled over his knees. "When you come to the end of the wire, Skipper," Howard had instructed him, "just touch these wires from the batteries to the detonator poles. Negative to positive: positive to negative." It was not that easy. In the cold his fingers were stiff and clumsy. Shifting winds repeatedly confounded his efforts to spin a wing nut over the battery pole. After several vain attempts the nut slipped between his fingers and was lost somewhere on the ice. Improvisation consumed more time. When the circuit was almost closed Awesome rotated on his heels toward the spot where *Amundsen* had gone down. Wind or no wind, he couldn't destroy her with his back turned. He stretched the wire full length between his hands, carefully directed an exposed end over the appropriate pole, and made contact. A stiff air current swished through the fluted pressure ridges and partially muffled the delayed thud beneath him as the first charge detonated in *Amundsen's* bow. The water pressure (at her depth, approximately 120 pounds per square inch) reduced the explosive thrust. Powerful sound waves alone escaped the physical implosion at *Amundsen's* grave site.

The ice above the submarine had already levitated several feet when the second explosive discharged amidship. An enormous lightning-shaped grid knifed along the surface of the ice around the polynya. No sooner had the mantle above *Amundsen* settled to its original plane when the stern charge detonated. The aftershock produced new tributaries in the frozen canopy. Brash ice commingled with floating debris that had escaped from the wreckage beneath. Then, as quickly as the disturbance had begun, the ice stopped shrieking. Its final groans were absorbed by the relentless winds.

He glanced at his watch: 1802. Only three minutes from the prearranged time to contact his crew. The power switch and volume control on the transceiver were easier to manage than Howard's detonator. It had been only three hours and four minutes since the crew departed, though it seemed like days. He could scarcely wait to hear their voices. "Bill . . . Bill . . . Awesome here. Come in . . . come in. Can you read me?" It was a full ninety seconds before the stipulated time; nevertheless, he released the transmission switch, urging Schroeder's reply and straining to hear a voice among the monotonous crackles of polar static.

"Men of the *Amundsen* . . . do you read me? . . . Come in. . . . Come in. . . ." He huddled tighter against the wind and yelled into the speaker, unconsciously calling over the ice in the southerly direction of Kolguyev Island. "Come in! . . . come in! . . ." When he looked at his Rolex again it was exactly five minute past the hour. "This is Captain Awesome. Do you read me? . . . Come in! . . ." Four more minutes past the designated time. "Come in, *Amundsen*. . . . Do you read me? . . ." Static alone filled the airwaves.

He hid what remained from the lead wire and detonator in an ice fracture. Within hours the polynya above *Amundsen* would have the beginnings of a new frozen crust. Days later there would be little superficial trace of her grave site, leaving nothing for the enemy to pick up from her remains. Awesome turned, once again, to the south. The tracks of those who had preceded him were still visible in the failing light. With some luck and a good moon one could follow them for hours.

Progress was frustratingly slow until Awesome learned to shift his weight far forward over the toes and almost fall into the path. After twenty minutes he found the first of Sergeant Diller's red dye markers left for his benefit at five-hundred-yard intervals. Through a region where hummocks were too high for scaling, the path became circuitous. Each step forward toward Kolguyev required six or seven steps laterally, and somewhere in the rills and channels he lost Diller's trail. At 1905 hours he tried to contact his men, and for the second time failed. Perhaps high pressure ridges were responsible for the radio interference; perhaps abnormal atmospheric conditions. Sooner or later the icescape would level off and permit communication. Even if it did not, the wounded could not be transported after nightfall. By morning he was certain to overtake their bivouac.

The chronic pains that had never been reported to Dr. Greerson returned to plague his thigh and gradually shifted higher into his hip. The straps on the knapsack dug into his bruised shoulder, exacerbating the relentless ache. Yet despite these discomforts, Awesome managed to increase both the frequency and the length of his stride.

By 1945 hours, light was fading. The violence of the wind abruptly abated, and the cold became more bearable. He found himself on the summit of a twenty-foot ridge that, in the twilight, appeared to drop precipitously into a flat ice field and extend south to the Kolguyev shoreline. The moon did not rise in the eastern sky. Perhaps it would later. Awesome needed rest and the bluff provided a fine location from which to make radio contact with his crew. Better to bivouac there until morning and resume his march with the sun.

He settled on the escarpment. Without the wind there was a timeless serenity about the polar world. Arctic peace calmed him and for a long time he sat quietly enjoying its tranquillity. At 2005 it was time to establish contact with his crew. "Bill, do you read me? This is Awesome. . . . Men of *Amundsen* . . . this is Captain Awesome speaking. . . . Do you read me? . . ." Only static. Always the same damn static. But this time its crackle was noticeably fainter since the electrochemical charge in the dry cells was weakening. "Where the hell are you guys? . . ."

he cried. "Damn it, Schroeder, come in. . . . Schroeder . . . this is Awesome. . . . Goddamn you, why don't you answer? Where the hell is everybody? Come in. . . . COME IN. . . . You've got to be out there. . . ."

When no contact was made at sixteen minutes past the hour Awesome switched off the transceiver. Sheltered by an extraordinary ice configuration jutting skyward like a giant monolith, he warmed himself by his Sterno stove and closed his eyes. Gentle heat from the flame soothed his wind-burned skin. Cuddled into himself, the outside world was bearable. Dreadnought's way.

Perhaps, he speculated, Schroeder had misunderstood the time to make contact. If so, their messages had been crossing at unknown intervals. To test that hypothesis required using the transceiver at different intervals during the hour and further draining valuable power in its batteries. A costly gamble, but one he had to take. Awesome tried for two hours, with no more success than his previous attempts. Fatigue eventually overwhelmed him and he curled into his parka to sleep. Somewhere, lost in the vast darkness beyond, *Amundsen*'s crew was also at rest. He imagined their heavy breathing in the stillness of the Arctic night and small fires from their bivouac punctuating the black icescape. His own sleep was short and very fitful.

Early sunlight bathed the ice pack in gentle gold and silhouetted Kolguyev's hills against a dark horizon. Far faster than at the equator, the Nordic sun rose like a fireball, perching for but a moment atop the island hills before leaping into a still-clouded sky. Awesome greeted the dawn with relief and quickly gathered his gear. As he shrugged the knapsack over his parka, a faint growling noise penetrated the background whistle of the morning breeze. It originated in the north, in the direction of *Amundsen*. Pitch and volume rose simultaneously until the distant rumble turned into a screaming, steady roar. Jet aircraft! Nothing could be seen through the thick cumulonimbus clouds above, but the din of their passage and the howl of their afterburners were impossible to mistake. At first they swept past individually at high altitudes, their echoes lagging several seconds behind. Later they streaked by closer to the ground in wing formations, leaving wakes of reverberating thunder. Judging by the direction of their flight and the high-pitched growl of their engines they were Sukhoi and MiG fighter-bombers, probably from the Soviet airbases at Ut'tsilma and Mezen.

As the roar of the engines waned, more horrifying sounds came from the distance: intermittent thuds . . . flat and dull . . . individually and then in rapid succession. . . . Isolated on the icy plateau, Awesome peered through the morning dawn. He could imagine, too clearly, Kolguyev's tundra exploding with white-phosphorus fire and smoldering with the afterscorch of napalm. One after another he saw enemy jets descend beneath the clouds, dipping under a thousand feet as they approached the target zone to align their sights. Thud . . . thud . . . thud . . . Awesome wailed in response. "God help me . . . I'm too late! They won't know to surrender!"

"Bill . . . Bill . . . Do you read me? . . . Do you read me? *Amundsen*, come in!" Awesome cried into the walkie-talkie. "Why don't you guys answer me? . . .

Christ, why don't you guys talk to me?" He fumbled frantically with the antenna, pointing it in several directions. How fast could they have traveled with the wounded? Diller had marked on the map several possible bivouac sites. The men had to be at one of them, but why weren't they answering?

More jets screeched overhead, so close to the ice pack that Awesome thought he saw their silvery undersides through the clouds. A few words of prayer snagged in his throat and refused to reach his lips. "Men of the *Amundsen* . . . come in. . . . Come in, *Amundsen*. . . . Come in. . . . Come in. . . ." The static sounded louder and was accompanied by a pit-pat . . . pit-pat sequence that continued to repeat itself. That was something new. And it was coming through the walkie-talkie! Hastily he turned the antenna back and forth, trying to tune in.

Another jet dipped below the clouds, temporarily distracting his attention. A portion of its fuselage and tail was visible as it banked south toward the tracking station at Kolguyevskiy Severnyy. He crouched over the radio; the pit-pat, pit-pat was all too familiar. Small-arms fire! "Come in. . . . Come in. . . . COME IN, *AMUNDSEN*," he howled.

At the other end a voice was pitifully weak. "Elisha . . . Elisha . . . Do you read me?"

Awesome switched for transmission. "Yes . . . yes . . . Awesome here. . . . Awesome . . . here. Is that you, Bill?"

Amid the patter of gunfire the voice faltered. Its first words were lost. ". . . mas . . . Thomas here. . . . Thomas . . . Can you read me?"

"Yes, Thomas . . . go ahead! Go ahead!"

"Sagi's dead . . . strafed by fighter planes. We're under attack. They're coming in wave after wave. No let-up. We can't hold on much longer. Hundreds of planes. They must think we're the whole American Army. There's no cover. The men are scattered with nowhere to hide. Elisha, we've stumbled into a new guidance ground station for the SS-20. The whole island is laid with camouflaged grids and radio dishes. Intelligence was right. We were twenty miles from our prime target all the time. The Russians must have understood their vulnerability at Nar'ian Mar!"

The bombardment at Laycook's end sounded sharper and closer to his transceiver. While Awesome waited for the noise to recede he weighed the extent of *Amundsen*'s tragedy. Laycook's revelation explained the unexpected massing of the Soviet Navy in and around Kolguyev Island. Since the Lumbrovskiy Channel the Russians had appeared at times aggressive and at other times uninterested, but always in greater numbers than anticipated. *Arktika, Dskari, Svetlivyiare* crisscrossed the Barents, constantly changing course. Icebreakers from Severodvinsk on the White Sea debouched into the Barents. Submarine chasers and attack submarines maneuvered south of Bugrino.

No one understood the Soviet Union's vulnerability during the transition period better than military authorities in Moscow. A task force from the Baltic Fleet had been assembled in the Barents to stand guard while electronic equipment was being transferred from Nar'ian Mar to Kolguyevskiy Severnyy. The influenza epidemic on the Kanin Peninsula had been fabricated to seal off the area while critical equipment was being transported to Kolguyev Island. Through it all, *Amundsen*'s presence had never been discovered! She had been positioned right where Gaffy intended her to be—only her Tomahawks were programed for the wrong target!

More explosions near Laycook drowned out his voice. Between blasts Awesome heard blood-curdling human screams and felt himself in the midst of the fighting; the heat of the flames searing his own skin, smoke clouding his eyes. "Thomas . . . Thomas . . . surrender. For God's sake, surrender."

"We can't . . . napalm . . . they're massacring us!"

Incendiary detonations interrupted communication for several more seconds. Laycook's voice returned, remarkably stoic. "The men are burning. Elisha, it's a holocaust. . . . The men are burning. . . . The men are burning. . . ."

"For Christ's sake, Thomas, surrender. . . . Do you understand me? Surrender. Save yourselves. . . ."

There was no immediate response—only the increased rumble of rockets and now . . . mortars. Each round sounded closer.

Laycook's voice was faintly audible and fading. "No surrender . . . they won't let us. . . . Sokorski was machine-gunned with a white flag. . . . We've tried a dozen times to surrender. There's no mistake. They want to massacre us. No prisoners."

Awesome repeated to himself the words, no prisoners. . . . The myth of *Amundsen*'s burial near the Azores in January now served *both* superpowers. Just as Underwater Strategic Services could not publicly admit its cunning, so the Soviets could not admit that an American submarine had penetrated its defenses and threatened its vulnerable missile-guidance centers. Both militaries were careening toward nuclear cataclysm, but as far as their civilian governments understood, there was no *casus belli* and no provocateur! What stood between combat of unimaginable proportions were 104 lightly armed, poorly clothed, and non-combat-trained submariners on a remote, desolate island. Since neither military admitted their existence and neither government knew of them, they were less than what military tacticians categorize as expendable. NO PRISONERS . . . NO RECORDS . . . NO EVIDENCE. *Scorpion* had died a decade before; now it was *Amundsen*'s turn. Her crew had months before joined the roster of those "Still on Patrol."

"Where are you, Thomas?" Awesome called over the ice field.

"One mile southeast of the tracking station . . . on a two-hundred-foot hill . . ."

Vibrations from the intense mortar fire rattled the speaker. Through smarting eyes Awesome watched an ocher-colored halo rise over Kolguyev's northern shore. Like flames bursting from the sun's corona, streaks of orange fire flashed over the horizon and soared high into the atmosphere. Somewhere above the island they merged into the light of dawn.

"Only six rifles left . . . one grenade. . . . Diller is gathering the men now . . . thirty men . . . Elisha . . . Elisha . . ." Laycook's voice was now almost inaudible amid close explosions. "Tell them at home they wouldn't let us surrender . . . tell them we fought to the end. . . ." Awesome heard Sergeant Diller in the

341

background calling his warriors from shelter in the shell-pocked tundra to their final offensive. He pictured the remnants of his crew running, tripping, firing, huddled together, shooting with rifles at the sky.

When Diller could no longer be heard and Laycook returned to the walkie-talkie there was a calmness in his voice Awesome had never known before. "I'm sorry, Elisha, for what happened between us. . . . It should never have occurred. . . . When you see Nick Gaffy, tell him all about it. Don't spare anything. Then tell him for me that I finally came to know what he was trying to do here. He was the only man in the Navy who really understood these bastards." Communication from Laycook ceased abruptly.

Had the circumstances been different Awesome might have used the remaining moments to enlighten his executive officer about the man he esteemed. But attack on the hilltop fortress suddenly intensified, with artillery fire closing the ring. In that moment when there was no time, when the last of his men were dying, Awesome detested Gaffy as much for what he had done to Thomas Laycook as for the perfidy committed against himself.

Laycook apparently kept the open-circuit transceiver strapped to his body as he followed Sergeant Diller, for it was possible to hear the shrieking of jet engines and the intermittent cries of desperate men. Diller's magnificent call to arms was the last voice from *Amundsen's* crew. And a gallant voice it was. But soon it was lost in battle. No friendly eyes witnessed the result.

Awesome heard the afterburners of a jet climbing back into the clouds, presumably banking to the southeast en route home. Then Laycook's walkie-talkie went dead. Shortly after, winds diffused the thick, asphyxiating smoke, and Awesome smelled it in the air. There was a rich and pervading quiet over the island as the sun climbed higher in the northeastern sky, burning away the clouds.

During the course of an hour Awesome's trans-ceiver returned only static until its own weakened batteries faded and died. He ate canned fruit and drank tepid tea warmed by the last heat from the Sterno's flame. The sun, now high over Kolguyev, suddenly broke through a cluster of clouds and with a shaft of light painted the icescape a golden hue. It was the first bright sunshine he had seen since departure from Scotland eighty-eight days before.

In the morning's light he flipped through the Bible's pages, occasionally inserting his forefinger to stop at a familiar and once-loved passage and feeling amply rewarded for having carried the heavy book. Yet the words themselves seemed frozen to the printed page, neither vital nor relevant, and no longer able to raise his spirits. Even the sagacious Koheleth failed to console him with his magnificent poetry. Deliberately Awesome ripped clusters of pages from the leather binding. Piled over the Sterno stove in loose stacks, the gold-rimmed leaves resisted the fire beneath for several seconds. Gradually a white smoke crept between the pages; they curled and caught fire. Section by section, book by book, he committed the entire Bible to the flames. Its heat was warm and, though gone too soon, a blessed relief from the cold.

Nicholas Gaffy's letter survived until the end. Awesome turned it in his fingers, resisting an urge to reread its familiar passages a final time. Manipulator that Gaffy was, his words were nevertheless not inauthentic. On the contrary, they represented that part of the man which drove him to scurrilous acts for high purpose. Under the flap of the khaki envelope (12th Submarine Squadron) Awesome's forefinger touched the heavy stationery and retraced a section of Gaffy's shaky pen line. Perhaps, Awesome speculated, Nick understood in his prophetic manner the course of future events. The man had an uncanny grasp of history and an unholy ability to manipulate it. Awesome remembered the sadness of his voice as he stood on *Amundsen's* bridge in Holy Loch.

For half a minute the letter remained on the cinders as though miraculously protected from the pyre. But when it could resist the heat no longer, the envelope crumbled into a sepia roll and was instantly engulfed by fire. In the metallic blue cone of the flame Awesome pictured Gaffy's face—his lips parted and speechless, his eyes lowered in shame.

The cartoon of the admiral alone remained. Somehow the cartoonist had captured in Gaffy's caricature his expression of defeat. Skillful as he had been, his caption was still not correct; it was untrue that Captain Awesome was a bigger prick than his commanding officer. It seemed fitting that Gaffy's caricature should not be destroyed. Awesome lodged it face up in the ice for judgment from above. His last thoughts of the admiral were neither affectionate nor hostile. The bonfire flickered; Gaffy's letter had been reduced to embers.

"You'll have to go on your own, little fellow." He removed Dreadnought from his breast pocket, balanced him on his palm, and fingered the scalloped shell. His lips remained close to the creature's head, now poking curiously forward. "This time I can't save you. You'll be better off without me." He gave the turtle a kiss on his soft underbelly and set him upon the ice. Hesitantly, Dreadnought thrust his head and legs from the shell, explored the frozen surface with experimental steps, then halted and peered back at the tall figure hovering above. Awesome was looking to the south and squinting into the sunlight. Kolguyev looked so far away.

With no further regard for his body's deteriorated condition—fingers numbed by frost, feet and ankles anesthetized, lips parched and bleeding—Awesome marched into the flat ice field toward the island. Its background hills were the beige of Maxine's skin; its coastal tundra, the pastel green of early spring.

He had not gone far when between himself and the shore he saw an irregular mass that appeared as a dark blemish against the icescape. The new form fitted no recognizable pattern. The object appeared to move slowly, erratically, haltingly in his direction. Finally it stopped altogether and remained motionless. But it had once moved—of that he was certain.

Mindless of the slippery path before him, Awesome trudged forward. Whenever it was possible to lift his eyes from the ice while still moving, he examined the curious form. The distance slowly closed. His heart suddenly palpitated and his brain swirled. Was it possible there was another human being on the ice pack? Could there be a survivor of the massacre? Two hundred yards farther, a man was balanced on unsteady legs, yet he continued to advance. Then he fell to the ice, stood up, and staggered forward again . . . and again . . . and again.

Awesome plunged into the separating gap, dragging his aching legs. During the final hundred yards he was barely aware of his feet touching the ice, much less the crippling pain in his hip and thigh. His wild shouts of joy were dissipated by the winds. The final steps seemed longer and farther than all those that preceded them. Both survivors traversed the last paces weeping and fell into each other's arms. How far they had traveled to find each other. Unable to speak, the two men clung to the black flesh that made them brothers.

Everett Young was hoodless, his scorched parka cauterized to his neck and wrists. Patches of singed eyebrows and a single tuft of an adolescent mustache had survived the inferno. Frozen bloodstains sealed his trousers to the legs beneath. As the two men embraced, Young's charred lips touched the swollen bite wound on Awesome's neck. Though cold and blistered, the sailor's lips transmitted what no words could about human forgiveness. "It wasn't our war . . . Skipper," Young whispered.

"We'll tell them that when we return, Everett," Awesome replied, then ducked under the submariner's shoulder to support his weight. They turned in tandem to the northwest. When Awesome had studied the Kolguyev map aboard *Amundsen* he had pledged that one day he would stand on the island's northern shore and peer out over the ice pack. Her Siren coast was only a quarter mile distant but he was certain never to stand on her mysterious, blooded tundra.

Arm in arm, the black men began their return to the sunken *Amundsen*, following the skipper's trail over hummocky ice. They rested on the twenty-foot promontory where Awesome had bivouacked the previous night. The sun, now high overhead, glazed the icescape with a crystal shimmer. The cold winds abated, bathing the survivors in luxurious warmth. The sky was rich azure; the ice pack, white. So clear was the atmosphere the eye could see beyond the horizon into distant space.

Leaving Young temporarily, Awesome maneuvered on the crest of the ridge for a final moment of solitude. Before him stretched a plain of fast ice, punctuated by irregular configurations from sastrugi and hummocks; beyond that, the verdant hills of Kolguyev. How far he was from Frankfort, Kentucky, and yet his father's presence comforted him. "When you grow up, Elisha . . ." he used to say before uttering something wise.

"Look, Pappy," his son proclaimed in a loud voice. "Look at me, Pappy, I'm on my feet!"

Twenty yards to the northwest, Dreadnought sniffed at the breeze until his snout caught a familiar scent. He raised his underbelly from the cold ice and, after confirming what instinct told him was true, turned about face and took the first small steps toward reunion.

EPILOGUE

(Patrol Polynya: 60th day plus 28 and 29)

To say what happened in the Barents Sea and at the Soviet satellite tracking station of Kolguyevskiy Severnyy had absolutely no witnesses is not entirely accurate. Indeed, no event with such potential for international conflict could be wholly quarantined to an isolated location. While *Amundsen*'s crew dug into the tundra and fought for its life, another drama was unfolding at 33,000 feet over the state of Kansas. As the deadline for the Soviet ultimatum had approached, Gaffy joined the President and his advisers aboard their 747 emergency command jet. The Soviets threatened and American nuclear retaliatory power mobilized in response. Countdown to holocaust. The path of madness was abandoned when both nations discerned simultaneously that the soberest policy was to do *absolutely nothing!* What stood between apocalypse and salvation was a single American nuclear submarine that was ultimately expendable. The Soviets knew it. The Americans knew it. Eventually Elisha Awesome knew it too. Once the irritant had been eliminated, both governments demobilized their strike forces and took the first steps toward *rapprochement.*

Aboard the presidential jet the mood was euphoric. Relief from the intense strain was so profound that neither the civilian nor the military advisers considered the genesis of the crisis. Gaffy was regarded not as a diabolical madman but as an international hero. He was revered for his role in defusing the explosive situation, not for having created it in the first place. But, as always, he understood what those around him did not. He knew that when the momentary euphoria waned and the country's leaders came to their senses and asked from what squadron *Amundsen* had originated, like her crew he too was expendable.

Immediately after landing at Andrews Air Force Base outside Washington, Gaffy transferred to a waiting Gulfstream executive jet and was whisked home to Scotland. It was late afternoon on the East Coast, and as far as the average American learned from the early-evening news it had been a normal Thursday: The Golden State Warriors defeated the New York Knickerbockers in the NBA playoffs; the OPEC cartel continued discussions about future rises in petroleum prices; Amtrak threatened to close down more passenger service if Congress did not approve new subsidies for the coming fiscal year.

An aggressive young newsman from the Washington *Post* with his own "Deep Throat" in the Defense Department scooped the mobilization story for the Friday morning edition. He found out about the nuclear alert; he learned scattered details of the President's personal response; otherwise his exposé was hopelessly muddled. Ultimately, the story served to confirm what *Izvestia* refused to admit: A mysterious submarine had slipped through the Soviet coastal defenses and then managed to escape. The story died there.

Met at the airstrip by his usual staff car, Gaffy was driven back to Underwater Strategic Services at Holy Loch an hour before reveille. A thick, tully fog blanketed the loch and extended inland for a half mile from the sea. The driver was ordered to fetch a candle for the admiral. Given the early hour, the seaman protested, he was less likely to find a candle on the base than a virgin in a whorehouse. Normally, the admiral would have run the young man out of the Submarine Service first for such impertinence and second for such defeatism. But the chaffeur did have a point; Gaffy was the last man in the world to demand a miracle.

Exhausted from the ordeal, he dismissed the driver and walked along to the dock where forty-foot utility boats plowed back and forth to the nest of submarine tenders in the loch. Due to the international emergency, U.S.S. *Millard Fillmore* and U.S.S. *Mako* had been ordered into the North Sea and the Norwegian Sea, respectively. U.S.S. *Yellowtail* had earlier been patroling off the Finmark Coast, but had been commanded to fall back into the Greenland Sea. Gaffy walked along the dock, gazing out into the loch where in January *Edmond Roald Amundsen,* or *Scorpion*, had taken on provisions and a new crew.

Did Admiral Gaffy truly recite a prayer, as he promised Awesome in his letter? He did. Not being accustomed to speaking with God (it had been more than half a century), he began with a sincere apology for his long absence. Whether it was from true piety that he spoke is doubtful. More likely, he prayed out of respect for Elisha Awesome who, he believed, would have appreciated the gesture.

From the quay, he walked along a gravel path past a semisomnolent guard to his office. A small desk lamp was his only light in the massive mahogany room. He loosened his necktie and dropped wearily into his desk chair, his shoulders slouching against its squared back, his arms flagging over the armrests. With closed eyes, Gaffy pondered the mystery of what had transpired aboard *Amundsen* after her departure from the Lumbrovskiy Channel. Because the Soviets reported monitoring an explosion *before* he ordered Tomahawk 6 to self-destruct, he concluded some of *Amundsen*'s crew had died innocent of his artifice. That was something of a relief, though Gaffy was not certain why.

He balanced himself on unsteady legs, cautiously inching around his wastebasket to a double Victorian captain's chest with antique brass furnishings. At the bottom hidden under personal effects from his earlier days at sea was a fifth of Dewar's scotch. Avoiding the desk blotter with his eyes, as he had done since his return, he poured one full ounce of whiskey and belted down the fiery drink. Fortified for what was waiting, he squared his jaws and lowered his eyes to the blotter. Just as expected—a communi-

351

cation from the Chief of Naval Operations in Washington. Sealed and stamped FOR ADMIRAL NICHOLAS GAFFY'S EYES ONLY: TOP SECRET. He knew what it was without reading it.

In those silent moments, Gaffy regretted his career-long feud with Robert Katzenback. What had begun innocently at Annapolis had been permitted to escalate throughout the years: the Korean War and the Vietnam War, up to the present. He admitted to himself something that he had hitherto entertained but dismissed as improbable. For a full decade he had argued that Underwater Strategic Services was absolutely necessary to ensure America's preemptive first-strike capability in modern nuclear warfare. As military strategy—perhaps. But there was also a personal dimension. Now that the Service was certain to be dismantled, he understood that he had created it not as a deterrent to the Soviets but as a beachhead in his personal war against Bob Katzenback. It was a bitter admission at the end of a long and successful career, when one's judgments of the past become more important than one's prospects for the future. Very soon Admiral Gaffy, like U.S.S. *Scorpion* and the U.S.S. *Edmond Roald Admunsen*, would slip below the waves and be heard from no more.

Gaffy settled the scotch glass before him and poured again. It was well known that he, as an example to other submarine officers, never, never drank more than a single scotch . . . and a small, one-ounce shot at that. True enough. He never exceeded one scotch—that is, until that early morning, April 16, when Nicholas Francis Gaffy drank . . . two.